# SAGA OF THE URBAN SORCERERS

## BOOK TWO

### THE RECKONING OF EMERALD TARRAGON

# SAGA OF THE URBAN SORCERERS

## BOOK TWO

### THE RECKONING OF EMERALD TARRAGON

# ALEX JAMES

**Novels by Alex James:**

**SAGA OF THE URBAN SORCERERS:**
Book One: The Summoning of Barker Moon
Book Two: The Reckoning of Emerald Tarragon
Book Three: The Shaping of Cheryl Equiniox (Pre-order)

**THE CHRONICLES OF THE TERRAGUARD:**
Book One: Maker of Rules

**THE ASCENSION SEQUENCE:**
VOLUME ONE
The Pandora Sequence
VOLUME TWO
Book One: The Pandora Inheritance
Book Two: The Pandora Arcana (Pre-order)
Book Three: The Daughters of Pandora (Pre-order)

**AMAZON SEVEN**
VOLUME ONE
Book One: Mission Queen
Book Two: Queen Renegade
Book Three: Intergalactic Ingenue (Pre-order)
Book Four: Princess Executor (Pre-order)

**DARK STREETS:**
Book One: Agents of Fear
Book Two: Avatars of Wrath (Pre-Order)

**www.GalexyTales.com**

(or search "GALEXY TALES" at Amazon!)

Saga of the Urban Sorcerers – Book Two:
The Reckoning of Emerald Tarragon



Cover Illustration Copyright © 2016 by Galexy Tales
Cover design by Michal Dutkiewicz and Alex James
Cover Art & Illustrations © 2016 Michal Dutkiewicz

Book production by Ingram Spark
Editor: Melissa Sheldrick
Editorial Consultant: Gretel Newman-Sugrue
Text layout: Adam Dutkiewicz

Galexy Edition 1.1

*Dedication*

To Adelaide,
and
Whatever It Is Here

# PART ONE
## GAME AND PLAN

# CHAPTER ONE:
# NAKED INSTINCT

This was it, Emerald decided.

She was going to survive.

Okay.

Okay, so that was decided.

*That was a decision, now?*

*Wow.*

So strange, the places you could get to.

*Deciding to survive.*

As in, one could get to a place. A little village, or a big city. Or, a little village within a big city. A mansion over a village, a mansion in a city that was like a tiny village, or a tiny apartment in a massive city that was like a mansion to you. All combinations of the above, and below, all perspectives valid. That is; you could quite easily live somewhere, and not even see your surrounds, because within, there was another life. Big, small, discovered or undiscovered, lived, unlived. You could even retreat to yet another place, within that life, within that place, yet again. A place that made you not see anything else; nothing around you, and to be honest, nothing much within either.

Yes, so strange, the places you could get to…

The places you could *retreat* to.

Be *hounded* to.

Places from which one might not even be able to see a future.

Not a future one wanted to live, anyway.

And so, one decided, or at least, one allowed, that one was not going to survive. And that made it okay. Okay for the universe to take you out. Simply; very well, take me out, however you like, I'm done.

I'll just… wait here.

Perform some tasks, take care of some small jobs, pass the time, and then, whenever you like, just; a click of the fingers, no flourish, take me out. Don't care if it takes a while, I'm good. I'm good right here, waiting. I'm done.

Everyone, Emerald supposed, who'd ever had even the hint of the black dog in their blood had been through that morbid desire. Everyone who'd faced constant hardship. Everyone who'd faced…

Well, she supposed this was abuse, really.

This constant hounding.

Now she came to think on it.

And she had meant it, at the time, absolutely; her desire to depart. She had truly felt it and wished it. At the time. And truly, that time had been from about three months ago, right up to…

Now.

Just now, sitting on the bed.

*Shit.*

She had decided, put it out there and waited. She'd quite settled on it since then, in the weeks and days. But just a minute ago…

*Shit. Shit.*

She'd seen a way out.

One could go to a place where you sat and believed you didn't want to be here anymore. Where one requested of the universe that it set a course, and make it so, without even really, not really, realizing that you had done it. And then, quite suddenly, you realize that you have actually been doing it, actively waiting; and it was only then, you really realized… there could be a way out.

Just in the way… the exact way… she just had.

And so, she would have to run again. One more time. Could she run again?

She could run again.

She could run, but this time; she would have a place to stop and turn and fight. It could be any city, any state, any country…

anywhere they had a centre for gambling. And these days, with the demons running the world, every city had one, every city had a casino. They were nothing special any more. Nothing illicit or profane, nothing romantic or even remotely exotic. The world was spoiled now, and she was spoiled for choice.

The plan was dark and daring but it was doable and… suddenly she had begun to hope that her death wish was reversible. Of course, it would have been ridiculous for anybody else to even consider that a death wish would really come true. Or any kind of wish for that matter. Wishes didn't come true. Not without a lot of luck or effort or practical design. Wishes required infrastructure in order to be made manifest.

Only, for Emerald, wishes were different.

Emerald was a sorceress.

The barriers between the power of Emerald's will and the material universe were much thinner, much looser and more malleable for her than they were for normal people. For her kind, wishes – sustained wishes, could absolutely become real. More often than not, if one wished a certain way, she supposed, with a clear mind and honest heart and true spirit and a connected soul, these wishes could manifest. They did manifest, one way or another, more often than not. They could and did come true. And sometimes, if you hadn't been careful, they came for you.

Emerald was hoping now.

She had not been careful, regarding that for which she had wished.

The wish had been morose. It had been… not actual self-pity, but a surrender of sorts. The result of a sustained psychological beating down that… she didn't want to think about it.

About the thing.

The thing that coveted.

It was not wise, not now, to feed it any more.

But she hoped now, really hoped, that after summoning and accepting that path, having laid down her defences and having allowed her morose desire to be heard, that after not having

countermanded the order, not for some thirteen, fourteen weeks…
that she could, quite quickly one hoped, simply duck down a side
street, off the summoned path, and avoid the oncoming train that
she had been actively awaiting all this time.

Could she?

Was that allowed?

Because now… now she really wanted to stay.

Now, she had the idea.

The idea that would mean she could survive, and live, and
prosper, and in the end, maybe even find… maybe not joy, and
probably not even simple happiness. But – satisfaction. That, she
could see. That, she could manifest and hold. Behind the light that
was careening down the tunnel toward her, behind the oncoming
train; she could see a city of satisfaction, where she could build a
home, and a life, and be… be what? Just be. That would do.

She was naked on the giant bed.

She had intended to shower.

She'd started showering a lot.

Just standing there.

Hot until she couldn't take it anymore.

She wanted to get up now. Get up, and shower, not just to
feel something to distract her from the nothingness, from the
hounding; but to shower, to get ready. To get ready… to go? To
go, she supposed. Yes. To go.

*To run, again.*

She didn't know if a sorceress, one as ostensibly powerful as
she was, could reverse something like this. She had never been
as tired before, not as she had been these past months; she had
never been that done. Never felt that world-weary. Never this…
just, *done*. Fucking… *done*. So, *could she* avoid the oncoming train
now? Her home-made destiny-killer? The slo-mo ejection seat
that she had deployed, the anonymous assassin she had hired
from the ether, like a terminally ill billionaire? It was like a stupid
thriller; *the prognosis was incorrect! How do I stop the assassin?!*

*You can't, Miss Tarragon.*

*That was part of the arrangement.*

*You placed an order.*

*That order cannot be countermanded…*

*And he absolutely will not stop…*

A deal with the universe. And now your assassination, the one you requested, is part of the fundamental structure of…

She got up.

She did it.

The bedroom was big; now it seemed enormous.

A big empty room with a giant bed in it. And stuff. Other stuff she… hadn't ordered, didn't want. Like everything in this life, at least, in this last part of this last version of her life; there was nothing here she had desired, had ordered, had accepted or embraced. She could take her things, her few *real things*, and leave without sentiment or remorse.

The walk-in wardrobe, several paces from the end of the bed, was as big as a large suburban bedroom. She didn't look at herself as she slid the mirrored door across and entered. She had always been tall, and thin, and she had been admired for it; but these months she had become lanky, and gaunt, and hated herself for everything. She walked in, realizing (another in the cascade of personal wake-ups the evening seemed to have prepared for her) that she had hated herself all this time, all this fifth time.

That had stopped now.

Just like that, just then; stopped.

She had seen a blurred flash of her own image in the mirror, and averted her eyes. All that it had made her think was: *wow that woman needs to eat something.*

*Who's looking after her?*

Was it possible? *Was it possible?*

Could the oncoming light at the end genuinely be light, and life, and not an oncoming train? Weren't there angels, weren't there spirits who could step in and pull you from the curb before the morbid daydream manifested and had you bleeding out on the street, or toppling onto the train tracks? There were, she knew.

Which made her wonder as well: where the hell had they been all this time? Where had their divine intervention been while she had fought this thing.

This *fucking thing*, five times now?

Five times!

Jesus!

She could feel it in her shoulders, in her neck, over her scalp.

She didn't know.

There was no telling.

But she would find out, soon enough. Because tonight was a nexus. She could feel it, she knew it. This was one of those nights, and there was nothing she could do about it. Something had woken her up, and on every level demanded to know; *do you really want this?*

But the train was coming.

And tonight, for now, she knew and could see; Manny was the train.

# CHAPTER TWO:
# BAGGAGE

Damn.

It was all so clear now.

She should never have tried to love again. She should have buried her optimism and just remained pragmatic. But that was the way with romance, with attraction, with emergence. One placed all of those things; the pessimism, the cold reality, off to the side, and focussed on the source. The source of the optimism, the potential, the heat of the moment. Things could work out. Things did work out, for a lot of people, one way or another.

And things had started out so well with Manny. Started, sure. Enough for her to think; this time will be different. But every single time, her lover chose the demon.

The covetous *thing*.

And was this really… the fifth time? The fifth time that she had found herself, standing in the room that was nominally the bedroom of the home of the life she shared with her lover of long-standing, asking; what clothes can I wear that will hide the most of the things I don't want to leave behind?

*I walk out.*

*I never come back.*

*What I take, I keep.*

*That is all.*

She was a bit dizzy. Naked in the wardrobe now. Not cold, not warm. The cream carpet had changed to stained wood, the colour of expensive milk chocolate. There were wardrobes and open cupboards right the way around, cream again with bronze trimming. Her deep lime-green crocodile leather shoulder bag was on the floor, but her handbag and purse were beside each other, sitting on the polished wood surface of the chest of drawers in the middle of the room, exactly where she had left them whenever she had last come in. Probably when she had last gone out for a packet of cigarettes. Days ago.

Manny had loved making this room for her. Stocking it with whatever clothes she desired. Manny loved money now though. More than her.

She opened her handbag. Nothing useful in there really. Cash, a fair bit. But lots of traceable cards that were useless now.

*Take five…*

*And – action.*

She slid open the two main inner-wardrobe doors. Not that she wanted to take all her clothes. She just did not want to be distracted again by the image of herself there in the two mirrors. She turned and opened the top left drawer on the tall central chest. Underwear. Top right drawer. Socks. She left them open and went to the other side. Top left. Jewellery. Mostly rings, earrings and things. Top right. More jewellery. Necklaces and pendants and bracelets and…

She didn't want any of this.

Besides, if she took any of the jewellery he'd given her, he would chase her for longer, use it as an excuse, just as the others had. Not this time. She went back and lifted the presentation insert from the ring drawer. Quickly she checked off her handful of magical items, her charms, one by one. Nothing Manny had bought her, none of the things she had bought herself while she had been with him, were magical. None of them had properties… but these were the *real things*. Her sentiment, her channels, her sources, her lenses… her arsenal.

…although?

She looked back into the insert.

…hmmm.

That one.

That one was becoming something.

She reached for the ring, but her tired fingers fumbled, and the tiny thing fell, rolling into her magical-containment drawer below with a smug little rattle.

So; that was something.

But it wasn't something green.

It wasn't totally obvious to anyone, at least until they saw this room, but Emerald kept to greens. Greens complemented by whites, greys and blacks. Greens right across the spectrum though, so that her wardrobe could stray into brownish or blueish, but always a tone anchored in some kind of green base. Degrees of green, shades of green (or no green at all, just black, or white, or grey) depending on intent, and stunning-green to seduce, kill or conquer. She knew them all, all the combos, and they were all right here before her, starting from the aquamarines and almost-blues to her left, through to the most powerful, the most striking greens straight ahead in the middle, to the olives and almost-browns to the right. A whole other wall for the steel-greens, almost black greens, faded and pale so as to be almost white greens. For her name was Emerald Tarragon, and she was a sorceress; the name had stuck, it had altered her, it had seeped into her core to reflect back into her material reality. Her name was twice green, and she had gone with it, because that was who she was, and what she was meant to be.

This ring, though. This one that was becoming something; it wasn't green. She had collected a few things that weren't over the years; gifts, and the odd bit or piece from here or there. They meant nothing; she would abandon them all, as she would abandon anything associated with Manny and his money, and the *thing*. However, a television actress had given this to her; it had been a nice gesture from a comrade, a memento, but it hadn't been her colour, nowhere near it, so she'd simply popped it into the drawer, along with all the other bits and forgotten about it. But now she could tell, the way it was when a talisman emerged, that it had become some kind of focus for the lessons she had learned here, with Manny. From him and despite him. It was definitely resonating with that experience now, buzzing with her recently hatched ideas, even as she picked it up again, inspected the deep amethyst core, and confirmed it. Just this one, just this once, she would welcome to the costume of her armour. This one would become the reminder of her time with Manny; and Giancarlo before him, and Horst, and Steele and poor Josef.

*Never again;* the jewel would enforce; *they always chose the demon, and they stopped you being Emerald.*

The amethyst would symbolize that. Pinkie finger, left hand. She slipped it on; a promise to herself. If she survived, there would never be another lover. It wasn't fair on either of them, on anyone or anything they did. Never, ever.

The tension came down from her scalp and shoulders, across her chest. Her heart; she could feel her heart as it felt the promise. Never. Her heart, tight, as she crossed her pinkie fingers across her chest, forcing the ring right down. Never again.

She released it, let her arms drop, and returned her attention to the task at hand, feeling just a tad angrier.

The bag. What could she fit in it? She scooped it from the floor and dropped it on the surface before her, beside the unwanted jewellery, the handbag and purse.

Security would not blink at the crocodile bag. That was her everyday bag, it was a longstanding habit that she took it everywhere, whether she needed it or not. But this time, she had to fit everything in it; whatever she wanted to keep.

Manny had added some new guys to the rotation a few weeks ago, doubling the roster, and Emerald knew this pattern of paranoia from her lovers. The new arrivals were the ones trained to analyze her behaviour. Anything that looked like she was about to leave, or even make a run for it. Anything planned, anything spontaneous, and all stops in between. The world was full enough of wealthy men like Manny, or rather, Hermann, who had trouble letting go of women who'd had enough of them, that there actually were niche divisions within most high-end security companies that specialized in the prevention of such separations. She knew all too well; Horst had run the world's largest one.

There was another wave, another realization, another shock.

She suddenly found that she detested Manny, just as she now detested Horst, and had for some time. Manny must have sensed it. He had certainly sensed her… she hesitated to call it depression, but she supposed that's what it was. But he had kept his distance all this time, since she'd allowed herself to know, on some level, that she wanted out. Wanted out, but… simply couldn't face the running again. Running from a man she'd once thought she could spend the rest of her life with.

Emerald looked back, into the bedroom. She had been in there, she supposed; ordering meals, ordering movies, binge-watching TV series, catching up on her reading, for… Jesus, *weeks* now. Weeks and weeks, and she'd barely seen him. Thinking on it now, Manny hadn't slept at the apartment in ages, and she hadn't really reacted, or noticed, other than to be unconsciously relieved on some level.

Of course she had come and gone, and he had come and gone. She had left the room, left the apartment, but only out of necessity. She supposed that was true for him as well. She left only to stretch her legs, feel the cold, buy cigarettes. Manny had, ostensibly, been working nights all that time. It was an easy tale to tell oneself; you could work nights here but it was hard, the sunsets and sunrises were too strong, the sun blasted in like a stadium light and locked one too solidly into standard circadian rhythms. To work long hours, at length, it was easier to find an office, a bunker, and hunker down.

So, they were avoiding each other.

And she'd been entertaining herself, for three months, to distract herself from… that. And the fact that it was over; painful. And the fact that Manny had succumbed; depressing. And the fact that she would have to run again.

Unbearable.

Until just then. Just… fifteen, twenty minutes ago now, she supposed.

She looked down at the pinkie ring.

There were no tears.

Maybe that's why she had watched all those sad movies last week. Three days' worth. To purge all that?

Every sorcerer, sorceress… why did they insist on us all being called *sorcerers*?

'I'm a sorceress…' Emerald uttered to herself.

Every one of them had a greatcoat. Hers always hung just inside the door to her wardrobe, as was tradition, and as she walked out she embraced the heavy, dark-green wool and lovingly allowed the garment to engulf her. She went past the bed and across the carpet, past the bureau to the French windows and out, onto the balcony to see the last sunset she would ever see from here, across Central Park.

# CHAPTER THREE:
# CHURNING

The high, cold wind blew in, the central heating gushed out.

The apartment was relatively newly renovated; Manny had purchased the place two years ago when he'd realized he would be spending a lot of time in New York, then redecorated all the rooms in either bronze and tan, cream and beige, or gold and white. They'd met here around then but had lived for most of their time as a couple in San Francisco, where all the big games companies apparently liked to be right now. They'd come and gone for a while, but eventually settled here, as he'd become more involved with the business, less with creative. Their (or his, really) apartment was the whole tenth floor of a very old Fifth Avenue building, not quite the penthouse but more easily updated and as a result much better equipped. Even so, whereas several other nearby buildings had been completely reshaped in recent decades, this one had maintained its separate brownstone balconies for each separate set of French windows. Maintained its façade.

Keeping cool, maintaining a façade of normality; that was something she was going to have to do this evening, this hour, soon. The act was always going to have to fool the security team, and stay in place for her to resist any local psychic security; perhaps the mask would even have to hold for Manny as well.

Manny. It felt ridiculous to call him that now.

He would go nuts like the others, but this time she was reading the writing on the wall much earlier, and he would not react as big. If she got out now, his business would recover. She had given him enough for *Primagineer Experior II* to be a massive success, but not enough so that all future versions would depend on her continued involvement. Even if they did, she could help him from afar, open the realm to him again so he could see another...

No.

Clean break.

That was, after all, where most imagined realms originated anyway; quite naturally, from dreams or flights of fancy, and the normal connections true imagineers were born with and developed over a lifetime.

She hadn't *really* done that much for him.

Just a peek. Just a tiny cheat.

But the demon had whispered and, yes; the perception was that she was now indispensable.

His RPG Rapunzel.

It was terribly cold out on the balcony, still January, and the icy stone was a shock to her bare feet. There was a slow wind, but that was all, no rain or snow. The sun had set and the sky was invisible; everything was reflecting orange and pink and yellow off the chrome and glass and metal of the darkening exterior cityscape, and golden-pink off the many white and pale-stone buildings that bordered the treetops of the enormous park. There were radiant sunset clouds, as far as she could see, and as she angled her neck upward, widened her eyes and raised her chin to see more clearly, she caught more of the Manhattan soundscape as it carried up; traffic, and traffic and traffic on top of the more traffic that was drowning out the traffic.

The discordant symphony of a metropolis; she'd liked to have said she'd miss these daily spectacles, all of them at all the big times, but she'd been in such a slumber here she had never really... bothered, she supposed, to appreciate them in the first place. That in itself should have been a literal wake-up call, but of course you never got those when you were under. Just a pile of urgent messages on the other side, most of which were now... redundant.

She walked to the edge the balcony, still feeling that ghastly slow-wittedness but also feeling better, like she'd just awoken from a long jetlag sleep. She took her cigarettes from the inner coat pocket. It was nowhere near time for her third and last regimented smoke of the day. She had that one after dinner; but this would just have to be one of those rare days where she had four. Dinner tonight would be later, on the road, paid in cash. There would be meat and cheese and bread. She flipped the packet; there were just a few left. Another reason her departing would not seem suspicious; it had been at least five days since she'd last ventured out.

Her long, thick hair blew in the solid chill, but away from the click and the flame.

When she lit up, she knew he was home. Home, or coming home.

She tried not to think about it.

That façade absolutely would have to fool Manny.

Dress, just the main outfit, and run – *dash!* – run now with the bag and the arsenal.

Instead she found her yoyo, in the pebbles under the bare branches of the potted Mr Lincoln rose, and began to play. It was the bright lime one, the same colour as her cigarette lighter. She tried to keep things clean like that; uniform, symmetrical.

Her mind cleared some more as she did.

She could view it; sense it; knew it.

Manny was here.

He was home.

To a place that was not home to her.

Time to go find a home, Emerald.

Time to find one, and go there. Or, go there, somewhere, and make one. Regardless; this time, she was going to go there, and stay there, no matter what. Go home, and stay home.

She looked back into the bedroom from outside.

She could see herself in the glass, but the sunset was obscuring anything sharp. She just looked like the outline of a hippy; big coat and cascading hair. The orange of the inhale glowed in the glass. She watched the yoyo rise and fall. Fling, spin, hover, yank, snatch; left and right and out and up. As though with a will of its own. She hadn't practised for months. But she was still good.

She left the bright lime yoyo, still her favourite, on the stone ledge of the tenth floor balcony, satisfied.

'Still got it, sorceress.'

She stared at the ashtray on the garden table, surrounded by the expensive, comfortable garden chairs, with their expensive plastic covers. That expense that made them almost look like they didn't have that nasty, cheap, waterproof look. All of a sudden, the fakeness of it was shockingly apparent. Not that there was necessarily anything wrong with it; it was that or nothing, like so much of the idiotic quality they demanded in this class. But it reflected back her own lack of personal integrity, just a plastic, outdoor, water-resistant chair, because that was where she was with her life.

She drew and exhaled, paused, drew and exhaled, and realized she was not enjoying it. She wasn't even savouring the special extra smoke.

She wasn't even watching, enjoying, her last sunset in Manhattan.

Smokes and sunsets went together; every romantically inclined smoker knew that. But she hadn't regularly watched them since she'd made the three-a-day vow, since she'd been a pack a day girl, hustling the halls –

Shit.

Her staff was here!

Hiding in plain sight!

She stabbed the damn thing out.

She'd become set here. Virtually ingrained within an unsustainable environment. Almost stagnant. She turned her back on the City That Never Slept and went back inside, to where she had slept for three months.

*Unsatisfied.*

Obviously, she couldn't take down an extra bag, or pack a fat, overstuffed case, but that was her childish instinct. That was what twenty-one-year-old Emerald had done with Josef, and almost twenty-five-year-old Emerald had done with Steele. Fuck; she had spent three years with someone actually called Steele. She could barely summon his face now. God she wanted to do that again; the temporary, infantile satisfaction of *fuck you I'm leaving*. But no. Only she could know the truth; that from here, her everyday crocodile messenger bag was her travel bag now, her escape kit; her swag.

Just as it had been, thrice before.

Just as it would be, one last time.

Decisions now; just the essentials.

The money, the gun and run.

For most of her kind there were special clothes, but above those there was an outfit; not a costume, not a uniform, not truly a look or a style, but something else. A kind of armour, a kind of veil, a kind of symbol, a kind of statement. A favourite shirt, accessory, belt, trinket in the pocket of those special jeans. The one, specific, sacred, sorcerer ensemble. Different for everyone. It was telling, no doubt though, that she was already wearing her greatcoat; the modern cloak, hiding in plain sight, under which those special clothes would be worn, that was, in the end, the same for everyone.

Sorcery was as much about symbols as anything, and this to her now symbolized the same thought again; *main outfit, and run, run now with the bag and the arsenal.*

She could leave now – *dash!* – with the bag, the handful of items, and that would be all she required. The veil, the armour, the uniform, the misdirection; all practitioners of the arts had a different collective name or notion for the distinctive items that they wore, and they all knew which were the combos and alternatives that worked; where, for what and why. Worked, not simply as in fashion, as in 'popped' or 'that's you' or 'your colour'. Worked as in… the other element. The magic; the symbol they generated. But for most of them, the coat, the evolution of the ancient robe; all else could be lost and rebuilt around that.

*So… why wasn't she leaving?*

*Why was she standing here going over what she already knew?*

*Rebooting? After three months?*

*Maybe.*

Her fingers played at her sides, strumming the surfaces of her thumbs as her wrists brushed against the thick wool of her side-pocket flaps. This was hers, and it had started as something, and come with her the whole way; stitched and restitched, recrafted, amended; worn and re-worn and re-worn again; re-worn and reborn; carried and packed; rolled and pillowed and thrown and tossed; tucked and spread, sat and slept on, weathered and huddled in; loved, fought and worked within, in every possible respect; this coat had kept her warm, proud and herself, even as the coat had evolved, from one thing into something else, it had been with her, on her, part of her, all this time.

Needed a dry-clean, too.

But now it was on, so was she; she was activated.

And something was bugging her.

Something was… *stopping her?*

She was pretty sure, *pretty sure*, that Manny had not yet bugged, teddy-cammed or nanny-cammed the apartment. Certainly not the bedroom or bathroom; he would never share that aspect of her with security. Besides, sorcerers had a sense for this as well; they almost always knew when they were being watched.

And yet, there was still something… niggling.

Manny knew that she was a sorceress.

He might, just might, have taken advice…

Emerald knew; the sorcerer's awareness of being watched could be circumvented. If the cams were added in a certain way; slowly but not too slowly, spaced apart so that one did not feel an immediate new invasion of mental focus upon them… it was possible. Horst had thought so, when she'd asked. It was possible; she could see it. She had told him. She had helped him work it out. If it were done slowly and carefully… then yeah. You could surveil a sorcerer without him knowing.

Sorceress… without her knowing.

She'd never mentioned this to Manny. She'd been ashamed and angry for working it through with Horst, because the sick bastard had used it on her not six months later. But if Manny had somehow worked out how to do it, sometime during her funk, it would be working right now. It would fit the pattern, in the progression of sociopathic cohabitation.

She and Horst had supposed it would work much better if the sorcerer had been weak, or if the cams could be somehow shielded with powerful spells without the target realizing; how powerful depending on the weakened state of the sorcerer.

One way or another, she was weak now.

Even now, she was second guessing herself, one part of her mind telling her that it was nothing, all part of a general sense of paranoia, the kind that, she knew, came at the end of a toxically co-dependent relationship. Telling herself, but not… knowing. For sure. Not knowing… before it was too late.

Almost.

*'Almost…'*

After all, hadn't that been part of it?

The never-knowing?

Hadn't that been how Horst had almost trapped her forever, at his whim?

*I had to test it honey,* he'd smiled. *It might be worth something…*

So. Were there cameras in here, or not?

Had Manny let them all see her, naked, showering… or not?

She looked back out.

Wednesday sunset.

Still orange and pink outside.

Fading.

Bye-bye.

Bare feet, great coat.

Fingertips strumming on thumbs.

It didn't matter. She didn't have time to find pinholes, nor risk the chance of him seeing her looking for them. He was near; there were minutes.

Time to wake; fire up; think.

Think; the apartment was secure. Out, down the hall, double back through the second kitchen, out into the middle lounge, past the pool table that nobody ever used, grab her stash, then from there to the elevator vestibule.

Easy. Nothing she would even think about on any other day.

But today; go through it. Always one of Manny's men there in the vestibule. Pizza Guard, as she thought of him. Past him, down to the elevator vestibule in the lobby. One permanent security dude there, Button Guard, employed by the building but always there to push the buttons for you, and by now tipped extra, on top of whatever else, by Manny to report her movement if he asked.

*Manny*; she could not lose that. Huh.

Hmmm.

A third, Micro Guard, just outside the vestibule, was one of the recently added security force; she was the one employed to watch her closely, observe her moods and micro-expressions, and in the end, she supposed, alert Manny and The Trolls to her escape. That was what it was, after all. She had been through it enough times to know that was what one felt like; and that's what it was. An escape. Again.

There had always been four of Manny's plain-clothed private security people downstairs, to 'manage potential fan incursion'. She'd laughed, but it happened. There were fans, and some of them were, it had to be said, not entirely in touch with everyday rules to do with personal space. The four were stationed; one in the café, with three others doing the same for other celebrities who lived here, the second outside, and the third across the street and the fourth on the edge of Central Park, behind the stone wall. They were always there, always of a type, always looking like Jerry Seinfeld, or Ray Romano; or Sarah Jessica Parker or Kyra Sedgwick. Regular building security was always there too, but in uniform and just for show. Then there was the concierge and the doorman.

But there were four extra now in addition to that, four extra hired by Manny, so far as she could tell; not to make sure nobody unwanted got in, but to make sure nobody unwarranted *got out.* She called them The Trolls, because the vibe, the clear reading she had gotten from them every time over the last... how long had it been? How many weeks? Four? *A month?*

*RUN.*

*Dash!*

– was that they *fucking hated her,* and mentally trolled her whenever she came and went. She'd unintentionally named them in her mind, in their nondescript black business suits and slicked-back hair, after what they thought of her; generally, their first thought as soon as they saw her. The woman who shadowed the lobby was *spoiledbitch;* the woman who shadowed the door, and the doorman, *doucheparasite;* the man on the pavement, *wontfuckingforget,* as in; *ten minutes alone with that one and I'll give her a bruising she...* and the man across the street, on the pavement near the park, was simply *gagonit,* so; all totally mentally stable, sexually balanced, class acts, to be sure.

If they busted her escaping, they would chase her... but she was not sure how far. How much was them, how much was money, how much was how much they hated *her.*

Manny's ordinary security men didn't know that the new people were there to keep an eye on her; Manny would never want his people to know his trophy lover was unsatisfied. There was not to be a show. The lookalikes would follow, and trace, and track so far as they were not physically endangered. So, no running across traffic, no running through crowds. After that, she would know how to throw them, so long as she knew what it that was being used to track her; her phone, her laptop, whatever. And then she would weave a web, that did not look like a web.

But; not arousing suspicion in the first place?

That was the main play.

If that worked, she was gone, without fear.

But the Trolls… they were the wildcards; she just didn't know.

Lunch-to-afternoon shift generally shared a smoke with evening-night. So there would be more of them if she walked out now, maybe twice as many. But that meant more to be distracted by each other. She could time it, stagger it, make sure. They swapped ten minutes apart but if she left… in about three? That felt right, by instinct.

But what if she *was* being watched?

Wait; what was happening?

What was it – that kept *making her think that?*

How would she look through the pinhole cams, now, just standing and thinking?

She suddenly realized. The extra cigarette; that would be a big warning sign that she had become restless. She hadn't done that, had the extra one… since moving here. Deciding on the interior décor. That he, in the end, had already decided.

But that was okay. There was a precedent. Creative thought; the classic trigger for a cigarette. *That was the cover.* She moved, did a little performance in case she *was* being watched, like she had forgotten something. She usually did most things alone. So, oddly, all she had to do was perform as herself now. Not too much, not overdone, naturalistic, and…

Check the phone.

Do normal things.

*He hasn't cammed the bedroom, but just in case he has cammed the bedroom, from here on, you are on, you are performing for him, and them; session times; yeah, that movie you wanted to see, could make it but you have to hurry…*

She actually did want to see this thing. All those old Brits hamming it up in Tokyo. *Lost in Translation* meets *Budapest Hotel.* Who knew? Maybe she'd see it on the plane. But; no, not a plane. Order an Uber, and a cab, and take neither.

*Run.*

Do it like in the movies. No. Don't think. Stay spontaneous.

*DASH!*

What? That word again… was it…? Something? A word she never used, coming up… a third time? She shook it off, feeling weird. She had to try and maintain focus. The fact that she had a genuine intent to see this movie about the elderly characters in a fish-out-of-water scenario would help to cement her alibi, her *story*, and cloud any spying that might have been, but probably, *probably* wasn't, happening.

Unless they're hired *psychic spies?*

In the end, she had suspected that both Horst and Giancarlo had employed psychics to read her mood a few times a day. She knew… didn't she? Some psychics made a good living doing that; Sybilla… back in Vancouver. Hadn't she claimed to have bought a decent house on the lake, funded (*again*) by the fear of bolting spouses?

Psychic businesses.

She had had an idea, and that… yes, that was what had awakened her from her depression.

Psychic business… but not like anything before.

*Don't think.*

Music.

She slotted her phone into the nearest cradle.

Manny had the cradles and TVs hooked up to everything, throughout.

Anything that was a random combination of iconography could be used as divination; she hit random on *Tarot 12*, the twelfth iteration of the massive playlist that she was constantly adding to, and hoped that her divinatory dip would be kind.

Al Stewart's *The Running Man.*

Okay.

She stared moving to the song, allowing herself to take that as a good omen, holding the intent of seeing all those dear old things in that predictably lovely British formula piece, as she calmly, calmly, collected the clothes she wanted to wear, and yes, to take, as though she were simply, clumsily, dopily sorting through all her things, maybe rearranging them; yes, *rearranging them*, for no good reason, no good reason at all, all the while disconnecting any lingering attachment she had to them as she deployed them as a smoke screen.

Fashion, she could replace. There was no lingerie she felt attached to; at least not since Manny had turned. She had to be pragmatic. She put on her most comfortable sports bra and underpants, because it might just, *just might*, be possible that she would have to actually run through a crowd, through traffic (would not be the first time) and surreptitiously tossed a few spare pairs into the croc bag as she made out like she was sorting out all the old ones she didn't want any more.

She performed as though she were layering up for the cold outside; tight thermal top, fave tee, shirt, waistcoat, jacket, tie, scarf… okay, scarves. As she dressed, she found herself dancing a little more wildly, flamboyantly covering the clothes she was squirreling by making piles as she picked out her escape outfit, her everyday sorcery ensemble, with camouflaged precision. The thermal, the tee, the shirt, the waistcoat, the jacket, the scarves; they were it. She was throwing things on the floor; slacks, blouses, jackets, and throwing other things on chest surface, near her bag, around her bag and yes, woops, oh dear; *some things even in her bag*, but she was dressed, dressed as the sorceress and –

New song.

She held her breath in the two-second gap between.

Golden Earring. *Twilight Zone.*

Two songs about hit men on the run, time running out.

*Dash! Dash!*

Okay.

*Okay.*

She upped the performance.

*Where's my card? Oh there it is* – switching the phone to Bluetooth, then the elaborate dropping of the phone, and the looking up the session times again…

*She could feel it.*

*Something… off.*

…and the changing of the boots again (into the ones she actually wanted of course) and putting the purse in the handbag, and the handbag into the croc bag, stuffed down with the alternate jeans, and alternate boots – oh, the clumsy, the muttering, *damn I want to see this thing, don't want to miss the trailers!* (more than she remembered, slipping, sleight of hand into the pockets, the bracelet from Adelaide and the nipple-rings from Sydney…) I am so busy it might be the last chance I get… (there, that is enough, enough – *enough* – go! *Go!*)

Keeping on dancing with the bag out to the bed. Manic, she was having a manic episode. Anyone watching would think that. Flipside of the depression; and hell, maybe that was true? Maybe that's what was happening; but it didn't make it any less practical, or her decision any less real.

She looked at the bag. It was overflowing.

Okay, so… maybe she really was *genuinely* a little bit manic.

Maybe there were a few extra things she *did* want to take.

But she had to go.

*She – had – to – go.*

She grabbed a few scarves out of the top and stuffed them in her coat pockets. Shirts and blouses flew out with them.

Too much!

Why couldn't she go?

So her armour had variants, worth keeping. Big deal.

But, if anyone *was watching*, now it really looked like she was planning to go.

Or, like she was completely breaking down.

Which was it, she wondered?

The epic song was reaching the middle bit.

This performance had taken too long.

*She was taking too long.*

Way too long.

*Why couldn't she go?*

Her instincts were raising the alarm.

Her skin was crawling.

No, no, it's okay.

A few minutes… then go.

At least the stuff in the bag was the stuff she liked, *narrowed down*.

She looked at it again.

*Could she* take it?

Fuck. It looked *exactly* like she was going away on a plane *forever* and could only take one bag.

She grabbed it, upturned it, shook it and dumped all contents on the bed.

The song was ending; the next song would be the third and that would complete the reading, the divinatory trinity of pop culture iconery, and that would tell her what was happening *next*. If it was a good one, she'd go.

She'd go then.

She put the phone on the cradle by the bed.

Why – *why?*

*Like she wasn't going to leave!*

She sorted through again, purging the stuff that was nothing, that she merely *liked*, but did not *require*. She saw the ring on her pinkie. It was darkening.

Amethyst to burgundy.

She stood straight.

She was a sorceress. Dressed. Prepared to leave.

She looked at the bag again, stared it out.

You could still tell that the bag was full!

It even looked, somehow, exactly like it had a change of clothes in it.

*It was way more than you took to see Dame Maggie and Dame Judie.*

Library. That was the key.

But; her hands were shaking. She could feel her teeth chattering.

She was terrified.

And then, she knew.

She upturned and dumped the bag again.

She went back to the walk-in, and took out the inserts.

She had intended to do this last.

She should have done it first, and last.

This was all.

The rest was fear.

Fear of the thing.

The demon.

*The coveting thing.*

She dumped all the stuff, the scarves and stockings, the thermals, all the light stuff from her coat pockets, all the stashed jewellery, on the top. She took her three yoyos, the three rings, the earrings, pocketed the doubles, wore both the pendant and the chain, both bracelets and the watch. She put the cufflinks in, and the tie pin.

She wore them all.

She went back to the bed and opened the croc bag. She put in the black variant and the best green variant. Some white. Rolled them tight. Minimal, practical; only half the bag, without it even looking odd. She opened her bureau drawer and shoved a few notepads, her chargers, her tablet and laptop, all of them on top of the… *Jesus, that had to be three changes of clothes really, and a pair of sneakers…!* …and told herself she didn't give a shit, that she wasn't afraid, that she was going to the library. Then she shoved a second pair of boots down each side.

'Going to the…' Emerald uttered under her breath. 'Going to see, then…'

Could she sell it?

She looked in the mirror.

She was dressed; the real deal.

You could see the rings; slightly unusual, the extra jewellery, but no red flag – she always dressed to go outside, and always looked like this. Always –

*Fuck that. She didn't care.*

But seriously. Jesus. She looked okay. She didn't look like shit at all.

Thin, yes.

'Burger and fries for dinner, Miss Tarragon?'

She blew herself a kiss.

'Don't mind if I do Ms Emerald!'

*Fuck security. I can fight my way out if need be.*

# CHAPTER FOUR:
# VOICES

She snatched her phone from the cradle as the second song ended.

She killed the playlist.

She didn't want to know.

She called him.

She heard his phone ring a few rooms away; chambers, really. They were too big to be called just rooms. The ring tone, the theme to the new game, played almost to the point where she knew it would cut off, then he answered at the last beat.

'I thought I could hear that down in the lounge?'

'Yeah, Em, I'm here. I thought you might be sleeping, didn't want to wake you.'

'I'm just heading out, I'll come see you.'

'Well, I'll be here.'

She hung up. That didn't happen often but it was far from the first time. She fought back fear again. No. She did not have to try and make the turducken croc bag look less heavy, or less full than it was. She would go with it. Say yes, as the improvisers taught. It is clearly more than usual, and she could tell him why. Make something of it. The library.

She left the bedroom without the slightest sentiment, and as she walked down the cream-carpeted hall, lined with frames of all the art from the games Manny had grown up with, she thought that she would have to map out a quick route in her mind, get to some kind of casino; three, five trips away, and make some actual cash there. Put some distance down. No fake ID this time, but she had the cash in her purse to be getting on with; Manny's paranoid switch to greed and control had come on more quickly than the others, and along with the downtime, a first for her, she hadn't had the uptime to source someone reliable to make her anything fake.

With Manny, she *really had* thought… fifth time lucky.

But the thing that covets would always find her, always ruin things.

Over her twenties and into her thirties she had sought security in a variety of places, with a variety of men, in a variety of worlds. Always, the *covething*; that was what she had started to call it, that was her weird name for it now, the thing that was scaring her, keeping her trapped in her bedroom, keeping her mentally paralysed over choosing between things she didn't want, didn't even need; the thing that coveted, the *covething*, always it would whisper in her man's ear.

*She is so beautiful*
*She is so powerful.*
*So unique.*
*She will not stay.*
*Not with you.*
*Never with you.*

*No woman is satisfied forever*, covething would tell them. *Normal women stay, because they know; satisfaction never lasts. Normal men stay because of the same; you know this to be true. In the end, companionship, comfort, shared memories. These are the things that bind. But the beautiful; the truly beautiful, the gifted and the uniquely gifted; they do not have to rely upon these bonds. They can move, and move on, and move on again, many more times than the ordinary, the plain, the nothings, before they settle for mere love, mere memories, real life.*

She had heard the voice the first time, just faintly, with Josef. She had the power to hear telepathic voices, spirit voices or voices from the ether; that was one of the things sorcerers did. But she had not wanted to hear it, and she had ignored it.

Then, the second time, she really had heard it.

Still, she had ignored it.

She had hoped Steele would resist for her; make a different choice.

The third time, she had heard it enough to know what was happening, definitely know what was happening; and to try to will him against it. *Please, Giancarlo, do not submit.*

The fourth, with Horst, and the fifth now, dear Manny; the same.

Too late, nothing could convince them. Giancarlo and Horst had nearly killed her; she was lucky not to have killed Giancarlo, and had not cared less whether she'd killed Horst. Something deep within her still hoped that she had. But this time she'd known she'd been pushing her luck, and now she knew that she had just, sadly, almost pathetically, been treading emotional water until Manny had heard the *covething*, fallen to its whispering words, and turned down the dark path.

*I can give you what you need to keep her.*

She had known, and when it had happened again.

And she had given up.

She had retreated and acquiesced her own cosmic assassination.

Five times lucky.

Fifth time the charm.

Nope.

Fifth time the curse, and she had prayed, essentially, to be taken, to be wrenched from this mortal coil and...

And now, of course, she realized, as she walked on down the hall; *Coveth* lied.

*I can give you what you need... to drive her away.*

*So that I may once again pursue her.*

Coveth.

She stopped in her tracks.

A proper name.

The thing was closer, more real, more entrenched now in the material plane, more eager for her, than she had known. Now the game, the chase, was real.

*Was that...?*

She took another step.

Her leg jerked, then stopped.

*Was that… what was happening?*

Yesterday, she had found herself sitting on the bed. Drifting, asking passively yet again, to be taken out of the world. Sad, deeply sad, and tired, so very tired, without the will or the energy, or the energy to will. No target, nor the desire for that will, even if she had possessed the energy, for which to get up and go. Just, sadness; all that was still there, over emptiness.

But then, somehow she had seen it.

She had been struck with an idea.

An exit, a solution.

A plan.

And if she was using the last of her will in asking the universe to execute her, then she could bloody-well change gears, change course, and use it to execute that plan. But now…

Now, it seemed…

Coveth.

Coveth was real, and trying to stop her.

That was it. That was happening.

Coveth was behind the door, at the end of the hall.

# CHAPTER FIVE:
# EPISODE V

Five times, the man she loved had turned. Five times, Coveth had appeared to convince him, and it had always started the same way.

Manny had asked for a little push here and there; the thing she said she really didn't like doing. But, he would ask, could she just cast a little spell? Just for him? Make this person act this way, just this once? And then, just this once again? Make that person sway another way? And once again? And again? And; *you don't mind really, do you? It's not – so bad – is it?*

Change people's minds, change people's circumstance, change people's reality; *changing reality itself.*

Part of the problem was that she was such a Samantha.

There were sorcerers who had no problem being that kind of sorcerer; they just got out there and did it, hid it, glamoured it all away. Took over a beach town and made it their kingdom. Took over a son and made the business their own. Settled into a little community. Ran it. Took over a store in the middle of nowhere and never went broke. She had even done a bit of that herself; enough to know; no, that wasn't her. She wanted a relationship, and she wanted a man who would accept her as a sorceress, as someone whose will, properly summoned, focused and channelled, was naturally able to enact change upon the physical realm. But also; she wanted someone who did not want her simply for exploitation. Want to exploit her, or others.

*Yes, yes.*

*Good luck with that.*

*Ha-ha.*

Now through which door do I pass in order to exit this stage forever?

She stared at herself again in the hall mirror; she looked concerned, intense.

Thirty-three. She was too old to start again as a fashion model now, but she was not too old to revive her acting career. She still photographed well, and once Horst had given up on her, she'd put herself back out there; made a few calls, hustled a few meetings, and gotten back on the books. She'd left Berlin and returned to New York, happy to become lost in the crowd, lost in the casting calls amongst all the other telegenics and hairstyles and cheek bones and jaw lines. After calling in a favour she'd landed a decent agent, and after the excitement of being back in the city, and back in 'the biz', and back in the casting world had worn off, the agent had come through and managed to help her genuinely not waste too much of her time. She'd taken a few okay meetings, competed in a few high-end auditions, but in the end the producers and directors and money people had mostly just wanted to know where she had come from, in her thirties, such a striking actress, out of nowhere. But then they had not hired her, because she had no track record.

She hadn't cared; this had always been how it was going to go.

Someone would give her a break eventually.

Manny had hired her in the end, to be a full-spectrum model for a new lead female character in his upcoming RPG sequel Primagineer Experior II; mo-cap, live action, art, promotion; she was it. The fact that she was experienced, yet essentially unknown, was appealing to him, as was the fact that her voice was just as enchanting as her looks (his words) and right for the character. The fact that she was indeed very beautiful, and immediately attracted to him too, didn't hurt either. In the end, the fact that Hermann 'Manny' Devane was actually dating, then had shacked-up with his most famous and popular character, IRL, only boosted his cool factor with the young men whose demographic bought most of his product, and also, if the niche demographics were to be believed, was secretly appealing to many of the gamer-chicks as well.

And she had fallen, again. Allowed it, hoped it.

Coveth was a lazy demon though.

Her admirer had the patience of his kind, the patience of a thing that lived forever.

Again, she had not allowed herself to see that, although it had been there, the whole time. Of course. Coveth had waited until she had done all the work; until her lover had done all the work. Only then did it go to work.

Not everybody famous and hugely successful is paranoid, insecure, and egomaniacal.

But it helps.

She smiled at herself in the mirror.

And it doesn't take much, if the person in question is spiritually unawakened, or unprotected, for a demon to manage it, to bring it out, to…

*You have made her into an idol. Now, many other men covet her. This is your doing; now it is your task to protect her; from them, for herself. Just for you.*

She'd heard it whisper in his mind, as she'd lain awake.

Like it didn't care anymore.

Like nothing, let alone her, could stop it now.

And now… was she hearing it again?

The door at the end of the hall was closed. It was a narrow hall. That was unusual, for the door to be closed.

*For you, just for you!*

Was she hearing…?

*What* was she hearing?

She had been so stupid, agreeing to help him with her sorcery. *So stupid.*

But she always did. And now she had, *again*. She figured she was cursed. She fell in love, and the demon ruined the man she fell in love with. Clockwork demonic influence. Always the men who were already there. Who didn't need her. Who were more attractive to her, because they didn't need her. Already making their way in their chosen field with only themselves to get in their way.

It always worked. Always, until the demon, until Coveth, interfered.

Five times it worked, five times… Coveth.

That's how demons got you; they saw patterns. Your only defence was to recognise them yourself, and see the devil in the details. She knew that. Everyone knew that. But hope, and desire, even loneliness; they all made you think that you could do better, that you could outwit the *things*.

Things always started going better around then, when she agreed to use sorcery to help her man get ahead; but 'better' always needed sustaining. The demon, she now, finally figured, stepped in and helped about then. Little demon miracles, to make things happen. Then, when those little miracles stopped happening, when the demon withdrew them; when the growth of the business, the growth of the success, levelled out, that was when he asked. Whichever he; he always had, eventually.

You know the Samantha thing?

They always ended up asking.

How… how much wriggle room?

How much… *more?*

So then, *she ended up being the demon.*

Maintaining the growth that the demon had begun.

Going back on the Samantha thing; triggering the beginning of the end that had always been predestined.

She called it the Samantha thing.

It wasn't strictly. Samantha had always at least attempted to acquiesce to Derwin's insistence that she did not use her witchcraft; that she tried to be normal. But in the end, she could never help herself. So, she called it her Samantha thing because, once they believed her, that her sorcery was real, once she had proved it, she had told them;

*Look, you know how Darrin never wanted Samantha to use her powers?*

*Well; I want you to be Darrin.*

*I don't want to use my powers to make you rich, or more successful. I don't want you to want that for yourself. You get it? Nor for me, and not by me. For yourself; or it will never sustain you. I want to be honest with you about who I am, and what I can do. But I don't want to be with the kind of man who wants me to cheat for him. I want you to be you; and do what you do, and have your own success.*

Of course they agreed.

She was strikingly, Spanishly gorgeous and this was a deal breaker for her.

They would always agree to anything at that point; she recognized that now. She would never again underestimate the power of self-persuasion that lust and desire created in the human male, even the nicest, the most innocent of them.

So this time around would be the last; really, this time.

But this time around, she would do something different.

She would look for a different kind of man.

Be a different kind of person.

A different sort of sorceress.

Be modern; call herself a sorcerer, not a sorceress, like the social controllers wanted.

Find love, maybe.

But find, and make, a different kind of love.

Business love.

She turned from the mirror and stared at the hall door again.

*Why was she thinking all this?*

So she'd made herself indispensable. To him, personally, and to his business.

*Like someone was... telling her?*

Then, the extra security. It had been easy for Manny to justify because this was New York and although he was hardly John Lennon, he was worshipped by a lot of very intense gamers. Then more, and then the psychics.

*Just here to make sure nobody interferes with you.*
Wait; had he… *told her that?*
Half asleep, weeks ago; had he?
*Had he?*
Suddenly she felt it.
There was a low-level dark sorcery all through the apartment.
But… what else could she have done?
Not done it, was the answer.
Not acted like she was normal.
Not gone forth with an open heart, like a normal person.
Admit that she was not normal, that she, her life, could never be normal.
That Darrin was right.
That Samantha was a fool.
But that had been a sitcom; there was no comedy in the real world. Comedy existed outside of it, to critique and sometimes define it. But there was none in the world.
Mel Brooks had said it best.
*Tragedy is when I cut my finger. Comedy is when you fall into an open sewer and die.*
There were all sorts of things to be mined from that quote. But the main thing so far as her world went was that it was all tragedy. Comedy was perspective; comedy was tragedy when it happened to somebody else, and the more appalling, the better. But there was no comedy in her using her powers, having that backfire, then cleaning up the mess in order to save the one she loved. He had pleaded with her, she had acquiesced, he had become a raging monster of possession, and now she had to escape – *Episode V.*
So here she went; through the door.
She took one last look.
The coat.
And the tie.
The belt.
And the charms.

She could have managed, rebuilt, just with that.
But she would take the three changes, and the rest.
Just a crocodile skin messenger bag.
Not that much, really, in the end.
She opened the door and went through.

# CHAPTER SIX:
# COVETH

Immediately weird.

She adjusted to the feeling and got her bearings.

This was one of the main rooms, the north-western corner. North, facing the city; west, the park. Balcony landing all the way around through one door in the middle of each wall; high-arched, gold-framed windows all along. The southern wall, right over there past the coffee table and big dining table, all bookshelves. Couches against every wall, smaller coffee tables that could join or separate to accommodate any number, art everywhere. White, white, white. Lovely. Clean. Such a big space. She had always known that, but this evening, *weirdly huge*. It was night now, just into the first few minutes of full darkness …

Something was *really wrong*.

Keep calm.

To her immediate left the wall went straight out to the first arch-window. There was a 'fun' bathroom back there that they never used anymore; spa and bath and… then, to her immediate right, the room spread back into the apartment's second, lounge-attached kitchen, as opposed to the main one at the other end of the 'house', with the long kitchen bar separating preparation from socialization. Beyond that, the big pool table, the wet bar and another lounge, further within, and past them; the elevator and escape.

It was big, open.

She could see it all from the kitchen corner here, by the hall exit.

Manny was at the bar, sitting casually on a stool with his elbows spread, facing away from the white windows, toward the table and elevator. He was flicking through something on his tablet with one hand, eating what looked like a hastily prepared ham, cheese and lettuce sandwich with the other.

Façade.

She carried the bag around the corner and into the kitchen, placing it down on the bench corner, away from him but in his eye-line, not hiding anything. Then she leaned over his tablet and kissed him on the cheek.

Manny smiled. He had dark hair and a thin but friendly face; a bit like that young French race driver she liked, a bit like that older British politician she liked physically but loathed philosophically, but his smile was nicer than either of them, his eyes more cheeky and his manner less stiff. He was still a geeky guy; very literal with a straightforward sense of humour, and you could still kind-of shock him with a well- placed swear word. Before Coveth, this had been simple, uncomplicated, and endearing; especially when his heart had been so open, so ready to share and understand.

'You said you wanted to see that old British-biddy comedy. The one in Japan.'

He said it in a way that made him seen casually smart, and intuitive. Like he knew her, like he still cared enough to remember what she liked, and what she'd said; and he had anticipated her movements. It was supposed to mean he felt close to her, instead it made her skin crawl, just a bit.

'Then I'm going to the library. I want to continue researching that book I keep threatening the world with.'

He looked up at her as she went to the fridge. She glanced at him, holding steady; his face was passive, but his resting face was good looking, and she remembered, as she looked at him for what was hopefully the last time ever, the many times they'd made love in this place. Right there, where he was sitting, on the bar. It seemed another life now that she could be that heated, that limber, that eager and energetic. That woman, she supposed. But it had been sweaty, and sweet, and satisfying. He was no animal, he didn't have that in him, but he was attentive, and had technique, and when he was really switched on, he really meant it. In the end, that was what she liked most.

'Book?'

She closed the fridge without registering the contents, becoming angry and restless.

'Remember I started it, a few months ago? I've been in a bit of a funk, but I'm feeling a bit better now. I think I just need a project. You know, all the gear from the last time I went down there is still in the bag… I think there are library books at the bottom I'll be fined for keeping so long.'

'Shall I call a driver?'

'No. I'll walk. I like the cold.'

'You're rugged up enough.'

'Plan ahead. I always say, you can always take off a coat if you're too warm; but you can't put one on to get warm if you don't take it.'

'You're still too young and hot to be dispensing grandma advice.' Manny smiled, nicely. He'd had a good day, it seemed. She hadn't seen him in a while, but she hadn't seen him like this, casual and almost charming, for a long time.

She faked a sweet response. 'Being hot, is the point, my genius boy.'

That was what she had called him, started calling him, early on. He'd always liked it. It felt like they hadn't talked for weeks. She was pretty sure they hadn't. It still seemed very foggy.

*Just here to make sure nobody interferes with you.*

No – wait.

'*…yes; she knows…*'

Who – who had said that?

Manny suddenly sat up. 'Got your phone? Cab if it's too cold. They say snow after midnight. How long will you be?'

'Not – not that long. And I will certainly cab back.'

She took the bag again by the long handles, came back around the bar, and kissed him on the cheek again.

That was it.

Last kiss, last word, last goodbye in five, four –

The screen on his tablet had gone blank.

No. The screen was… the tablet wasn't even turned on.

Manny huffed. Like he was sad all of a sudden.

'So, he says you will *think* that you've have been having revelations.'

She was still standing beside him, looking at the blank tablet.

'But it's really just him, scanning your mind.'

She stepped back, away, out of arm's reach.

The fact of her fear becoming reality sharpened her mind incredibly quickly; she immediately felt a psychic presence take flight as her mental defences kicked in, the defences she was not even aware of having let drop, like someone had twisted the dimmer on a light switch to high all of a sudden. But she did not truly register anything anywhere near as acutely as the question of whether or not she would have to fight Manny, to get back past the kitchen bench, and into the elevator vestibule.

How much extra security would be there now?

In the vestibule, in the lobby, on the street?

'…*yes; ha–ha! She knows, she knows…!*'

She didn't have to ask, and there was no point. She knew exactly what had been happening now; what *was happening* – *right now*. In her depressed and weakened state, Coveth had been reading her; not her deep thoughts but her strong ones, and relaying them to Manny out loud. Genuinely reading her like a book. He, *it*, had been speaking openly to him when he was alone. She had been picking up Coveth's psychic scans as her own mental churning, as her own thoughts or insights, even as revelation; as 'help from above'. But in the end, all those thoughts, all the regurgitation of her fears, back and forth in the wardrobe… she'd just been hearing what Coveth had churned, as he was scanning and rummaging and trying to figure out what she was going to do, relaying it to Manny, hypnotizing him with his bullshit. In the end, at the very least, Coveth would have told him what to expect from her; he would have made him order extra physical security, and extra psychic security.

How much extra would there be?

There would be a lot.

'You don't have to go to the movies.' Manny smiled, calmly. 'You don't have to go to the library. You can have anything you want, streamed or delivered here. You never have to leave here, not if you don't want to. The level of security around *Primagineer Experior II* is massive; there are crazy people, obsessive nerds, who will be waiting outside; they will follow you down the street, get in your cab, hold you at gunpoint, just to find out where the game story goes.'

Her hand tightened around the bag handle.

That was mostly true, at least potentially, but she didn't care.

She hoisted the croc skin and put it on her shoulder.

Coveth had kept her befuddled in her own weariness, in her own mind; second guessing, swirling up the mud in the water, as he determined her intentions and motivations and told them to Manny in real time.

Her mouth had gone dry and she gulped.

She took a shot and walked to the fridge.

She took out a bottle of orange juice and opened it.

Clear path to the elevator.

She gulped, and swallowed heavily.

'I call it Coveth, Manny. At least, I do now. I've escaped it, and the man it controls, four times. You are the fifth man I have loved, that it has turned against me, and now I have to escape *you*. That makes me sad, I admit.'

A little flicker of a smile slashed his lips.

'Not sad enough though.'

She looked him in the eyes. There wasn't much of him left that he hadn't allowed Coveth to infect.

'No. Not sad enough.'

She tried honesty.

'I am not going to play the game this time, Manny. I am leaving. I am leaving now. I told you about it, I told you not to listen, I even told you, after our first few times, about my abilities, about my culture, and about the problems it had given me in the past; I told you not to listen to it. Part of it is my fault, for helping you with sorcery. But even after that, you still didn't have to go the way he offered; you could have told me, come to me.'

'There was no need. I had it all under control.'

She sighed. 'Coveth did things to make things temporarily easier for you.' Then she huffed. There was no point. 'When it stopped, I did love you; so I stepped in and helped you. It's a trap it sets. I fall for it every time.'

'It's helping me now. I wish you could understand.'

'I understand exactly.'

'It says that the creatures of its realm are misunderstood. We're going to make a game about them.'

'Sympathy for the Demons? Or is he a Djinn? In the end, they are always out for themselves, Manny. And even the Djinn are three steps ahead.'

'He's helping us. But, you won't help anymore, he says.'

She suddenly realized something about him. 'Manny; are you awake?'

'No. No, of course not.'

'Of course not?'

'No. I'm dreaming. We always talk like this in dreams. Like, when you say you're a sorceress, and you help me by casting spells. You're not really a sorceress; there's no such thing. Just like Coveth isn't real; he only talks to me in dreams.'

'Manny, I'm leaving. He will leave you, and follow me. At least, he will eventually. It happens every time. You'll be free after that. It shouldn't hurt you too much; most of it's happened under the influence. Once I'm gone, it can stay like a dream and you can go and find –'

'You can't leave. This is a dream; this is *my dream*. He's taught me how to control my dreams, so only what I want to happen –'

'He's lied, Manny. This is reality. You let him in too far; he's getting stronger. *It's* getting stronger. He's defining your reality for you… look, there is no point to this. This is over, and the only way to help you is to leave. What can I expect downstairs?'

'You won't be going downstairs, Emerald.'

'I told you; two years ago, I told you. I nearly killed Giancarlo, and I did my best to kill Horst. I still don't know if Horst is alive, and I don't –'

He walked straight in from the elevator vestibule.

'Care?'

There he was.

'Ozzie! I'm so hurt!'

Horst.

Horst was alive.

She hadn't noticed until then that there was another man, too. Pale and all in white, so much so as to be nearly camouflaged, sitting in the far corner, on the couch by the bookshelves. He, *it*, seemed to have come into focus with her shock, with the shock of seeing Horst. But she quickly put it together. That it was him, *it*, she'd seen, but not seen, when she had first entered the room. Or rather, his presence, to which she'd responded; to which she'd been responding all day.

'At the risk of cliché…' Horst smiled, charming as ever. 'Ozzie, my darling, I run a security company that specializes in finding runaways. I have a psychic division. Even before you shacked up with one of the three most publicly recognizable billionaire game designers in the world, I was closing in on –'

'No, you weren't.' Emerald was starting to snap. In a bad way, or good way; that was yet to be determined. 'You didn't know where I was until I went public with Manny. And even if you had known, you never would have come after me. Something has changed.' She gulped again. 'That's him isn't it? Sitting down, over there? That's Coveth.'

Coveth stood, and bowed.

It felt like he was standing right in front of her. It was even a little too real, like he was standing right there, between her and the kitchen bar and Manny, standing just an inch too close, just a fraction into the limit of her personal space; but he was still there, at the end of the room, still.

He arose from his bow.

'You named me.'

Coveth's lips seemed to move a little clumsily, like a badly dubbed movie, but its psychic voice spoke crisply, and directly, into her mind.

'You have slowly, ever so slowly, succumbed to my emergence. Just as each of your successive lovers have succumbed more deeply, surrendered more completely, as you have exposed me to each of them. You fully accept me now, as a reality. I am so pleased. It is very difficult for us to work our way up these days. We are legion, and there is so much competition; so many spaces that practically every djinn, every dark spirit, every demon and succubus must fight for attention. Constant jostling! But then again; there are so many avenues now! The rise of the anti-spirit movement leaves so many unprotected! But, there you have it. I am clever. I am better at this, it seems, than many of my brethren-competitors. And now, I am Coveth.'

Despite herself, she whispered. 'Coveth...' Immediately she registered a terrible, bone-chilling self-disgust.

'That's the name you gave it...' Horst spoke, reverently. 'It told me you would. I can't see him, but I can hear him talking to you.'

'They're intimately interconnected...' Manny looked to Horst. 'More than she could ever be with any mortal. They sense each other.'

Emerald nearly threw up. 'Jesus Christ! Did it tell you that?'

Manny stared accusingly at Emerald. 'It knew what you were thinking, didn't it?'

'You're jealous of it?' Emerald guffawed. 'It knows the shape of my thoughts, Manny. At least, it did until I just shut it out; but it doesn't know anything, didn't read anything, deeper than...'

Manny smiled and finished eating his sandwich as she indicated it sharply with her ringed hand.

'…that I might want a sandwich, because I see you eating a sandwich!'

That wasn't strictly true. She understood now that he had been churning those thoughts, *I want a sandwich because I see a sandwich* thoughts, *I want to take that tank top because I see that tank top* thoughts, *I want to leave now because I feel like leaving* thoughts, to try and get deeper, churn the mud, see what lay beneath.

It hadn't worked.

Had it?

'Don't be angry…' Manny shrugged. He put the tablet down and looked up at her. 'He says, I think, if I understand correctly…' Manny wiped his mouth with a napkin as he finished chewing. '…he says that you found me so I could have you. You want me to have you. Otherwise, you would not have kept looking for a man.'

'You even found one called Manny,' Horst guffawed. 'A man called Manny!'

Coveth took over, and the two men fell silent, as though they were listening to, and trying to identify, a distant song.

'You looked for a man who could satisfy your desires, Emerald, did you not? Not just sexually, but your life desires. You had looked so hard, so long. You know that I can have Manny build you a green screen up here. You can mo-cap your role for the next game from here. That will satisfy your need to perform; and you can talk to your fans, all from here. Nobody in this world *really* needs to go out any more; and you don't even *like* going out. Your isolation will help maintain the mystique of the game, as well. You'll be reclusive. Security will have to be raised; as you've intuited, Horst is already helping with that. I had Manny buy a stake in his company, so we can expand it. His psychic agents already tell Manny that you're very restless, and you were… so manic this evening.'

'Are there cams?'

Manny's distant gaze broke. 'They say you tore your wardrobe apart. All that; just to go to the library. That's why I came home.'

'Who said?'

*I was naked.*

'You're restless, I get that…' Manny stood, as though he were about to reach out and touch her. She flinched, and this time the juice really came up in her throat. 'There are nerds and geeks and gamers; violent, sexist, rapist gamers out there. You don't want to be chased again. I know you don't want that.'

She swallowed back the sick. 'You don't know anything!'

'He does know a lot, actually…' Coveth seemed to smile.

She stepped forward, toward the demon, addressing Coveth directly.

'These are all his worst impulses; his darkest desires, his base *uses* for me! You're just… feeding each other!'

Horst stared at her. 'It's not like you to go out without makeup, Ozzie.'

God that made her ill.

'You must be very feeling very out of sorts.'

'He makes you ill…' Coveth noted. '…but he did not, before, when you were together. Interesting. I learn more and more. I can help you to find him appealing again. Both these men have agreed that the choice is yours as to sexual partnership.'

'*Coveth…*'

The use of its name, with such bitter fury, genuinely seemed to startle it.

Then she saw; it liked it.

'…*listen*. You don't want this; you don't want to possess these two men. You just like *chasing me* –'

'Yes! I did; but I have evolved. Now, this is what I want. To feel what they feel, to share their desires. Yours, too.'

She gulped back more bile.

There was no getting out of this.

It could have them kill her.

Right now.

They could try; if she couldn't get to the pool table, they might succeed. She didn't know exactly how weak she was. But more likely, it could have them keep her here, wear her down, until she agreed to allow it to… what? She'd heard of a dozen different things. Some of them had been made into movies. Any of them could be made to happen in a private billionaire's apartment, in a city like this.

Except…

No, wait.

*Who had been telling her to run?*

Back in the room, while Coveth had been feeding from her fear, and insecurity?

Something; something had been telling her to run.

*Run!*

But not just to run – *to dash.*

Dash; a curiously old, eccentric word she never used herself. She looked to that word in her mind, but felt complete terror, externally, *from another local source,* as Coveth moved toward her and made half the distance between them in one step. It was terrifying; jolting… but it had seemed urgent for him.

A desperate… *misdirection?*

He wasn't really there, she saw now. He was some kind of malformed hologram, a trick of the light with no real characteristics or detail. But there were illuminated flickers, coming off of something that was hovering about it, about its basic, essentially formless energy body. She could see them, make sense of them. She knew straight away what they were, what this was, what these tricks were, what *it,* what these creatures, could do, and did do, to appear real. It was collecting motes; particles of dead skin and insect; all the grim and unseemly dead and inanimate things that dust was made of. It was starting to manipulate it, the old, dead matter; the smallest matter, and use it, levitate and congeal it, mingling it with the humidity, the water particles in the air, to make clay, make a form. Soon, he would appear as though something humanoid. The more people recognized him as such, the closer he would come to being able to walk the Earth, and pass for human, like so many other minor demons who had worked their way up. Some of them even believed they were human after a while, taught themselves to forget their demonic base. And this one seemed to learn quickly, very quickly; he had his hooks into her; into her psyche and well into her world. In that respect, although she could understand what *it* was doing, she didn't really know what that meant, what the consequences would be for her, or her personal world.

She'd never seen this or been near it, only heard and read.

And it was true what they said.

Hearing and reading wasn't the same.

*Maybe she'd been right to ask for an out...*

Coveth smiled. He couldn't tell what she was thinking anymore, but he still seemed to get the gist. She flinched as her phone vibrated in her coat pocket. Coveth stepped forward again, a shorter step this time, but much closer still. His unformed, quivering hand lurched out, as though...

The phone?

Did he want the phone?

'So this is the full costume?' Horst asked suddenly. 'Don't think I ever saw this.'

Emerald uttered. '...shut the fuck up Horst...' Two years, and he'd succumbed, or betrayed and agreed, almost straight away.

He laughed and she glanced back at him, despite herself. He'd moved to cover the exit from the kitchenette at the other end. Closer now, she saw that Horst remained a classic example of Teutonic handsomeness. But he'd visibly aged, with grey streaks having sprouted at the side of his dark blonde hair. As though to compensate, he had a kind of almost-Hipster manicured beard, thin and dark brown with white patches at the sides of his wide, square jaw.

'Your smile doesn't reach your eyes any more, Horst.'

The narrow, piercing blue eyes were just cold now; the smile was just a sinister stretch of his Joker's mouth, and a baring of his clean, shining-white fangs, pushing back his tiny ears and visibly stretching his scalp, creasing his high, imposing brow.

Her hand reached up, to her breast, for the phone.

Horst barked. 'Don't let her touch anything!'

He almost grabbed for her but simultaneously, as he obviously considered it, took a couple of unconscious steps backwards, remaining bizarrely with his arms outstretched. Coveth moved again; it flashed in a full ninety-degree arc to her right, as though she had become its centre of gravity somehow, maintaining the same distance between them, but now on the other side of the kitchenette, placing it fully between them to stand in the kitchen area between lounge and pool room, almost exactly between Manny and Horst. Manny spun on his barstool and turned to it, puzzled and oddly concerned. Coveth examined the group strangely, not quite sure what was happening but wanting to be close. Emerald wasn't really sure where it was exactly; its pure, manifested energy form might still have been way off in the corner, it might just have been moving its physical manipulation, its tulpa, around the room while it sat tight, far away. Creepily, this felt even more as though he was starting to insinuate himself, genuinely and physically, into the scene between the human trio.

It looked at her.

He was giving himself *emerald eyes,* Emerald saw.

Oh God. She tasted more bile in her throat.

And the look… what was becoming his face.

Did he think… did he think they were friends?

That they were… *all friends?*

'It's my phone…' Emerald snapped. '…you fucking moron.'

Horst was suddenly nervous, frightened even.

'She has a power! Devane! Has she been *touching anything* around here lately?'

Manny guffawed. 'Touching anything?'

'Is that so?' Coveth came further forward a little more.

Emerald gasped, she couldn't help it.

Horst was speaking urgently now. 'We need to get everything away from her; now! You don't know what she can do – didn't you get that message?'

Manny took out his own phone. 'Message?'

'Give me your bag!' Horst threw out both his hands with the demand, but kept his feet planted solidly where they were. 'Now!' Still keeping his distance, in his fabulous grey pin-striped business suit, he looked utterly ridiculous.

Emerald felt her lip sneer up. 'I can't believe I'm looking into your face again, Von Wertheim.'

'Now!'

His arms jutted out further, which made his posterior stick out as well, like his feet were caught in mud and he was trying to reach the branch she was extending, to help him out. Only there was no stick, no help.

Manny stared at his phone. 'There's nothing here about...'

Message...

Emerald looked at her screen.

She had a voice message.

Coveth held up what looked like a pale, cautious hand. Like he could suddenly see how things could go wrong. Emerald raised her hands as well.

'What... what is she doing?'

She quickly slipped her ear-buds in.

'At the end of the email I sent you, Devane! Didn't you read the whole thing?'

'This is a damn essay, Horst.' It was tedious to him, reading what people had bothered to write him. 'I never read a message any longer than five words...'

The voice message came through... and Emerald sighed. She recognized the voice. It was the mild, female, recorded, automatically-dispatched voice of her service provider. The men were shouting at each other over the top of it. She couldn't hear, and everything seemed distant.

Coveth was staring at her, anxious, almost angry.

Horst's face was getting redder.

'Well I didn't think you'd really show up!' Manny protested. 'It's not like she's going anywhere, anyway; she's weak as a puppy! The thing's worn her down! We can do what we like with her!'

The two men stared at each other, both incredulous with rage.

The message voice said: '…balance and recharge…'

That was all of the message she heard; but it spoke to her as though an angel with a loudhailer had just appeared between herself and Coveth, addressed her with those three words, and vanished.

Maybe that had actually happened.

She ended the call.

'Not show up!? Look at her!'

Her music player was set to resume at the end of a call.

She left the buds in, hoping that it would be something immediately loud and immersive, that would stop her hearing the two monstrous fools before her as they barked at each other. At first, feeling weirdly distant again now, she didn't hear anything.

'I do look at her! All the time! She's a goddess! I have her fully-rendered for eternity in digital bliss!'

'Who cares about that!? She can be our slave – real and physical! But we have to contain her!'

'I have contained her!'

Suddenly, a weird, high strumming out of nowhere.

'…and the thing says we can have her for whatever we want!'

Did she… really hear that?

The tune was building.

Like, some sort of song that began with just a crescendo.

She looked down.

The Eagles – *Journey of the Sorcerer*.

Okay.

What the fuck was that?

She didn't know it.

But; okay. There were more than three thousand songs on *Tarot 12*, after all, and some were just albums she'd dragged and dropped at someone or other's insistence, things she'd added to see if she'd like them, or if they meant anything, when they came up. Somehow, at some time or other, The Eagles had gotten on there. It seemed unlikely, but, still; it also seemed… there was no denying the implication. Seemed she was off.

'You totally fucking deserve a lot worse than this.'

She had long legs, with good reach, and she quickly recalled the whole centre of gravity and pivot thing from her training, not *that* long ago, anchored the bag on her shoulder with a tight fist, and kicked up with her right leg. The bottom heel of her boot smashed Horst right in his mouth, connecting with his teeth and putting most of the front ones out, again, to the back of his throat, right through the direct middle of his ridiculous still-outstretched hands as her greatcoat billowed to the side, as though with the puff of a small explosion. Horst's neck jerked back and his pathetic hands came up to his face as he moaned, then howled and gushed blood. She skipped forward and kicked him hard again, this time in the guts. Blood plumed all over the white kitchen tiles as his diaphragm pulsed more out through his face, through his mouth and nostrils, between his thick fingers. As his knees buckled and he fell forward, she found that she couldn't stop herself and she kicked his crown, fucking hard, and heard something crack as he jolted backward and totally collapsed, face-first into a pile.

'Murder! How delicious!'

Coveth came even further forward, and for a second she thought his tulpa was going to jump the kitchen bench. Instead he stared down at Horst, crumpled closer to the middle of the kitchen floor, face down in an expanding pool of blood that was coming from somewhere out of his down-pointed head.

Manny was tense on his feet now.

'You killed him! Holy shit! You are crazy!'

Emerald ignored them both.

'What's that!?' Manny suddenly shouted. "There's something there!'

Suddenly he had no idea; no real idea about Coveth.

Not when things got real; not when his focus was on brute reality.

Manny had woken up.

'You crazy fucking bitch! You fucking killed him! You killed him in my apartment!'

She could only half hear him. The tune, it seemed, had no lyrics. It was really very eccentric and fun, a series of variant crescendos that were oddly stirring yet definitely, cosmically, mystical.

But now; the way Coveth was staring at Horst.

'Are you going to finish him, sorceress?'

'I didn't kill him…?'

It was a question, but because Manny was now fully conscious and blocking Coveth out, he also blocked out the inflection.

'Well he looks dead to me!'

She looked directly at Coveth. He was increasing in power. Becoming more inherently frightening. The next time they met, if there was a next time, it… he, would be so terrifying from this distance, even way over in the corner, that she would not be able to address him in any way as personal as this.

'Coveth… if you do this, if you do what you're thinking, it will be war between us; war like you can't understand. I don't know how to destroy something like you, I don't know if you can be destroyed, but I will find a way to do the closest thing possible.'

Coveth wasn't listening, though. He was hungry, desperate for the opportunity that was presenting itself.

'It is your right to kill this man; there would be no karma, no judgment, Emerald. Virtually no repercussions if you simply 'finished him off'. You nearly did once before, didn't you? Thought you had – and cared not? His plans for you were abominable; sinful. It would be a righteous kill…' Coveth's mote-glistening tongue licked his still-forming lips. It was the face that was forming first and foremost; that and the shining conceit of a white suit. He was starting to look a bit less like… *her*, she supposed, and a bit more – like Horst.

Emerald turned and gazed over the other end of the kitchen bar, to the pool table.

Could she?

She could.

She could end all this now.

But again, she remembered, there was something, maybe *somethings*, behind all this, helping her.

Telling her to run.

But she couldn't run and leave this as it was.

There was no way.

Even if it killed her, she couldn't.

She moved.

The table was Olympic standard and, so far as she was aware, had been made for the apartment and used only by herself. Manny followed her back to the table.

'Where are you going!?'

He was shocked, but coping.

'What is that thing?' Manny was backing up, unable to take his eyes off Horst and Coveth, but seeming to want to remain within her aura.

'You're pathetic.'

'You can't leave!'

She looked at him.

'You're transparent when you're afraid; I have never seen you this scared, but you are. You are thinking about the game. You are thinking about *PE II*. How this will impact things. You want to call your manager, and your lawyer. You are thinking about those Hollywood cleaners they have on television. *Don't tell me this is New York*. You are thinking that it may go either way.'

'I…'

She didn't know whether to do it in front of him. She didn't want him knowing about this; she'd kept it from him. It could come back, like Coveth would. But right now she had no choice.

She reached up to the lamp and withdrew her pool cue.

'*...and you are very seriously wondering whether or not it would be cooler to have this murder associated with me, as the badass actress who plays the badass star of your badass game...*'

She watched as Manny's eyes flicked around the room, trying to remember where the other pool cues were kept, thinking his lover was going to try and kill him, as well.

Now she really hated him.

'You don't understand what is happening.'

On the tip of the cue was a large ball of green wool. She removed it and Manny saw that it was a beanie; a long beanie that was the colour of her coat, streaked with the colour of her jewellery.

'I've never seen a demon do this; the beginning of his manifestation into physical reality. Hardly anybody ever has. Remember it Manny. Remember it.'

Emerald put the beanie on the table, along with the cue, and in a process that had come with years of practice, having hair down to her elbows, gathered it in a fast ponytail, then a quick, thick knot.

'I don't know why it's chosen me, why it gravitates to me, but...'

She then raised the beanie and scooped the hair knot in from behind, and brought the front rim down low, right to her eyebrows, to seal it.

'...but Manny, listen. There isn't going to be a body... not if I can help it.'

The elevator bell rang from within the vestibule and their heads both turned. Manny tried to snatch the cue from her. She spun it and cracked it over his knuckles. The beanie stayed it place; custom enchantment. It would not budge now, not unless she wanted it to. Manny squealed like a child, a child over-performing, and staggered backwards into the table, and she saw that Coveth was watching.

A security man came through the sliding, double vestibule doors, directly across a wide carpet and into the lounge area, with his handgun extended. He shouted.

'Where is Mister Van Wertheim?'

Emerald pointed the other way, toward the bedroom suites.

'There!'

'We have a report that is heart rate has dropped dramatically; I need conformation that the area is clear and a direct route to send the paramedics.'

She sensed that the two paramedics, and two other privates, were waiting in the elevator. Emerald moved quickly.

'This way…'

She walked steadily and swiftly past the table, toward him as he covered her with the weapon.

'Ma'am, can you please put the pool cue down – '

'Oh!' She acted as though she wasn't even aware that she had brought it with her. 'Sorry.' She turned to walk back, to return it to the table.

'Right there on the floor, ma'am.' And then he spoke to Manny. 'Is this the assailant, sir?'

She spun back. She had been going to do it anyway. She'd just been waiting for his attention to divert one iota. The cue came down, the heavy end, on the collar bone of his gun arm; then she came down on him with an open palm to his temple and *pass-out* zapped him unconscious to spare him the pain.

She turned and walked back to the table and picked up the white ball, turned and threw it with all her force as the first of the awaiting privates came through. It broke his nose and rebounded back into her palm with a cold, satisfying lap that stung quite a bit. Then she was down behind the kitchen bench, with Manny screaming something. The elevator dinged again. The second guy would be preparing to take a shot through the kitchen bench, but he'd spotted Coveth's tulpa and mistaken it for Horst.

'Mister Van – '

Coveth turned and looked at him. He started crying and wet himself as he dropped his gun.

'Manny don't look at it!'

She didn't know why she warned him; old time's sake maybe. But she heard him scream and drop to the floor.

Fuck, it's right behind me.

Coveth is fully powering up and he's standing right...

*RUN.*

She stood, turned and slammed the tip of the pool cue through the tulpa. It was too late. It disintegrated like a house of cards, made from dust, as Horst rolled over, a bloody, toothless smile gumming up at her through his idiot, handsome face.

'I agree, I agree...'

She kicked him in the face again and put the cue through his chest.

She heard a lot of clicking, as though some odd mechanical instrument were winding up, and looked over to see three private security guards, their guns pointed right at her over the kitchen bench, all three repeatedly pulling their triggers, all three with their guns failing to fire.

She threw her arms out, palms up, and shouted at the ceiling, at the sky and the cosmos beyond.

'Do it! Do it and I will run like you have never seen!'

The building shook, the power went out, then there was the brightest flash any of them had ever seen as a strike of lightning appeared to run through the cue.

Somebody cried out. 'Lightning!'

'...lightning's not green...!'

'Where is she!?'

She – could smell burning flesh. In the pitch dark she reached back. The cue was still there. She pulled it from the corpse and heard the squelch, then scampered across the floor to the other side of the bench, leaped, grabbed her bag, and fell over the other side. Gunfire began, loud and crackling, hurting her ears in the enclosed, echoing space. She stayed low but moved instantly, across the floor, kicked open the hall door with as much noise as she could, slammed it –

'She's through!'

– didn't go through and ran to the bathroom. She pushed the door quickly and gently and was through even as they went straight past her. One of them had the same idea she did; she side-stepped and turned as he entered, palming his forehead before she even really knew she was doing it, spelling him into unconsciousness, snatching his gun from his hand before he hit the floor. His bio-readings would instantly go back to central, and they would be satellite heat-reading by now. She assessed, pinging out with her intuition and accepted something like ninety seconds before the building's power returned. She hoisted the bag again and summoned some raw energy. She felt it in her chest, in her palms and the soles of her feet, behind her eyes and in her throat, then she summoned some more. It had been a while, but it was like riding a dragon; you never forgot.

Okay.

You wanted the sorceress.

She went out and around again, firing the gun high and unlikely to hit anyone or anything other than the wall down the other end, but the brilliant repeat-flashing of the muzzle, the crackling of the constant fire startling them all, hoping to scare them like fuck to empty their cartridges down into the lounge, into the windows, maybe break one or two, *where is he?* but not succeeding.

They weren't returning fire.

She pocketed the gun, piping hot on her upper thigh, even through the thermals, not caring, then took the cue in both hands. She spun it like a quarterstaff over her shoulder and before her, aided by the heightened awareness that the summoned energy gave her, along with her general familiarity with these surroundings after all the afternoons alone, practising with the cue. The combination of all that excited her mind and body, heightened her spirit and focussed her soul; allowed her the precise dimensional presence to negotiate with her will, and rekindle now, totally, her suppressed determination to survive, to run, and to find out, to learn, to know, how to kill it; *it*.

*Where is it?*

Hand over hand and moving, hearing the cue swipe and whistle under her control, within her intimate physical space, confusing and confounding the physical space with the anger from her chest, and the alertness from behind her eyes that let her sense, see in the dark, knowing none of the security operatives knew where she was, or what she was, or what they were supposed to do about her. *Did she still have the gun, or the weapon; what was that weapon? Was it neurotoxins she was spraying?* The order through their earbuds not to risk firing until central command had identified the weapon, and through her earbuds that long, jolly, repeated mystical crescendo of that Eagles song fading out. Wondering what would be next.

Here it was though; the start of the journey of the sorcerer, just as the song predicted, just as it ended.

The instinct, the keenness of her sorcery, projecting that the song was something else, was owned by something else, and it would be something for her, something down the line, some kind of *cosmic journey joke*. And; everyone's eyes had at least partially adjusted by now, in the here and now, but she had completely confused them for the second it had taken her to mystically maintain the spinning of the staff in the space before them, and so she stepped aside and went for the elevator.

They would be expecting that, and it dinged; there were more. No turning back, she went on, ducking and running as two panic shots in the dark nearly killed her, then sprinting, powering energy into the sound of her clopping boots to instil terror, then into the vestibule, the pool cue the epicentre of her focus. She knew where the panic button was; but there was an equally well-informed security guard standing right before the hatch, where the button was hidden. To her surprise, it was Pizza Guard, the normal guy from the elevator vestibule.

What were they thinking he was nothing more than an everyday doorman!

And they'd put him in the firing line – *Jesus*!

Pizza was terrified, and he didn't see her coming; she smacked the two others who were paid for it and they fell, then she pushed Pizza aside, and hit the panic button. Steel doors slid across the vestibule entrance. A shot went off and ricocheted inside the chamber.

'*Fucking idiot there are civilians in here!*'

She turned and crouched before Pizza. 'You okay?'

'Whuh?'

'Are you hit?'

'Huh – how long you gonna keep me in here? You gonna ki – ?'

'The killing's over.'

'Who – who…?'

'They were trying to keep me up there. I got carried away. It won't matter.'

'Whuh…?'

'Listen; have you ever been spiritual? Religious is okay, but have you ever felt protected by… anything?'

'Whuh…'

She focussed her sorceress psyche on him and –

*soothe>myvoice<soothing*

'…protected by anything beyond just yourself…?'

– cleared him of his panic.

'Yeah…' Pizza started breathing again. 'I…'

'Call it now. Summon it now, no matter what it is, it doesn't matter.'

*Manny was out there, and once he remembered the cancel codes…*

She let Pizza sit with that, and stood.

The panic button signalled the elevator's safety clamps to bolt to the inner walls of the elevator shaft, making it essentially immovable. The doors were also bolted closed over the normal partition, likewise until a technician was called in to open them.

She'd been here when the panic room had been installed; it had taken three days and they'd had to crane in the metal via the top of the elevator shaft.

She looked up to the unseen stars again.

'Okay!' Emerald sparked. 'I'm running!'

Pizza stared up as well. 'Is there someone up there?'

She'd cast the equivalent of a mild sedation on him, but it didn't help make someone brighter under siege.

'No; the upward address is like summoning an altar that's always ready in your mind; no matter where you go, no matter how low they bury you, the sun, the sky, the stars, even the clouds, are always there, like a permanent symbol of...'

The two security guards on the floor started to groan as they came to.

'Stay down...' She ordered them.

'You cracked them pretty hard...'

'It's nothing permanent, I know what I'm doing.'

She crouched and reached out with both hands, placing the cue perpendicular to her feet. While they remained groggy, she placed the base of her palms hard on each of their foreheads.

'Listen to me; Horst Van Wertheim is dead. He made a pact with a demon that got him killed; if he's still out there, if he reappears after what I did to him, that's not him. Remember; *that's not him*. I am telling you this –'

She looked across the small chamber at Pizza, eye to eye. Good; the energy she'd brought with her had allowed him to summon something, something important to him, something that would do its best to ensure that he didn't get killed here.

'– the three of you, because that idea needs to be *installed*. You don't have to believe it, or even remember this, but you need to *know it*, on some level, and act as well as you can to protect the other people that are going to end up working for him.'

Coveth hadn't been there when she'd come out shooting. But it, *it*, Coveth, *had been* there, in that room, somewhere. She would have known if it had gone, and it hadn't. Therefore, she knew;

there was only one place it could have been, one thing it could have done, to explain why it wasn't coming after her right now.

She stood smartly, snatching up the cue. Quickly, with long, nimble fingers, she unscrewed it from the middle, then held one half firmly in each hand and turning to the closed elevator, placed the central, metal end upon each of the doors.

*Open*

It was as though the hands of a giant, invisible trauma surgeon had applied heart paddles, then cracked open the ribs of its mechanical patient, as the doors lurched apart, just half a meter, crackling, sparkling and grinding. Emerald stepped away.

'You three stay.'

She went in.

She could see herself in the mirror. She looked a thousand times better; she was glowing, looking stunning in her emerald cufflinks, tie pin, buckle and buttons, adorned with her cloak, and armed with her staff as she screwed it back together.

No makeup. None required.

Hair everywhere, like a hedgehog. It would settle once she got outside.

The two halves reconnected, tight.

*Force, brute force*

She brought it into the chamber. She felt it shake the cage, and effect the clamps, but she drew it with all her will, into the cue. She held it there as long as she dared, with the stress, like the elevator clamps transferred to her temples, and that same giant surgeon, slowly turning the screw. She held the cue with both hands when it became extreme, then knelt when it started to feel heavy. When it was a burden too heavy, and the magical weight of the cue made it almost contact the metal floor, she released it. The energy shot up, singeing the very edge her eyebrows and eyelashes, but she had done this before (only thrice, though, enough to be nervous) but enough to know; she could do it and it would work. The ceiling of the elevator vanished with the concentrated upward blast of magical force, followed by all the barriers between herself and the sky.

Then one of the clamps gave way, then another, and in a second the cage would start to fall, which she had not foreseen.

Oh fuck, this was going to take everything.

'Get out!' Pizza yelled.

She did.

She held the cue upright and looked around, gazing intensely over the molten edges of the cage, quickly searching for the service elevator.

There it was; on the far wall.

She reached up and touched the end of the cue to the closest rung.

*Hold*

Then she moved to the side of the cage, hoisted her bag back up, high over her shoulder, and grasped the handle of the cue with both hands, sensing Pizza's astonishment as he scrambled around to watch the levitating, apparently glued stick hold her weight as she ascended it like a rope climb, and was gone.

As she cleared the roof, she felt the third clamp go, then with a nasty crash to the side, the fourth gave out and with a millisecond's grace she watched as the carriage plummeted from beneath her from the safety of the service ladder. In response to the upward billow of air through the shaft, she sent a psychic zap down to Button Guard; *clear the door!* – and hoped he got it. She had watched him watch her and registered his face often enough to summon it now. She hoped, she hoped. She had no idea what something like that would do when it fell ten floors.

One of the guards poked his head up and saw her. He pointed his gun but she ignored him and hooked an arm around the ladder rung, then hung on tight with that while she unscrewed her cue again.

'Don't move, lady…'

'Don't be an idiot, man…'

'I'll shoot…'

She looked straight at him. 'You'll miss.'

*Fumble*

He went to say something and dropped the gun down the shaft. 'Fuck!'

Then the cage hit the ground. She hadn't counted on basement floors, on the carpark and storage levels below. The smash echoed up like a nuclear blast, and shook the ladder so hard she nearly lost her grip. She did lose her grip on one half of the cue but her response; a tense, extended arm and a claw-like hand, fingers curled so tight they resembled advanced arthritis, was so quick that her magic –

*Stop!*

– held the half-cue there, hovering in mid-air. She leaned down then, hanging by one hand's grip, and the closer her talon hand got to the hovering half-stick, the more it seemed to reciprocate by coming closer to her. Her sigh of relief when she finally grasped it once again almost made the watching security guard weep, such was their mutual relief.

'Go…' The man uttered. 'I'll remember what you said. I know what I saw.'

She pulled herself back, slipped a half-cue each into two long pockets, each down the inner side of her greatcoat, and started to climb up.

# CHAPTER SEVEN:
# MO-CAP

It was freezing on the roof.

She knew the vestibule doors would be open by now, and that the paramedics would be working. Whatever the situation, Coveth would have to start again, start working on… whatever.

One thing or another; he would be preoccupied.

Now she just had Horst's bastards to deal with.

If they were still coming, they would be coming as a matter of professional pride.

She looked down on Central Park. Across at the buildings. The naked winter branches, and the lush evergreens. She should have resonated with the gardens, and the park lakes, not to mention the culture, the whole time she had been here. So… somebody far away had told her, once, long ago it seemed; that it was the earth, and *hard nature* that she should try to… anyway. Here, in these comatose months, she had instead resonated with the building itself, with the stone and the shape and the enclosed space. The cave; the rock. What she had thought, at least at first, to be a protective…

She turned back; something had moved on the roof. A flicker of light. There was nothing. She went to the corner; corners were usually the best, and moved the cue toward it. Again, in had been a while since she had scaled, but it was nothing that made her frightened any more. She had just faced a demon. A child demon, an infant almost, but a demon nevertheless. Almost no sorcerer ever survived that sane.

Maybe… she should find some of the ones that had.
*RUN!*

Ah. So, was that the deal for opening the channel, friend above?

The friend above showered her with endorphins, just to confirm it.

That old metaphysical chestnut-command; *find the others.*

*Dash!*

She heard clanging behind and looked over her shoulder. They were coming up the shaft ladder, she could hear them swearing at each other. But that wasn't it; there was the ghost of an old woman standing there. A real, fully luminous, old woman in a flowing nightgown, her face filled with concern, but also... affection? The old woman's expression became shocked as she realized that Emerald could – finally – see her. Her old, wrinkled, liver-spotted hands went to her face as her mouth formed an excited oval and her ethereal eyes twinkled.

'I can see you!'

The old woman's spirit suddenly raised her hands; they were trembling with excitement as she extended the index finger of each, and pointed down, stabbing both elderly fingers down, down, down, nodding as though it were vitally important that Emerald understood something. She mouthed at her, so urgently.

'Dash! Dash! *Dash!*'

Emerald nodded at her.

'I'm going, I'm going!'

Then the old woman looked up, as though responding to a voice from above. She looked back at Emerald with a sweet affection, that somehow only old ladies can summon, and put both her hands to her mouth, and blew her three big kisses, throwing both hands out to her each time with such a warm, loving, encouraging smile that Emerald heard herself splutter, and choke just a little, as she almost burst into tears. Then the old lady was gone, her ethereal form dispersing and seeming to fly out, and around, but mostly upward into the night sky, like a dandelion in the wind.

Emerald was frozen a second.

She had just seen something very rare. An earthbound spirit being 'called home'. And, just before, employing the last of her earthbound energy to…

She looked back to the corner of the building.

The pool cue stood there, upright on its own.

*Fly down*

She stepped off the side of the roof, holding the cue outward at forty-five on the tip, bracing her heel over the thick end that was still attached magically to the stonework on the building's upper corner. Then she descended, the end of the cue sparking slightly as it slid, magnetized to the building's edge, her hand tight, some kind of gravity bubble holding her there, as though she were hanging from the speared prow of a ship over the water, descending onto the street, through the darkness with the pedestrians below oblivious, everybody's attention at the main entrance to her building; some of them looking up, but looking up to the very top, around the lobby canopy, to where they imagined the roof of the collapsed elevator's shaft to be, where Horst's private security guards would be emerging now, one at a time, pissed off and trigger happy, confused and angry at all the weird things going on that they couldn't nail down, punch out or shoot through.

The cue slowed. She protected it and it protected her, and it intrinsically understood what she wanted. The commands were unique between them, verbalized expressions of her will as channelled through the cue, passive communications that formalized condensed ideas; the renegotiating of earthly reality that she and the pool cue, her sorceress's staff, did as one.

She came down on the street corner unseen, and stepped onto the street as though she had stepped out of the alley, down the side of the apartments.

The lobby had been evacuated, and the apartments were in the process of following suit. The lower eight floors were rented, the higher four owned. Manny had been the youngest inhabitant by far, and the purchase had seemed much less ostentatious than many of his gamer-lord contemporaries, back a few streets on Park or Madison, or across the park on CPW.

She remained by the corner, and took a breath as she unscrewed the cue. It was almost one and a half metres long, the wand end slightly shorter than the club. She'd had secret, inner sleeves sewn into the front-collar hems of her greatcoat, beside the buttons and button-holes. They'd come in handy to hide the staff in a pinch, but their weight made the coat hang strangely, made it too unwieldly. The halves were too long to hide up her sleeves, unless she could go without bending her elbows, and so in the end, she had gone with simply carrying the two halves in one hand; looking quite innocently like someone heading for a pool hall who'd forgotten their case.

She gathered herself and gained her bearings.

She would have to move, soon and quickly, she supposed. She'd channelled a lot of power just then, more than she had for at least two years, and from a source, benevolent she was sure, that was nevertheless strange to her. It would take time to recover, for her mind to adjust, and the new pathways to settle down. A figure approached. She reached slowly to separate the two halves, hold one in each hand, defensively, but instinct let her know it was okay, even though she now saw clearly who it was.

'You're finally making a break for it?'

It was Micro Guard, the woman she was sure Manny had stationed between the elevator and apartment lobby, employed to observe her moods and micro-expressions, and report back.

'Finally?' Emerald asked.

Micro was silent for a few seconds.

'Miss Tarragon, if I may say…' She was New Yorker, with a broad accent and a vital, Mediterranean glint in her eye. '…that is a most excellent winter coat…'

'Thank you.' Emerald frowned. 'But; finally, you said?'

Micro nodded and smiled knowingly. Emerald considered that a second.

'You're… responsible…?' Micro nudged her chin skyward. 'For the cage crash? I figured when you did make a move, there would be a kerfuffle.'

Emerald looked at her, scanned her psychically.

'Oh…' Micro nodded. 'You are one of them. I thought so.'

'Was anyone hurt? I tried –'

'No. Nobody in there but me and Curtis, and we were having a cigarette.'

She took out a packet. Emerald accepted, even though she was breaking her ritual a second time that day.

'He knows, doesn't he?' Micro asked, lighting up. 'Mister Devane?' She re-clicked and held the tiny naked flame out for Emerald, and she leaned in without taking her eyes from Micro's; brown and clear. 'Don't worry, Miss Tarragon; you're out. My only duty is to report that you're leaving the building, in my professional opinion, forever, and…' She exhaled. '…with extreme prejudice.'

'Call me Emerald.'

'…then, my work here is done. You can read my thoughts if you really like, but I would rather you didn't, and from experience you'll hurt me if you try.'

'I'm sorry.'

'We both have our crosses to bear.'

Emerald hoisted her bag. Micro nodded at it.

'Amazing what you can leave a billion-dollar apartment with and still be satisfied.'

'How did you know…?'

Micro smirked. It was an appealing smirk. 'Well; I am almost never hired for nothing. You lasted in the mood you're in for longer than most trophy wives, and I've watched my fair share.'

'Trophy wives.' It wasn't a query, Emerald had just wanted to repeat it out loud.

'If you'll forgive the expression. For six months you've been getting less and less happy. More and more dissatisfied. But; along with that whole *determination thing*. I don't see that very

often. You stayed much longer than you needed. Like you were…
waiting. Determined to *prove something*.'

Emerald nodded to herself. 'I guess that's true.'

A bullet hit the ground between them. They dropped their
cigarettes as Micro pulled Emerald aside, then the pair ran across
the alley, to the opposite block corner, and on to the front of
the building. It was another old apartment block, where several
people, four elderly couples, it seemed, were waiting for a cab
beneath another old-fashioned, heritage-green, classic New York
canopy. Micro pulled her in again, under the canopy and a few
steps into the lobby. She was much shorter than Emerald, but
strong, and confident with what she was doing.

Inside, Emerald looked around; this apartment lobby was
much older, far less-modernized than Manny's had been. There
was a small, dark bar and the lighting was low all through the
lobby as well, as though to suggest the anonymity of late evening.
Micro pulled out her phone, and the moderate glow was sufficient
to seem almost bright.

'Look, I get a fifty grand bonus for this call. Won't affect you.
It's just a formal thing.'

'Okay.'

Emerald still had her phone; she needed to ditch it, but
somewhere smarter than here. Micro made a call, and when
someone answered she rattled off a long list of numbers, then
gave the word Baum, and spelled it out, as some kind of mission
name or code.

'Yeah, look…' Micro suddenly became less formal. 'She's left
the building and she's not coming back. No. No. Impossible to
determine. No.' There was a pause. Emerald could see that Micro
was itching for another cigarette, hated not finishing that last one.
'Yes. Approximately two minutes ago; there's been some kind of
incident, might have been part of her leaving, but I clocked her
and made contact; there's zero chance of a rebound.' She paused
again, and ground her teeth, listening. 'Yes. Yes, definitely. No.'
Micro looked at Emerald and rolled her eyes, like the questions

were an idiotic waste of time. 'No. No. Yes. No. Undecided; and…
I don't think she'd tell me if I asked. That's correct. Absolutely
negative. Negative. Neh – gah – teeeve. Understand? Okay.
Bonus confirmed? Okay, accepted. Accepted. Confirm that. Yes,
accepted. All good? Thank you. Okay, Baum One out. I'm taking
a month.'

She hung up. The light from the phone was gone and they
were once again in the dimness of the old lobby.

'I'm taking a life.'

'Retiring?'

'Okay; three, two, one; my money's transferred. I can tell
you this now; and you need to know this. The four from central
casting, the look-alikes? They'll look for you, and they'll try for
whatever reward Devane offers, but they're freelancers, they'll
give up after a while. But those four who came in, the extra
security, they mean business.'

'I could read their dislike of me without trying. I call them
The Trolls; they just want to… *hurt me*.'

'He's mad to have hired them.'

'I'm not sure *he* did.'

'Whatever; but you need to get out of here. I need to get out
of here, too. I've seen enough of those types; those two women
compete between themselves, they hate each other, but they'll kill
a target rather than let the other one capture. The two guys are
just monsters. They know I know them now. I barely got out last
time they decided I'd clocked them once too often; never again, I
shoulda bolted yesterday.'

'You're leaving the life?'

'I'm opening a pie shop in Nebraska. That's slang, it means
I'm changing my name, burning my shit, and starting over as a
waitress.'

'I know. I've done that.'

'You'll do it again, right?'

Emerald squeezed the two cue-halves in her right hand.

'I've never changed my name. But I have a plan, I just need to get out of the city.'

'Then you shouldn't be huddling in a corner of a lobby here listening to me, sweetie.' She was keeping one eye on the lobby entrance. '…Devane wants you under lock and key, or else nobody has you. And right now, those psycho goons are operating under the assumption it's the latter. You need to run sweetie. Unless…' Micro reached out and placed a firm, but somehow soft hand, low on Emerald's right hip. '…Miss Tarragon, you'd like me to get us both out?'

Emerald was sort of flattered. Micro was masculine, but striking. Definitely attractive. She nodded. 'Thanks. But that's not how my magic works.'

Micro nodded back. Disappointed; she'd taken a shot, it hadn't played. No hard feelings though, Emerald read. Then she sighed, reached up, and placed the same, equally soft hand upon Emerald's upper arm.

'Nice watching you walk the lobby. Another life maybe. Now –' Her brown eyes blazed. ' – run!'

Micro turned instantly and took two steps, then scanned.

'Bye Micro,' Emerald whispered.

Micro turned, eyebrow arched.

'Bye Mo-Cap.'

# CHAPTER EIGHT:
# THE RUNNING MAN

Emerald watched as Micro crossed the lobby, then slipped past the concierge and vanished into the bar. She would find her way through some circuitous route to safety, Emerald knew. Then it was her turn to scan. Two of central casting were out there; the one that looked like Ray Romano, with Kyra Sedgwick right behind him. Jerry Seinfeld and Sarah Jessica Parker would be scouting the other side of Manny's building.

She pushed herself back into the corner, which had a magazine rack that nobody ever touched, and a lounge setting that nobody ever sat in; scarlet with gold trim. She suddenly felt lonely, and looking around realized that Micro had vanished forever. She told herself not to feel lonely, to channel her emotional energy into her abilities; into her instinct, her powers, her escape. But her heart was still sinking.

Alone again.

Running again.

*Never again.*

So, what could she do now?

Big magic on a rooftop was one thing; to escape a demon, sure, essential.

But there was no using higher-channelled energy down here.

But that was okay; *that was okay.*

She might have been an RPG Rapunzel, but she'd scaled down the castle wall and now she was free. This was New York; here you used your wits. Magic only if required. She just needed to place one block between them, and she could get herself lost. One block.

*Assess, Emerald. Focus.*

Okay. Micro had likely gone within the hotel. If she followed, she would risk fucking her over. Life was long, and maybe she hadn't vanished forever; they'd bonded, and that meant Micro was a potential ally some time down the road. Stranger things had happened, did happen, all the time. So, not out the back. Outside to the left; no way, the alley would be crawling. To her right; she would have to wait until Romano and Sedgwick doubled back.

She gazed out from her shadowy corner.

The concierge was pretending he hadn't seen her, but he was right across there at his desk. Romano passed back.

*Shadows*

It was half-hearted; the scaling had taken a lot.

But Romano went on; he'd looked in, but hadn't entered. Where was Sedgwick? She might have, *might have* gone before him, just as she'd taken her eyes off to check the concierge, who was clearly on the verge of calling his own security to have her removed.

Okay. That meant she looked desperate, and probably that her attempt at camouflaging had made him instinctively wary of her; made the hairs on the back of his neck stand up, something like that.

Contain it. She inhaled, deeply, slowly, stood straight, adjusted her neck, her shoulders, her total stance and posture. She allowed her grip on the bag to relax, then she released the deep breath and cast her eyes calmly, if not casually, around the lobby again. She put the two halves of the staff in the bag, so the ends stuck out, and smiled to herself.

Almost immediately, the concierge reciprocated and relaxed as well.

Not even a spell; just people.

It was a lobby; she could wait all day if she liked.

Think some more. Right about now, Manny would be calling in reinforcements. He'd be persuading the security up there that this was a situation they had to deal with themselves; security guys loved that, but they had a limit. Something would need to be done with Horst, no matter what condition his body was in. One of them would get nervous, think of their wife or their kid, or a potential sentence, and they would call it in. Then the cops would arrive. If she heard that; the sirens, the cops or an ambulance, she was in bigger trouble. They'd cordon the block and start a witch hunt, literally, although they wouldn't know it. And what about Manny's goons? The reinforcements would have any back exits covered; Micro had known when to move. This place, and all surroundings, would be stationed with security back to Park Avenue by now, and all through The Park itself, and his men, or Horst's, would be walking in here any minute like they owned the place. Manny would have told them not to be slow, that Emerald would cover a lot of ground; *she's an athlete, she uses enhancement drugs…* some such bullshit that they would find easy to believe.

From outside, there came the sound of a cab horn close by, then another. Suddenly there were a dozen outside, all at once. She risked it and left the corner, walked swiftly, closer to the entrance. There were yellow cabs backed up all the way down the two lanes of the one-way avenue, all heading south and facing to her left. She'd seen this before; there was an event ending, a benefit or something at one of the galleries or museums. Suddenly the pavement was filled with people; from the types, it looked as though they were coming down from the Guggenheim, which was just up the street, chatting and talking and looking for one of the competing cabs to get out of the cold in. Fifth Avenue would be in chaos for the next five minutes as the wandering patrons and benefactors briefly ran into the evacuees from Manny's apartment block, as the cops and ambulances arrived, as they casually, competitively sought their way home.

She ran for the closest cab.

Out the door, under the canopy, past two middle-aged men in expensive suits who were just opening the cab door, and in she went, fast, ducking. She was in, almost rolling across the back seat.

'Jesus, lady!'

Then another cry.

'Hey!'

And she knew someone was behind her. Her hand was on the other, inner handle, she opened the door, and felt someone grab her calf, tight but unstable, their hands slipping as she wrenched her leg back, then grasping again, trying to take her boot. She let her bag drop behind the driver's seat and scrambled over, onto her back. It was *gagonit*. She kicked at him, just as the open door swung out behind her and her head and shoulders lurched backwards. Her left hand went down to the asphalt and, as she managed a quick, rough balance, the heel of her right boot caught him across his mouth, swiping his lips but nothing else, and he swore with a streak of furiously disgusting filth. Between her legs she saw a flash of metal; she reached down and grabbed the handles of her bag and quickly raised the other hand, pressed hard and painfully on the asphalt of the road beneath, whipping it up, scuffing the base of her hand and the top of her wrist, and allowed gravity to take her down, hard onto her back. With the backward momentum she raised her knees and kicked out again, then curled and half-rolled sideways, half-manoeuvred backwards out of the cab, dragging her croc messenger with her as both feet slammed him full in the face and retracted as the knife that he held high came clumsily down, between her heels, missing everything, even the back seat upholstery, in what he'd intended to be a wild, downward stab, idiotically and psychotically aimed right at her crotch.

The cab driver was shrieking at them in a foreign language, but staying put behind his glass partition, and the two men behind who had intended this cab for themselves were shouting at him, frightened and appalled, in upper-class astonishment. She caught this in flashes, then she was on the road, rolling about between two rows of honking stationary cabs, and *gagonit* was coming out, scrambling on all fours, exiting face-first, snarling with the knife; a long dagger really, still clutched tightly in his big fist.

*Gagonit* moved quickly, and he was halfway out as Emerald was on her feet and had her bag slung back over her shoulder, ready to run again. Furious and desperate for a kill, he grabbed the top of the cab door with his left arm and rose up, pulling himself to his knees on the edge of the cab seat, raised the knife, which was clearly some kind of long, tapered thing, a nauseatingly homicidally-designed custom job, and went for a swipe that would absolutely connect; she saw it coming, there was nothing –

She remembered her balance and pivot, and without thought or hesitation Emerald ducked back and side swiped the cab door with a savage kick, right on the edge with all the force she could muster, that once again brought her down to the asphalt. She heard the metal *pound* her kick made, and something almost simultaneously *crunching*, as her footing slipped and she dropped, almost a free-fall, to face the asphalt on her hands and knees, and then the closest cab driver in the other lane cry out;

'Ohhhwwww!'

Then she righted herself and looked back.

*Gagonit* was still there, balanced on his knees on the edge of the back seat of the cab, with his left arm ostensibly holding the cab door for balance, but with the door now squashed into his chest, and the weird dagger held high, but holding there, his right hand squeezing it, just as he was squeezing his jaw, clenching his molars and baring his fronts, his lips curled back, tight in pain. Somehow she'd crushed his chest, and the door was holding him there in that position.

'That's what you get!'

There was a driver, a heavy-set woman, leaning out of a nearby cab window.

'Oh yeah! That's what you get you Norman Bates knife-wielding motherfucker!'

But *gagonit* couldn't hear her, or anything. Emerald had killed him.

She turned to run, against the traffic, but from behind the cab, the Sedgwick look-alike appeared and pulled a gun. It was small, silver number that she probably had a license for, and had probably purchased legally and responsibly, and had trained to use in a crisis, maybe even as a prerequisite of her security license. Emerald would never get used to America, and their guns; but she could deal with them, given half the chance. Sedgwick had seen the incident, and reacted lawfully, in the line of duty.

*Where the hell were the cops?*

Emerald stopped, took a breath, and put down her bag, right at her side. She lowered herself to her knees, and raised her hands above her head.

'I saw it…!' Sedgwick gasped, but with a professional certainty.

'I'm sorry.'

'I saw him, he came after you in that cab, with a knife, I saw him take a swipe…'

'I know. Really, I'm sorry.'

Sedgwick was nervous, sympathetic, but determined to make things right, in her own way. 'That's okay, that's okay; you're sorry, but I think you killed him; and you have to answer for that…'

'I'm not sorry for that.'

'…but I'll testify it was self-defence, and you were… what?'

The Sedgwick lookalike seemed to realize a few things all at once; the odd way that Emerald had simply raised her hands, and not interlinked them behind her head in the customary manner; the way she was not actually looking at her, but seemed to be looking somehow beyond her, maybe… above? And then, the way her right hand seemed to be moving, along with her eyes, like… hand-to-eye coordination, or –

And then the excruciating pain as her right shoulder was dislocated by a sudden impact from behind. She dropped the gun and howled, screaming in agony as she fell to her knees right before Emerald, virtually face to face. Emerald moved forward, kneeling up on her left side with her right leg forward, her foot down hard as she reached for the poor woman, who'd had the misfortune of getting in her way, and fallen victim to a foresighted trap intended for someone much nastier than herself.

She grabbed Sedgwick with her left hand by the scruff of her shirt and scarf, to stabilize her more than anything, then pulled her forward and grasped her forehead with her right hand.

'Find me peacefully and I will make amends!'

*pass-out*

She whipped her scarf from Sedgwick's neck as she allowed the woman to fall into her arms, then lowered her swiftly but gently onto the street, and stood. There were bloodstains on the scarf from where Emerald had scraped her hand on the street; she couldn't leave that. She reached up with the scarf, turned and took the knife from her would-be killer's grip; immediately the door opened and he fell like a sack of potatoes.

The driver yelled out. 'Cops are on their way, lady! Better get clear!'

Probably a dozen cab drivers had witnessed this. She left Sedgwick's gun where it had landed, but dropped the knife along with the scarf into the croc bag, pushing her hand after them and secreting them down low. Her fingers touched the lime yo-yo and despite her hurry she paused to pull it out and hold it, balled in her fist, to her cheek.

'...*didn't think I'd leave you behind beautiful...*'

Then she pocketed her favourite toy, made sure the two ends of her cue were sticking out, like two tight horns from the front of the bag, and was moving again, keeping low between the two lanes of cabs. There was honking and shouting all round, then the second, inner lane was moving slowly in the opposite direction. Emerald was moving against it; one, then two, then three cab drivers, the second being the heavy-set woman who had yelled out in vindication, glanced down at her like they hadn't seen the violence she'd wreaked just seconds before; like she was just another mad New York arts patron, an artist trying to avoid the payer of an unfulfilled commission. Then another Troll, the female security guard who thought of her as a *spoiledbitch* was ahead of her, just skip-stepping, stopping and searching, coming straight out between the next two cabs along. Emerald whipped the club from her bag, grasped by the protruding thinner end, and brought it up in a swift arc, neatly collecting *spoiledbitch* under her chin, sprawling her and her neat black business suit backwards onto the street.

The cabs in the first lane started to roll slowly forward not a second later, and Emerald's boot moved the hunter's arm aside, nudging it out of the way of an oncoming tyre. She looked left, to Central Park, but two buses were coming fast down Fifth Avenue's third, bus-only lane, right between her and the low stone wall she needed to alight on the other side. Turning, she saw that the traffic was moving because the driver of the cab she had moved through had, apparently, dumped *gagonit's* body and just kept driving. Now both Seinfeld and *doucheparasite*, the pro who had shadowed the doorman all week, and who had apparently teamed up in the middle of the crisis, were coming right for her, straight down between the cab lanes, straight over *gagonit* and poor Sedgwick without a second glance. They were still six or seven away. That meant, she was sure, *wontfuckingforget*, the appalling dude with the rape fantasies, Romano and Parker would not be far either.

What would they risk?

How much was he, either Manny or Horst, paying them?

She suddenly recalled Horst bragging.

'If anyone takes me down, all my people know there's a reward…'

It didn't matter.

They were coming after her, and she had to place distance and make time; that was all.

With *spoiledbitch* still at her feet, she turned toward the park with her instincts spiking; that they were closing in, seen and unseen, from all directions. Seinfeld and *doucheparasite* were trying to get to her before the second bus passed, *doucheparasite* having spotted *spoiledbitch* and running full-pelt at her now, coming up on her, determined to stop her getting into the park. Emerald stepped between cabs and to the edge as the first bus trundled past at speed. If she kept calm, they wouldn't get to her, and they could see it, but it would be seconds. She bolted as soon as the second bus roared passed, feeling the hot air of the backdraft, the smell of the diesel exhaust and its roar in her ears as she ran directly through it, and she was across the bus lane, over the sidewalk, across the grass, over the wall and *down*.

The wall was stone, three huge rock bricks high, with a solid ledge, all about a meter high. This section of the park was lower than the road, so the drop to the grass and ground and litter and twigs and rocks and dirt behind the wall was deep; more than two meters. She was ready for it. The boot heels dug into the earth as she landed, but she kept upright, folding into a deep crouch. She kept moving, low and along the lower edge, back-tracking; one of them leaped right over her, but kept running into the park, assuming that's where she'd gone. She heard them yell, something awful like, *split up she can't have gone far!* but she kept scampering, as the ground along the stone wall began to taper upwards, heading toward a common park entrance, a formal gap in the stone wall, that led in from a Fifth Avenue zebra crossing straight to an intersection of three different paths through the park. As soon as she was able, however, she reached up for the ledge, gripped and jumped, hooked up a leg and hefted herself onto it with all her might. Then she was on top of the stone ledge, crouching a second, then over it and back with her boots on the solid pavement of Fifth Avenue. The cabs were all still there, lined up and honking, but she had doubled back, past Manny's building and was another four or five down. But *doucheparasite* had predicted her move and was coming toward her, running low along the pavement, keeping to the stone wall, taking out a gun in her right hand, her right side in shadow from the street lights, from the park lights. Panic spiked in Emerald. Was this genuinely to the death?

She dropped the bag as she snatched up the halved cues from it; the wand by the tip-end, the club by the screw. Her hands went up, backwards, over her shoulders as her elbows arced up.

Her right leg stretched and came down before her as her left knee knelt and with full force she arced her arms back down and released the two sticks. They soared at her would-be killer as she raised the gun, as Emerald saw the silencer attached, and the intent in her eyes; *to take out this douche parasite and do the world a favour.*

*Disarm / Silence*

Emerald had expected the tip to penetrate her would-be assassin's shoulder, the club-end to knock her out, bash her temple or something. But sometimes she underestimated her own will, and her own unconscious anger. The club smashed the gun from her opponent's hand. Emerald heard her fingers break. The tip penetrated her mouth like a spear, and stabbed the back of her throat into her neck, stifling her initial cry of pain. The horrible mind of *doucheparasite* froze as she dropped upright to her knees on the pavement in dumbfounded shock, jolting her whole body again. Emerald bolted from her one-knee-kneel like an Olympic sprinter. The club rebounded toward her hand and she snatched it from the air. As the woman fell forward, the cue still protruding from her open mouth, Emerald wrenched it back out, creating a simultaneous arc of vomit of blood, then left her there as she fell flat on her face, already, somewhere deep, abandoning everything she thought she believed about herself, her skills, her trade and her commitment to it.

Emerald quickly eyeballed the lane for buses and sprinted again, jay-running a good three cars' distance from the zebra crossing, then was bolting down the pavement on the other side of Fifth. She made a hard left down one of the East side-streets, with no idea which one it was, toward Madison Avenue. She kept running, in the night, under the street lights, passing three, four buildings, and stopped outside the fifth, about halfway.

Seinfeld was one building behind her, running, crazy-eyed.

He had a hands-free and was shouting to his comrades.

Again, she threw the club like a knife.

*Balls*

And he was down; scraped but merely painfully disabled, as the club rebounded and was back in her hand.

'Don't come after me any more!'

She turned back again. The East street to here was all side-entrances to apartment blocks. The second half of the block, further down, was side entrances to Madison boutiques. *Boutiques.* She turned and ran again. Thursday night, very late. Last she recalled, things were open, but not many, and only by appointment. There were two side-entrances on each street wall; many of the store fronts on the actual Avenue were just advertising. You walked in, and you were partaking in a kind of installation. For platinum and diamond clientele, these were the actual entrances. The first on the left was shuttered; the second manned by what resembled a prison guard. She crossed over and found the closest side-entrance on that side closed but with the sense of activity, on a quick psychic scan, that was a little dramatic.

Emerald huddled into the *shadows* of the alcove and buzzed. Nothing.

She removed her beanie. Her thick hair cascaded down again, across her breasts and down her back. She pushed it all back, away from her face, over her shoulders.

She buzzed again.

One of the goons would be down here soon.

There; Sarah Jessica Parker ran past, but she was too eager, too pumped, and missed her in the shadows. But *wontfuckingforget* would be furious, out for rape, and *spoiledbitch* would have regained consciousness by now and be out for blood. Maybe one would get *doucheparasite* to an ambulance, maybe another would care that she had crushed *gagonit* in a cab door, but more likely the task of dealing with all that, and relocating Sedgwick's shoulder, had fallen to Romano. Or maybe they'd just left all three of them there on Fifth Avenue to be run over by the next cab, or bus, or…

'Yes?'

'Emerald Tarragon.'

'Who?'

'Manny Devane sent me to get something for the premiere.'

'The what?'

'Google it, stop wasting my time; hurry the fuck up.'

Nine seconds and the buzzer sounded. She pushed the door and entered.

# CHAPTER NINE:
# TWILIGHT ZONE

The alcove inside was better-lit than the dark glass had given the impression, and she moved quickly up the old wooden stairs before Parker doubled back, having heard the buzzer, and suspected what was potentially happening. But there was no clue, and she would give up. It was late; the job was over, she wanted to go home.

Two flights up and the door to a warehouse was open. The private showroom was a partitioned space of a larger warehouse, this section offering long windows that looked down to Madison below; long racks down the inner-partitioned walls; four long, tall mirrors propped in a square in the middle; and a long-limbed, swan-necked supermodel standing in the corner, smoking a cigarette in her plain beige lingerie, beside a tall coffee table, the only feature of which was a tiny, gorgeous, lotus-shaped crystal ashtray. The supermodel stared at Emerald as she entered directly by the top of the wooden stairs, inspected her with an auto-pilot disdain as she looked around, then dropped that and regarded her curiously, and a little defensively, as she walked across the plain concrete floor. Beneath Emerald's coat, and the layers of clothing, the supermodel was seeing, sensing, almost recognizing; one of her own? Was she…? What *was* she? No; not one of them, but once? A model; maybe?

Emerald went right up to her.

The supermodel watched like a good-natured dog, with no sense of guardianship of their own household, watching a stranger enter and approach. Emerald barely registered the mix of confusion and disbelief as she went directly to the high, tiny table and took out one of her cigarettes. Shit, how many was this now today? Five already? Only a couple left in the pack. But the fourth she'd only… Jesus. Did it… yes, it did matter. Ritual was important. She had to be careful.

She lit up anyway.

The thing that looked like the most beautiful female version of a human praying mantis possible stared at her. She was famous, but one of the new social media models that nobody over twenty would recognize. But Emerald liked to remain aware, and had kept abreast of the so-called new media. Exactly; for right now, just such an occasion.

She exhaled her fumes away from the mantis.

'How many followers now?'

Emerald didn't engage her directly. She remained aloof, preoccupied, but asked so casually, as though they knew each other, as though they were picking up exactly where they'd left off, like old friends.

'Two point seven something.'

Hundred thousand. That put her firmly in the middle bracket.

Emerald turned and looked her right in the eyes. They were around the same height.

'There's nothing here for you. What is your favourite thing?'

Emerald's temples seared. This was taking a toll; she would soon have nothing left. This level of psychic exertion, combined with this amount of sheer sorcery, plus the pressure of the pursuit and the stress of the consequences should she become recaptured…

The eyes of the mantis trembled, side to side, as she found she could not escape Emerald's gaze.

'Cherry Coke.'

'Really?' Emerald was surprised.

Her voice was light, and essentially friendly. But she was scared now.

'Gavin. Princess Diana. Pearl Jam. Romance porn. People leaving me alone.'

'Where's your phone?'

'I hate my phone.'

'Give it to me.'

The mantis turned and went to the corner of the warehouse. Her cigarettes and a small clutch were on the floor there. She removed a gold-trim, caseless phone and came back to the table, handing it to Emerald.

'Don't tell anyone I said that. I didn't even know myself. I do though. I can't stop looking at it. It's like a dominatrix and I don't know the safe word.'

'Social media's like that,' Emerald confirmed, somewhat sadly. She could see that this girl could not escape it. Her addiction was primal now; maternal, paternal, her whole self.

'What are you doing to me?'

She asked it so simply.

'I am exerting a very powerful psychic control on you; it's simple because your thoughts are very easy to read. They are honest and focussed and passionate and direct, almost completely unfiltered. I won't hurt you; I have to stop bad people hurting me, though.'

'That's okay.'

'I know; I wouldn't do it otherwise. I can read it in you. You're a good person. You have a true heart. You want to help.' Emerald picked up a thought and couldn't help express it. 'Suddenly everybody wants you, but in school they called you The Giraffe.'

'They called you Eerie Emerald.'

'You can see that?'

'I can see things, back in your past, that are still…' The model squinted curiously at her. '…whirring around. Like windmills. That's an old song isn't it?'

'I… think, yes…' She knew damn well it was, she had it on her playlist.

Her playlist that had stopped at some point, without her realizing. She still had the earbuds in, but the jack had been yanked out, probably back at the elevator. It was funny how you could forget.

'You have to run. The friendly thing in the sky, it's telling me, you have to run, or you will run out.'

'Run out of time?'

'No; run out of you.'

The mantis, whose name was Galena, seemed to balk.

'I'm sorry Emerald; that frightened you.'

'Yes.' Things were worse than she thought. She cracked the back of Galena's phone, removed the battery, and then the SIM. Then she took out her own, and did the same. Then she swapped the SIMs, and as she did so, she told Galena this:

'Galena, I need you to move very fast. Can you do that?'

'I have a driver. I can tell him.'

'Go to the club you know that is the furthest away, where there are the most people, very quickly, and get a Cherry Coke. Stay and drink it. Is Gavin at home?'

'Yes. He'll be hungry, and lonely.'

'Go home then, and –'

She smiled, distantly. 'He'll be sleeping on the end of the bed by now…'

'Gavin is…?'

'My dog.'

'You have a dog called… I guess you do.'

'I know what you want me to do. You want them to chase me instead of you. I have a job in Seattle, the day after tomorrow. I can go early. It would work out.'

'Really?'

'And the thing, the thing that's chasing you, won't come after me instead, it will keep looking for you. That's what I was wondering when I saw it there, windmilling in your mind. But, the thing in the sky says –'

Galena turned suddenly, like a schoolgirl caught talking over the fence, and a woman appeared from the other end of the partition. Emerald could read her like a cardboard sign in a TV studio. She had kept out of the way to make it seem like it didn't matter that she was here; that there was no hurry. But there was all sorts of passive-aggressive patterning within her; how the store needed the celebrities as much as the celebrities needed the store, but that the celebrities who shopped here, who were more often than not afraid that they would not find anything to suit them in the store, and thus be left out of the rapid, tri-weekly, high-fashion cycle this store catered for, were… *God, Emerald just couldn't be bothered.*

She took out her purse and looked inside. The new woman, the shop assistant, Emerald wanted to call her, could not believe how gauche that was. Emerald didn't have time, or emotion, or anything. She had nine hundred bucks in cash, and took out three, in three bills.

'When I give you this money, you will go. She was never going to buy anything tonight. She is lonely and wanted company. Take this as a commission.'

Emerald extended the money.

The woman immediately took it, huffed resignedly, turned and departed. She went back the way she had come, around the partition, and was gone again, muttering something to herself about time-wasters.

Emerald turned back to Galena. She had put on the summer dress that she had apparently worn here, and was pulling a winter coat and scarf over it; all beige, like her underwear.

'The thing in the sky says what?'

Galena slipped into some flat shoes. 'That you missed something; a hint, a help. That you still need to run. Really, run.'

Emerald took her phone, containing Galena's SIM, back from the table.

'You should…' Galena was dead serious. 'You should run.'

'Galena, I will, but I have to disappear. By the time I resurface, I will be ready for them. When I do, feel free to come find me.'

'Do you want to sleep with me? I want to sleep with you.'

Her natural hair colour was beigey as well; she was growing it out, from having thinned it with over-colouring; halfway down the edges were violet and bright blue and pink.

'I think sometimes that gay women find me more attractive than straight men.'

'I want to see you again…' Galena had a smitten look in her rare, hazel eyes. 'I will find you.'

Emerald sighed. 'Look, you've got my SIM. Find my details, then, if you really are willing, take it to Seattle. If you remember any of this by then, then; you have one of the… clearest spirits I've ever come across. I'll be far away, but…'

'The world is tiny to me. Run, Emerald. Now. Before you run out.'

# CHAPTER TEN:
# JOURNEY OF THE SORCERER

Emerald turned and ran. She ran around the partition, where the shop assistant was closing down her computer. She went down another two flights of steps at the front of the building and across the show floor. She easily unlocked the front doors then was across Madison and running, her heels clip-clopping, louder the faster she ran, running as fast as she could, down two more blocks before she knew it. There were people leaving restaurants late, lovers walking hand in hand, weird folk wandering, day-jobbers working late. But there were not many, and none of them seemed to take anything but a passing interest in her. She saw a squad car in the distance and turned sharply down another avenue and sprinted another block to Park Avenue, almost exhausted now, but determined to keep going, past empty buildings with all the lights on, past offices that were shut down, and closed retail outlets that would be thriving in a few hours. It had to be very late by now; she didn't want to look at the phone, and there was nobody around – even as the minutes passed there were fewer and fewer people around. After another block, still seeing nobody, not even passing cars, she saw a cab and pressed herself into an alcove as it passed, puffing hard, wondering if she was being paranoid, or if it were possible to be paranoid enough where demons were concerned. Then a few more cars went past. The lights had changed somewhere down the street. There were still people, still cars. She collected herself enough to buy a bottle of water from the next 7-11 she passed, just walking swiftly now, and some energy bars and two packs of cigarettes.

'You okay, lady?'

Her mind's eye didn't even register what the guy behind the counter looked like.

'Time…' Emerald puffed as she accepted her change.

'Time is a river. Keep hold the rudder.'

She waved in approval over her shoulder, but by the time she was moving swiftly again down the street was determined to remember it. She kept her music off to remain alert, was immediately revived by the water, and kept moving as she munched the bars, zig-zagging down the streets, side-streets and avenues where she felt she could, then she ran again, and kept up her pace a good while, until she found herself slowing down as she approached yet another big intersection. It had all blurred; she might have levitated a little, just a little, down some side streets, past a few homeless, a few skaters, a few roaming insomniacs and druggies. But now she was at East 63rd and First, and there was a half-decent franchise hotel. She replaced her beanie, reconcealing her mass of now utterly unruly hair, paid cash for a room and ordered a club sandwich and a Cherry Coke, which she devoured sitting cross-legged on the bed, watching on the local news; a report about how a drug deal in a Fifth Avenue apartment block lobby had gone bad, right in the middle of people leaving a Guggenheim benefit, and how four people were now in the ER at Mount Sinai.

Emerald stopped chewing her club sandwich for a few seconds.

So… *gagonit* lives?

She checked that the notepad app on her phone still worked, even though she had Galena's SIM. It did; she let out a sigh of relief, then burped from the Coke. A while back she had written down all her important numbers and details, by hand, into that program. Her audio material was all still saved as well, and so were her playlists. She fell back on the bed and went within, then scanned psychically. She could not detect anyone watching her, anyone closing in, any hostility. The concierge thought she must be a Hollywood actress he'd never heard of. There were eleven other rooms on this floor, none vacant, all singles sleeping.

Nothing.

She had no choice but to risk sleeping for a cycle, and set her phone alarm for ninety minutes. She was pretty good at power naps and self-programming, but in the end she still had to trust the phone.

She woke one minute before the alarm and switched it off before it sounded. But she hadn't been easy with the risk of using the phone. Manny might have been rich now but he had remained very much connected to his ubergeek roots; for all she knew he had set the phone itself to ping cell-towers, as opposed to the SIM, which was her limited understanding of how people were traced. So far as she knew, you turned on the phone, the SIM pinged the nearest tower, that was recorded, or reported if necessary, and as soon as you passed another tower or two they triangulated and they had your position. But that required the chip in the phone to be powered. She suspected that if it were at all possible, Manny was capable of devising something that did the same thing, the tower triangulation thing, whenever you just turned on the phone; she didn't trust Google, or paranoid forums, to be right about it either.

So. That was that. She would not turn her phone on again. Not until she was safe. Perhaps not ever.

She did not feel better for the sleep; worse in fact, and her legs and lower back ached from the running, but she knew that the sleep would count, that it would help, if it had not cost her.

She held her breath and scanned again.

It hadn't cost her.

Nothing had changed.

Emerald Tarragon remained AWOL.

She departed the hotel for good near four in the morning, asking the concierge where the nearest chemist was, claiming she had a migraine, which was a lie that was so close to the truth he totally bought it and utterly sympathized; if anyone came looking, she was still checked in. She walked another half block then hailed a cab that had just dropped someone at the same hotel. She asked the driver to roam a while, but then stopped him when she saw some garbage collectors, got out and threw Galina's SIM in the next lot they would collect. Then she got back in and told the driver that she wanted to buy a car, that she needed to drive to Trenton in a hurry, that her maniac husband was getting out of prison early, that he was a drug-dealing con-man and that he would be able to find her if she wasn't careful. She had a sister there, who has just moved out from Washington, and it would give her a few days head start until he found them. Her brother-in-law could protect them all anyway, he was ex-military.

Yada yada.

The cab driver said he could help for a decent tip, whatever the hell her story was, and drove about twenty minutes in almost no traffic to a fairly okay-looking used car block, in an area she didn't know that looked pretty much the same as all the areas she didn't know; old but thriving, unwashed but liveable, just like this part of every inner city she'd ever been to. The driver left her in the cab while he went into the front office, where the light was still on. He told her to stay in the cab, but she got out anyway and had her sixth cigarette for the day; it was the first day in four years she had had more than four. But what the hell, she'd slept, it was almost five in the morning; screw it, it was tomorrow already.

The cab driver re-emerged and stood by the cab while she negotiated with the owner, a big man she thought was no more or less trustworthy than any other of the used car dealers she'd dealt with in her history of escaping the thing she now called Coveth. She was offered three hundred for a ten-year-old – she didn't know what make and cared less – that would get her to Trenton, about eighty miles away, but not much further.

'Trade it when you get there, you'll probably get half that back.'

She thought that was probably bullshit, and told him. She'd been in this situation before; she reckoned she had one level of bluff to work with. He laughed her off, but offered the same make, the same year, but one that would probably get her to wherever it was she actually wanted to go, and run her around a while when she got there, before it would need some pretty serious work.

'GPS?'

'No; but it's got a USB jack. I dunno if it works, I dunno anything about all those sticks and stuff. Just give me an old fashioned CD player, me.'

He had another, regular model of these cars.

'Get you to wherever you want to go, get you to work every day a while, wherever you're going, set yourself up before you get something more your style? Two grand?'

She didn't have two grand.

She would have to see to that.

She offered him two hundred cash for the second one, gave the cabbie a fifty, and she drove it inland as the sun was coming up, following signs until she saw one to Pittsburgh. She got there, leaving New York over a long bridge and then just driving all day, thinking and watching the road, but once she was there it started making a noise, and smelling of fuel. She traded it and a hundred for a smaller car, because by that time, with the fuel leak and realizing she was going to have to buy food the whole way, she was down to nearly five hundred, a long way to go, and seeing a day fast approaching when she would start to run low on cash. She spent another hundred on a pillow and duvet set, slept uncomfortably in the back a few hours, then drove that smaller car three hours to Columbus, and traded again, another hundred for an even smaller car, for the afternoon drive to Cincinnati; all cash.

It was Sunday night by the time she arrived. She found a decent tapas bar, ate her fill, then walked two miles to the Jack Casino and briefly assessed it from outside. It didn't take her long, not any more at least, to find the closest relatively high-class bordello.

'I like women who look like me.'

'Can't say I blame you, honey.'

Panther had about as much Spanish heritage as Gwyneth Paltrow but there was a passing Eastern European resemblance and they were almost the same height and exactly the same size. In Panther's room, she gave her the rest of her cash in return for the rest of the night, her least slutty sporty-girl outfit (including a pair of sunglasses) and they passed a few hours while Panther smoked some weed, combed out and braided Emerald's hair, tried it on and was politely rejected twice, then stitched up her highway cop costume while they both watched the old film of Bowie's last Ziggy Stardust concert on Panther's laptop. At first light Emerald departed with a mild contact high, having made a new friend, and a USB of current American alt-pop and alt-rock that Panther played in the background when she did her weeknight webcam performances.

Emerald walked back to the tiny car and drove it to an empty Wal-Mart parking lot where, cramped and awkward in the back seat, she changed into the white costume; girl's polo shirt, V-neck jumper and long cardigan that went down the to the hemline of the sexy little school girl tennis skirt.

'I look like Nancy Drew, off to see her tennis coach…' Emerald had commented when she'd tried it on for Panther.

'Sweetie; don't you think that was exactly the look I was going for?'

The sneakers and the cute little white socks were a bit tight, but fine as she drove to another spot two miles out then walked briskly back to the casino, busting the lenses out of the sunglasses and arriving with a light sweat in what looked like ordinary nerdy specs. She made herself seem a little nervous, then plunged and ran the tables there, skipping out with five grand from her last twenty bucks. Risky after just two days, she supposed, but nobody stopped her. They seemed kind of excited for her, truth be told.

She went immediately back to the tiny car and drove a few suburbs to some place she'd never heard of, found the local postal service, packaged the majority of her most precious and distinctive items, and sent the parcels on. She would miss her real coat, and the empowerments, but with the powerful protection spells she had cast, they and she were safer with them in the air.

The amethyst ring remained on her finger and was fully burgundy now, and the cue remained zipped up in its leather bag, in the bottom of her croc bag with the changes of clothes and little else. She also kept the beanie; it would take her ages to weave another hair-containment spell that intricate.

After dropping the pillow and duvet set off at the nearest homeless shelter, she drove back to a strip mall she had passed earlier, still in the tennis gear, and bought three pairs each of blue jeans, thermal tops and leggings, plain white tees, plain blue jumpers, plain sneakers, then a half-decent wool coat from a boutique further down the road, closer to the city. Then she drove to the main bus terminal and found a girl with a black eye in line to take the coach to Nashville. Three behind her was another girl with a split lip. She put them together, bought them each a coffee and gave them the keys to the tiny car.

'Swap stories on the way; it'll be good for you to hear.'

Then she gave them a grand each.

She waited until they'd gone, then paid cash for the overnight coach to Indianapolis.

She missed her music.

She hadn't turned her SIM-less phone on all the way here, not since she'd checked it back in the Manhattan hotel. The commercial music on the car radio had driven her mad all the way from New York, even though it had been slightly better than nothing. The coach took a few hours and all the music on offer was easy listening, interrupted for ninety minutes by a family-friendly edit of a lowbrow American comedy she would never have bothered with anyway. It completely depressed her, so much so that she almost turned her phone back on; she desperately missed having a filter for her personal world, her mind and emotions, and wanted these random hits and pieces, chosen by corporate suits for social control (so she was told) to go away.

At Indianapolis she walked around until the shops opened, and bought a decent generic tablet with some prepaid data; the man there was sympathetic and explained how to keep everything anonymous, keep it off the cloud, prevent tracking and create fake email addresses. It had been a few years, but all the processes were as she'd assumed, but it had been good to double check.

It had also been depressing.

As it had been, back in the Fifth Avenue apartment, naked on the bed.

Running, again.

On the Tuesday afternoon train to Chicago, without a credit card to access the iTunes store, or any music store for that matter, she used the Wi-Fi to access various pirate sites and re-downloaded all her favourite songs, starting with an Al Stewart discography and going from there until she almost ran out of data. At the hotel that night she reconstructed her playlists, deciding that she was going to keep this thing, keep it anonymous, and use it purely as a jukebox.

She slept all night, then in the morning ran the blackjack tables at Rivers for three more grand, then paid cash three nights in a row at three different, low-end motels that she walked to for at least three hours each day, until she was sure she hadn't been followed.

She still carried her cue, and all the while she walked along with her croc bag over her shoulder, she was thinking her plan through. She almost had it worked out now, she was sure.

Despite her paranoid precautions, she remained edgy that Manny or Horst would somehow have spies, have alerts somehow, on… she didn't know. Certain kinds of wins? At certain kinds of casinos…? Who knew; Manny was a master of algorithms and had told her several times that he could hack most of the world's data if he really wanted to. Plus, she had told Horst, but not Manny, about the potential for sorcerers, and some ordinary psychics, to skim off the luck of others…

If they had been working together it seemed more than possible that Horst might have told Manny about it, especially if they had been drinking together, so for the rest of her time she found bars, and hustled pool, like she had back in Madrid.

She didn't like doing it, but she didn't like the idea of dying either.

Lonely, she thought about maybe sleeping with some of the guys she met, but always thought better of it. She almost never did that, hadn't done it in a decade, and when she had become that girl, and done it just a few times, way back when, sometime between Steel and Horst, she had always pretended that she had been someone else, made up a whole story, and in the end wished that it had been real, which had made her even more depressed.

Even without doing that, she was becoming melancholy. She'd had too many hours to walk around and think, or sit on hotel beds and go over her plan too many times.

She bought another car, a good one, for two grand.

'Does it have a USB?'

'Sure.'

'How much?'

She thought about taking it and leaving it at O'Hare. She still had a few grand left, enough to fly anywhere. But Manny would certainly be watching the airports, even if the cops weren't. If there had been an APB, she would have had to zap some cops by now. But there had not been, and no mention of her either at "the Fifth Avenue drug deal gone bad", which had surfaced that night on the news and, so far as she could tell, buying what print newspapers this country had left to sell as she had proceeded through it, never been mentioned since.

Manny wanted her all to himself.

One way or another.

She drove the good car through Illinois to Iowa and took three days to hit three more casinos in Rockford, Davenport and Cedar Rapids along the way, then laid low in Des Moines for another three days, actually going to see that movie the old lady ghost would have loved; catching a superhero blockbuster that was better than it had any right to be; then a remake of a classic romance she never should have taken the chance with, that *they* should never have taken the chance with, and as it turned out, hardly anyone else in the world had taken the chance with either. She then drove all afternoon, night and morning to Denver, where she bought more pillows and blankets, slept ten hours in the back of the car, which was a lot more spacious than the back seats to which she'd recently accustomed herself. Later that night she drove to the casino in Black Hawk, Colorado, a tourist mining town that existed purely for the sake of the casino, then drove less than two miles to its rival casino in Central City, which was almost exactly the same. She slept in the car, then the next day she did the same, but backwards.

This would be obvious to anyone tracking her; with more money than she needed, her plan was to hit Vegas next, then get down to Los Angeles. She would get lost in LAX, and somehow manage a flight from there without anyone knowing. Maybe she was even planning to lay low and start again in California. Maybe the Bay Area, maybe Seattle. Regardless; that would be where to look for her, on her way through Vegas maybe, where she would be out to make her final fortune, then headed for the west coast. It almost sounded good.

She rested a few days in a small town outside of Denver, near the highway, and on the third day left a credit card that she'd been saving all this time in a roadside diner, to get stolen by someone heading to Vegas.

She thought that she'd been running more than three weeks now, although she'd kind of lost count.

Was that enough?

Time for the big move?

How long did grudges last, anyway?

How long would he grieve her loss?

She knew the answer damn well; it all depended whether Horst was alive, and where Coveth was, and what was left of the real Manny after he'd been exposed to both of them.

But; here it was.

The first of the risks, in the first part of The Plan.

Nothing ventured.

The Garbage track *Paranoid* played as she turned from the diner, heading away from Vegas, away from Denver, and she committed to the two thousand mile drive to Montreal. She let it play on repeat for an hour, before she hit random again.

Time passed strangely; she seemed always to be either driving to music or sleeping in the back seat of the car, but she was eating okay, buying food and sugar drinks, and rugs and cushions to pad the whole of the back seat, from farmer's markets and artisan fairs she found along the way. She tried not to pay attention to anything else, especially anything related to her kind, or potentially connected to her kind, which was difficult when she was making all her purchases from nature people. But she managed, she thought, despite the fact that she was desperate, deep within her soul now, for spiritually or mystically nourishing company, especially after the dark, draining energy of all those casinos. But she couldn't help notice the broad changes in the landscape as she went, and draw energy from some of the monuments, and her proximity to areas of vast natural density. The closer she got to Canada, the colder it became. Toronto was freezing, but she couldn't risk a hotel, and then it was horrendously cold once she got to Montreal itself, and impossible to keep sleeping in the car.

She arrived in the morning, driving extra-long on the final stretch to finally get there, but still didn't risk a hotel; rather, as the day revealed itself to be cold, really too cold to sleep, she drove down to the Old Port. It had been redeveloped, and not much of the connection to the old world remained, but it was still there, basically as she'd been told.

She found the pub, at the back of the least redeveloped section of the wharf. The signage claimed that it dated back more than four hundred years. It had just opened and she went inside. There were only a couple of other people. She took a booth to herself with her back to the corner, then ordered a big pub burger from the young waitress, one with proper European chips. When it came, again with the Cherry Coke habit she seemed to have developed, she devoured it, then sat waiting.

It didn't take long for someone to arrive.

# CHAPTER ELEVEN:
# BURGERS OF THE THIRD DENSITY

'I've felt your approach for days.'

The man sat across from her in the booth and looked into her eyes. He felt to Emerald as though he were in his… mid-sixties? But she couldn't see his face; at least, could not discern any distinct features.

Emerald was almost too scared to ask.

'Was I followed?'

'You tell me.'

'Did – *it* – follow me?'

'Ah. You're there.'

She still couldn't see him.

'Yes. I'm there. You know that. You felt me coming.'

'Pursued?'

'And you're one of the Fur Traders.'

'I am.'

Emerald sighed. She let go of something deep within her.

She'd made it.

The sigh kept coming.

She'd made it.

She choked, holding back tears.

'Go back and sleep in your car tonight. Come back here tomorrow.'

'I… I don't think I can…'

'It will be okay.'

She found that she was standing, finishing her Coke, and walking out, walking away on autopilot. The car wasn't far, and she sat in it, wondering whether that had actually just happened. Wondering where the hell she was going to drive now, that would be safe, to sleep. She had assumed he would deal with her immediately, that she would not spend another minute in Montreal, outside of the pub, once she had entered. She put her hands on the wheel. She knew this car really well now, but like the others, the make still hadn't sunk in. She'd seen a lot of others, this white colour, on the road, but she still didn't know. But, still; she'd know *this one* anywhere.

The passenger door opened and the Fur Trader got in.

'It's okay.'

She lost consciousness.

She woke. It was still daylight, but late afternoon now, and he was still there.

'Sorceress. You sleep very deeply in the presence of...' The Trader smiled. 'Anyway, that is a good sign.'

'I still can't see your face.'

The Trader reached over the seat between them, grabbed something from the back and handed it to her. It was her regular bottle of water, half full.

'You've done well. Timed your fresh food without proper storage, eaten hot food when you could; kept to your good diet.'

'Even the Cherry Coke?'

'Indulgence in moderation is the key to sustained discipline.'

She wanted to write that down on her phone, next to the thing the 7-11 guy had said about time.

'It's been freezing cold most of the time; fresh food storage hasn't been...' She looked at his fuzzy face again. '...you just watched my journey like a movie. I can feel it.'

'On fast forward.' He smiled. 'You needed to sleep. You looked pretty bad when you walked in. Sometimes; a long drive, thinking desperate thoughts; one focus, a plan going over and over... I have seen a lot of that in my time, just from running a pub. But when it's a sorceress running from a stalking demon...'

'Then, is it true?'

'Yes.'

She felt another level of stress evaporate.

'You can help?'

'Yes.'

'Can I…?' She still hadn't had that cry. It was still choking a bit, deep at the back of her throat, resting just above her heart. 'I suddenly feel like…'

'Yes.'

She slept again, awakening from early evening to night. This time her neck was sore to the right, and her leg was a little numb. She'd either slept in a bad position that had woken her, or so deep, and long, that the bad position hadn't mattered.

The Trader was still there beside her.

*It was true.*

That was her first thought.

There were three apparently; old sorcerers who'd lived here since the days it had been a fur trading port, before London, or Paris, or any of that. They'd seen it all. They'd fought demons, channelled angels, changed governments, spawned generations, and they, well, at least one of them, could open portals.

The Trader seemed to be watching the street light against the backs of the buildings ahead of them in the parking lot. 'You can't kill them.'

'I know. They're un-killable.'

'They're not alive. Not like we are.'

'But they're not immortal, are they?'

'I don't think anyone's ever proved that.'

Emerald drank some more water. 'Right…' She didn't feel so much like crying any more. She wasn't tired any more. 'But they work their way up, right?'

'Yes. And you can…'

' – send them back?'

'Not exactly. You can remove their structures. They can be made to descend. But, it must be done early. There is still time for you.'

'How much?'

'Keep drinking your water.'

She obeyed.

'I have seen your plan, Emerald.'

'I thought you might have. Do you disapprove? Even if you said you wouldn't help me, I think…'

'You are irreversibly committed to it. Yes. I think it will bring change, and change brings pain; some change however forges a path toward the ultimate wisdom, where the causes of pain after change are better understood. This plan of yours… I think it is worth pursuing, to see. But even if I didn't believe that, Emerald Tarragon, I would still help you. Would you like another burger, for breakfast?'

The pub was just there.

'Have I slept that long?'

'It will be sunrise soon.'

The car hadn't moved while she'd slept; they were still in the parking lot of his pub. She opened the door beside her and all of their collected body warmth vanished. Her leg swung out, stiff and weird-feeling. She had to put her hand on the upper doorframe and pull herself up, and out. She was still in her Cincinnati coat, her jeans and jumper and sneakers. Still in her magic green beanie. She raised herself and found she wasn't so bad, not so stiff. Her body was more than willing to stand, her lungs grateful for the deep breath of frigid five AM harbour air.

He appeared at the bonnet, or the hood as the Americans called it, then she followed him to the back door, reminding herself that she was no longer in America, and hadn't been for days now.

The pub had been renovated, quite recently she saw, to look like a Ye Olde Fur Trapper Pubbe. She hadn't seen that yesterday, it had seemed almost real. But she had slept almost a whole day since then. She saw what he'd meant now. She'd been wrecked, depleted, possessed. But now she was vindicated.

He went behind the bar and she stopped, and watched.

He was so normal for a sorcerer of more than four hundred years; he used keys, and walked about in shoes, and clothes. He'd had a haircut recently, but was unshaven. Had it been real time in the car? Had he sat there with her, as she'd slept for… two lots of…?

'Oh, you were in another place when you came in last night. You were fading in and out of the astral.'

'I was…?'

'I had to sit with you while you slept; you were in danger of letting it all slip away.'

'Slip away? How? Letting what slip away?'

'You. Your dreams. The plan. I had to ground you.'

He put a glass bottle of Cherry Coke on the bar, cracking the lid with an old steel opener. It fizzed, and dribbled a bit.

'Burgers and Coke. This is very third dimensionally grounding.'

She raised the bottle and swigged. It was amazingly fizzy, and tasted like…

'This is old. Like, good old.'

'Come out back.'

She could feel that she was walking a little like she was in a dream still, but he cooked the burger himself as she watched. The stool and the short kitchen bar where she sat, quite comfortably, felt as though she was not the first he'd sat here and cooked for, but also as though this wasn't done all the time. It was casual, but it was a privilege, and sacred.

'They leave us alone now, here. We take little interest in the affairs outside. They had us renovate this place, and we did, to keep the peace, but it's still the same; now nobody suspects even the slightest, and we hide even better.'

Something occurred to her. 'You don't sound Canadian.'

He said something in French that she didn't understand.

'How's that?'

'That sounded French.'

'Change, my dear. We all do it, and we all adapt, or we wither and become obsolete. The demons are especially good at that; adapting, adopting, being adored. This one I think will go far if nothing is done. It's right he should be taken down, now. You can do that; he doesn't know it, he may even have completely forgotten about you by now, but I can see it. Then again, I keep out of these things, these days.'

'But, you're the one who's defeated them before, aren't you? If you keep out of it, then how…?'

'I will send you somewhere. You won't be alone. It's part of something much bigger, but you will be someone there. There is someone, someone else there, who is… younger than me. Keener.'

'I don't need keen! I need –'

'To decide, yes. If you decide to go, when you are there, I will trust you to make more of the right decisions. It will be a reckoning for you, Emerald Tarragon.'

She stared into his face.

He looked like an old guy who had run a bar for years. Like, the kind of old dude who still owned the bar, and still hung out at the bar, but left the actual running to his…

'That sounds ominous.'

…protégés.

Hmmm.

He put the plate down softly in front of her.

'There is a man there. He repelled a demon. He and his group. But; mainly him. He will be able to help you more from there, than we can from here.'

He indicated the burger, and the chips.

'Same as before. You seemed to like it.'

'Thankyou.'

She had no choice; she took the meal in both hands and began the process of devouring it once again.

He held up his hand in front of her face.

'Will you allow me?'

She spoke with her cheeks puffed, her tongue pressed down with burger.

'Of course.'

Even as she swallowed, and bared her teeth to bite out another huge chunk, he placed his palm on her forehead, and she felt him take a very deep reading. Later, when he removed his hand, she realized that she now knew what it was like to know when a four-hundred-year-old sorcerer was taking a very deep psychic reading, and that in itself, as if the burgers had not been enough, had been worth the entire drive. But for now, he left it there while she ate. She was surprised at how odd it didn't feel.

'We'll be easier to contact now. You weren't supposed to remain there with that computer man. Devane? But; there is deep karma. You needed to prove something to yourself.'

'I think I figured that out as I was leaving.'

The Trader smiled. 'The old woman, she had passed, and he bought the apartment not long after. She was so concerned for you. She stayed longer than she might have, because you did as well. But she has moved on now, and is pleased you have escaped.'

'I wondered why I was so keen to see that movie about the old people having a last romp.'

'Life begins at sixty, don't they say now?'

'Do they?'

'You were wise to divest yourself of your trappings; but you must reassemble yourself now. You have safe places where your things have been sent, but when you get to the destination, and take on your new assignment, you must have them returned as soon as you can. You can draw energy from where you are going, but you will be far from fully protected.'

He removed his hand.

She was halfway through the burger now, and had forgotten his hand was there.

'Can you see it now, Emerald? In your mind? As though you are recalling it?'

She was a little startled.

'That's where it is?'

'Follow the arrows. Drive through it. It will take you where you need to go.'

'I understand. Thank you.'

She allowed herself to lose herself in the burger a while, before she remembered something and looked up at him.

'Oh. The trade?'

She'd neglected the chips. They were thick and crunchy on the outside, fluffy within, and miraculously, still hot.

'Of course.'

Emerald shrugged. 'What would you like me to do?'

'Two things. One for us.'

'The three of you?'

He nodded. 'We want to see it.'

'See it?'

'In the end. *At* the end. In the end, at the end, we want to watch. That has to be made available to us.'

'And the second thing?'

'Cahokia wants a word. They have a condition.'

'Cahokia…' Emerald uttered. 'The Mississippi?'

'Yes.'

Cahokia. Like London, or Rome, or Babylon – and others that she'd never encountered. All through what the Europeans called the Piscean Age, the past two and a half thousand years, the Mississippi had spawned a succession of massive Native American cultures; Cahokia had been a temple-city at the heart of one of the largest.

Emerald spun backwards suddenly in her mind; she had been born in Madrid, but had spent most of her childhood in Sydney. Back and forth into adulthood, then America had entered the mix. But her blood, she had always assumed it went back to the Spanish invading South America somehow, back to conquering the Incans, who had all-but created the Mexicans, but now she saw that it went back further, it traced further back, up to the north, up along the Mississippi… to when her earliest maternal, shamanistic ancestor had come down, and exchanged with the Incan shamans, and –

The Trader snapped her out of it.

'That is the trade. Cahokia has a condition.'

'I can't refuse you. I can't refuse them.'

She had just been all over North America. Crossed the Mississippi twice, and its massive tributary, the Missouri; on a map, the enormous river system split the United States like a lightning strike. The rivers had been just some of the natural monuments from which she had drawn energy. Even though she had tried to lay low, and not pay attention to anything mystical, or shamanistic, or related to sorcery… she had drawn attention. You could not avoid the natural monuments. They would see you, no matter what. She had been noticed.

'But, as nice as you've been, retuning me and all, that is not a trade. That is a bribe.'

He did not disagree. 'Stay here.' He shrugged, perfectly happy to accept an alternative arrangement. 'I need a new waitress. You could live out your days quite safely working here. We have karma magic; we can attract you someone you need to burn with, to create with. It would be very satisfying. Children, a house, never unemployed. I will train you. In twenty years, you can be standing here, talking to people, people just like you, helping them the way I am helping you. There will be little you can't do by the time you pass on, and you will pass on a great grandmother, able to take most of your mystic knowledge directly into your next birth.'

Her chewing had stopped. There was still a chunk of spiced beef and bread roll between her lips.

'Cah… cah I hah thah…?' She chewed quickly, and swallowed hard. 'Where I'm going? Can I still have that?'

*Home?*

'More perhaps. Or, you will fall in a great battle, protecting other great sorcerers. Or someone you love will fall, protecting you. And still you may live, and create, just as I have said you might here, but there. Stay here, I can guarantee it. Go there; you gamble. A lot more, a lot less.'

Suddenly she wasn't hungry any more.

He placed his old hand on hers, as they came to rest on the table.

'You're here Emerald; you've evaded them. Even when they realize where you are, they can't remove you from our sphere of influence. Any more than you can extricate poor Manny now. People make choices; your pain, his pain, they are coming. The lines have been drawn. Each to their own.'

'So Coveth didn't follow me. Manny didn't follow me. None of those psychos followed me.'

The Trader sighed. 'I am saying; they cannot hurt you under my protection. Remain here, work here, help others here, and they, it, will never harm you again.'

It was sinking in; but she could still feel what he'd left in her mind.

'The map. I drive there and…'

'Whoosh. Through. It will stay open until you find it, and close immediately behind you.'

Emerald nodded. He removed his hand, and she began eating again.

As she finished the burger, from another room, k.d lang's *Constant Craving* started up; someone at the jukebox in the bar.

'Good burger?'

'The best.'

'Would you like another to go? They're good cold, too.'

On the long drive, even on the last stretch without hotels, she'd always found places to wash, and keep clean. But the shower in the staff bathroom was the best she could ever remember having. Coming out, she went commando, but replaced the same shirt, and the old jumper, and the coat and jeans. She felt great.

There were people in the bar now.

It was daytime.

Around eleven, she guessed.

The Trader was behind the bar, talking to a woman who could have been his sister, who was drinking some kind of vodka and lemon on the other side. When she saw Emerald come out, she necked it and smiled at her as she walked away, toward the pool table at the back of the bar.

'It's a good plan, Emerald.'

The Trader handed her a brown paper bag. She looked inside. There were two more hot burgers, a couple of plastic takeout tubs of salad, and some cold fried chicken.

'My sister likes it as well…'

He handed her a second bag.

She looked inside that as well, smiled, and shrugged.

'Thanks, but I won't drink that much in a million years.'

'It's not for you. You'll know who, when the time's right.'

She accepted both bags, put them down on the bar, lifted the counter and came around. She gave him a big hug, held him tight a few seconds, and then departed, closing the counter and grabbing the two brown paper bags, walking across the creaky wooden floor without looking back.

She knew that his face was starting to become misty again, shrouded. She'd already forgotten what he looked like. Just; his face had been wise, leaning toward kind.

When she reached the door, he spoke. Although he was far away now, maybe not even there anymore, she heard him as though he was speaking right behind her.

'It's a two thousand and five Ford Taurus.'

'Pardon?'

Her hand was on the door.

'Worth twice what you paid. I thought you should know; you're going to need parts.'

She nodded, and smiled, and pulled the door open.

She was feeling a lot better now.

# CHAPTER TWELVE: PARANOID

The back seat of the Taurus had become a bit of a mess, she saw as she approached, so she opened the back door, folded all the rugs so they stacked neatly, shifted her few storage boxes, stacked the pillows, and pulled the cue from beneath the driver's seat. There were some empty water bottles, and a couple of stray plastic bags, so she walked across the empty parking lot and threw them in the dumpster, along with a few stray wrappers from the feet of the passenger's seat. There wasn't much; she was disciplined, and always kept a neat base of operations.

More blankets than she had thought though, she saw upon her return, looking in.

It had been bloody cold and, she had to face it, she had been losing it a bit.

Not going mad, not crazy; just tired.

Weary. Weak and alone, uncertain but determined.

A neat base. Yes.

A tidy home.

Home, anew?

Maybe.

From here?

The Trader had placed the directions to the portal directly into her head; a kind of psychic module she supposed. A kind of spell so precise that it made her realize how much she had left to learn. That she'd left behind?

She started the car and pulled out.

It was a busy city, nearing lunch time.

As she drove, it felt to her as though she had always known where it was. And yet, she was aware that it was simply a psychic patch, a unit of another's memory, neatly filtered and edged, so that it was clear but unfettered with anyone else's memories or emotions.

Four hundred years plus, she supposed.

That was where it got you, as a skill-set.

She drove out of the old, remade section of town as though she were driving to an old favourite picnic spot. When she got there, it was as she remembered it, even though she had never seen it before. She took her ticket from the machine and the gate went up. She steered the car up, and up, until she had cleared five, six, seven levels. Then more, until her arms were a bit achy, turning and turning, ten, eleven, twelve.

The sign outside made her realize that these places had been called something different everywhere she'd lived, although she'd forgotten the Spanish now. Car park, parking lot, parking garage, and now parkade. Up and up, to the sixteenth, (was it *estacionamiento?*), seventeenth, eighteenth level.

And then, there it was.

Another curved concrete ramp incline, up to the nineteenth level – that nobody could see but us mystics. That nobody but mystics, psychics or sorcerers, who had been given this patch, had ever seen.

She didn't hesitate.

Up, and up.

The top level of the nineteen-story parkade, that she knew but had never been in, was completely empty. The floor was there, physically, in the real world, but its entrance had been obscured with a powerful spell.

So, they owned it, the Traders. They had built a parkade here, in order to hide the dimensional portal that opened up here in the sky, in plain sight. In fact, the parkade was a sort of… secret temple. It had even been built over the ruins of a temple, she… thought she… remembered?

So there it was.

Right there, in the middle of the concrete space, in the very centre of all the pillar supports, glowing bright purple, circular; ready to drive right through, like the world's simplest car stunt. She followed the arrows, as instructed, slowly to get a good look at the thing. She supposed that the arrows had been arranged so that anyone driving through it would drive through it in the right direction. The arrows took her along, and past it to her right. It was right there; a *real* special effect, a tyre, donut, of blazing, circular energy.

Bright purple.

Real.

The arrows turned at the end of the building, which looked out over the midday skyline of Montreal, and now she was turning, and passing it again, closer, to her left, slowly down the lane, her engine running smoothly. It was shining energy, rippling, a central white circle, billowing the purple energy in deep tones right by the central white, then violet, and calming into lavender out at the edges. She passed right by it again, then turned left at the end, curving one-eighty into the central of the five lanes.

Still there.

Right in front of her now.

Just – drive in a straight line.

Straight through.

She drove halfway toward it, a quarter of the lane, and stopped.

She stared at it.

A portal. A doorway between dimensions, directly. One place, directly to another.

Between being killed in a battle, and generations of children.

Or, not.

Not?

She heard herself breathing.

Heard herself shift slightly in her seat.

All these years, she'd never seen one. They were rare, but they were around, a bit like diamond mines. She'd just… never needed one, she supposed.

Some led to other dimensions.

She'd heard.

She wasn't even sure if she believed that.

She cracked the handle. It sounded like someone opening a manhole cover in the middle of the night. She got out of the car, leaving it running.

The demons, devils, djinn, whatever; the ghosts of old women, and these; she could see how they were all just part of one dimension.

She walked closer.

It was real.

Like electricity, like fire, like… gravity.

It was something, it could be studied and explained.

There was no need for anything else; all this mysticism, and spells. It was… science. Formula and language. It was that, for the human will, which was radically misunderstood. That really was all; will and focus by people whose minds and bodies and chemistry were able.

It was all science, all explainable; but the people who wanted it secret, kept it clandestine, they held power that way, through fear and ignorance. They held power at the expense of others, the lives of others, sometimes.

And that was the plan.

To stop that.

Expose it.

Find a way to…

She was quite close to the energy ring now.

She knew better than to touch it, although she wanted to.

She turned sharply and walked back to the car.

Determined.

She didn't even see him as she got in. It wasn't until she sat and looked up, preparing to drive forward, that she saw him. Standing there, blocking the way.

'Manny.'

Then there was movement behind her as, it happened, the absolutely most dangerous of Manny's hires revealed themselves. Not more blankets in the back seat than she'd thought. Someone underneath them, someone who'd climbed in while she'd gone to the dumpster. A handgun extended through the middle of the two seats.

'We meet again, Mo-Cap.'

# PART TWO
## PLACES AND BETS

# CHAPTER THIRTEEN:
# BRIXTON ACADEMY

Bach was on her side, her back wheel still spinning, some distance in front of him. The knife, the glistening silver dagger the maniac had taken out, was embedded deep in his shoulder, and had severed an artery. Barker was bleeding out, unconscious, his blood flowing in an ever-widening pool, spreading all over the street like broken, crimson-black wings, shining in the neon and the darkness, and the dirt of the asphalt.

'It might have ended here; there, tonight.'

As Barker watched, the moustached detective from the lights raced up to him, talking on a hands-free headset as he knelt and examined Barker's wound.

'*Who is that guy?*'

'This is Chief Inspector Parry; I need Extension Twenty-Three-Hundred. *Yes, it's a bloody emergency!*'

Barker could feel a pounding in his chest. How, he wondered? It must have been some kind of spiritual muscle memory. A phantom heart.

'Might have ended?'

Brixton sighed, almost melancholy. 'Barker Moon can end in all manner of ways; you know that my friend. But your vessel and your soul are moving forward, through one stream of linear time; so you cannot, outside of extreme psychic exertion, truly know the future. But something you did, a while ago now, back through the fog, has stopped Barker Moon checking-out tonight, even though it is, quite delightfully; the reason for that happening tonight.'

Barker looked back to Brixton. He was out of the limousine and standing beside him now. They were the same height, about six feet, and he seemed almost normal. Although, he also seemed to be partially composed of mist as well, which was odd, and indicated to Barker that normal was different here, wherever here was. As though he could tell what Barker was thinking, and was pleased by it, Brixton grinned at him with tremendous charm, and a slightly cocked head, which seemed to accentuate the wide, slender beauty of his eyes, his sharp cheeks and the explosion of smile, frown, and crow lines that helped radiate an incredible sexual handsomeness. He was, quite simply, sculptured charm personified, and Barker was caught by that.

Caught somewhere; being shown something.

And it all seemed eerily familiar.

'Your body, your Barker Moon body will perish, my son. In one way or another. But as I said, you won't be forgotten. This planet makes vessels and in those vessels there is a brain and in that brain there are programs that run and the combined running of those programs creates an ego. The ego taps into the programs; some never do anything but run in the background, but some are right there to use, right away. Some are hardwired, some the ego hardwires itself; some it ignores, some it erases, some it improves, and some it gets from outside, and installs over the top, over time, over and over, upgrading until the whole thing just starts to lag and decay.'

There was music coming from the bar behind the limo.

'There it is…' Brixton grinned. 'Ooh, I like this one. Some of mine in that; some of my mate's stuff; and some of it they found all by themselves. My stuff's the stuff that makes it soar though. Wouldn't you say?'

'I can't quite…' Barker still couldn't get a fix. 'You have an ego, I see? It's not just us?'

'Dear me, of course not! I am, as you would see it, mostly spirit, and you can't have an ego without a spirit. Or is it the other way? I tell you what…' Brixton made a face as though he had just thought of all this, rather than having had it clearly rehearsed, and probably having had performed it many times. '…let's say, it's something like; as soon as the vessel is born and the ego starts *singing*, the spirit appears and starts *playing*. Are you following? Your human ego goes out and uses everything it can to complete its mission, to record its oeuvre; it assesses what it's been dealt, and plays its hand, and with that hand it learns its instrument. Instruments, sometimes.'

Barker felt something was happening nearby, something he needed to see.

He turned from Brixton's hypnotic performance and saw that Chief Inspector Parry had moved away from Barker's body. Paramedics had arrived; an ambulance was tearing around the North-East Terrace T-junction. But Parry was moving closer, talking urgently. But as he drew closer, he seemed to become less well-defined through the fog.

'…Moon's down. Yes. No, I tracked him on his phone. I don't know. Look, I've trusted you a long way to here, and you said if he dies, everything goes to –'

The arriving ambulance drowned out his voice, and then the whole scene started to vanish in the fog.

'…what's happening?' Barker heard himself ask.

'Your ego isn't responding to your imminent death; you're not afraid.'

'Is that real? What's happening?'

'Well, let me put it this way. *Continue* – to put it this way? The ego, you remember the ego? The ego creates a personality and tries some life experiences. We got that far, didn't we?'

Barker nodded, but Brixton's gaze wasn't as transfixing this time.

He thought he could still see Mainwaring, sitting on the war memorial.

'The ego extends its personality and sees how it goes; it uses its powers of persuasion to acquire things, like status and knowledge and possessions, and it uses its defence mechanisms to prevent those things being undermined or removed. It seeks pleasures and pains, and records it all, makes notes as to how it might improve the likelihood of success…' Brixton winced. '…oooh, yes my friend, all that pain, and pleasure, and all the little morsels in between, everything that is based in what you are physically, in your mad little vessel, created by your mother planet womb, ignited by your cosmic father spunk; everything you've genetically inherited from your ancestors in those pesky, complicated little spirals, the aforementioned cards with which you were dealt…' Brixton huffed. '…eventually, you forget what you came for. The game's rigged, you see. You get caught up and keep playing and before you know it, there's debt, there's karma, and…. I'm sorry, Barker, am I keeping you from something?'

'I…'

The fog was clearing, more of a mist now, and there was nobody else about on this plane; even the homeless man in the park was gone, and from what he remembered of this stuff the severely mentally ill were usually more here than there, as were many animals. So, why was there a woman sitting next to Mainwaring on the Light Horse Memorial, decked out in full biker leather, streaked with lime green?

He couldn't completely make her out through the mist, but she seemed to just be sitting, one leg out, one leg up, with an elbow on her knee. She was watching, waiting them out, totally cool with it all.

'Oh…' The Rock God took a step back and made a polite gesture, as though to excuse himself after a slight misunderstanding. 'I'm terribly sorry.' He put his hand softly over his vest. And, presumably, if only symbolically, over his heart. 'Do stop me if you've heard this one? Just a deity stopping time and space to impart the spiritual wisdom of the ages…!'

Barker looked back at him. 'I'm sorry, it's just… she saved my life I think?'

'Only a – a – '

'Timeless personification?'

'Yes, thank you! Only a – *timeless personification*, my son, of a *sacred aspect* of the *ultimate eeee-go* of the Greater – Cosmic – All

– ! Nothing more than that, my dear, sweet, child-prodigy of the mystic occult…!'

Barker wasn't buying the performance. It was way too theatrical and self-conscious.

'Look, Brixton, where are we? Where is everyone?'

'Everyone?'

'All the spirits. This is somewhere on the lower astral, right? There should be…'

Brixton suddenly stared at him very hard through sly, narrowed eyes.

'…ah! Ah; there, Barker! There! So you do know! You do remember it!'

'I do?' Barker wasn't sure if he did or not. Was this a secret that needed remembering? Didn't everyone know…?

'Lower astral…' Brixton offered. '…quite correct. There are usually ghosts everywhere.'

Barker nodded. 'I remember this; now I'm here. I mean, these are the old east-end market lanes; this might be the better end of town but it's one of the oldest places in the city…' He scanned up and down. '…there are still usually dozens of restless spirits just wandering the parklands... not to mention coming in and out of there…'

Barker pointed across the intersection at the Botanic Garden gates.

'…not just…'

Looking over to the gates, he'd drawn his attention to his own dying body again. It was just there now, as it had been to begin with. No Parry, no ambulance, just him, bleeding out.

'…not just us.'

Barker took a few steps over, to the edge of his blood, and looked at his face. He was pretty good looking, after all. His resting face was quite handsome. He'd never quite believed it. It was just that he was always so tense; always thinking, frowning, worried and concerned.

He asked quietly. 'Where are they all then, Brixton? All the parkland ghosts?'

Brixton stepped up next to him, and looked down at the body as well.

'We're just one plane removed. The ones on this level; I'm rather afraid they are all hiding from me.'

'Why?'

'Well, I am a deity.' Brixton placed his thin white hand gently on Barker's shoulder. 'Barker, there are no reals once you get past the science and materialism of the human incarnate dimension; I mean, you did know this once. The human Earth plane is all about how well you can manipulate ideas and make them solid, in those three hard dimensions; musically, narratively, lyrically… even mathematically. It's all maths, some of them say. Equations; balances and imbalances. And you are an unsolved equation, my friend, in any of the abstract languages.'

'I am?'

'That's what I was saying; before I was distracted, by you, being distracted… speaking of which…'

Brixton's gaze had arisen and was staring at the other side of the road. It was the start of East Terrace, the northern end, where Barker had fallen, and the outer terraces were almost all wide roads, with double lanes and gardened medium strips; the ones on East Terrace, being the better end of town and all, were paved and well-tended. But Brixton was not looking at that; he was looking at the two men who were standing on the other side.

'Who…?'

'Yes….' Brixton uttered low. 'Them.'

'Who are… they?'

'They – are they. They are The They, capital T – The, capital T – They, "The They" that when you say 'They want it that way', and people say, 'Well, who's They?', these are They. The They.'

'The They.'

'Or just They; let's not get too specific.'

'They look like…'

They were shifting. One of them moved forward, over the edge of the parklands and onto the footpath.

'…Edwardian?'

'I've seen this one before…' Brixton didn't sound pleased about it. '…they have been stalking the grounds around me, wherever I show, like vultures, waiting.'

'Stalking *you*?'

'Do you remember? Earlier in this Earth year, one or two, or two or three, rather large portions, along with some rather fine entrées and a sumptuous dessert or four, even a cheese and cognac or two, all aspects of the veritable banquet of my Earthbound-self, departed. Some of the larger portions, rather unexpectedly. Since then… they seem to think I'm weaker somehow. Like my influence will somehow… fade away.'

'But, surely, that can't happen?'

'Well, you see; that's the thing about this plane, here and now, well into the start of the twenty first century; as I was saying, nobody remembers why they're here anymore.'

'Everybody's distracted…' Barker uttered, still watching the Edwardian interlopers.

'Everybody! You're all lost souls, just like the wandering ghosts in the astral. Just stumbling through the density of the human Earth plane, bumping into things, making noise; bumping into each other, and complaining! Litigating! And consuming, consuming, *consuming*, to take away the pain of it all!'

Barker glanced at him again. 'Too many people? That's an old one.'

'Not really. It's quite a new thing, actually. You had a good solution but you stopped it. The forces of evil – that these creatures represent – shut it down; now you have to wait for the planets to realign again…'

'What; wait for the Age of Aquarius to kick in?'

'No; well, in a way… but no, I was speaking more materially, Barker. I meant space travel. You had a shot at lunar colonization, at Mars and Europa, before one shot blew another; the shot heard 'round the world blew the shot at off-world colonization. Then just as things were kicking off again, those poor bastards on the Columbia were all killed. So very tragic, Barker. So. Very. But you still need to get off this rock and start spreading out. That was a real option back then; a trajectory for your people, your planet as a home base for everyone, rather than just a home.'

'They say there's nothing out there.'

'Nonsense! You don't believe that!'

'No...' Barker looked back at The They. 'They say there's nothing out there.'

'Well...' Brixton seemed impressed. '...precisely! And what you would find out there, almost immediately? Well; that's a story for another time. But! Now; you have to start that equation all over again. Until then, this planet just gets more and more dense.'

'So what can we do?'

'It's like the sages have always said; start with yourself. And, like the equation of the planet, you, yourself, are imbalanced, Barker.'

'I know, you said, but...'

'The fusion of ego and spirit, my son, can sometimes be separated. The part of you listening now is the dislodged spirit, not the ego. Although the ego patterns most certainly still remain...'

Barker stared back. 'I totally *did* know all of this once, didn't I? Not just the words, but the actual, *practical* applications...? I knew it, didn't I?'

He noticed then that the second of The They had begun to move forward. Barker returned his gaze to Brixton.

'Speaking of outer space... I was sorry when that part of you died. I think the whole world was; you made rock stars like they don't make them anymore. But, why does that make The They think...?'

Barker had an idea and looked back at them suddenly.

The one at the front was certainly somehow late-Victorian, or Edwardian. He wore a charcoal brown wool suit beneath a long black coat with feature-lapels and massive black buttons. It looked tailored, fitted; another thing that they didn't make like that anymore. The high collar of his white shirt was turned up to his jaw, and closed very tightly at his stiff neck with a black cravat over a faintly patterned, perhaps dark bottle-brown waistcoat. His face, which to Barker seemed eerily featureless, almost part of the surrounding fog, was very definitely streaked with a thick black moustache, beneath a tall, black, stovepipe hat. The long coat didn't move in the wind as he took another step forward, with the black-striped trousers ending over glistening black lace-up leather shoes, and black spats, as his long golden cane tapped, with a supernaturally violent crack, on the asphalt before him.

Brixton spoke softly now.

'They made themselves, those larger aspects. I served as their muse. But those I made, and others of my kind, that we shaped almost two generations ago now, shaped in order to shape the approaching millennial turn… they were not appreciated by The Establishment. Conservative forces preferred things to remain as they were; as they had been all through the Piscean Age and through most of the Arian and Taurean. But this Aquarian Age will see all of that pass.'

Barker stared back at the man from the turn of the twentieth century.

'He wants revenge? He thinks that while those pieces on the board have been taken, have passed on, you're weak?'

Brixton smiled. 'This one is from The Establishment. It is a division of The They. Agents of The Establishment are powerfully Conservative. My pieces; my avatars, helped flaunt and destroy the Conservative Hold, at a time when it was required. When it was crucial. The Establishment has a long memory; these demons have long lives. They will do anything now to restore the Conservative Hold. They will leave the New Age in ruins, use science as a force of destruction so that it becomes taboo, raise temples in their last days to human sacrifice so that the notion of spirit is once again synonymous with terror and restriction.'

The man behind him was taking shape now as well.

'I knew this…' Barker uttered.

'We all knew it. We all *know* it,' Brixton insisted. 'And with a little bit of luck, and a bit of push and maybe a shove, perhaps even a kiss, you will know it again before it's too late.'

'Too late?' But Barker shook it off and ignored him. 'But, consciously; to the extent that I could employ it. Exploit it… I really knew it?'

Brixton cocked an eyebrow. 'We all come here, incarnate here, knowing it. But as I said, we all get distracted. Those men over there make it so. They have done so for six or seven thousand years, give or take. And they are backed by alien forces you would not at this point believe. But Barker, you happened to have come here, to this plane and place and time, knowing it all very well indeed; so the people who wanted to stop you were forced to distract you very effectively.'

Barker looked back down at himself again, still bleeding out.

Parry and the emergency workers from ambulance seemed to be working in slow motion around him. His blood on the asphalt was a silvery-claret colour.

'I was a sorcerer. And I let myself get beaten. Let myself forget…'

'It happens. The ego gets bruised, and retreats. It just happened to me; the restless spirits of these parks aren't intimidated by me. They are terrified of Them.' Brixton smiled his charming smile again. 'The spirit gets crushed, and deflates. That's what the sad songs are for. It happens; it's part of it.'

The second man was modern; an American Psycho banker.

And he spoke.

'Is that him?'

It sounded as though he were speaking underwater, but Barker understood.

The older Establishment figure seemed to sneer. It was amazing that although both had the fog-disfigured faces, their expressions were still easily readable.

'They're worried I'm going to turn you into some kind of new rock star; rock their boat again.' Brixton smiled.

'Are you?'

'No; too much of me is dislocated right now. I'll be moving on soon, back up to sleep a while, and dream up something else. But, when you remember what happened, you'll remember why I have time for you.'

Both of them; the Edwardian and the Psycho, also had an uncanny knack of being able to look down on them. As though to address this, Brixton took a step forward and spoke slightly, but definitely more deliberately louder.

'That young one is new; these are the money ones. The Accountants. There are also The Enforcers, and The Authority; but the worst are The Arbiters. There may be other Establishment departments, but those are all the ones I have come into contact with. It's not good that they're here.'

They sneered. Barker ignored them as best he could.

'That ghost tonight at The Lion and Unicorn. He was just ego. Just what was left of that guy's ego.'

'That's right. The ego writes onto the spirit. When you die, the vessel ceases to function and the ego stops generating. Obviously; the brain turns to dust. But it's all been written to the spirit, and the spirit goes back. The pen runs dry, but the writings remain. The spirit flows back, slowly, over minutes, hours, days. It's spiritually alchemical; and sometimes if there's a very dark or powerful emotion left, that process leaves a residue. Sometimes it's just… toxic junk. And it hangs around. Sometimes it is love, powerful love; and it is still connected to the spirit of the loved one. Sheer will, and need, can play a part, from both ends. Love can remain, connected by a slender thread. And sometimes it takes on a life of its own. Sometimes it's benign, just a watcher. Sometimes it's almost deliberate, a flower from the mulch; a guardian spirit or something. But other times, when there is no love, when it's just toxic resentment, or regret or bile, it's like a patch of mould left behind, that was growing underneath something that was long ago removed, but it keeps growing, even after that. That part can keep a larger part of the departing spirit tethered here as well; bound in the astral, and that animates the nastiness that's left behind, anchoring it here… and the more dense the anchor, the lower the level its departure is limited to. Get a demon whispering in their ear, and… well,' Brixton laughed, a little huff, '…they make movies about that kind of unpleasantness, don't they?'

He nodded across the park.

Some of the ghosts were starting to emerge from behind the trees, as though what he was saying was of great interest to them. But they were keeping well-clear of the two Establishment figures. There was an old woman in a nightgown, a pretty girl in a sheer nineteen seventies disco dress, and another man in an Edwardian suit, but this one was clearly some kind of lower-class worker.

'In simple terms, some spirits, some *people*, really, get stuck. In the end they get mad when all the mortals they knew move on…'

Barker nodded. 'And then, someone like me, or Cheryl comes along and…'

'That's right. Brings them back and makes them…'

'Remember. To clean up their mess…'

'And that untethers them. And on they go. The anchor dissolves and… Hey, Saint Peter.'

Barker gazed out at them. 'What happened to me? I still don't remember that night; I don't remember… can you – ?'

'It's better that you remember yourself, Barker.'

The girl in the seventies dress seemed to make a decision and walked boldly across the road to them. Both her low-cut cocktail dress and her classic mid-seventies hairstyle were gold and glittering, shimmering even through the classical blue-grey, ghostly glow that was all about her. She was squeezing a thin, gold-chain clutch, seemingly for dear life, and was bare-foot. But over her wrist, dangling by their slender straps, were a pair of shining gold stilettoes.

'Excuse me…'

'Yes darling…?' Brixton asked.

'I feel like I've been waiting here for ages! Where have all the bloody cabs gone?'

Brixton smiled at Barker.

'Well, my son… you're on!'

# CHAPTER FOURTEEN: WELL

'You have to turn your phone off.'

Cheryl was being told this by someone she didn't know. She'd been with Shirley in the back of the van; there had been a bright white light, and then…

'I can't…' Cheryl responded. 'Everyone's going to think the worst if I do that.'

…she couldn't recall what had happened then. Now there was just black asphalt and grey concrete. White neon. Walk lights on a pedestrian crossing, stuck on red.

The other woman shrugged. 'Let them think the worst. Just for an hour or two.'

Cheryl sighed. 'It's a bit convenient, isn't it? That your salon's just over the road from the casino?'

'It's not my salon.'

'Then…?'

'People in this town know Shirley. When Shirley calls, I come.'

'You and Shirley work together? At the salon?'

'Kind of. Look, apparently there's three of you receiving boons tonight. The others will be here soon. I might have to do you all at once. You don't mind, do you?'

It was kind of like an alcohol blackout. Cheryl knew that something had happened in the back of Shirley's white van; she had done something to herself, it had altered with her brain chemistry, but because of that, she now couldn't recall what had happened during the time she had been under. When the drug, or in this case, the magic, had been working.

'Like an alcohol blackout, yeah? When the magic finds you?'

Cheryl nodded. 'And you wake up in only a coat and some… itchy underwear a strange woman gave you…' She grimaced. '… how long ago was that?'

'Best part of an hour, I'd say. Maybe a bit more.'

'An hour?'

It felt like whole night. At least there was that; just an hour.

'Shirley called me when it happened. That was elevenish. You were asleep in the van when I got here. It's almost twelve now. But the higher forces can do that; hype you up right away, sometimes for days. Or put you to sleep. Sometimes for days. You were lucky. At least for now.'

'What do you mean?'

'I mean, next time you go to sleep, don't make any plans for the next day. Or two. Or week. And don't do anything until you've had that sleep – that's important.'

'Great. We have two gigs next week.'

'Maybe not.'

'What?' Cheryl still wasn't quite sure who she was talking to.

'This kind of thing, a spiritual boon, doesn't happen lightly. Have you seen that thing that's closing in around the city? Maybe, before you turn off your phone, check the weather radar online. They say it's a freak storm. One of those 'perfect storms' closing in from all fronts. It's not. Something's going to happen. I'm staying in here tonight, in the city.'

'In the city?'

'I have a place. Don't worry. There's room.'

They were sitting under a bus shelter, on the downward slope of North Terrace just past the intersection of King William, right near the entrance to the Railway Station, and the World Casino. Someone had bought her a takeaway coffee and a chocolate brownie, which she didn't feel like, but was eating anyway. Just about finished, actually. Maybe she had felt like it. Certainly looked that way.

'This isn't going to get me totally high is it?'

'The brownie or the magic? One of those is, yes. Or I should say, already has, yes.'

'Right.' Cheryl nodded. Magical high. 'Has this happened to you?'

'Sure. But… not quite so big, and not such a big load.'

'Load? Who are you again?'

'Karri. Karri Cork. I'm here to do your hair.'

Cheryl nodded. 'Right. Okay.'

'I saw the white light hit the van. It came straight up from the beach. You could smell the ocean. The salt and the sand and the seaweed and the seagulls.'

'Really?' Cheryl finished the brownie. 'Huh.'

Some time, probably not ten minutes ago, Cheryl had regained consciousness in the back of the white van. The garments had still been there, lined along each side, but the back doors had been wide open and there had been a large wooden chest, like a pirate's treasure, under her feet when she had gotten up on her bottom, and tried to slide out at the end of the van's fancy red carpet. It was on the pavement beside them now, but at the time she had hit her feet on it as she'd swung them out, and the sound had attracted Shirley, who had been nearby on her phone, awaiting with the coffee and the… it had been a cheese and spinach filo.

So, who had given her the brownie?

Shirley had immediately hung up.

'How much do you remember? Do you remember picking out the clothes? The magic seemed to take you; you seemed to know exactly what you wanted. Or, needed, which is usually the case. You took more than I usually provide, but when the magic is that strong I don't charge extra. We can say you owe me a favour. Nothing major but a solid. Deal?'

It had been.

'Who do you work for, Shirley?'

She'd shrugged. 'The universe, I suppose. In the end. I need to go, but I'll be back. There are two more boons tonight, I'm sensing, but I need the other van. Can you believe it? Three in one night? It's all happening! This is Karri. With a K and an I. She'll do your hair.'

Karri had offered her the brownie.

Cheryl remembered that now.

'Is it all starting to come back to you? The casino café is actually pretty good with sugary things. Pastries and cakes. Anything sweet that keeps people docile but awake.'

'Thanks.'

Karri was a bit older maybe. She was busty and hippy, with a broad, fleshy face that made her immediately seem very sensual and friendly. Cheryl could have imagined her with big hair, like Shirley's, in any of several bygone fashion decades. Clearly Shirley had been there, in one of those, and stuck with it, made it keep working. As a stylist however, as well as Shirley's apparent junior, Karri had moved with contemporary fashion and had, as the fashion had been for a while now, straightened and bleached her hair almost white-blonde, with the length resting just over the top-curves of her bust, with a severe down-part sharply highlighting her best side. She was definitely attractive but that look was… ever so slightly pushing it. Just a bit. Maybe. She's not going to do that to me, Cheryl thought. Too loud, she realized. But then she also realized; Karri either wasn't telepathic, or wasn't listening.

'You are one of us, aren't you?'

Karri's long, narrow eyes creased at the sides with a welcome warmth as she gave Cheryl a wide, full smile. Her tiny button nose and her dimpled chin and cheeks somehow belonged in another age as well, along with the imagined bigger hair. Only slightly more glamorous makeup would have, upon reflection, seen her crowned queen of any bygone era typing pool in no time.

'Sure I am. You'll see.'

They hadn't bothered with the pedestrian crossing. The walk lights had remained red as they carried the chest between them, by the handles on each side, to the empty North Terrace tram stop in the middle of the city street, with barely any traffic in sight and certainly none to impede their crossing. Karri was shortish, and stocky, but very much in shape. As she easily negotiated the tram platform with half the weight of their odd cargo, along and over the tram rails with an almost athletic grace, her balance and direction were unimpeded by her black-suede pixie heels. Cheryl noticed that Karri's calves, beneath the sheer black stockings and thick, black-wool, knee-length one piece, were toned and hard.

Cheryl recognized the salon, just down but essentially right across from where they'd been sitting, as one of those small, major street frontages that people forget are there. This one was squeezed between a renovated now-corporate hotel and a huge colonial bar, and upon entering, the place seemed much bigger than it first appeared from outside. It stretched back past a reception corridor that was barely wider than the front door, but then expanded out to double the width after about ten meters into a ground-floor cut and wash space that almost comfortably fit six basins and two big dryers. There was a tiled, black and white checkerboard floor the whole way through, accented by a chic, non-chromatic colour scheme that extended even to all the basic utensils.

Cheryl was continually reassessing her first impressions of Karri. As she unlocked the entrance without pausing to lower the chest, then hipped the door to the side in one fluid movement, she saw that Karri's natural hourglass dimensions had not been put out to pasture, but rather, that the dress fitted and flattered her completely. From several angles too, as there were mirrors everywhere, of course; ample for Cheryl to assess herself as well, as they made their way through. And yet, there was something new within her that seemed to make turning away from the mirrors, and not seeing herself almost naturally easy.

It freaked her out, but she went with it.

This newness within her was urging her: *don't look yet.*

*You're not ready.*

Beside the six wash stations, stairs ran along the wall to the left, leading up to a mezzanine with several more cutting stations, and behind the furthest bank of wash-stations was an open door, disguised only by the angle of its allotment in the grand design, leading back again to another room. They put the chest down, with Karri's assurances that it would be safe, and went through. This next room was three times as wide, with another four cutting stations and doors leading (Cheryl realized as she was led through) inward now, toward what must have been the back of the hotel. Her best guess was that these warrens had been standing in this form since the colony days, and that the salon bathrooms were connected to the same plumbing as the hotel backrooms, which would be on the other side of the far salon wall. They went on however, past these executive wash stations, still further back, through the tiny staff room (an antechamber with a small, square, pale-yellow laminated table, three terrible metal-framed kitchen chairs that looked as though they had been with the place since an early sixties renovation and would survive a nuclear apocalypse, and a proper working coffee machine) to an emergency exit door which Karri casually pushed open.

'This place is enorm…'

Cheryl caught herself.

'You caught yourself, didn't you?' Karri asked back, as they walked down another short but much more sparse, plain red-brick corridor. 'You were going to say enormous, weren't you? Some do, some don't. It's not, of course, when you think about it. Everything seems larger when you first see it; property that is. It's like how time gets faster the older you get. Property seems larger at first, because everything's new. Every room is new as you walk through it. Same as when you're young. Every experience is new; or newer. But if you reflect back straight away; like you did just then, you realize, it's only a few small rooms. But it's long, and in a row.'

'But it's still a lot longer than you expect.' Cheryl looked back as the emergency door swung closed behind her. There was still light coming through, however, through the cracks. With that light, she was able to notice that here, in this small, enclosed section at the back of the salon, the short red-bricked hall looked old, but also new. 'This wall looks like it hasn't seen sunlight since they put it up.'

'A hundred years ago, right? We like it.'

'We?'

'Well, I might not actually work here permanently… but that doesn't mean I'm not one of the girls.'

'The girls?'

'I can cut. I make some extra cash that way when they're in a jam. No magic required. I did train though; I am a proper stylist.'

'Then, where are we going?'

'I don't know about you but I love all this history shit.' She grinned cheekily in the dark. 'You know where we are? This was an alley. Used to come right in here off the street, used to be the side entrance for the pub on this side, and the brothel on the other; there's still doors all through, they're just blocked up. The brothel's that hotel next door now, but it was a brothel all the way through to the forties. Survived the Great War but not the Second. Kept running out of men. Became a makeshift repatriation hospital when they all started coming back; straight off the wounded carriage and over the road, you see? Get them indoors, quick as possible, out of sight. Missing limbs, missing minds. Slowly became a legitimate establishment. Pub right next door didn't hurt. But even before all that, the pub made a deal with the apartment store at the back here, that comes off Hindley on the back flipside, like, in the twenties, and they sealed the alley up. People kept getting away to more than the front bar, apparently.'

Karri's smile became more wry. It was a smile Cheryl wasn't sure what to make of. It told her that Karri wasn't going to explain what she'd meant by that, and that Cheryl could make of it what she would; she seemed very sure. But the smile, which had as many components as this salon, had also seemed to add that Cheryl absolutely would work it out later.

'That brick wall used to be the alley wall. It's the only bit that's still exposed. There are other walls like this but they've all been encrusted with decades of traffic smog, and city shit, since the start of petrol traffic, industrial shit and all that, just about; this is still, pretty much, what it looked like when they put it up.'

Cheryl was a little nervous. They seemed to have been standing here, quite close, for just a bit too long. Still, she put her hand on the deep red brick, because it seemed to be what Karri wanted her to do. It was quite nice, actually. Beautiful, if she thought about it. So smooth, and cool. Yet it felt somehow brittle as well, but then again, it was more solid than anything she'd ever felt; like nothing else she'd ever felt. Amazing. Wonderful. Words like that came to mind that fell, meaningless at her feet like the fine layer of dust her open palm had shifted. Her old world seemed so far behind now, back beyond those three long rooms and the closed door with the cracks of light coming through.

Cheryl noticed all of a sudden that there was one last door; off to the side, to her left, going inward.

Karri was waiting for her to respond.

Cheryl looked up. There were the edges of wooden beams up there in the (now she perceived it) insanely thin ex-alley space; massive and solid. They extended over the inner wall, into wherever. The beams were newer than the well-preserved wall, but still very old. And high. Very high, supporting a floor above.

'What's up there? On the higher floor, in this space?'

'Nobody ever asks that.' Karri nodded. 'Through here.'

She opened the door to their left and immediately Cheryl felt a wave of cold, then acute nausea. Her gut twisted and her knees ached as though someone had squeezed them tight all of a sudden. She was short of breath, and her hands trembled, but something compelled her forwards and she stepped onto what felt like the slats of a wooden balcony.

Karri flicked a switch on the inside wall and a stark, naked bulb came on, hanging high up and swinging with some unseen whisper, illuminating a giant chamber that seemed to Cheryl immediately like a bizarrely tall, but very shady interrogation room.

She realized quickly; that was exactly what it was.

Cheryl stepped in anyway; Kerri was not out to hurt or trap her. This was something else. Something she needed to see.

The landing beyond stretched right around the square chamber, with a dual stairway ascending and descending against the wall on the other side. Up another floor, the same pattern repeated; stairs and an enclosed landing, zig-zagging all the way up, with each level of the expansive shaft, perhaps seven or eight meters across each wall, interconnected perhaps… it was hard to tell; five or six floors high?

'The landings and stairs are safe. You can get up to the roof for a smoke from here. Or down to the sewers as well, if you really want.'

Cheryl couldn't stop shaking.

She felt as though she were losing blood.

A lot, fast.

Bleeding out.

Dying.

'How many people died in here?'

# CHAPTER FIFTEEN:
# IT ALL WORKS OUT

'I'm on?' Barker demanded. 'On what?'

Brixton maintained his smile and turned benevolently to the early-seventies party girl.

'What have you been waiting for darling? A cab you say?'

'There's no cabs! There haven't been any cabs for… bloody ever! And it's freezing out here!'

Brixton turned to Barker.

'Can you tell this dear girl her story?'

Barker could. He could read it and knew it right away. He turned to her. She could have been one of Charlie's Angels.

'You stepped out to hail a cab…' Barker spoke evenly. '…do you remember? You were sick of them passing by and ignoring you?'

'Too right, mate; they just wouldn't bloody stop! They never bloody did!'

'You'd had some coke.'

She frowned. 'So? Everyone does a little these days…'

Brixton sighed sympathetically. 'But tell me; what days do you think these are, my darling Earthling?'

'I don't know…' She seemed taken aback. She even stepped back, frowning deeply. '…what days? What kind of a question is that?'

'She was a mess. The drivers could all see,' Barker grumbled. 'But she just wanted to go home. Be in bed. Sleep it off. But she was so coked-up, and fed-up, that she stepped right out in front of it. Over-stepped. Stumbled. Ankles weak from dancing all night in high heels.'

'Who did?' The girl demanded.

'Do you remember?' Brixton asked. 'The coke must have numbed the pain; it must have been very fast.'

The girl looked up and down the road. Then at the massive pub behind them.

'Everything's different...' She suddenly started to cry, started to break down, then an avalanche of frustration crashed in. 'Every time...! They just – drive straight past me! *Every bloody weekend, it takes me half a bloody hour*, I just wanna *fucking-well go home!*'

Her voice echoed through the park, up and down East Terrace, like thunder from the approaching storm. She was standing there, shaking, shimmering gold, as though she were the only person on the street.

But everyone on the lower astral; the other ghosts, the Establishment duo, Barker and Brixton, were transfixed. Then Brixton took two gentle but confident strides forward.

'I can give you a ride sweetie...' He smiled, just a bit, and when he caught her eye, he winked. 'Why don't you hop in? There's music in the car. It's warm. I'll make sure you get home....'

'Hey...' The girl gasped, and immediately stopped crying. Then she squinted though her red eyes. 'Aren't you...?'

'That's right. He is me and I am him.'

'Wow...' The girl giggled, and the door of the limo opened on its own. 'Wait til I tell my Mum who I got a lift home with...' Her bare feet padded nimbly across the asphalt, toward the open limo door. She had one slender blue leg inside when she turned back. 'It was nineteen seventy-six... almost Christmas.' She thought for a few seconds more. '...suppose she must be dead by now too?'

'Probably, darling...'

'Oh...' She recalibrated very quickly, having realized what she had just said.

Brixton smiled again. 'I suppose you'll find out soon enough?'

Then the girl shrugged. 'It all works out in the end then, does it...?'

Brixton shrugged. 'We'll see, darling. We'll see.'

Then she bobbed down, sat, and was gone, into the limo as the door closed behind her.

'You see; she just wanted that cab. She was so angry. The anger kept the…' Brixton waved casually at the limo. '…coked-up and self-obsessed aspect of her here. If we hadn't come along, she'd be stuck here, with the pub, until someone tore it down…'

'And that… clogs things up, doesn't it? Up there?'

'And down here. She was Party Girl. The Party Girl vessel is gone forever, forty-plus years gone; but her experiences could not be fully recorded, nor the final track laid down, or the song of Party Girl released, because she had not signed the final release form. Like a lot of people… she had last minute reservations about her contract.'

'But…' Barker quickly side-tracked the obvious allusion. '…if we all come into this plane with a mission, what was hers?'

'Who knows, Barker? This world is well on the way and every spirit, every aspect of The One…' Brixton made air-quotes '…that incarnates here, is already burdened with karma, with anywhere from just a few, to hundreds of previous mission results. Seven billion incarnations here now, out of a total of one hundred and eight billion who have *ever existed*. At least, in this version, this incarnation, of humanity; but let's not go there just yet. I mean, basic maths; if it's all even, which it isn't, and it was all limited to this planet with no-one from anywhere else coming in, and no-one from previous versions of the Earthling race you may or may not, for your own good, have been forbidden, or let's say *blocked* from remembering; even if you don't include all of that, even if you don't include Inner Earth entities and Higher Planes Drifters passing through, who you may or may not also be, or have been aspects, or incarnations of, or even piggybacking and sharing an existence with; even without all that, you lot *still* have, each on your own, basic maths; all been here *fourteen times*, fourteen times *each*, before now. So, sunshine, anyone born on this planet, on this plane, this far into this history, is already an amnesiac continuation of so many other lives and existences that if they tried remembering them all with their little dense and gooey human brain, there would be nothing but constant bedlam.'

'That's why we don't remember them in the first place… right?'

'That's right…' Brixton's eyes narrowed. 'But you are still able, when required, to have a sense of them. That's how it's supposed to work. Not the total memories of fourteen, forty, four hundred lives; but at least a….' Air quotes again. '…life library, eh?' One of the quotes tapped Barker's third eye. 'How much is in there still, able to be read, I wonder?'

Barker placed his own fingers where Brixton had touched him.

'So, in essence, Party Girl just… forgot? Through the shock of it? A sudden death?'

He looked down at his body again.

Time seemed to be standing still down there, on the asphalt.

The blood had ceased to flow.

The ambos had stopped moving.

Parry was still, frozen, staring.

'Like I said, everyone forgets these days Barker. Though hers was not a wasted life, necessarily. Neither has yours been. She's a young soul, from a young soul cluster. Down here, a beautiful vessel emerged; an aspect of The One that wanted to play. So it sent one of the new souls from the Goddess down here to be Party Girl in Adelaide in the Nineteen Seventies, to see what it could do. A free spirit emerged from the vessel. Maybe the oversoul believed it could make the world happier, freer by example. Maybe she was supposed to marry someone and make them happier and freer. But that new, young, free spirit accidentally went and got the vessel destroyed. Cocaine is evil. The free spirit was distracted from its mission and captured by evil and that led her to an early death.'

'Weakness!' The American Psycho across the road, it appeared, had been listening. The old woman and the working Edwardian vanished immediately.

'What?' Barker addressed it directly. '*What the fuck did you say?*'

The American Psycho sniggered and continued to look down his nose at Barker, pleased that he had angered him.

'What is that rancid smell?' Barker demanded.

'Eighties aftershave…' Brixton uttered.

Barker stared at the horrible young man again. He looked as though he had stepped right out of that film. His outfit, with the white shirt and navy pinstripes, the thick tie and golden pin, were essentially just updates from the Edwardian Establishment Figure.

'We create poverty…' The older man spoke.

Barker gasped. Jesus; he was awful. His voice was rasping and made Barker feel immediately empty. Immediately; … *worthless*. And yet the voice was crisp and precise, and could not be discounted. Barker had a sudden sense of him. He was The Land Lord, and his companion was The Creditor.

Brixton placed a soft white hand on Barker's shoulder again. It seemed to break the spell they had on him.

'Some free spirits are so shocked by the outcome of their endeavours that they have become trapped on this plane by forces that don't care if they live or die, or express themselves as they intended, or complete their mission; so shocked by the outcome that they don't even realize it has happened. By the way; what did you come here to do Barker?'

'I came to make sure they get through okay…'

'They? Wandering spirits like Party Girl in there?'

'No, the Old…'

'The Old what?'

Something in Barker's mind snapped back. 'Damn! I nearly had it!'

'Nearly.' Brixton nodded. 'Party Girl is whole again now. She always would have been eventually, but you and me being here, doing that work, means a free spirit has two hundred years more, in the grand scheme of things, to help others; she will probably come back, and learn to drive a cab.'

'Two hundred years?'

'More or less. Until an earthquake levels this hotel in twenty-three eight –' He glanced at his wrist. 'Dear me, is that the time?' There wasn't a watch there.

Barker looked up at the beautiful old Colonial structure and tried to imagine it lasting another two hundred years.

'Nothing lasts forever…'

'But some things endure. Maybe Party Girl's soul comes back through a spirit that becomes a long distance driver, who as it turns out always picks up hitchers, but never knows why. Who knows? But it won't take her soul long to figure out what happened, and to come back, and try again. You can go back now Barker, too. If you like. You too came with a mission, and you too have failed.'

'I have?'

'But you learned this.'

'Learned what?'

'How to fade away gracefully. Seven years, isn't it?'

'But I…'

'Whatever you were, you tried to execute your mission, and evil got the better of you, as it did Party Girl. It happens; this is a very dark age.'

'We create poverty…' The Land Lord spoke again. '…and we can create it in you, Moon. We can create it in your world, all around you, and make you impotent and worthless.'

Brixton ignored them and continued. 'Your ego was bruised and your spirit fled. This happens sometimes too. The ego-spirit fusion, it is an element of consciousness that becomes its own energy; that is how the soul comes through. When all this is in alignment, there is nothing that will stop you getting in your own way and completing your mission. But you have forgotten why you came, Barker. Maybe it is best to go back, debrief with your Higher Self, and return replenished… the Barker Moon spirit will go to the eternal record, and reside there, content in the light, as a living history. Others might be able to channel and consult him; whoever you return as might want to do that too. Perhaps that's the smarter choice?'

Barker kept staring at his own body. Then at the Edwardian Land Lord, and The Creditor. But there were other figures there too now, more ghosts emerging from behind the trees. The Edwardian worker and the old woman were back. They had all seen Party Girl get into the limo.

'Why am I so blasé about this?'

'You are basically disassociated, right now, from your ego. You can still feel it, but not as acutely. But the main part, Barker, the part of you that remains in pure source, always; that is your soul. The soul doesn't care that you have died, here and now. The oversoul knows; it is a necessary part of everything that you must return at some point, with your spirit imprint, the record of your adventure, your studies, your results… and there will be no judgment. Once you get as high up as an oversoul, none of this happens in a linear pattern, so why should it care how many times anything happens?'

'Is that where you're going now? How high up does Brixton go?'

'Oh, I've been high Barker. Believe me; more than most. But Brixton is one of those beings who is spread about, over a lot of territory. He senses the comings and goings; he's picked up a lot of hitchers. How ya doin'? Where ya been? Where ya goin'?' He grinned. 'There are many different kinds of vessels, of conscious beings, with different kinds of egos, and identities, and spirits and connections to the divine ego and the eternal spirit, and I am just one of them. But I am one of the ones who can see more of you than you see of yourselves.'

'Then… can't you just remind me? What I came to do?'

Brixton grinned again. 'I told you. You're losing the back-beat Barker. You lose the back-beat, you're in trouble. You can't lose that. You have to remember yourself!'

'But you're a God!'

'I'm a deity, an icon; a personification of a broad concept that can mean and has meant many things to many people over a certain period. As a being, I am… somewhere in between all of that meaning. But higher up, where you and I have both been before; those who are there permanently, they see the whole of all your lives, and they know everything. Me; I get suggestions from up there, so I can just pop in here and there; a few decades here, a century there; and say; listen, I think you can do more. I think, if you just hold on another day, the right girl will show, or the bleak mood will pass, or just let you know; you're not the only one, you're not alone. I can do more, sometimes. I can mass-produce musical vibrations that carry those notions, make sure everyone gets the chance to be reminded; oh no my love, you are *not alone*. Or, maybe you should talk to that person you know you need to talk to.'

Barker took that personally. 'You mean… talk to *her*?'

'Which *her*, Barker? It might be a good idea to talk to the blossoming witch. She may or may not need you right now. It may or may not be a good idea to speak to the young beautiful one, the one who hurts you, even though she doesn't want to. Or the young beautiful one who wants to do nothing but hurt you. Also, the mature beautiful one; the one who will do anything not to hurt you. It might, also, be an idea to pick up the phone and call your mother once in a while. But if I were you, one thing is for sure; I would keep them all apart, and I would speak to the object of desire, and the dread mentor, sooner rather than later.'

Barker scowled.

'So this is really what I think it is? A deity intervening to tell me to talk to the girl, patch it up with my friend, call my mum more often, and deal with the ex? And then get on with the thing I came to do, that I haven't gotten around to doing yet?'

'Barker; sorcerers are not Party Girls. Actually, scratch that. They are by no means exclusively Party Girls. They are not young souls. They do not drop in, to become free spirits, to make people feel better by making the vibe more strawberry. You came from one of the mystic oversouls, but I think you came here, now, to see if there was anything you could do about the density. And you decided you could, and you started to do it. Then something stopped you. Dark, dense things have a vested interest in darkness and density.'

He pointed at the Establishments.

'Those two certainly do. And they have come to see me, in my last days here, and you, in your last minutes. But now you must decide. This is the fork in the road; although it is a T-Junction. You can go down North Terrace, and onward into the belly of the beast. Or you can go into the pub and remain. A ghost. Ponder at the bar where you went wrong for decades. Centuries if you like. The ghost of the poor fucker who saved a girl from being stabbed outside the pub, but got killed himself. Or, there are the gates to the Botanic Gardens. In the astral, that is a path to other realms; they are the Astral Gates. That's why they have…' Air-quotes again. '…The Fringe, here, annually. This is, air-quotes Barker, The, definite article, Fringe. Some traditions remain, some areas remain true to their purpose. Every city has a gate like this, but this is world-recognized, because it is one of those places.'

'Simple as that? Go through the gates and I reincarnate?'

'End here, and go back. You will go back and consult with Rasputin and Crowley and Dee and Parsons, and all the other occult maniacs, and all the other secret ones nobody ever knew, and remember what you came here for, look at all the tools you have, the programs you downloaded, and the cards you were dealt. You will no doubt, as everyone does, become angry or disappointed; you will ask yourself why you didn't employ them, or employ them with greater skill, develop them more, reveal them to others with more flourish and better timing. The answer is always fear. And because you became afraid, you searched for distraction and suddenly … thankyou Adelaide! You've been a wonderful audience! Good night! Woo-hoo! The concert's over and you didn't even know it had begun because you got too high and blacked out. I've seen it a million times; literally!'

'Jesus…'

'And you will come back to try again, to fight that fear…' Brixton cupped his hands over his mouth and shouted out into the parklands. 'Encore! Encore! More! More!'

The dozen or so ghosts who had now accumulated simultaneously panicked and vanished back behind their trees.

The Land Lord cupped his free hand around his moustache and shouted out.

'Ah-boooooo! Ah-boooooo!'

Brixton turned back to Barker, cocking his eyebrow again.

'But you will be different. And once again, you might remember in theory that there were other yous, but you will not fully believe it. In this life, Barker, you have echoed that. You have been told that, in this life, not before this life, *but in this life you are living now*, there was another you. You do not remember that very well; so you believe it in theory, but you do not trust it, and you do not act as though it is true. Life is a dream within a dream, Barker. But you are living a dream again, within the dream, within the dream.' Brixton smiled sympathetically. 'People tell you that you were someone else. That someone else was a greater version of who you are now, but because you do not remember, you do not truly believe them, and if you do, it is just a conviction towards an imaginary past, that people have helped you build.'

Barker's adrenalin was peaking; he could feel himself getting angry again. He really knew better than to be facetious in the face of… whatever Brixton was. But he couldn't help it

'I know I was someone else! Another me! All this stuff you're telling me; all this spiritual bullshit, all these rules and pathways; I don't need to remember all this; it's in the world. You can Google this, read it anywhere!'

'You need to be interested first. To know it's there in the first place.'

'But isn't that just… life? Isn't that what the control matrix is all about? Red pill, blue pill? We could all be greater version of ourselves, but the control grid stops it?'

'The control grid is the density.'

'But, that's hardly occult knowledge anymore! At least, not if you take occult to mean 'secret'. Turn off the telly, go off the grid, don't sleep with the phone near your bed, don't buy a house next door to an electrical transformer, coffee's good, red wine's okay, dark chocolate's better than milk chocolate, research organic, don't eat processed, smokes give you cancer, alcohol's a depressant, weed makes you crazy, cocaine is evil. But meditate, eat right and the path opens up to you?'

'You were just thinking about a grid, were you not? On your way here?'

'I...'

'Things must happen here. The grid was created for that. It doesn't have to be dense and restrictive; you came here to take part.'

'But; what's your play in all this? You're a twentieth century rock deity at the wrong end of your time; I admit, I'm spot on your demo, but... I'm not a muso or anything...?'

'You'll figure it out. This city is a grid. An arena. People watch what happens here.'

'People?'

'Yes. Gods are people too.'

'That's...' Barker knew it was true, but could not suppress his belligerence. 'Here? But nothing ever happens here!'

'What better place for the most important things to happen, than a place where nobody thinks anything ever happens?'

Barker was speechless.

'I don't remember that guy. The guy I was. How am I supposed to...?'

'Yes, you do; but, the problem is, all you *can do* is remember him.' Brixton nodded back to Barker's dead body. 'He is dead, that version. Good riddance, I say. His fear almost got you killed. It was not his fault, yet his decision led him to that end. Yours can lead you there as well.'

'But that's it, isn't it? I don't want to be that other guy again; he was reckless, he was dangerous!'

'Barker; clearly, this version lying dead before us is way more dangerous. Your true self, the dormant Barker, yes; he is still dangerous. But you need him to be dangerous to your enemies, not to you, or to your allies. Not to get you killed!'

Something in Barker's gut twisted.

His allies… were dead.

'Barker Moon; there are people trying to force you to remember. However, there is one person who can help you remember; just like that.'

'I had power. I took responsibility. And people got hurt. People got killed. I can't open that door again.'

'You risk even more, trying to force it to remain closed.'

Barker shook his head. 'All of that, my involvement with that, it was too dangerous. I don't want to remember; if I do, more people will die.'

'People die all the time, every day. If you had not been at the head of what had occurred, seven years ago, even more people would have died at Bridger Mansion…'

'More…? But, so many, already…'

Brixton scowled. 'They didn't all die, Barker. You want to believe they did; if you believe that, it makes it easy for you.'

'Easy?!'

'To never go back. Never remember, never reclaim your own life.'

Barker stared again at the illusion of his dead body, prone on the street. Now it was solid, real, but everything else, everyone else that had surrounded it was gone. It was just him, dead and alone.

'Barker, they were not attempting assassination. They were, they *are* attempting to lure you out. They are trying to make you angry. But have you considered this, Barker? That more of your friends may die, if you cannot protect them? The people who would force you to remember; they do not care that you do not wish to remember. They will put you through great pains to force you to remember, and they will not care about you. They wish only to provoke you into *what you can do*. And if there is anything they can do; damage, destroy, hurt, kill, anyone, to make you remember, then...'

'Then they will.'

'They will.'

'Then, I…have no choice…'

'Yes you do. You can be passive, and you will be made into a new version of Barker Moon; your enemies will do that, and you will not like the version who is born from their provocation. He will be bitter and resentful and mean. Or, you can reclaim your memories, reclaim your strength willingly, step back into your power, and remake yourself. Be the version of Barker Moon that is required of… what is to come. You do have a choice. And that choice is yours.'

The light behind Brixton's stormy eyes sparked with lightning.

'Make, or be made.'

Bach stood and stepped off of the war memorial.

Mainwaring sat up as well.

They were awaiting his decision.

The Rock Icon grinned again.

He had a great smile; great teeth. Money, Barker assumed.

'You bet quite a lot, Barker Moon. And you lost. We've all been there, done that. But you still have allies. In the strangest places, but you have them. It is time for a reckoning Barker Moon. Are you ready?'

# CHAPTER SIXTEEN: SEEING

'How many people died in here?' Karri repeated Cheryl's question, then nodded. 'A lot.'

Cheryl held her breath. Karri kept talking.

'I thought you'd know what to ask. There used to be actual floors. It goes up six, and down two or three. They used to have beds down there too, in the sewers, in the dirt and the mud.'

'They?'

Still almost naked beneath her blue coat, she suddenly felt severely underdressed, disrespectful somehow.

'There are tunnels under North Terrace, from the old railway stations. Line extensions, where they stored the carriages. The creeks and springs still run; the large ones are sewers and storm drains now, but there are still a few too small to bother with. They survived on them; the women in the flop houses, the brothels, or just the ones who came to the end-of-the-road smoke houses, where they gave their last pennies for enough opium to drift themselves into final oblivion. This wasn't the only one. There were spaces like this all over, of course. This one near the railroads, the others near the big industrial blocks. Every city is the same, was built the same, to have brothels for the workers, along with everything else that is planned. Boys too, of course. But really nobody speaks about that.'

Cheryl was speechless.

'The thing about this is…' Karri spoke slowly now. '…very few cities are planned on an actual grid, and in even fewer cities, are the grids built on active energy lines.'

'You mean, an actual, activated magical grid.' Cheryl nodded. 'How many…' She gulped, hard. 'How many cities actually are built on *activated* magical grids?'

'That we know of? The Vatican is the only one we know for sure. Parts of London, Rome. There are permanent portals on every continent; and most of the major cities have areas that are activated in some way. But there is nothing like this one; this one isn't the only one of its kind, but it is unique. This shaft is just part of the mechanism of course. That's why we've cleaned it out.'

Cheryl looked up and down.

'You said there were floors?'

'Makeshift floors. The space was, and is, just a pointless gap. Or it would be, in any other city. An empty space between a brothel and a bar, not even good for storage. Owned by nobody, desired by nobody, useless to everybody; except the dying and disenfranchised. There was a warehouse store behind that wall. We think they might have blocked it off for an early influenza outbreak. Multi-storey car park now. They don't even know this is here. Freyanna has legally purchased them all, all these spaces throughout the city. Cleared them and left them.'

'Freyanna?'

'Yes.'

'The?'

'Yes. The Freyanna. If you've been fully activated as a witch, or a sorceress, or whatever you have been activated as or want to call yourself, you're going to need to deal with her from now on.'

'Deal with her?'

'Who do you think is paying for all this?' Karri smiled.

'The renovations?'

Karri smiled. 'Everything, Cheryl.'

Cheryl looked out again, then behind her to the lovely brick. 'You'd never know an alley ran behind that wall. Or that there were hairdryers through that wall, a carpark through there… or just a… space. In here.'

'The centre square. The ninth space. Not all blocks have them. Usually one of the outer blocks would consume it. But sometimes; it doesn't happen. The city doesn't want it to happen. And this city has its fair share of them.'

Cheryl looked up again.

'Are they all… like this?'

'We don't know what half of them are. But no; we think some were, but others have structures inside them. What they are, exactly, is any sorcerer's assumption.'

The hanging, naked light bulb was softer than she'd first thought. It was attached to a long thin, white-plastic cable that came directly out of the wall just near her head, and had been stapled to the wall in metre-long gaps, right up one level, across and then wrapped around the central beam by some game monkey-climber and left there to dangle, right in the middle. The single, central beam that supported the light diagonally dissected the ceiling plane of what would have been the next floor up. It was the only thing that did.

'You've cleared out all the floors. Just left it a space. People used to put planks across, didn't they? And string hammocks. This was part of why London sent people here, because back there, they were living like this all through town.'

'And New York. Probably everywhere. In London they stored convicted criminals in old ships, chockers full, before they sent them out there. Starving in their own shit, hanging over it, by the hundreds, sleeping on planks of wood and makeshift hammocks. People are amazing like that; they manage, they subsist. They still do it in India, in China. Goddess knows where-else.'

'All through everywhere…' Cheryl uttered. '…all through time…'

'Through Empire. Women with no choice but to bear children. Children outside of light, grace or divinity.'

Cheryl felt herself gulp again, swallow dry. Jesus. What kind of hairdresser didn't offer a glass of water or a coffee?

'I've seen enough,' Cheryl turned back.

'Okay then…' Karri smiled sweetly, but a little forced. 'Let's go get your blonde on.'

Karri seemed disappointed as they walked back into the small, brick space. She closed the doors successively behind them, casually starting the coffee machine as she passed. Cheryl was still feeling very unwell, sick to her stomach in fact, when Karri finally led her to one of the first six wash stations, and at last offered her a glass of water. Cheryl still avoided the mirrors beyond as she stood and watched Karri's back, listening to the spring water dispenser gurgle as she stared down at the chequered floor.

She drank heavily as Karri gave her the glass, and another smile, this one pleasant but blank, then refilled the tall glass without asking. Karri absently offered to take her coat and Cheryl was halfway disrobed, revealing her new underwear, before she knew it. They both paused, then Cheryl shrugged.

'What the hell. It seems so important to everyone to get the whole picture.'

Karri lowered the coat off her shoulders, then vanished from view momentarily again as she hung it in the staff room.

Cheryl relented in the last few seconds before Karri returned, and glanced up at her reflection.

Something was wrong and she immediately glanced away.

She did not take in any information.

She was tired; it might have been good or bad, what she'd seen, she simply did not know.

Karri assessed Cheryl openly.

'I thought Shirley gave you new lingerie?'

'Well, truth be told, I don't think she's fooling anyone that they're not just off-the-rack bra and undies.'

'New things look special. They're not tat, if that's what you mean. But she usually gets it so right…'

'That's funny. Because now that you mention it, they don't feel right at all.' Cheryl stood perfectly still. 'Karri, in a fucking hall of mirrors like this one, why is it so difficult for me to even just catch my reflection?'

Karri smiled; serious but in control. 'It's happened before. These boons come in bundles; one thing at a time, some things slow release… part of what releases the next module might have something to do with… seeing yourself, in a… new look. At a certain time? That might be important?'

'Do I look that different?'

'A bit.'

'How…? It's not…?'

'No. Just a bit. But for all number of reasons, it might be important for you to see the changes at the right time. So let's assume that there's a spell, in the bundle that's being released and installed, that prevents you from seeing your reflection, until that time comes.'

Cheryl could feel a tightness in her chest. It was the edge of panic.

Still Karri did her best to reassure her.

'Look, don't worry about the undies. I can see plainly; the bra is too big. And the bum on your nickers is loose. Shirley never gets it so wrong. The spell must have changed you more than the…'

Cheryl turned to the mirror, but Karri stepped quickly across and reached out, grasped her hard by her forearms, then reached up and placed her hands on her cheeks, so that Cheryl was forced to look into her Karri's eyes, not her own.

'Cheryl? Really? Trust me. Best not to mess with it yet. How about we just…?'

She guided Cheryl effortlessly to her seat, and somehow relaxed her backward into the clean enamel headrest.

'Let me just wash your hair. Then you can look.'

'Is it that bad? What's it done? I… I don't think my mind can…'

'It's okay. It's not that your mind can't take it. It's…' Karri splashed the water a bit, testing the temperature on her wrist. 'I think the spell altered your perception. I don't think you can see it just yet. Not as you should.'

'I thought I saw something. Not me. Something else.'

'Don't think about it. How do you know Freyanna?'

Cheryl allowed her eyelids to relax as the sensually hot water suddenly splayed down her crown, along the back of her head and neck, threading soothingly through her locks.

'I don't. We've only met a few times to say hello. But word is, she's like the Tony Soprano of witches in this city.'

'Don't be afraid of the shadow of Freyanna. She's just quality control.'

Cheryl nodded. 'I'd heard. Or, assumed.'

'She's not as scary as her reputation might have led you to believe. She's powerful, sure, but she's okay. More than okay. We're friends. But I'll let her tell you her own story.'

Cheryl winced. 'The most powerful witch in the city is okay with random boons, empowering people?'

'White witch, Cheryl. That white light that hit you, up from the shore; I mean, I saw it. I don't think you and she are going to have any problems. I think she needs all the help…'

Karri trailed off suddenly.

Cheryl was drifting now, but she understood, and let out a sigh. 'Good.'

'Although…'

Cheryl opened her eyes. 'Although what?'

She instantly felt Karri's fingertips on her scalp, massaging and easing her, seducing her almost immediately back into relaxation again. Cheryl closed her eyes again. Karri's tone of voice, near her ear, was calm but firm.

'…you… you really didn't see the kid?'

'The kid…' Cheryl uttered.

'The child? Out in the old space? You didn't see the little girl? Or the mother, or the old wise woman?'

Cheryl laughed. 'Just one of them?'

'No, I mean, it's unusual.'

'For what?'

'It's… kind of a test. You take the new girl out there. So many women died back in that shaft. Men and kids too, don't get me wrong. But, overwhelmingly women. Settlers, convicts, immigrants, Chinese workers, Indigenous…'

'Yes. A lot.'

'That's right. And, usually… to someone with your kind of reservoir… one of them makes themselves known. It's almost like a Sorting Hat kind of thing, which one you see.'

Cheryl shrugged as best she could in the headrest.

'That's what I said.'

Karri didn't understand. 'What did you say?'

'I said; just one of them?'

'Just one of them?'

'I was asking; do people usually see just one of them?'

'Well, yes. One or two, sometimes all three, but that's very rare. Why…?' Karri began to massage her scalp a little harder. 'How many did you see?'

Cheryl's eyes squeezed more tightly closed.

'All of them.'

'All of them?'

'Yes. I saw all of them.'

# CHAPTER SEVENTEEN:
# WORLD

'You know, Colonel Light decided that Adelaide, unlike most of the other major Australian cities, would be built inland. Why do you think he did that? Not a port city, like Melbourne or Sydney… very unusual for the time.'

Barker heard himself speak.

'My friends are in trouble…'

Then he realized he was in the front bar of the Botanic Gateway, sitting in a booth with nobody else around, except…

'Knife attacks tend to steer people clear of hotels for a while, in my experience'. Parry had a wry Australian drawl, the earnestness of which was difficult to pin down. 'I told the manager you were a person of interest. I told him that if he would be so kind as to allow me to interview you here, on the quiet, I wouldn't need to report anything like a mad occultist trying to take out another mad occultist outside his hotel, on a classically quiet old Tuesday night in good old Adelaide. He's agreed to throw in free drinks while we talk. Some people might think that's a bit of an abuse of power, but personally, I think it's just keeping things in perspective. What do you think, Mister Moon?'

Barker checked his bearings again. They were in an open pub booth. Someone had propped him up, unconscious in the corner.

'Did you prop me up here?'

'Seemed like the decent thing to do after you moved to save that pink damsel. I draw the line at claiming she was in distress. Others might see it differently; but eye witness accounts only carry weight in America. And most of the time, only on American television.'

Barker noticed suddenly, as his consciousness drained back into him, that Parry was holding the silver ceremonial dagger that the man in the suit had thrown at him. He was just holding it, quite inoffensively, by the handle with the blade resting flat on his middle fingertip. He was also, apparently, halfway through a pint of ale.

Barker tried to respond. 'Colonel Light?'

'I hear you're a fan.'

'Not... not really. Just... peripherally. But... in answer; in the early years, our horse and cart forefathers, to use an Americanism...'

'Must you?'

Barker grunted as he tried to sit up. His ribs were killing him, the slice-wound was stinging, and now his shoulder, on the opposite left-side, felt like someone had taken a sledge hammer to the back of it. On top of this, his body was still stinging, still tense, still searching for an outlet for The Ox. He got the message though; Parry was one of those Aussies who resented American cultural imperialism.

'A bit sore?' Parry questioned.

From behind, someone put a beer down in front of him.

'I don't drink. Can you do a latte? Biggest mug you've got; strong and milky?'

There was a grumble and the beer was removed.

'Thanks.'

'You were saying?'

Barker settled on a position in the corner. 'Well, when the ships came in, obviously the traders would head down to the port. It was a whole thing; who got there first, to see what they had. The merchants had look-outs and... anyway. Once they got their goods off the boats, the stuff they'd ordered and the stuff the ships had to sell, these *early horse and cart settlers* had to come back up from the main sea port...'

'Creatively called Port Adelaide. Very strong local footballers.'

'If you say so; along a direct route that was named, with appropriate flourish, as you would no doubt agree...' Barker grunted as he shifted again, this time leaning in a little and finding some comfort. '...the Port Road. Port Road connected Adelaide with incoming cargo, precisely via its north-west chessboard corner.' Barker pointed outside, west along North Terrace, which he was now facing. The Gates to the Botanic Gardens were just in view; even at night it was really quite nice.

He was trying not to wince as he pointed.

'The opposite northern corner from here, right down there, about a mile away on the other end of the main Adelaide grid.'

Parry nodded, but his face was impassive.

'Well done Mister Moon. Did you pay attention in your Australian History classes, or is this really all part of your weird and wild world of personal interest?'

'It was of interest, a while back, to the extent that it directly served my interests...' Barker smiled. 'I could really do with that...'

The frothing of the coffee machine exploded from somewhere behind them.

Barker nodded to himself. The booth was bench-length and his newly-injured shoulder was leaning against the cold of the glass. As well as the gates to the Botanic Gardens along the line of the window ahead, he also could see the eastern parklands directly outside. Over the top of the street benches and the long concrete pots that were filled with high ferns and low-hanging ivy, he could see the same stretch of park where he'd seen the ghosts, and where the Establishment Figures had appeared, the street where he'd stood with Brixton, and right there; the place where Party Girl had died, forty-odd years ago. Bach was parked on the other side of the road beside the Light Horse memorial, and so was Parry's white car. But he could no longer see the spirit of the leather-clad biker-chick. Parry waved the dagger toward one of the white, wooden veranda supports. Covered in ivy, it was at first difficult to see what he was getting at.

'That survived.'

It was his branch, propped up there.

The not-yet…

'…but your koala went up a tree.'

Barker kept staring out at Bach.

'He's not mine. He comes and goes as he pleases.'

'If you tell me you were headed for Waratah National Park, I really will have to take you in.'

Barker chortled, and it hurt. Parry just observed, although he seemed to be assessing something, slowly but keenly. 'What else do you know, Mister Moon?' Barker sensed movement behind him and a large mug of latte was placed on the table before him.

'A bit late for that, isn't it?' Parry sounded genuinely concerned. 'You'll be up all night, surely?'

'Thanks,' Barker called over his shoulder. 'Can't be helped, detective.'

'That would be Chief Inspector Parry to you.'

Barker gulped down some latte. It was just right

'Sorry… but, why the history quiz?'

'I heard through the grapevine that Barker Moon was fascinated by the shape of the city. I just thought I'd test you to see if your brain was still working.' He placed the dagger down on the table. 'What do these markings mean?'

Barker examined them and answered honestly. He figured that was the safest hand to play. Perhaps, at this stage, his only play.

'They're glyphs; maybe sigils. I'd have to google the glyphs. If they're sigils, their exact intention is anyone's guess; it'd be like trying to guess what's in a cocktail, with potentially hundreds of ingredients, just by looking at what people do when they drink it.'

'Sigils, hey?'

'Very densely packed symbols; a focus for power, or acquisition. At least, that's what these ones are.'

'Because they're on a dagger?'

'Yeah. The dagger isn't necessarily meant to be used to try and kill.'

'But it was. Tonight.'

'It may have been. There are some people, I think, who are trying to make me very mad. I think.'

'You think?'

'I think.'

'Moon, I'm going to make you an offer. I am going to take you down the other end of North Terrace, to the north-west corner where our colony's early lazy capitalists first rejected Light's perfectly logical vision in favour of what quite frankly is still to this day a bloody decent ale, and I am going to deposit you in the care of the nurses at our enormous, brand spanking new, global-contagion-and-aging-population-ready hospital, because I am fairly certain you have at least one broken rib, a shoulder that might need some serious attention, something on your other arm that is clearly still bleeding underneath the massive cut down your clothes, and perhaps even a small concussion. If I do that, can you assure me that you will be there at first light when I come to interview you about what may or may not be occurring under the radar in our fair but currently very grim grid of a city?'

Barker nodded, leaned in and smiled.

'Are you a gambling man, Chief Inspector?'

# CHAPTER EIGHTEEN:
# EYES

Karri's scalp-massage was sending Cheryl into a sleepy trance, but she didn't want to close her eyes again. She kept seeing them. All the women, and the elderly, and the kids. All the dead from the old makeshift flop house. They'd been like a giant cloud in there, an explosion held in temporal stasis, just after detonation. One massive cauliflower cluster of broken spirits, all still asking the same eternal question, with the same one word.

'They wanted to know why…'

Cheryl uttered the statement softly. Karri continued to massage. Cheryl wondered if it wasn't the only thing holding her brain together right now.

'Have you…' Karri fished, not quite nervously. '…dealt much? With lingering spirits?'

Cheryl gave a little shrug against the porcelain headrest.

'I'm aware of them.'

Karri's massaging slowed a little. 'Every psychic is aware of them. In some way or other. I'm asking if you've… *dealt* with them.'

'Yeah, I have. Here and there.'

There was a strange pause. Cheryl knew what was coming next. It had happened several times before. Barker was coming next. And so, Karri asked softy; respectfully, at least.

'You were at Bridger Mansion, weren't you?'

'I sure was.'

There was another strange pause, longer.

'Freyanna always says we're not to approach them unless they approach us, especially the very powerful ones; unless there is a clear indication that there's an extradimensional request.' Karri paused and there was a further odd vibe. 'I think you were heavier. I think the boon, whatever you received, must have taken a lot of fluid, or body fat, or something. Shirley got it right; she always does. But then you went down a size after the light hit the van.'

Cheryl tried to look down at herself, but she was at that weird angle; half-seated, half-reclining, with her head right back and her… pale throat fully exposed.

'No offense. I've seen you around, you always look like you're in good shape.'

'Not really. I walk a lot.'

'Witches do, don't we?'

'Nature…' Cheryl offered. '…n'all that.'

'I am too. In good shape, I mean. But, I was born round, and curvy. What's your natural hair color?'

'My…?'

'Natural hair color?'

'Can't you tell?'

She could feel Karri starting to lather her scalp up, sensed a hand move away and squirt some shampoo from a pump.

'It might have changed. With the boon.'

'Changed?'

Cheryl was lathered up now, but sat up a bit and tried to look sideways again into one of the mirrors, a little keener this time. Karri held her down again, just lightly, professionally.

'Just wait; I want to see something… can you glance down at yourself? But – don't look in the mirror?'

Cheryl really wondered if she could.

'Ummm…? …okay.'

Cheryl raised her neck a little and stared down her middle. She reached for her now too-loose new nickers and flipped up the elastic, gazing along, between her breasts, under the new bra (that seemed not to be doing… anything much?) and assessed her skin… which seemed… maybe different? But then, how often did she see herself so broadly lit from this weird angle? But was her belly… flatter? And just under the elastic, was there… nothing? Like; she couldn't see anything. No pubes at all.

'Oh, no; it hasn't *plucked me* has it?'

'No!' Karri was almost too quick to respond. 'But… it might take some getting used to. Hang on; I'll just rinse you. Not sure it's made any difference, but you were on the floor of the casino loo, and besides; that carpet in the back of Shirley's van has seen a lot of…'

Cheryl heard a hiss. She thought it was the shower-head getting ready to rinse her out. Then she realized; it was a sound that had been building now for some time. It was coming from outside, from the street. Then Karri started the water, and that hiss momentarily drowned out the other.

'Yeah…' Karri seemed to pick up on her concern. '…wind. Big storm on the way. Worst we've seen in decades.'

The warmth hit her scalp and was immediately, involuntarily relaxing.

'Has my hair gone *vomit-green* or something…?'

'Well; *something…*'

Karri ran her hands back over her scalp, rinsing out the shampoo. Cheryl could hear the light gurgle in the drain under her head, then again as Karri re-ran the warm water. This was always the sleepy bit; the bit designed to relax you. But this time, it made the rest of her body feel colder as the wind outside become louder, now whooshing right over the sound of the water.

'It hasn't made any difference…'

It was strange. Karri didn't sound alarmed, or even concerned. More; mildly fascinated. She started patting Cheryl's hair dry with a towel, then sighed.

'Well, I suppose you should see it; so to speak.'

'So to speak?'

Cheryl sat up this time, with no resistance, and turned very definitely as she swung her legs over the side of the vinyl chair and stood.

It was alarming to see yourself in the mirror, and not quite recognize yourself, Cheryl realized. Not like, a full spy-move face-off, but... enough to make your mind double-take. She straight away flipped the coat open, so only she could see, and took her whole self in.

Her whole, altered self.

She immediately recalled, just a few hours before, assessing herself in the mirror at the casino, with Shirley keenly co-assessing. Now she had another strange woman with her, perhaps not assessing as keenly to see what she looked like, but rather to gauge her response. Regardless; chaperoned the whole time.

The first thing that was apparent was that Cheryl was still herself; still with the wide cheeks, round jaw, button nose, and dark, sunken eyes. Nothing to be done; she had told herself that, a thousand times. The mouse-brown hair however, was gone. And the brown and white and grey and pink tinges of her pale Polish-Russian skin...

'What...' Cheryl uttered. '...what do you think happened?'

'I don't know...' Karri uttered lightly. 'But it looks...enchanted.'

Cheryl took a few steps closer and fully opened her coat. Through the loose underwear she could see that her body did indeed bear some token signs of rapid weight loss. She reached behind her, irritated by the bra, removed and dropped it. The knickers needed just a push down her hips before falling to her feet; she kicked them aside. Karri picked them up, diligently.

'Don't be shy. You're beautiful, okay, but I'm not here for the perv.'

Cheryl turned to her. She could see that Karri was transfixed, just waiting to see what Cheryl would make of her new self. But nobody had ever called her beautiful before. Well, not really. Men had lied, in bed. To be polite. But to say it, matter-of-factly, like that; as though it were a foregone conclusion. Apparently, her beauty was held in Karri's eyes. She liked Karri, a lot now. Couldn't help it.

Cheryl turned back, braced herself, and removed the coat.

As soon as she did, the door opened at the front of the salon. A gust blew in, powerful and cold, right up the monochrome corridor.

But it was too late; Cheryl didn't care who it was.

She'd seen herself now.

'Cooh-ee!' Shirley called out an old, traditional bush-greeting that Cheryl had not heard since childhood. Cheryl just stared at herself in the mirror. When Shirley came around the corner with two men in tow, Cheryl did not flinch. She just kept staring at herself, right into the depths of her colourless eyes.

# CHAPTER NINETEEN: DIRECTIONS

Barker stepped outside. It was freezing cold; the chill was shooting up North Terrace like a well-designed, open wind tunnel.

'I wonder…' Barker mused as he grunted his first few steps. 'Did Light see that? The winds, straight up the plains from the ocean? Was it planned that way?'

'Cleansing?' Parry shrugged.

Barker looked at him as he collected his not-yet staff from where it had been propped up outside the window. He grasped the wood and the roughness felt good in his hand. They were all the same height, him and Parry and the not-yet staff, although Parry was maybe a decade or more senior, a hard decade by the look; in his early-fifties perhaps. Thin and unfit, with an unconcealed but not disgraceful beer-belly and worn-out posture over his decent but almost overworn steel-grey suit. Under that, Parry wore a clean but crumpled white shirt with a white-grey chequered tie that Barker suspected someone else had picked out for him. There was something about him though that Barker liked a lot, and he really hoped that he wasn't Black Prax.

Right now, what he needed was an ally in the real world.

They went to the intersection and stood on the corner, then waited for the lights to change.

'Cardinal directions, that kind of thing; big symbols like planets…'

'Moons?'

'…moons and stars, snakes and scorpions, wolves and lions…'

'…koalas?'

'Okay, koalas and roos and kookaburras; they're very important in mysticism, if we're going to look at things that way.'

Parry nodded. 'Obviously, you're aware that this sounds completely mental.'

'But it isn't. Nothing is ever just one thing; there are different levels to everything. The normal world occurs on two or three; mine occurs on more than that.'

'You really don't remember anything, Moon? About what happened at Bridger Mansion?'

Barker stared at the huge wrought-iron gates to the Botanic Garden.

The apparent Astral Gate.

'I remember the version of me that existed here, and concurrently on those other levels. That other me; he lived around, or at least he had permanent access to that other Adelaide.'

'…that other Adelaide.' Parry repeated.

'Well, technically, the other, mystical-dimensional plane. Adelaide just happened to be where I accessed it. And where I spent most of my time. It's the mystical dimension that is just under the surface of everything; the one where big directions and big symbols matter; the mystical city as opposed to the ordinary.'

The wind behind them was really picking up, whipping Barker's coat around his legs.

'Did you know the man who threw the knife at you? Which Adelaide was he from?'

'Dagger. And no. Never seen him before. The girl in the fuchsia dress was a decoy. So, somebody knew I was going to be there. Somebody told them I was coming down Magpie Road.'

'Any ideas?'

'Some suspicions.'

He looked across at the diagonal lights, to the section of the street where Parry had pulled up beside him.

'Where did you come from?'

'You mean which Adelaide, or which suburb?' Parry gave him a friendly smirk. 'I was following a lead up in the Hills. But then there was a report that someone might need help with a rock slide up on Moon Road.'

'Where did you say?'

'Moon Road. The only reason we're waiting here at these lights in the middle of the night with absolutely no traffic around is because I'm a cop, right?'

The walk light turned green. Parry went straight away but Barker paused a second.

'I mean, it's almost midnight. The night is over; there's pretty plainly nothing coming for miles.'

Barker didn't answer. '…it's really called Moon Road?'

He stepped off the curb and took a few long strides to catch up to Parry.

'That crazy one that goes up to the Lion and Unicorn Hotel. I thought you'd know that; you just mentioned it. It's where the merchants used to station lookouts on moonlit nights, to try and get an early jump on incoming tall-ships. Are you alright?'

'I – just…'

'They should close Moon Road for a year and put proper modern roads in. But the locals would go bananas.' He looked back at Barker, slightly incredulous. 'You know the Lion? The old pub with the view. I thought maybe you had something to do with it. The landslide, not the pub. I don't suppose you have anything to do with either, do you? Moon Road; Barker Moon. That would be a bit too much of a coincidence.'

'I really need to find Cheryl and Carlton.'

'You really think your friend Cheryl is still at the Casino?'

'I'm pretty sure.'

'And you think the same people who… staged that fight, and tried to kill you, will be in there, trying to kill her as well?'

'I hope not.'

'But you think so. Look, Moon, you keep your side of the deal, okay? If nothing else, it's duty of care. I may not have formally arrested you, but from now on essentially, from a certain, if I am to be honest, quite malleable but very short-term-enforceable legal point of view, you are what might quite liberally be referred to as being 'within my custody'.'

'And?'

'And; should you die in my custody, the form-filling, hitherto the digital replacement-term for the once-classical 'paperwork', would not be worth the time it took to go to the shop to buy the milk for all the extra coffee I would have to drink in order to get through it in one night. What's with you and the coffee, by the way? People seem genuinely surprised that you ever sleep at all.'

'You seem to know a lot about me…'

'I'm a Chief Inspector.'

'Point taken. But; what's your point?'

'My point is; you need to go to a hospital, Moon.'

Barker turned around. Just past the entrance to the Botanic Garden was the old hospital, a higgledy-piggledy pile up along a whole city block, with architectural styles featuring everything from stunning Victorian and Edwardian veneers to ghastly nineties pre-fab kitsch. It was empty and lifeless now, but… it *had* been built right beside an Astral Gate. It almost made sense.

'I will go to hospital; as soon as we find Cheryl.'

They passed the Light Horse Memorial and reached the Chief Inspector's new, white, unmarked police car. Bach was parked right beside it.

'Somebody I trust told me that it was probably a good idea to trust you; if I could ever actually find you.'

Barker shrugged. 'Trust has to be earned, CI Parry.'

He turned back and stared at the Gate again.

'…Colonel Light's design had been that the incoming carts carrying the incoming cargo would take them to the centre of the city, to Victoria Square, right in the middle of the mystical chessboard. Victoria Square was where the major retailers and investors were going to build their city's new shopping precinct; a thriving central market, around a massive city park that formed the heart of the urban board.' He turned back to Parry. 'But what Light called Victoria Square also happens to be the central focus of mystical energies for hundreds of miles; there are other pockets all around here, but that's the centre of it all.' He nodded at the Gate. 'Someone I trust told me, very recently, that one level of consciousness up, that gate over there is some kind of entrance to the mystical plane.'

'The Astral Plane?'

'If you like; but just saying "The Astral Plane" is like saying "The Ocean", or actually, more like, "The Sky".'

'Point taken.' Parry sniffed, his nose already becoming red with the night's cold. 'And so if… what? You're mad enough, that gate is a psychological symbol that makes you think you'll go there? If you go through in a mad enough state of mind? Maybe that's why the other name for the eastern parklands here is The Garden of Unearthly Delights?'

He looked back and saw that Parry was, in fact, gazing out into the eastern parklands.

The old bagman remained there, asleep.

'The Indigenous folk have a name for it…' Parry uttered. 'I can't remember it.'

'For what?' Barker gazed around with him. You could almost see the cold. His hands were chill now. It was time to get going. 'The Garden?'

'No. For Victoria Square. It's about thirty thousand letters long, and doesn't sound even remotely like Victoria Square, if that helps. It's as though the Indigenous Peoples didn't even know who she was.'

Barker's fingers tapped the long stretch of branch in his right hand.

'What is happening, Chief Inspector? What are you chasing?'

Parry kept staring out. 'Deaths. Disappearances. The kinds of things that have always happened here. Weird Satanic rumours everyone knows are true but nobody can ever substantiate. Everything from secret societies in the higher echelons to purpose-built ghettos in the outer suburbs where the fourth and fifth generation unemployed create easy-pickings victim farms, and a general circle of damnation and torment; inbred children and ice-babies. It's only in the eastern suburbs…' Parry kept

staring out into the sometime Garden of Unearthly Delights. '…
right there past the eastern parklands there, where that hasn't
happened yet. Otherwise there would be a quite convincing
Circle of Hell on Earth, right around the outer city.'

Barker stared at him, grim-faced, as Parry turned back,
resolutely deadpan.

'I don't get creeped-out easily, Chief Inspector,' Barker uttered,
as though to imply that the opposite was starting to occur. 'But…
let's assume you're talking to me now because all this is connected;
or because, you want to find out from me whether or not it might
be connected.'

'We could try assuming that. See where it gets us.'

'Well; for almost two centuries now, since the mid-eighteen-
hundreds, since Adelaide has existed as a city-proper true to
whatever age it was in, the heart of Adelaide has not been located
in its grid-designated centre, Victoria Square, as Light intended.
Because, once they got back to town, none of those early horse
and cart settlers could be bothered going the extra mile, or half-
mile, as it were, into the middle of the city; to Victoria Square.
Rather, they just came along here, right along North Terrace,
all the way down, and sold their cargo stock along here, to the
people who were waiting. Some of them had warehouses here
anyway, along North Terrace; but those that didn't soon did.
Anyone else who wanted first dibs on the cargos being carted up
Port Road soon did as well. The North Terrace warehouses, right
along there, started to form their own living, thriving, organic
town centre that had nothing to do with Victoria Square. This,
North Terrace, became a major artery that had grown itself,
despite Light's planned grid, and it brought in, and bestowed
wealth, upon anyone who had the quick wit and fast finances to
set up a store here.'

'There was a lot of money here once. A planned city, in a
wealthy new world.' Parry stared past the corner of the Botanic
Gate. 'This is Adelaide lore and legend, Moon. There is no single
proven theory as to why this happened. Why the city came out

this way. Some say it was because North Terrace was closer to what was the Torrens River. The horses could drink there. The warehouses were close by, it just happened. The river's the reason the city was put here in the first place.'

'Was it? The river didn't always reach the ocean; it spread out into wetlands before it got there. And horses couldn't drink here in the summer; it was nothing but a stretch of billabongs in summer. So they say. You could dam the main flow with the palm of your hand.'

'So they say...' Parry smiled and proceeded. 'Some say it was the brewery, just over there, on the other side of the Garden of Unearthly Delights; that after the long ride in, and the selling and unloading, they couldn't wait to get there for a cleansing ale. Fresh, spring-water ale; first port of call out of the port. Adelaide was famous for it, even back then. Alcohol is a very persuasive argument to the working classes; just ask any taxation department. And that path to it just happened not to go through the centre of the grid, but along its northernmost edge.'

'Whatever happened; one thing is for sure...' Barker offered, sounding distant. '...they didn't head for Tarndanyangga.'

Parry raised an eyebrow as Barker recoiled slightly at a realization.

'I just plucked that out of thin air.'

'Apparently, Moon.'

Barker turned back and looked further up East Terrace. There was another, more regular intersection, just a little way up.

'I mean, look at that; Rundle Street. Tiny.' He turned back. 'North Terrace. Wide by design. They came up here; they dumped all their stuff on North Terrace, and the warehouses here had no choice but to unload into that; into Rundle. Light's Grid was laid down in alternates; boulevard terraces around the edges and dissecting the middle. Then a larger street, then a thin street, repeat and so on, in grids right through. But, as a result of being the major zone of unloading directly from the port, North Terrace storehouses became show-houses, and their back doors, that exited out onto tiny-little-thin Rundle Street, had to become the front doors for what would become the major department stores. It completely warped the grid's intended purpose. Adelaide lore and legend again, if you like. But they didn't even give enough of a shit to unload on Rundle, just one street, *one street* over. I mean, you'd think someone would be able to persuade them of even that; just one street over, so that the most logical backup plan, the most practical dimension, given what was occurring, could...'

Parry had been listening. 'Could what? I suppose I can see; the big road should have become the one for department store traffic, not the much thinner one.'

'...the most practical dimension...'

'Yes, you said that...'

'It's not just off-centre, shoved up one end, Chief Inspector...'

'No?'

'It's off-centre, shoved up one end; *facing the wrong way.*'

'Facing the wrong way?' Parry looked back and forth; Rundle Street to North Terrace, then nodded. 'I suppose there's a logic to that. An actual twisted logic. Figuratively speaking. But on the whole; a twist. But not one that would have passed un-noticed by anyone local with a passing interest in urban planning.'

'And how many of them have any knowledge of the occult?'

'The Rise of Rundle Street; intentionally inconsequential, meant to serve as nothing more than a slender strip of central-vein, a mere utility road; a fast route out of town and into the eastern suburbs, unfortunately but forcefully bestowed with the burden of becoming, *heaven forfend*, a thriving central shopping and entertainment precinct. Now, instead of Victoria Square, right in the middle, the de facto 'centre of commerce' becomes the second street in, along the top of the grid.'

'Why?'

'What do you mean; why? We just came up with quite a few very compelling reasons. You don't actually need the occult to explain its occurrence.'

'No; but as a good friend of mine is fond of pointing out, sometimes if you place occult knowledge over something that essentially makes no sense, the occult starts to make more sense.'

'Look, Moon; clearly Rundle Street, as iconic to Adelaide as it's become, has for years provided a service that it was never intended to support. It was in fact so legendarily insufficient at maintaining its new status that in the mid-seventies they had to permanently cut off traffic and turn the whole middle part into a mall.'

Barker sighed.

'Detective Inspector Parry, I realize that this is all just – stuff. It's all just stuff that happens when people design things and other people start using them. They get refined and adapted, no matter how perfect the intention of the original design is. In the end North Terrace is just one big 'desire line'. But nothing is ever just one thing; everything has layers.'

'Well, the first part is certainly true; the city is quite clearly not as it was intended to be. The merchants completely screwing with Light's original intent; whether that was to just build a local, functioning, planned urban center, or…'

Barker shrugged. 'You see?'

'…or, to build a modern city on a massive astral energy field, totally centred and totally energized by this – Tarndanyangga?'

Barker shrugged again.

Parry hummed. 'Difficult to prove.'

'Well…' Barker sighed. '…this stuff is notoriously difficult to prove.'

'I don't know Moon; but…'

'But what? Why do you care, Chief Inspector?'

Parry put his hands in his pockets and looked down at the ground, nodding to himself.

'It is true, Moon, that according to most people who give a damn, common knowledge is that for two hundred years the general no-nonsense exhaustion of the early horse and cart settlers did indeed quite unceremoniously, but quite organically, supersede Light's design. North Terrace and Rundle Street are indeed collectively considered one of the world's largest and longest desire lines. But still; I know there's something wrong with this city; something that shouldn't be, but is. Very wrong.'

Barker turned around.

'That hospital was never supposed to be there. Look down there; North Terrace has been forced to accommodate, in one tight side of the whole city's square mile, all the things Light had intended to be spread evenly and sensibly throughout the city.'

'You really believe there's something in that?'

'I think, Detective Inspector, that there is indeed – something in it.'

Parry stared at him then. Just for a second, he seemed extremely concerned.

'The thing that always struck me as odd is; this is a city. A whole city that was planned. Designed and surveyed and; what have you. The streets were carved out, the intent – and I know that's something big with you oddballs – the intent, of having the city planned was there. Not a town, not a suburb even; a capital city in a major new colony. There were police, there were troopers. There were officials, Colonel Light himself; and yet, none of them said anything. They all just stood by and let it happen. Allowed the grand design to be...'

'Warped.'

'Thwarted, right under their noses.' Parry looked back at Barker. 'A whole city, just allowed to slide so many blocks north, then turn about face? I just don't buy it, Moon. I just don't buy it.'

Barker met his gaze approvingly for a second, then gazed out into the parklands.

'You don't have to buy it. We're standing in it. Right here.'

Parry hummed, darkly. 'Well then. Shall we go and see if your friend hasn't gambled her life away?'

Barker grabbed the passenger handle.

'Mainwaring!' He cried out into the parklands. 'Watch Bach!'

As Barker laid his staff along the base of the Light Horse

Memorial, rendering it virtually invisible, there came a rustling from atop one of the parkland gums that he accepted as acquiescence.

Parry didn't question. He just stared.

'Mainwaring…'

Barker returned to the passenger side of the car and stared back over the roof.

'He looks like Arthur Lowe.'

'Yeah. Well, I'll give you that. It's uncanny how many of them do.'

'But this one really does.'

'I can't say that was *not* something that was almost immediately brought to my attention upon first meeting him.'

'So that's what I called him.'

'Not a pet though?'

Barker shrugged as he opened the passenger door.

'Waratah.'

# CHAPTER TWENTY: PESTS

Cheryl stared at herself.

Her eyes were colourless now.

Not albino, just white and black.

It was unnerving to her.

But at the same time… kind of cool, actually.

She was aware of Shirley and two others standing behind them, but she blocked them out, and asked of Karri, hushly.

'You think I can make this work?'

Karri remained quiet, looking. Then she reached across her body and took Cheryl's right hand with her own. She couldn't have been much taller than a metre and a half, the old five-two or three, and Cheryl almost felt as though, between waking and meeting her, and seeing herself in the mirror now, that they had become two different species now; even though the changes upon Cheryl's physiognomy had been upon her that whole time, and Karri had said nothing. Karri raised Cheryl's hand to her lips, and ran the tops of her knuckles lightly across them.

Then she whispered, confidently.

'Don't be scared.'

Karri seemed to have made the gesture almost unconsciously, as though she were accustomed to children, and by the time Cheryl realized that it was perhaps just a little weird, or over-familiar, Karri had released her and it was done; almost as though it hadn't happened.

Cheryl looked back to the mirror, and was staring into her new eyes again; her new white eyes, where there remained only a sharp, black line around her stark, still-black, but almost pinpoint pupils, to divide them from the whites.

But her eyes were far from the mystical makeover's most striking changes. Over her whole body, where her skin had previously been a mix of various Eastern Euro tones, her surface was now so pale as to be almost translucent, although far from transparent, but somehow giving the impression that she was somehow glowing from within.

She put her hand to her cheek.

She felt the same.

'Not albino...' Cheryl uttered to herself, through her new, diaphanous lips.

'No. Different.'

Her hair was still there, but it was almost invisible, as though she were wearing some kind of giant, reflective-camouflage Rasta-beanie that was partially invisible, yet which reflected enough light to give shape, and outline form. She raised both her hands and touched it, ran her fingers back through her temples. It still felt almost exactly like her hair, moved and flowed like her hair had, but somehow it had become possessed with more body than her... she thought of it now as 'old hair', would have had.

'Basically...' Cheryl said to herself. '...new, virtually invisible hair.'

Her hand moved down to her right breast, and she cupped it.

'They're smaller...' Shirley told her.

Cheryl could still see her, behind in the mirror, in her periphery vision.

'I *know*.'

She hadn't looked Karri in the eye, in the mirror, yet. She seemed better, straight away, at blocking things out. No; at focusing. Was that new? Or was that happening as a result of the stress of the evening; the stress of *this*? Or rather; the *pure fascination* of this?

Shirley took a step forward, away from the other two, whom Cheryl had not even properly looked at yet. They were men though; she could feel their gaze. She didn't care. This was beyond any of that; any of those feelings.

'From the look of you…' Shirley's refined but suburban accent was somehow comforting. '…whatever the boon did, it's like you spent a week at a very diligent health spa. You see what I mean? You've lost body fat; lost whatever water you were retaining. Your DNA has been tampered with and it's triggered at least one, very apparent, dormant non-human trait. What you're looking at is a base-level hybrid fairy body; like your boyfriend Moon, way back when. You've been made fit-to-purpose, so you can handle the fight.'

Cheryl looked down.

'There are stretch marks where I didn't have them.'

'They look fine, woman. They'll probably even pass; you're more than human now, you don't know what you'll end up looking like; sure as The Devil, darling heart, you won't be complaining when you find out what you can do.'

'Do?' Cheryl wondered. 'Depending on what kind of fairy I descend from – ?' Cheryl's eyes flicked to Shirley, back through the mirror. 'Do you know already? Have your people been watching me?'

'No. I don't know. Freyanna might. You'll have to – '

'So I'll just have to wait and see what they were able to inspire out of my genes? What great, great, great Polish grandparent mated with what kind of… what? A Russian fairy? They have them, right?'

'Very good. Most people assume, stupidly and incorrectly, that they've been impregnated. Raped, some of them. Some think it's like being probed by aliens. But to do this, you already have to have had it in your blood.'

Cheryl still felt a little violated about it all.

'So it was just my grandmother a few generations back who was raped?'

Something happened then; in her eyes. She knew she was being ridiculous. Knee-jerk. For a start, female fairy folk were just as renowned; to mesmerize or glamour. To force a man to want them against their will. Who the hell knew which way it had gone down? And what had made her go straight away to poor Russian great-great-great granny being ravished by a centaur, or a troll?

Fear, she supposed, as ever.

That famous human trait; going immediately to the worst case scenario, searching for the greatest, most tragic, most outrageous drama. And dread, of course; that she would end up with the worst end of it all, and nothing to be done.

'People used to marry them and keep them in disguise…' Shirley proceeded, the edge of caution in her voice. 'Men and women. Kept their children hidden. Got away with it. Kept away. Cabins in the woods. For generations, some. Still do, although it's easier to blend today. Difference, novelty, is slowly being filtered through.'

But; hadn't she…? In the end, sure, but; hadn't she been given this boon without consent? Hadn't she been, essentially, violated in some way? Even if it turned out she could do cool shit?

She looked again, behind her in the mirror at Shirley. The older woman smiled, sympathetic but hardened.

'Are you going to tell the higher forces of good that you feel violated, darling heart? Or shall I? Given that they either can't hear us down here, or can't do anything, even if they could get through?'

Cheryl turned to face her.

She spread her arms.

'Can't do anything?!'

Shirley was a little shocked, and stepped back again.

Karri's voice came from beside her.

'They have to make big moves when they can, Cheryl. When they *can* get through…'

'You speak as though…'

'I had one. When I was little.' The wind whistled outside, high and fine and wild, as though catching the sharp edge of a thin sheet of metal. 'You get used to it. You change with it. Sometimes life seems like it's nothing but being lumbered with burdens, or boons, from people with more power than we have; things we didn't ask for, from people we barely know, who don't even pretend to understand us, or connect with us. None of us know what's happening, what's coming. In the bigger picture.' The howling whistle came again. Cheryl glanced back to the door, where the two men, handsome men, stood. They hadn't reacted. But there was something strange about them. 'Any more than we know what's really going on in another country, with another political system…' Karri offered. 'Or in the middle of a war, or a… we just don't know, Cheryl. We just have to believe it's for the better, because everything they've sent us, every way the boons have changed us, just our little coven, has been for the better. They have empowered us to fight the powers that commodify and dehumanize. That…' She looked across at Shirley and smiled. '… monetize and monotonize. That's one of yours isn't it?'

Shirley smiled just as Cheryl's attention was again caught by the two men Shirley had brought with her. Shirley glanced back over her shoulder at them.

'I had high hopes for these two here, but it turns out all they can do is see through each other's eyesight, which is basically a small step above what we can all do these days on our phones. Still, might be useful. Some boons are delivered to lay the ground for others. Some….'

Shirley noticed that Cheryl had frozen.

When they had accompanied Shirley inside the salon, Cheryl had paid little attention, but she had received a fleeting impression of two relatively young and fairly handsome men, maybe in their mid-thirties. But that glamour was cracking now; actually flaking. Their facial skin, their cheeks and brows and chins, were peeling, the top layer shedding and falling to their feet, onto the shoulders of their suits, their weird old suits, now Cheryl looked. It was becoming very clear that beneath, they were considerably older; still attractive men, but now with the weird peeling, revealed as perhaps in their late sixties. They were still relatively fit and healthy; silver and sleek now with a wiser, more wily look rather than the plain-hungry one that their younger veneer might have expressed. But still, somehow, obsessed, possessed now, it seemed, by the notion of sexual conquest and gratification. She wondered what had happened to them; what they had lost and needed to bargain for, what –

And then she saw that their penises were jutting out of their trousers, both of them red and purple with bulbous heads and veins, erect and grasped casually in their right hands, as they both slowly masturbated without a care in the world.

'Great saints!' Shirley gasped.

The first one broke their spell of isolation.

'See her arse in the mirror there?'

He asked this of the second one, as though there was nobody else there.

'Hope she doesn't move, that's a fucken great angle…'

Cheryl realized that they were talking about her. She flashed a look behind her and saw her own… weirdly pale buttocks, tinier and tighter than they'd been since her twenties. God, she was different now; younger but older, fitter but stranger, so much stranger. A stranger to herself.

She looked back at the two perverts.

Strange, as well.

Disgusting.

'Put those away…' She snarled. '…you're utterly revolting!'

'Put what away?' The first one asked as her reached behind him and pulled out a long ceremonial dagger. His partner did the same, then sniggered.

'The pork swords or the silver ones?'

Cheryl suddenly saw them starkly in her mind's eye as men who had once been Princes of the City, with some kind of low-level gangster-celebrity connection perhaps, or maybe well-known business owners… one of each, or both, even? But there, in their eyes… she could hardly look as they stared at what, even to Cheryl, at least for now, must have seemed like a very strange, lithe and glistening naked form; right there was that wily glare of desire that some sixty-something men possessed. It was the 'still burning' look that some older men could still exploit to seduce, it had seemed to Cheryl at times, even very-young women. Held with the right combination of dignity, confidence, reserve and desire, that wily look could be experienced as a vintage projection of the great male urge that was potentially, absolutely, under the right circumstances, attractive and desirable to women and men of all ages; the very essence of attractiveness, some would claim.

'Don't move, luv. We're just getting going!'

But here, it was not that; here it was leering and crude, totally base and debasing. It was all in their attitude, all in their manner, and particularly in their intent; just to utilize her in an act of objectification and gratification, without her consent, or even any suggestion of her permission as to her participation.

Shirley stepped immediately away from them, toward Cheryl and Karri.

'Oh Christ, it's The Old Pervs!'

Karri was flustered. 'Shirl! You let 'em in, Shirl!'

'It's a weird night – ' Shirl shook her head in plain disgust, and a little in self-disgust. ' – and that was a fucking powerful glamour to get past me!'

'Shirl! You never swear in the salon!'

'Well maybe it's past fucking time I did!'

Cheryl reached for her coat, but it wasn't there.

She had not felt truly exposed until now.

She had been in the company of fellow-practitioners, whose only notion of judgment or objectification had been in an attempt to help her discern and adjust what changes had come over her.

But now, these creature-men had made her feel totally uncomfortable, if not utterly freakish.

Fuck them, Cheryl cursed, and their demonic projection of the male gaze.

'What are you?' Cheryl demanded, angry that there was nothing within reach that she could cover up with; not to mention the fact that she now felt as though she had to.

They just smiled and sniggered, groaning and grunting a bit, as they looked her up and down, raising and twirling their swords threateningly. Then she noticed that there were odd bulges developing beneath their skins; under their shamelessly weaving wrists, and along each of their squinting temples. Something bulging from under their throats, too.

Outside, the wind gave a monstrous howl.

They kept staring at her, staring at Cheryl as though they were somehow drawing power from her. Although they stood close together, only a meter or so apart, they and their daggers were blocking both exits.

'What are they?' Cheryl asked shortly, nauseously unimpressed.

Shirley smirked with disdain. 'A remnant of a bygone era. Dirty old bastards, sick old Peeping Toms, they thought back then. No impulse control, we'd say now. They hang around outside, across the street, at the tram or the café, at the station or the casino, watching the women come in and out; them and their kind. Pretend to read the paper. Keep their business going underneath.'

'What!?'

'Every salon attracts a few Old Pervs, but when you're in the city, it's easier for them. And when it's a salon run by a coven, well; you attract Old Creature Pervs, I suppose.'

'Are you *serious*!?'

'There's never been more than a few – like stray dogs. But they've never made a move like this. Not out in the open, never come inside…' Shirley sneered. 'Been hanging around for years, haven't you!? Keep coming back!'

'*What*!?'

'Salons used to expect it in Freyanna's day. Even as late as the early eighties. In what we now call 'a simpler time'. Freyanna used to keep a basket of rotten eggs to throw at them if they ever came too close to the window, or got too frisky.'

Cheryl guffawed. 'You don't still have it, do you?'

'I like it when they talk to each other…' The first said to the second, under his breath.

Shirley snarled. 'They'd be good and ripe by now, wouldn't they? I brought Freyanna a cattle-prod back from my brother's property, when I first started here.'

'You worked here?'

'The cops took it from me, the first time I used it.'

Karri responded. 'We all work here, on and off. You should have been here, Cheryl. Seven years ago. Freyanna was expecting you. When you came back from… that place.'

'You can say it. You can say Bridger Mansion.'

'Take yer's back there…' The first Old Perv uttered. 'Back home…'

Cheryl was taken aback. Surely he couldn't have meant…

'That night changed everything, Cheryl. Tell her, Shirley…!'

Shirley scoffed. 'Don't put ideas in her head. There's enough myths been created in this city as it is. She had a place with us if she wanted one; I wouldn't call it destiny. Just planning, just… expectation. Although, we didn't know what to expect, really. We just thought you might seek us out, after all that. You went another way, and now you're back. And now, we'll see.'

They were friends somehow, Cheryl felt. Something had happened; all three of them had become friends somehow, bonded by the disgraceful scene before them. She heard Karri give a nervous giggle, and that somehow confirmed it. They were friends, or they would be, after all this.

'They look so bloody stupid…' Karri scoffed. 'Dicks look so stupid, don't they!'

Cheryl didn't answer. Friends, after all this.

If there was an 'after all this'.

After all that, at Bridger, they'd all meant to be friends, too.

After all this, in the City; they were meant to be friends.

If.

Always if.

'She got another one, Shirl. Another cattle prod. But she hid it. She thought you were enjoying it too much.'

'I was.' Shirley took a tentative step forward and stared at their faces, one at a time. 'Where'd she hide it now?'

'Whoar...' The second one grunted. 'Not bad for an old bird.'

Shirley stepped back.

'Cops say we can't actually stop them loitering, as long as they actually catch the tram every now and then. But they always come back. They had a young glamour on, but it's them, they're the same Old Pervs. Same ones from when I was first here, when we were young. Always old, looking like this. Must have been something in their time; whenever that was!' She yelled at them. 'Well what have you got to say for yourselves, before we throw you out, you sick bloody sex pests?'

Cheryl was becoming more angry now than uncomfortable, or concerned by the daggers, and chanced to step closer for a better look at the bizarre creatures.

The first one, who had a finer jaw and more of the silver hair, looked at the second, who was more rugged-looking, but had less hair and a harder, unshaven jawline. The powder left from the crusting flakes of their glamour lent them a ghostly pallor, almost like corpses made up for viewing.

'You look like bad cosplays for *Interview With The Vampire...*'

This anachronistic funereal effect was aided by the fact that they were both wearing new suits that didn't look right on them; that they'd just bought and worn straight out of the store. A new suit to be buried in, along with new, but generic lace-up shoes, with pale coloured work shirts, all off-the-rack from Suits-R-Us or something.

Someone had dressed them.

She didn't want to know their names, or anything about them, but she found immediately now that she thought of the darker-complexioned one with the strong salt and pepper hair and navy suit as Cruise; and the other, paler and ruddier, with a white five o'clock shadow in the dark-brown suit as Pitt.

'They're not coming closer…'

'They're talkin' about us!' Cruise sniggered.

'Coming…' Pitt grunted. 'We're not coming…'

'Not yet…' Cruise smiled.

'Jesus can't we stop them…?' Cheryl demanded.

The daggers glinted in the light.

'We don't know how strong they are…'

'You have to stop that…' Cheryl ordered firmly. 'It's inappropriate…' She thought she might as well give fair warning, in case this was all an illusion, or a trick, and they were genuinely mentally ill.

'So's being half-invisible when ya got no clothes on, fucking tease!'

The way Cruise accused her, he really seemed to believe he had a point.

'How old are they?' Cheryl asked, stepping back even further. The furiousness of their strokes had increased, and so had their personal energy somehow. They seemed bigger, and more furious. Cheryl was looking for scissors, or sharp objects in the corner of her eye on the cutting stations behind them. She saw that Karri was already wielding a pair of scissors, then she handed Cheryl a leather satchel filled with scissors of all lengths and size. Cheryl grasped a pair in each hand as Shirley took the satchel and armed herself in turn.

'Shirley; they've seriously been hanging around here since you worked here in the seventies?'

'I've been coming and going since my teens…' Karri confirmed.

'Coming and going!' Cruise laughed.

'In and out of the casino during the day; watching the women there too, I bet.' Shirley was disgusted. '…bloody awful place that it is. They bounce back and forth, we shoo them away, the casino security kicks them down the street… they watch women walk around, all day, and at night from the tram stop. But they look as old now as they did back then, when I was a kid? Dirty *Old* Pervs. Always Dirty, always Old.'

The howling wind rattled the door now, and the windows in the panes at the front.

Shirley edged closer to Cheryl as well, despite herself.

Now they were all wielding sharp, long, cutting scissors like daggers.

Suddenly Pitt grunted and seemed to ejaculate. Except, it shot right across the room as though a glob of porridge from a slingshot, right over Cheryl's shoulder, snapping into the mirror behind her with a sickening squelch. She had the sense to duck and another blast flew over her head, then she heard the mirror behind her sizzling, like acid had been splashed on it.

'They've upgraded, the *bastards*!'

# CHAPTER TWENTY-ONE:
# THE GRID



Because of the median strip, it was impossible for Parry to turn directly north, down North Terrace. Except that he did; immediately after starting the car, he u-turned to face the wrong way and then ran a red light as he drove, again the wrong way, into the intersection, in order to cross into the correct lane.

'Perks.'

Barker found that he had grasped his thighs very tightly for a second. The other weird thing was that this rare view of the Astral Gate intersection was framed by the shatter-web of damaged windscreen glass. He thought he saw something through it for a second; on the footpath, on the other side. He thought he saw Party Girl, and an old woman, embracing. He immediately shook off the spray of deep emotions, like a gush of seawater smashing high on tall rocks, that came with it.

'What happened to the window?'

'I was sent a message.'

'By?'

'I'll ask the questions, if you're not fussed, Mister Moon.'

There were flats and offices on the left, opposite the old Adelaide Hospital. People who had lived there forever, doctors who had practised there forever.

'Can you tell me anything else, Moon? Anything else you remember?'

Why the hell was Parry asking about all this?

Brixton and the limo were gone.

Mainwaring and Bach were sleeping.

He suddenly felt alone.

Why *now?*

Why was this happening *now?*

'Okay, I mean; look at this. The main river, the Torrens, is just down there. Here's the main hospital; the bloody Zoo's right behind it...' They crossed the next set of lights. 'That road to the right goes straight down to them. And here; the University of Adelaide, right alongside.'

'...doesn't your mother have something to do with one of them?'

'My mother... doesn't think that the astral plane is anything sane people talk about.'

'Understood. Less said the better...'

'And here; the Freemasons building; right opposite the Adelaide University. Freemasons, Luciferians, Light Seekers, Light Bearers, Light Workers? These are all mystical, secret-society terms. Colonel Light? Building the city on the centre of an astral grid?'

Parry pulled up when the next set of lights turned red.

'It sounds completely mental, Moon. But; when you take a guided tour... it does seem a bit...odd?'

'It's like; if everything in Sydney was in one group of blocks, right on Darling Habour.'

Parry accelerated as the lights turned green again.

'Look; the next block. The Art Gallery of South Australia, The South Australian State Museum, The State Library, all in a row, all crammed in here...'

The stately institutions were all housed in gorgeous, massive stone buildings of imperious design, and had decent-enough reputations, so Barker had heard anyway.

'All crammed in...' Parry noted. '...crammed in, between North Terrace...'

'...and the river.'

'Yeah... okay. I've never really thought about that before...'

They were almost halfway across the grid now; at least, the top of the grid.

Barker pointed through the spider-web windscreen again. '...and here, opposite, along here; the looming rear walls of the central Rundle department stores. All these buildings along here used to be the colonial warehouses. This is where the early horse and cart settlers dumped their cargos. Look...'

Barker pointed up and Parry slowed a little.

'...you can see; some of their names are still engraved, in stone, up high.'

Barker watched Parry's gaze find them out; establishment company names, or old store titles, all familiar to older Adelaideans, some of which were now the only thing that remained of those nominal endeavours. Early South Australia had been very wealthy, and very progressive; the local pioneer companies had long since blossomed into state institutions, grown enormous and moved house. Either that or been superseded by national concerns and corporate, or even global conglomerations. One or two had been lost in some of the major stock market crashes.

Parry accelerated to another set of lights where the intersecting road, a lane though to Rundle Mall on one side, but a major city-exit road to the right, dipped sharply on the northern side, again down to the Torrens River. It was bordered by the State Library on one side and a massive War Memorial on the other; this one to the ANZACS. The memorial was so huge; a massive arch featuring statues of angels and soldiers, that it also housed a shrine beneath it, large enough to walk through, and to accommodate all of the names of the South Australians who had died in the Great War.

'Great had a different meaning back then...' Barker uttered.

'Poor, brave bloody ANZACS...'

'Pull over. I want to show you something.'

'We're not going in there, are we? Because going into a crypt in a war memorial at midnight is probably something best left to the mystics, Moon. If you know what I mean...'

'No; just down here to the intersection...'

They walked further along North Terrace, a short block covered in high buildings on the southern side, and the wide, leafy canopy that covered the boulevard on the north. Barker stopped at the next intersection; the great city crossroads, where the regal width of King William Street, Light's intended major thoroughfare for the centre of the city, met with the strange, organic power of North Terrace.

'One of the few parts of Light's great design that actually stuck.'

The breeze was virtually Antarctic now. Barker closed his coat, and Parry buried his hands in his pockets again. North Terrace came to a peak here; it dipped down as it headed west, as did King William Street as it crossed North and headed further north. But south, into the centre of the city, King William Street was broad and level.

The traffic lights were all red; the walk lights were all red.

Everything seemed to have stopped.

'This was supposed to be the central, top-edge of the city. Not the main intersection. Look at this; have you ever really looked and considered this?'

'No...' Parry mused. 'But... I think I see what you mean.'

'Down there...' Barker thrust his left arm south. '...a massive Dreamtime energy core, the intended city centre; Tarndanyangga. Then he waved his right arm north, so that both his arms were extended in a cross formation; Parry's gaze followed. 'Along here; a fault line. Right down King William Street. Under that, and superimposed over it; one of the strongest ley lines in the whole world, straight in from some of the oldest earth on Earth, through Uluru; right down the guts of the great outdoors and the outback, through the Flinders Ranges, right down here to feed Tarndanyangga.'

Barker's arms dropped.

'But Moon; seriously? The Astral plane?' Parry turned to him, straight-faced, giving nothing. 'Most people take that idea as a complete joke. They would say that you must be *completely mental* to take something like that so seriously.'

It was as though Parry were testing him, to see where the limits of his insanity might lie.

'Celestial, astrological cycles take roughly two and a half thousand years each. We're going from one to another; right now. We're living through it. How much has changed in the past; just five years? Ten years? Or even; okay, one hundred? The Aborigines were here for more than forty thousand years. A lot more, some people think. If they say they were familiar with the Dreamtime, which is basically a massive section of the Higher Astral that they colonised, then I believe them.'

Parry looked around again.

Barker almost had him; he could sense it.

'People don't get it, Detective Inspector; the Indigenous People lived mostly in the astral. We totally destroyed that for them; made it virtually impossible for them to access it easily, within probably just one generation. We severed the link for them so effectively that they've pretty much forgotten it themselves now, forgotten it ever existed. The British Empire did it everywhere, because they learned it from the Romans, who did it to the Druidic and Celtic cultures right throughout Scotland and Ireland; and their equivalents through most of Europe. In every age, there is always an Empire. The Empire seeks to control. It takes power; physical, financial, spiritual, emotional; which equates to the military, banking, the churches and the culture, dominates them, and crushes anything that challenges that domination. But look; what's here? Do you see it? Detective Inspector, look; really look. It's all right here.'

III

There were major banks, all the way down King William, right up to Victoria Square. He was old enough to remember when there had been more, others; in different buildings along the street, but they had always been there, along King William, along the mystical power line. They might have just driven up past all the greater cultural centers of the city; but here, on the intersection…

'Banks. With Government House nestled on the north-east corner, hidden behind a high wall, covered on all sides, even behind it, by massive war memorials. The home of the Governor; the personification of the city's connection to Empire, and all the…'

'…all the blood sacrifices…' Parry uttered.

'Behind that, down the hill, down King William, just down there, the city's first military barracks; still there, perhaps just ceremonial now, but… still there. Opposite that, on the north-west corner… the bold-faced, dark-grey marble arches of the Houses of Parliament. And beside Parliament…'

… the Beast, into whose belly Barker was headed.

'The World Casino.' Parry shrugged. 'Who am I to disagree?'

'I'm starting to wonder.'

'I just want to know what's happening.'

'That's what I wanted to know. That's how I ended up at Bridger Mansion.'

IV

The World Casino had been created over an older casino, a landmark of somewhat long standing, that had been constructed within the abandoned office floors of the Adelaide Railway Station.

'I was supposed to meet Cheryl there…' Barker checked. '… three hours ago now. She's still not responding to my calls or texts.'

'Then how do you know?'

'Now that I'm here, I know.'

The Adelaide Railway Station Building was a beautiful but austere neo-classical construction, more than one hundred years old, not bad for a city of barely two centuries. It was essentially a giant rectangular slab of four high-ceilinged floors that overlooked most of the western side of North Terrace, down which it was conspicuously flanked, if not ominously supported by, a huge conference centre and several major hotels. Two of those had also been installed within the shells of other heritage buildings; the rest were overbearingly, transparently modern constructions, within massive, stark-glass shells. This imposing strip of cosmopolitan Australiana also ran directly between North Terrace and the Torrens River.

'The Torrens comes in from the Hills. Tributaries from the Mount Lofty Ranges. It's all local. All the local energy; pooled here, in the artificial lake.'

In fact, one of the major catchments flowed via almost the same route Barker had taken, intersecting somewhere back in the middle of the eastern suburbs. He had followed that, via the major gully and the major road, into the city from The Lion, as much as he had followed a road.

'Everything ends up here, eventually.'

The World Casino, and its adjacent hotels and conference centres, were in prime positions to exploit the views of the Torrens Lake. The Torrens was a minor river, it had to be said, but it had nevertheless been weired in the early twentieth century, a little further down its north-west trajectory, in order to form the Torrens Lake, by boosting the banks of the creek to support rowing students and tourist boats along the back of Adelaide University. The weir was small, and had been rebuilt several times before the engineers had been around long enough to get a hang of the flood seasons, but eventually they made one that had now held for almost a century.

Old Adelaide Gaol brooded nearby, hidden now in a small but high parklands gum forest, extremely haunted, and haunted by nobody real other than ghost tourists.

The artificial lake also ran right alongside the Festival Centre, which was located at the lowest north-west dip of King William Street, opposite the old barracks. The Festival Centre was an avant-garde construction which radiated white, angular seventies architecture as though via direct lineage to its thousand-times more iconic cousin, the Sydney Opera House. The lake also divided Adelaide City from its wealthy, conjoined suburb of North Adelaide, well within the parkland district, as it curved past the massive Adelaide Cathedral and the Adelaide Oval arena.

Barker's best clients, the classic wealthy widow types, came from the inner northern suburbs, just up there; the wealthiest of the new warehouse millionaires had built mansions at the top of the northern incline, to look down on their stores from on-high, over the glorious parklands and the shining new lake and river.

And the grid.

The simple, square, Adelaide grid.

You could not, Barker knew, absolutely not, get lost in Adelaide.

And yet, seven years ago, he had become lost.

Or rather, he had lost.

Lost everything.

Maybe that's why he'd chosen the casino when he'd first arrived back here again, six weeks ago?

The chance to lose everything again.

Almost everything had changed since those early days of his life, but really, nothing had changed. Only since they'd built the casino, had… something else settled in.

In Barker's childhood, in the eighties, Adelaide had been virtually the same as it had ever been; Adelaide Oval had once been just a humble sports field for Adelaide's bygone tribal football, cricket and tennis scenes. Now it was a massive, all-purpose, world-class arena with a lighting grid easily visible from Mount Lofty, and curved, silver, Spielberg-like stands that hovered ominously over all the views from North Terrace, from the street to the conference rooms, like the occupying mothership of some presumably-benevolent race of alien overlords. The Corporate Empire had indeed invaded, but it had been some time in the early new millennium, when Barker had been preoccupied with his occult pursuits, either deep indoors or far out, so that by the time he had seen the new grandstand, and that things had so radically changed, it really had felt as though the city had been invaded.

A foot bridge had been constructed over the Torrens at the bequest of the casino's new owner, so that potential punters, after a day attending sports, and drinking, could easily, directly, and unthinkingly pour themselves over the river, over the bridge and… see what else Adelaide, and the evening itself, might have in store. The fact that the bridge led all but directly into the shining rear entrance of the casino… was just happy coincidence. Just another organic accident, the kind of which Adelaideans were by now so thoroughly accustomed.

In fact, all things had almost always led to the Adelaide Railway Station… which was now, essentially, simply an adjunct to the World Casino. And so, now, all things led there. The Railway Station was a genuine terminus, a fairly rare feature in a major city, but here all lines into Adelaide ended within the city, rather than passing through, and this had been yet another contributing factor in the strange ascendency of North Terrace. Having nowhere else to go, the incoming farmers had followed the lead of the merchants from the port, and unloaded their carriages of transported livestock and goods directly into the North Terrace warehouses and markets; one each at the East and West Terrace corners.

All energies coming in… remained, until they were spent, and the carriages were released once more.

Back in the car, Barker looked at the giant brownstone construction, easily visible down the sloping gradient from the intersection of North and King William, as he and Parry waited again for the lights to change, surrounded by almost nothing but white cabs. Now the building was terminal in yet another way; a heritage listing had made it immovable, irreplaceable. The Station Building would exist there until it died there, when it crumbled and fell to dust, condemned and unrestorable.

v

'I see it, Moon.'

'You do?'

Parry glanced back down North Terrace; east, from where they'd come.

'Culture; all down there. Government; right here. Financial; just up there. The casino, the oval, the arts… all there; all here on the centre of the top of the grid. Where the river crosses the ley line.'

It was as though Parry had been having the same thoughts, or had been tuning in on Barker's; he was perplexed now.

He was in.

Parry suddenly turned south.

'And right alongside; everything else.'

They were almost there, on the bad side of town now. The notorious Hindley Street; the direct, western, re-named extension of Rundle, one checker-square south-west across King William. Hindley was that place every minor city required, for better or worse; a sprawling patchwork of concrete car parks, themed bars, renovated colonial fire traps, and every variety of strip club. It was the kind of place that (despite claims of success at least once a generation to the contrary) could never, ever be 'cleaned up'.

Barker was starting to remember more now; still not enough, but there were other kinds of dens down there, besides those of everyday, everynight iniquity. Card dens, gang dens, drug dens, but also magic dens, witch dens, dens of sorcery and the dark arts. Certain so-called crime bosses from certain so-called cultural or ethnic enclaves were known to conspire and consult in the upper rooms of certain eternally open night clubs that, if assessed, had been serving the same purpose since the colony's inception.

Sure, some of this might have been urban legend, or mythological conjecture, but some of it was just pure fact. In the ensuing centuries, and despite all attempts to correct the situation, the other side of the same, grid-long street; Rundle, had been consistently pumped and nourished, and had quickly grown and become valuable. This eastern end, which led out into the wealthier suburbs along the foothills, had in the nineteenth century developed into a centre of music halls, arts and café culture. But the western end, leading out to the poorer suburbs, had been the complete reverse. Crossing King William Street, from the end of Rundle Mall, over to the start of Hindley, was like flipping a switch. In colonial times, the western end had become a thriving hub of burlesque halls, gambling and drug culture, and a general wellspring for all things illicitly procured by night. In modern times, it was the modern equivalent; the street where all things that had once been procured illicitly by night were now, more or less, procured quite openly, and open all hours.

Directly across from the World Casino there were side-streets that led through to Hindley, and more, further down, right down to the other edge of the grid, to West Terrace itself. Populating these side-streets were a few too many cheap jewellers, pawn brokers and duty free shops. Side-streets whose activity had eventually sounded the death knell to several major cinemas that had downturned after the e-boom and never recovered, especially when the level of activity required to make them seem alive and thriving and safe had dropped past the point where the junkies, drunks, procurers and the general parade of street people had become all too conspicuous. The empty shells of the crumbling urban cinema caverns still remained there; they were still used, still managed as private stages, if you knew who to talk to. Sometimes they served as altars.

Hindley Street hosted four or five good pubs, and several more dives, a dozen nightclubs, two or three good restaurants, some yiros and noodle and burger bars, and more cafes than could possibly be making profit; all housed in the shells of ancient buildings that had served essentially the same function since the dawn of electricity. And some before that. Behind, between and under them were the dens of crack and crime, brothels for every social tier and fetish, along with art installations, impromptu happenings, creative improvisations, and if you really wanted to know; guided walking tours of only the most haunted hot spots and gut-wrenching murder scenes.

'There's something here, Moon. I've lived here my whole life; but I've never…'

'That's the thing. You never notice.'

'But there's something else here, isn't there?'

Barker knew what he meant. All of that seediness, and a century-plus of layered vice; the way it all culminated to focus upon this intersection, where it all terminated and collided and unpacked and separated; where Parliament sat, arts were displayed and performances offered, where the river flowed through, the lake-surface glistened and reflected, and the Governor was housed; where the cardinal directions of the city's heart and soul were defined, split and separated, where the raw material that had created this weird but structured city had been dispensed and dispersed; spontaneously? Organically?

Barker wasn't so sure.

From here, immense wealth had inevitably been created. But there was something about the way the city's chosen identity and shape, albeit apparently in essence democratically arrived upon; the way it was broken off from the intent of its parent, its architect, right here to form a new, improvised off-centre hub, was, fundamentally…

'It's been managed, hasn't it?'

'I think that's what I thought.'

Parry nodded.

'There's a border here; it's undeniable. A powerful division, not just between the dark and the light, the crude and the refined, the yin and yang, and the id and the ego, but more so of the *suits*… the elemental forces and the powers they invoke.'

'But if someone was looking for power…?'

'Why not let the city remain on the ley line?'

'Well; that, I assume, channels more power than anything.'

'If you put the right symbols there, absolutely. So; why would someone want to do this?'

Had something else been here, perhaps? Something pre-existing? Somehow built upon the basic mystical principles that Barker had once known well…?

Was there a reason for this?

Not just North, South, East and West, but Earth, Air, Water and Fire… and more? There was time here, sacred passing, and art, for millennia, along the banks of the river. And then, something else again, something Barker had forgotten.

*People had always come here…*

He had been aware, very aware of this, once.

'All through Europe, when the Romans, then the British or whoever conquered a tribe or a people, they rebuilt the temples of their own Gods in the sacred places of the vanquished. People say; that's a powerful symbol of conquest. But they could just as easily have burned the places to the ground; salted the Earth. They could have built other temples, in other places, to other Gods. Within a generation, nobody would have remembered. Why didn't they?'

'You're going to say it's because those places were all on the natural energy lines of the Earth, aren't you? They were all something like Tarndanyangga.'

Barker smiled. 'All the churches of our major religions are built on the sacred places of the conquered indigenous because the upper echelons of the conquering races knew; they have always known. There is power in the Earth, and with the right symbols, the right buildings, the right mental focus condensed in the right places, it can be exploited; to control, and to rule.'

Parry shivered.

'Look up there; over the Torrens, on the other side of the King William Street Bridge. St Peters Cathedral. Up higher, into North Adelaide; Baptists, on top of the hill. And look; what lines up along King William, all the way up? The giant Church, the giant Sports Arena, the giant Casino; with the Arts sort of, shoved in, behind Parliament House. From the top of the hill up there, all the way down, coming in from the north, they look like temples, all in a row. Massive, fuck-off temples. Drive up there and walk down some time; see if they don't. Virtually nothing, nothing significant happens in this city that does not happen right here. And there's one last thing. What's at the base of the cross?'

'It is…' Parry nodded. 'It's a bloody cross, isn't it? With the crossing over, right here.'

'And the base of the cross is Victoria Square. And you know what's in Victoria Square, in the massive energy centre?'

'Aside from the Central Market? Of course I know what's there; the law courts, and police headquarters…'

'And; the main Catholic Church.'

Parry nodded.

'Lord help me, Moon. It's late and I'm tired, but… does all this really add up?'

'Adelaide Railway Station is, and always has been, a terminus. They built a casino on it, right next to the Houses of Parliament. They built a bridge – from the sports arena – across the river – to the casino. There's very little else so blatant in the western world. This city is dark, Parry. It's got a dark reputation, it's got a dark, corrupted heart over a massive, massive natural energy line. It's not enough that most western governments have legalized the two most noxious, lowest-vibrating drugs on the planet, and demonized all the others. It's not enough that the lowest vibration activity – gladiatorial sport – is the most promoted. You mix that, with alcohol, and channel the intended victims into a casino; that is evil. That is a city that had made itself into a machine of total, blind mesmerism, of misdirection and marks; it has become an evil city. All under the shadow of one of the world's most admired Cathedrals, in the self-proclaimed City of Churches. That is what it has taken whatever it is that lies at the heart of that building; or this hilltop, or that lake; whatever the hell it is, to build a spiritual trap that holds an entire city hostage, holds an entire state government hostage; and causes nothing, in the end, but pain, and torment, and misery, in the guise of entertainment.'

'What do you think it is?'

'I think it's a demon. I think it's a demon that waited a very, very long time, for the Indigenous Natives who controlled the Astral dimension here, for forty thousand years, to be displaced, so it could… I don't know.'

'Wait; you don't know?'

'I know; I remember, that I wanted to know, why it makes such a difference for all the energy to be centred here. But it cost me. I went to Bridger Mansion, to find out. To ask something; something there… to get the answers? I don't know. Whatever it was, it nearly killed me. And whatever it was… it wants me to go back.'

Parry stared at him.

'You really don't remember; do you Moon?'

'No, I don't.'

Parry nodded. 'No, I don't mean that. I mean, you don't remember me, do you?'

'We've met?'

'We've met several times.'

'We have?'

'I was the one, Moon.'

Barker's heart started thumping.

'The one – what?'

'The one who found you.'

'*Found* me?'

'I found you there, on the floor, in all the blood. I was the first cop on the scene, at Bridger Mansion.'

# CHAPTER TWENTY-TWO: ACTIVATION

'Retreat!' Cheryl backed right off. 'Upstairs!'

They ran quickly up the steps along the sidewall to the mezzanine, but the sex pests stayed down, just staring up at them. Now the glands on their cheeks had started puffing, sending up little shots of the hot, white fluid that hissed against the balcony rails. Some splattered through onto the floor in front of them.

'I can't believe this!'

'Why send them? Who sent them?'

'The grid, child!' Shirley insisted. 'Can't you hear? The grid is being activated!'

'The grid?'

'Well you didn't think it was going to be Christmas Lights in Victoria Square, did you? It has to be energized; natural forces must come to bear!'

As though to confirm it, they heard the wind pound into the window, like a person banging with their fists. Then suddenly, the sound of the wind actually was accompanied by a person banging with their fists. They heard the door open, then slam closed, but in the intervening seconds, they made out a howling blast.

'Shirl! Frey!'

Shirley rolled her yes. 'Oh fuck, it's Candle!'

'Candle?'

'One of the coven; she's probably come to make sure we're all okay – ' Then Karri gave an almighty shriek. 'Candle, stay back!'

'Karri!?'

'That woman is in great danger...' Cheryl looked at them both. 'Do you two have powers? Given that I don't know what mine are?'

'Can't you feel anything?' Shirley demanded.

'Well, I feel lighter, but heavier at the same time; just, *odd* really…'

Candle cried out again, but the two sex pests ignored her.

'Is Shirley with you!? Is the new girl there!? Is she dangerous!?'

'Don't come any closer, Candle!' Karri leaned over the balcony and bellowed. 'We've got an infestation of weird mystical sex pests!'

'Is there anything?' Shirley demanded of Cheryl again.

'Well,' Cheryl shrugged. 'I don't seem to care, not that much, that I don't have any clothes on in public. That's pretty much a first.'

'Candle! Get – help!' Karri leaned back in and turned to Shirley. 'You think she heard?'

Shirley was examining Cheryl.

'Well it's not really like you're naked; the reflection, the fluid quality of your skin provides for… well, more than modesty; you're more… *covered* than anything. What is that, anyway, on you?'

Cheryl tested.

'May I?' Karri asked.

Cheryl sighed. 'Okay.'

Karri placed her fingers over the top of Cheryl's closest breast. Cheryl thought it odd, but clearly Karri didn't. She almost caressed it.

'I'd almost say…'

'That'll do, Karri.'

Karri removed her fingers.

Cheryl finished for her. 'It's water, isn't it? Somehow? The missing water from my body, if you know what I mean? Somehow? Maybe?'

'I've seen weirder, to be honest…'

All three at once looked down at Cruise and Pitt. They were looking up.

They'd ceased to work themselves, now they were just staring.

Listening.

'…I think I preferred them the other way.'

'I'm really quite thirsty, now I think of it… I have been all along.'

Cruise and Pitt raised their hands and the glands on their wrists went off, spraying the white goo like one hard pump of a decent water rifle. Four globs impacted with the edge of the balcony, and it started immediately to sizzle. One lump hit especially hard and sprayed higher, and a few light droplets landed on the back of Karri's hand.

'Ow!'

Three spots on the back of her hand turned immediately a bright, scalded red, then they too started to sizzle. Cheryl grabbed her arm and pulled her toward a tap, twisting the cold water on with almost supernatural speed.

'Wait…!'

Karri tried to turn back. 'I quite like them now…'

Cheryl froze.

'What?!'

'I mean… come on.' Karri smiled. 'They're very handsome…'

Cheryl reclaimed a firmer grasp on Karri's hand, but as she drew it to the running tap she noticed that the redness had abated; in fact, it was almost gone.

'That doesn't feel too bad…' Karri told her softly. '…that actually feels quite good…'

'Stop that! What does!?'

Cheryl turned and saw Shirley, standing openly by the ruins of the mezzanine edge.

'Ooh, I see what you mean…'

The whole of both hands, and the side of her face was glowing red, sizzling and burning.

'No!'

Cheryl ran up to her as the sex pests puffed their weird glands with even more force, summoning even more goo, then dropped their daggers and raised their hands and shot poisonous acidic strings of white fluid toward the balcony. She saw the terrible white net as it gushed toward them, as it hit the horizontal metal bars and they steamed abruptly, hissed and started to melt as the rail sizzled and dripped acid. She grabbed Shirley and spun her away, instinctively protecting her from the spray, then felt the stinging lash of the mass across her back like a cat o'nine-tails. She cried out, more in alarm than actual pain, and under that heard the edge of the balcony fall and crash to the floor behind her, as the rest of the tiles and concrete and steel rods continued to sizzle and burn. Then she pushed Shirley again, addle-eyed, backward toward the washing stations.

'Not her you bloody dickheads!' Someone shouted from the floor.

Karri had the water running at the wash basin, but the two of them were quick to realize that wherever Cheryl touched them, their burns healed. Wordlessly, Cheryl applied her hands to Shirley's face.

'Where did those two nice men go?'

'It's some kind of neurotoxin…' Karri uttered. 'Like a roofie love potion… instantaneous on contact with the goo.'

Cheryl glanced. 'Chemistry?'

'Potions. Stuff acts differently under magic, so it's not technically chemistry 'cos no trained chemist would –'

'She's right…' Shirley snapped out of it. 'Good Lord how I wanted those boys to take me in their arms. Let's look at your back.'

Karri quietly assessed her, up and down.

'There's nothing,' Karri confirmed. 'She's immune.'

The same person shouted from the floor again. 'Working it out at last!?'

'Candle?' Karri called back.

'It's started!' The woman proclaimed, with a hint of unnecessary drama. 'The storm is here!'

Cheryl still couldn't see her over the edge of the balcony.

'What the hell? Who is this now?'

'It's Candle…' Shirley sounded nauseous. 'She's with them…'

Candle called up again. 'There is no Them; unless you mean They; and I am not with them!'

'What the fuck is she talking about?' Cheryl demanded.

'Cheryl Equinox; I have come to make you an offer. You have been charged by higher forces yet to be identified. Join our side in the war and you will live. Refuse now and you will be considered our enemy.'

'Our enemy? Whose 'our'? What the hell is going on with you Candy?'

Cheryl hadn't yet heard Karri quite so angry, so angry she stepped forward a bit to see over.

'Don't!'

Cheryl rushed down three of the eight steps before the sex-pests could splatter fire once more. They stared at her, Cruise looking angry now, and not too far from terrifying; Pitt's dark gaze filled an earnest but spine-chilling stare of longing.

'You're Candle?'

It was clear to see that Candle, presumably Candace, had gained her series of nicknames from her big-hair mass of wiry, true-orange locks, and her brightly-colored dress-sense; layered scarves and skirts and frilly shirts of pink and white and lavender for this evening.

Cheryl turned to the other woman who had entered silently alongside her.

'And so who's this?'

Karri remained glaring down.

'That's fucking Feather!'

Shirley was at her side now.

'Feather!? You!?"

Cheryl thought Karri was going to sprout fangs and jump down on them both.

'You stop practicing with me, and go practice with her, and now you do this!?'

Feather was very pretty, with tightly-curled shoulder length black hair and a moderate goth look, with torn black jeans and high black boots, and many layers of vests and open-shirts, black and grey, along with silver jewelry. 'I've been practicing to do this for ages, Karr!' She didn't sound too sorry. 'It just became obvious you weren't going to do it with me!'

Cheryl considered calmly. 'Does practicing mean what I think it means?'

'It doesn't mean doing gay sex,' Karri insisted. 'If that's what you think it means.'

'Doesn't it?' Feather arched a thinned, archly black eyebrow over the shining whites of her eyes.

'Does it?' Shirley was nonplussed.

'Not to your generation, old crow! And not to the new energies; to them sexuality is fluid, it doesn't matter!'

'What?' Shirley spat down. 'Fluid like these pathetic cum-sacks? Get over yourself sister, you little shitster hipster ! I've seen you out of those rags and you're not half the princess you want us to believe! Remember who gave you that look in the first place – twelve years ago!'

'Screw you, Sybil Fuckty! And while we're at it, if practicing *doesn't* mean gay sex to our kind, Karri, why did you keep trying to touch my tits?'

'I don't!' Karri gasped. 'I didn't!'

Cheryl heard herself speak softly. 'You kind of touched mine, Karri. I mean; not that I minded. I just thought, if it's not the first time, maybe it's a thing? But really, I didn't mind.'

'You didn't? I mean; no I didn't!'

'You do do that quite a bit actually, sweetie love.'

'Shirley! Really? I just…'

'Hah!' Candle gave a cackle through her slender, virtually albino throat. 'You need to sort that shit out before you step outside, Karri! It's not a place out there for magical people who aren't sure about who, or what they are; not anymore!'

Cheryl held up her hands.

'Okay, I seem to have booned into the middle of some fairly

personal pre-existing tension here that I may or may not have inadvertently become a part of ...' She took another two steps. She could see that the two sex-pests had been drinking in all of this lovely feminine sexual tension. '...and I feel it's very important at this juncture to state very clearly, for the record, that although you two up there at least seem like very nice people, I am in no way affiliated with any kind of...'

She threw the scissors, hard and with a solid arc, right at Cruise.

They impacted, a direct hit right in the weird gland under his throat. To the shock of everyone he gurgled and swayed around for a second, but then wrenched the scissors out and seemed instantly to recover.

The two of them attacked her in tandem. Cheryl nimbly missed most of their outpourings as she dashed back up the stairs, their sickening expulsions splurging not only from their wrists now, but also from their lower-throats and the sides of their temples. The blasts that did impact with her however seemed to hiss and bubble and evaporate, all in the space of a second or two, over the surface of her seemingly impervious skin.

Shirley and Karri were crouching at the back of the mezzanine and Cheryl dived to cover them, her arms spread, as a huge bite-like portion of the concrete floor sizzled, decayed and vanished behind them.

'No, no, no!' Candle screeched, completely dissatisfied. 'There aren't enough of you! Where are the others? I was told there would be more of you! Much more!'

Cheryl spoke quickly at Shirley

'Now the stairs are destroyed, they can't get up here; but that webbing; they're getting stronger. The more you argue with Candle; when we fight or get emotional, it powers them, it turns them on!'

Crouching beside her, loosely protected under one of her arms, Karri screwed up her face and growled.

'They're like Spider-Man Sex-Pests and we're their friendly

neighborhood Fuck-Flies!'

'That was a stupid risk…' Shirley scolded.

'A blob hit me before and I didn't feel anything. I don't think they can get me; at least not just two. But I'm starting to feel a little muddle-headed… so bloody thirsty.' Cheryl's tongue was smacking as she spoke. 'The boon; it's like a hangover.'

Yet even as she did speak, something glistening and snakelike streamed down from the basin above. It startled them all and they gasped.

Shirley snapped, almost angry. 'What the bloody…?'

The levitating snake of water came down from the tap in the basin above.

Cheryl glanced up.

It was full, but just enough so that the thin string, in a beautiful, glistening swirl, could spiral down to the ground.

Shirley hummed thoughtfully.

'Do you see? Do you see, girl?'

'Of course I –'

Karri put a hand on her shoulder. 'No, Cheryl, see; it flows magically, but it flows down. It's one of the first simple rules; water flows down, it takes the path of gravity, the path of least resistance; it finds a way.'

The watery string floated in the air before her, just above her head, pooling into a central pattern, like a wide corkscrew, then slowly increasing in size like a deliberately unraveled mat.

'Hold out your hand, woman; beneath the flow.'

Cheryl obeyed and the water turned instantly to her palm, but did not break and splash. Instead it continued to pool, using her hand as a receptacle. Cheryl leaned in and pursed her lips. The water kept flowing down her wrists, on the outside of her skin, but she did not feel wet, even as she could feel some of it being absorbed into her body, through her skin. The tendril of water flowed down to her elbow, down under her arm, down her side and over her stomach, downward all the way. It ran down her buttocks and thighs, between her legs, to her knees, where it again flowed, as just water, onto the floor in front of her.

She inched in and sipped again from her open palm. When her lips made contact it was as though there was a thin membrane around the liquid, and as she tipped her palm and drank more deeply, the water remained. The stream from the tap had ceased now, but despite this, the membrane's flow did not break.

Cheryl heard a sigh, and saw that Karri was having some kind of rapturous flight, just watching her drink from her palm. She moved her hand to her, offering her some, and Karri made a light squeal from deep in her throat. At first she thought that she was frightening her, but then she realized; Karri really did have a full-on crush on her, and this was… turning her on? Wow. How did she feel about that? Cheryl quickly considered and realized, bizarrely, that out of everything that had happened this evening, that might have been at once the most challenging and yet the most comforting surprise to have occurred. Karri sipped, and for a moment Cheryl thought she might cry.

'Are you okay, kid?' Shirley enquired. 'It's like you've never seen sprite magic before.'

'Yep…' Karri squeaked.

'Sprite?'

'Mermaid, nymph, selkie, siren… something with a water origin. Water sprite or water nymph I'm betting.'

Cheryl turned from them and looked to the mirror. She could see there, and just on herself, that her body was now covered in some kind of tight, thin, silver-white and half-reflective liquid.

'When did that happen?'

'Right when you decided to renovate the salon.'

'Huh.' Cheryl stood. 'Stay here.'

'As opposed to…?'

Most of the mezzanine mirror remained, and although partially cracked, she could see in a larger section that the liquid layer was bound to her, apparently, by its own volition, and her own increasingly conscious need to maintain modesty. The new outer-layer covered her feet, ended at her wrists and high under her neck, and seemed to almost match the almost crystalline translucency of her hair.

'It's like a wetsuit.'

She turned and went to the edge of the mezzanine.

The four of them were standing, looking up, waiting.

Cheryl spoke calmly.

'You can't touch me.'

Candle shrugged. 'We can touch your new friends.'

'But I can't touch you!' Karri shouted. 'Yes I think we've established that!'

'You're getting obsessed, sweetie love.' Shirley smiled sympathetically, then shouted into the salon. 'We were your friends too until this morning, you magical munter!' Then she turned back to Karri. 'Quite liked her this morning. Just goes to show.'

'And we can touch you, you coven snob cow, when the others get here!'

Karri pulled a face. 'Not liking her so much this evening though, huh?'

Cheryl was listening; they'd been friends, all of them.

This is what the sociopaths did; they broke up groups.

'Stay down there; we'll sort this, okay?'

Cheryl turned back to the newcomers, but suddenly the physical shape of the two sex-pests shifted as they shook, and their skin bloated out.

'Jesus!' Cheryl stepped back, staring down.

Shirley and Karri immediately disobeyed and leaped up to the edge to see down.

Cruise and Pitt were gurgling, re-grasping their erect dicks. But even as they kept grasping, the flesh of their whole bodies seemed instantly to turn inside out, bursting and ripping their clothes, as their weird glands exploded white puss all over. As she had suspected, the glands had been present all over their bodies, and as the goo blew out and streamed down their skins, all at once as though their entire system of internal organs had been producing it and storing it, they were suddenly gushing and flowing like a couple of man-sized white-chocolate fountains, until they were completely covered, like absurdly high, misshapen wedding cakes. Their feet hissed as they moved, shifting on the tiled floor, searching for stability, then they were still, right in front of the exit to the street.

Although Shirley and Karri had crept up to see, Candle and Feather had backed right away, toward the inner exit that led toward the haunted shaft.

'Those creepy, sticky little fuckers…' Shirley gasped. 'All this time coming into some kind of sick gestation; all those years – bloody decades! Right before our eyes!'

Karri was aghast. 'Why give a boon to those creeps…?'

'Because it wasn't, was it?' Shirley snapped. 'Either the ones who got it, they took care of, or they're hiding them somewhere, or maybe they stopped it; or maybe they found a way to steal it? Or maybe they *are* the ones who got it!? Maybe, the energies are changing and they're not so easy to read any more…? Maybe, this is the new energy, and these are the new rules…!?'

'Idiots!' Candle yelled.

'It's nothing to concern you, Shirley!' Feather drawled, loudly. 'It's time for you to leave the board and return home!'

'How *bloody* dare you!'

'We control these creatures, and believe me; they will keep coming, and coming, and coming, until you are dead, dead, dead.'

'You're really going to kill us, Feather?'

Her tone suddenly changed, and was much lighter.

'Look, it's okay, Karr. In the end, we all get reincarnated anyway. On the other side, this all seems like a play, like a script we were improvising!' Cheryl was amazed at how she could suddenly sound so scholarly, so reasonable. She was a total sociopath, remorselessly persuading them into their untimely deaths. 'Our master says there's too much old magic in the city, it all needs to go; all the old sorcerers, all the old witches; a whole generation needs to be sacrificed; they all need to go to make way for –'

'What is this?' Shirley spat. 'Mystical Marxism?! Who is your new master? Harry Pol Potter!?' Shirley cackled. 'You don't know what's going to come out, do you?' She cackled again. 'Out of those things? Those massive jism jars!'

Cheryl was thirsty still. She looked down. The two hideous white-slime snowmen just stood there, almost completely blocking the exit. But Candle and Feather could still flee, if they wanted. As she thought, and watched them, Cheryl held out her hand. It was almost like reaching for a cigarette. It was instinct; almost involuntary.

A stream of water, just a short one, splashed into her hand and held in a solid pool. It had come from nowhere, but everywhere, and without thinking, without second thought, as though part of some unconscious ritual she had been doing forever, she brought her hand to her mouth, curved in an open fist as though she had just cracked open a fresh bottle of vodka, and gulped it back. She didn't waste a drop; just three straight belts, and then her arm dropped to her side, and she made a sound as though an alcoholic, home from work, sated after a long day's drought.

'You're part of the cycle now, darling heart...' Shirley offered. 'We need to find out exactly...'

'They don't wanna go back out...' Cheryl reiterated.

She moved to the edge of the ruined concrete extension and found the edge of the central wall that separated the entrance to the tea room, then placed her left hand on it, the edge of her left foot, and stepped off. It was as though she had connected to a pole, as though she were a rivulet of water, and she slid effortlessly down to the floor to a solid footfall.

She felt the water within her hand and on her fingertips, and along the side of her foot; all through her body, electric and channeled, the natural flow of the revived energies within her rebooted body. The water; the flow of water, the downward path of least resistance, the force of gravity. And yet she could feel; there was more. She could do, she suspected, whatever water did, in some way, shape or form, but she would have all the vulnerabilities as well. And this was just the start.

She stood there now before them, confidently; invisible hair, white eyes and silver wetsuit. She noticed the ceremonial daggers that the sex pests had dropped. They would do nicely. Candle and Feather had forgotten them.

'You could leave…' Cheryl figured. '…but you went that way, toward the room; you'd rather take your chances with the angry spirits, climb down and go out through the sewer, than face whatever's out there; or, coming that way, in here…'

Candle and Flower looked back and forth, to both exits, then stepped back and watched Cheryl. Cheryl looked back up at Shirley.

'Yes…' Shirley smiled.

Cheryl turned back and pointed to the traitors.

'You're scared to go back outside.'

She moved quickly past them, through the door to the kitchenette, then further down the thin corridor to the haunted shaft, pushing the door. Her bare left foot was slightly wet still from the slide down; she had collected water from the air to do that, as she had when she had taken her shots. Or had it been something stronger than just water? She had made it, with her mind, and consumed it, in mime at least, like some kind of fiery alcohol, to give her strength.

She muttered to herself.

'It's still magic, still symbol…'

'You can't go in there!' The call came from behind.

'…I just drank rocket fuel, to give me courage.'

It was freezing; her thin layer of… whatever it was; her own water? Spellbound somehow? In some rudimentary unconscious-command fashion? Whatever it was, it seemed to find and hold the temperature. It didn't seem to care that it was freezing cold outside and bitterly chill from up the shaft.

She stopped and focused on her left foot.

The water that had remained there vanished.

No; still there. In some way, shape or form. Just reclaimed.

Into the layer, maybe? The wetsuit?

She stepped out into the shaft and let the door swing closed behind her, even as she heard her two enemies bringing up the rear. She switched on the hanging light and walked out halfway along the wooden balcony, the wood creaking beneath her cold, bare feet. At this thought, she felt a padding close involuntarily over the soles of her feet, another closed layer of liquid molecules, or something, but it wasn't enough; she was still too weak after the change, her personal energy too low to charge herself, to warm herself; to tell, to charge the suit to do that.

Still too weak for self-preservation.

Sheesh.

The door opened and Candle walked in, following her as though Cheryl had defied her not to. Feather remained by the door behind her, propping it open and watching her.

Like a proper little instigator…

Candle opened with bluster. 'What the fuck are you doing in here…!?'

But she'd left too long a pause for it to be even remotely effective. Still, Cheryl was about to answer, and it would have been good; but a howling, freezing cold wind billowed up from the bottom of the shaft at a terrible velocity, seemingly connected to the storm outside. Cheryl shivered so hard as it passed that she thought she might simply drop to her knees and topple; plunge to her death down the shaft. But she didn't; she held herself, braced herself in a stand, and ground her jaw to stop shivering.

She searched, but there seemed no help at all from the angry spirits, who remained right in the middle, just under the swinging bulb. It seemed not at all to matter that she was on the right side of things. They were still explosively furious, still a cauliflower mass of rueful, resentful demand for vengeance on a world that had a century-since passed them by, a world they had no place in and could not now or ever again enter in order to gain any genuine recompense.

'You think you can escape down there?' Cheryl demanded. 'When that shit in there comes out?'

She stared at Candle, pointlessly demanding an answer, trying to figure out through the cold why she had come into the freezing cold shaft of horrors in the first place. Only then did she see, did she realize where Candle had truly earned her name. There was a faint shimmering around her. She was generating heat; heat from the air, from around her, through her body. Cheryl could see it; she could tell.

They were the same, kind of, and might have been complimentary, maybe, once, if… if only if…

All that stuff Shirley had implied.

But they weren't.

That hadn't happened.

She hadn't stayed, gotten to know her, been part of the coven…

'Your Master; he's lying. He'll make you die for him. If reincarnation was supposed to be part of all this; if it were real and we remembered it, then the whole of third density would be different. It wouldn't really exist. But it isn't, and it does. Your Master. He's fucking with you. If you're so obsessed with the game and the grid and the rules; play them! Ignore him! Read and obey!'

'Master Shilling says – '

'Master Shilling?'

'Come with us…' Feather offered dryly from the door. 'Meet him. He has such amazing – '

'Fenner…?'

'You've… heard of him?'

'Fenner… *fucking*… Shilling…?'

# CHAPTER TWENTY-THREE:
DEN

I

Parry drove over King William, and a little further down North, then turned into the open lane that led to the casino. On the corner was the gaping entrance to the walkway decline, a clean, gleaming, concrete and marble tunnel leading down to the trains, and the eight terminals, and the station proper. It looked sterile, cold and empty; most of the departing trains would be empty at this time on an Adelaide Tuesday night.

There were only a few cabs lining the casino entrance, a little further down the open alley, down the end of which the white angles of the Festival Centre loomed, behind it the gladiatorial base of the alien overlords, above that; a starless, cloudy sky over the stately homes and Cathedral spires of North Adelaide.

Parry turned a circle; there were only two security guards out front, and… yep, a reader, hanging back in the shadows.

'I'll wait on the street over there. If you find your friend…'

Parry handed him a card.

'Put it in now.'

Barker obeyed, entering the number into his phone and calling Parry. Parry's phone vibrated silently.

'Nicely done, Moon. Now we're engaged. Don't tell your girlfriend.'

'She's not my girlfriend.'

'I didn't mean her.'

Barker stared at him.

'I'm trusting you, Moon. To do what's right. The night's not over and neither is our historical discussion.'

'I don't want to know, Parry. I don't want to know what was there when you found me. I can't face that again; I've spent years –'

'I know Moon. I understand; I have seen trauma before. But at some point we will need to discuss the true history of Bridger Mansion; whether you are ready to deal with it or not. Now, I can arrest you, but I haven't. I am hoping we can get to the bottom of the Bridger Mansion incident, and lay to rest the souls of the poor bastards who got caught up in it, at some point. Maybe not tonight. But soon. I trust we are of like mind when it comes to that hope, Mister Moon.'

Barker smiled. 'Well, Chief Inspector Parry; we can all hope.'

Parry seemed to like that response.

'Good luck, Moon.'

'I appreciate the sentiment. But please don't wish me luck, Detective. Luck has precious little to do with anything, especially in a place like this.'


II


As Parry drove off to find a park from which he could no doubt observe both main exits, Barker stood outside the primary entrance and waited for a second, taking several deep breaths. His inner voice had divided again.

Don't think about it – *it's starting again* – don't think about it – *but it's starting again…*

He knew. This sort of thing, this scale, had happened before.

Beings. Out of nowhere.

Forces of nature responding to warped abominations.

Brixton the Rock God.

Stopping time and giving him a basic refresher course…?

And now he was remembering the city. More than remembering.

He was feeling the city. Sensing its energy and history.

Feeling the Ox again, worse than ever.

Going a little mad, and spilling his guts to someone who could have him locked up. Out in Yatala Prison, or Glenside Hospital, for the loonies.

*Luck has nothing to do with things, Barker…*

He'd heard Heather say it many times.

'Least of all here…' Barker uttered again, this time to himself as he crossed the open alley.

Most times Barker came through the side door, or even through the cafe. Tonight though, he had wanted to enter the casino proper, via the front door. Casinos were designed to be easy to find, easy to enter, but difficult, or at least mildly confounding to leave. Everything within was part of a physical and psychological trap, to make it almost impossible to gauge time; once you lost track, there were no visual clues to get you back again. Strip clubs and night clubs were essentially the same. Remain in the dream; do not awaken. Keep spending, intoxicating; don't think, and if you do, no matter what you do, do not think clearly.

There were laws, though. People had to be able to leave quickly in an emergency. But everything possible had been done to prevent the execution of those loopholes as well. Once upon a time, those secret exit doors had been used by the smokers. Barker, now an ex-smoker, had come here on and off during those times, but back then a slave to the ritual of commercially prepared, corporate-peppered nicotine, and he had come to know all of the secret exits. But since then, the place had been remodelled, and those old junkie loopholes had been tightened. All the old side doors had been sealed over. Emergency doors were real now. Too many punters had been going out for a smoke, having a think, a change of heart, and not coming back in again. Snapping out of it, out in the cold, or melting away in the heat. Not anymore. In the new World Casino, roof gardens had been sprouted, and balconies created; new beer gardens and rooftop cafes which were technically outdoors, where you could smoke, but you didn't have to leave the building. Did not have the option, in fact, to leave the building. You couldn't even climb a wall and jump; the outer ledges were all spiralled with razor-wire.

Insidiously ingenious.

Still though, there were a few smokers right outside as Barker had come in. In daytime the open stretch of footpath past the entrance was a steady pedestrian thoroughfare, but at night it was a gathering place for the drained, for whom nicotine was base nourishment. They might have found their way out, but most would go back in, straight away upon thrashing out their desperate pleasure; Barker had felt them, paranoid that their favourite machine, that they had been stoking for the past howeverlong, had been stolen by another, taken over by a watching skulker, or their timing simply blown, by their need to step out and snatch a fix, or their perverse desire to know that they could step outside, right outside, any time if they wanted. But the magnetism of their other major addiction would pull them back, as it had pulled them out; from outside, from home, from anywhere in the city, any time, to here.

Barker had walked softly past the plume, holding his breath.

It must have been one in the morning by now.

It was Wednesday, almost certainly.

*Although the sorcerer's day did not start until sunrise. The concept of the day starting at midnight was a trick of the –*

Barker didn't want to check if it was Wednesday or not.

He pushed the door.

*Bong…*

Down King William Street, down on Victoria Square, the town hall clock struck.

He knew now, whether he had wanted to or not.

It was bitterly cold, but warm as soon as he crossed the threshold into the restored art deco antechamber. There was a heavy Maori-looking guy on the door, but he hadn't said anything, nor moved, as though his enormous tight-tux had been accidentally stitched to the wall that evening as they had sewed him into it, and they'd just left him there because it was Tuesday night. The antechamber had once been a kind of lobby, but since the so-called refurbishments, there was no desk, nor a greeter, nor grinning concierge. After all, this casino was not a hotel, as many others were. This comparatively small room, that had once been the moderately grand entrance to terminus administration, was now simply a fancy, faintly old-fashioned emptiness, with tall wood and glass panelled doors, each leading to various other immediate and much louder sections of the casino. Barker knew that he'd been spotted by security; he would have been ID'd outside straight away by at least a dozen cameras by now. He knew who had seen him, and what would happen as soon as he walked into the casino proper.

He knew his clothes weren't great. He knew he'd worn better, better fits and materials, more stylish, more thought-out. There had been a reason; it had all possessed purpose; Brixton had tried to remind him of that, too.

Colours, shapes, patterns.

Sounds, waves, frequencies.

It was all symbolic, communicative; it was all story, conversation, statement.

It was song, and music, and all magic.

But now… with these clothes? A tee, a jumper, a coat and old jeans, and especially the nondescript sneakers… he would not get in, dressed like this on a weekend. The coat though, it was good, it was Australian wool, selected and cut especially for him, and it had style; it, alone, even ripped down the arm, seemed to allow him to pass the threshold somehow. He pulled the long handle on the main door and the cacophony of light and sound, immediately more offensive than anything he could ever have imagined himself wearing, blasted mercilessly into him.

It reminded him of the night, two years ago now, that he had become friends with…

…with her.

He'd just been given this coat, he remembered.

It had still been the old casino back then; nicer, as colourful dens of parasitic evil went, although…

# PART THREE
## RULES AND ETIQUETTE

# CHAPTER TWENTY-FOUR:
# RITA AND MARIA AND RAYLENE
# AND PEGS

I

…the place has slowly fallen away over decades, Barker thought as he entered.

But word was, it was going to be sold and upgraded, soon, maybe within a year, and…

He didn't care. So long as the place stayed open, so long as he could keep coming here and… it didn't matter. He was getting a bit used to the old place now though. It felt almost good coming in tonight, wearing the new black coat over the best of his admittedly lesser clothes, all of which were just about too old now to be allowed past casino security. But the co-opted charm of the old railway offices had long since been corrupted. The dark brown wood, gold chrome rails and trimmings, the rich red carpet; he hated that, the pretence to royalty, to Monte Carlo and James Bond. He'd travelled, and although he remembered only patches of that now, he did remember that a lot of casinos looked like this, or were cut from the same cloth. People wanted them to look like this and it worked; and despite the fact that he hated it, it even worked a little bit on Barker.

Immediately, as he let his guard down to that thought, the terrible atmosphere of desperation struck him empathically, along with the horrendous, toxic wave of air conditioning. He always acutely felt both as he entered; he couldn't help it, even now, five years after he'd become a psychic cripple. Although; he kind of dreaded to think what this place would feel like if his powers hadn't been reduced.

Barker summoned his psychic shield, as dense and shimmering metallic psychological armour as he could visualize, and brought it in. He tried to block them all out; all the hurt ones, the lonely ones, the broken ones and the doomed ones, and managed after a few seconds of willpower to protect himself from all but the burning edges of the angriest and most bitter.

The main room was huge, and with his full psychic protection up and running he could quickly sense the ebbs and flows of willpower energy in the main room as he walked through. Not just the ordinary randomness, such as the little wishes and begs and pleas and pushes to whoever was listening, but the actual bursts, and the pulse of how each person's little psychic generations impacted upon and fed the greater field of consciousness; changed things occasionally, infinitesimally. As people would push, for a dice to roll on, or a ball to rattle further; one more turn, one more spot, they radiated this willpower energy. He'd remembered the name of it once, this energy, the proper name, the feel of it and how to recognize its subtle qualities, but he had forgotten it again, and kept forgetting it. When people were pleading, or demanding of God, or Allah, or Jesus or The Universe or whatever, it was whatever first came to mind when they let it, when they were pulling this energy toward them. This energy would materialize above them as though breaking through, into this plane of existence through a crack in the deeper rock of matter, and splash through like an underground spring, around them, sometimes beneath or beside them, and flow at them, forking, streaming over and into them like water over a rock. Most of the time it would just splash on past; people didn't know how to harness it once they'd summoned it. But when there was enough, the willpower energy started attracting and collecting, and running as one, with all the fluid psychic energy flowing together. It would coalesce, and stream in spirals over tables, gush along the bars and travel the floor with the tourists, searching for something it could exploit as a receptacle, hunting as though it were alive.

It probably was; spiritually alive, as much as fire or water or even the wind itself.

These streams of travelling energy were, unsurprisingly, white-gold in Barker's field of vision, and his mind decoded them to resemble tiny, individually transparent and translucent fish. The little goldfish would dash about, apart from one another, until they slowly came together, one by one, sometimes over an hour, sometimes with surprising immediacy. They would form a line, or a long string, sometimes shoaling or even schooling over one machine, one table, one player. Barker knew the little goldfish weren't real of course. But he also knew that neither were they true hallucinations. Barker's mind had somehow evolved in a way that meant he could see things that other people couldn't; things that existed, and were real, but for whatever reason had never become part of ordinary human perception. The goldfish were a symbol that reflected something only partly-manifested into this dimension, perhaps not even fully translated into three-dimensional matter, but which were nevertheless there and active, observable, and consequential; the presence of the goldfish was not essential for a win, but when they appeared, they absolutely guaranteed one.

Barker had seen other things around the place too. Things only he could see that were actually, physically real; at least, physically realer than the goldfish. Some maintained themselves in invisible but definitely physical forms, and some did not. Some were in disguise as people, and the punters simply chose not to see them, especially those in poor disguises. All of these creatures however were generally shocked when they realized Barker could see, or recognize them. Some ran when they did, some ignored him, others still barely acknowledged the fact that their camouflage had failed, and treated Barker like a bad smell. He left them all alone, these ghouls and wraiths, lower entities and odd interbreeds who could pass as human in a dimly lit room. He walked on by and did not look them in the eye.

*Once, Barker, they would all have fled your presence… they would have felt you entering and they would have run and not looked back. You would never have seen them; some great sorcerers barely know these gutter-dwelling parasites even exist…*

Not all psychics and sorcerers saw the energy streams, nor read the energy as goldfish. Once or twice Barker had raised the subject with some of the others who operated here. Most of them saw some kind of swarming, or schooling, and their minds went with the undersea motif, but some saw insects, some streaks of paint, some just undefined curves of swirling light. One had seen tiny sunflower cherubs. Whatever. It wasn't like they all hung out or anything, but it was nice to know he really wasn't crazy.

Barker never stayed long at the casino though. He'd have a few drinks, assess the goldfish, do a bit of psychic angling and reel in the line, or, if things went really well, draw in the net. He only took what he needed, just skimmed off the collected magical luck of others, because that kind of karma was okay. The heavy karma, however, could wait; he didn't go near the addicts, he didn't need the cosmic burden of riches leeched from the bank accounts, the lives, and the families, of the psychologically unwell. And besides, there were rules. This place was heavy with karma of that darker tier, and he did his best to ignore that, too. At least, he was told it was. He was told; stay clear.

He was also told that there was some kind of organization, based in Europe, who sent out older sorcerers, *much* older sorcerers, some said, who watched to make sure nobody ever gave the game away. Some were in person, some watched from afar, and some were self-appointed arbiter wise-men, of whom this old bunch of sorcerer judges in London, or wherever, seemed to approve enough to employ as agents when things went too far.

So he'd heard.

So he thought he remembered, maybe.

He never went upstairs to the matrix banks, to the rows and rows of poker machines, and never, ever, steered his mind further upstairs to the executive rooms. As it was, what he was doing was just a few notches above cheating the welfare system; that was it, as far as he could stomach.

And yet, like some of his friends who were actually doing that, there seemed to be something to do with the chance of it, the luck (despite Heather saying there was no such thing) or good fortune, even if all those factors were ultimately rigged against the consumer, that allowed for a kind of cosmic loophole; if you had been guided here and made aware, and took only what you required within that context…

But never too much.

Easier said sometimes, but it seemed to be allowed, and for the most part, he managed it.

Besides, things were okay these days. Cheryl had been managing him since she'd dragged him back from his three year Sydney drinking binge. She'd been able to source and secure him a few jobs per week; piecemeal but reliable. But he had been paying through the nose these last few months for a merely half-decent rental house. It had to be a house, and he had to have it all to himself, for some reason. Size didn't matter, nor rent. Just; his, in the eastern suburbs, near a stream and a forest, near a decent café. At the same time, he'd been trying to eat well, so with all that, things were a little tight. The two poker chips in his pocket, the two he'd taken home with him last time, were currently all he had to his name, and if he didn't spot any goldfish currents tonight, he'd be forced to cash them in, just to get home on the bus, then eat packet-noodles and drink instant coffee all week until Cheryl's next booking on Sunday afternoon.

But Cheryl didn't know about this; about his little trips to the den, nay cavern, of iniquity. The money he made here wasn't just to top things up and make life bearable. He needed most of it, the grandest part of the one or two he made, for something specific. Something he owed, a duty. Cheryl would freak out if she knew, but when those needs arose, he came here and he won. He won what he needed, and a little extra, and he left. He'd learned how to do this through a process of trial and error; learned that it was all he could do. Just what he needed; no extra bad karma, no breaking the bank, no shaking the pillars. The helpless cases down here on the main floor were bad enough; he had tried to help a few of them at the start, the real gambling addicts and compulsives, but it had always gone wrong. It had always backfired and they had always resented it. They had always lost the money again, and then, somehow, so had he. So now he did what he could, with what powers Bridger Mansion had left him, five years after he had gotten almost all of his friends killed.

He read the room as he walked in a little further, almost happy in his new coat.

Almost having put it all behind him.

On a good night he could make a thousand, on a very good night maybe two. Once a fortnight, a little closer sometimes. A little more some months. Play it safe, no undue attention, just loiter, skim and skulk away into the night.

He smiled to himself, sensing something on the way.

He'd had a feeling, and followed it, knowing tonight there would be a win, just waiting for him. Obviously, it wasn't all psychological damage and desperation. There was the chocolate wheel and baccarat tables and dice, there was fun, real fun. Adrenalin and alcohol; people winning. People walking away when they realized it wasn't happening, but still having had a good time losing; breaking even, even. There were memories being made, occasions being had, parties out and about. But in the end, Barker knew the truth of it; they were like sparklers, distracting you from the fact that, despite this being an endless party, the cake looked cheap and awful, the drinks were watered down, it all tasted terrible, and all the ingredients were toxic.

The trick was, if you could forget that and be distracted by the other, by a group-night-out or something, you could ride their wave, grab the dorsal fin of their happy dolphin, and keep hold for one rotation. You could use it as cover until the dolphin started to choke out on the toxins and fled out the window for the Torrens Lake.

There it was again…

Something. He could feel it. Something was about to happen to make it all better, at least for a while; to make it change, and offer the opportunity for abundance and restoration and…

…and there they were. Four young women, tonight's night out. Just leaving the main bar on a spirit and sugar high and ready to roll; pumped, gaggling and shriekingly happily as they negotiated the steps down to the main floor with their heels stomping. It was one of several classic quartet formations. The tiny hot seven was their leader, the tall doe eyed six was her best friend from childhood, the busty pretty six was her best friend from high school, and the serious, athletic seven who was unaccustomed to letting loose was her best work friend; the two sevens went out properly together on weekends, but this was something else.

Barker tried to read them across the room, but Cheryl and Carlton had both told him he had not been any good at that, not even at the best of times, and certainly not with all the extra psychic white noise in a place like this. Saturday nights were usually the best; the most people, the most cover. But this, a good fired-up foursome on a Thursday, was fine. So he circled a few tables as though he were looking for someone maybe, until he was sure that the school of goldfish would be attracted to the moving quartet. Sure enough, the silver, dolphinesque energy that had come in with them, around them, and had grown larger with them at the bar, was weaving faster around their heads. It was the symbol of the energy that had been created by their sense of friendship and bonding on this night, their enjoyment of each other and their sense of discovery, mixed with their excitement and anticipation. That alone was enough. They were who they were; punters, and there had been nights he'd followed a dolphin for hours with not a goldfish school in sight. He kept watching but didn't engage psychically more than that. He wasn't concerned much with who they were, or why they had come; just that they were here to bet, and that they had brought the happy dolphin with them, so he could catch their slipstream, join in, and help make everybody happy, as it rained scales of diamond.

Or something.

Whatever.

Look, it worked, Barker told himself.

And it was starting to work again, in fact, as he saw the collective glow of orange in his field of vision begin, once again, to sparkle. They could all sense, in their own ways, the presence of their burgeoning good fortune. It would take some time to build, but soon their whole collective aura would begin to shine with a slightly more golden edge, as the developing school began to follow them.

He saw Jürgen across the room. He'd been watching too. He didn't like Barker, and Barker could never work out why; they'd barely ever spoken. Jürgen turned away, back to the table he'd been lingering around, and resumed making normal bets, acknowledging that this one was Barker's.

He waited and watched another ten minutes while the four women went from table to table, feeling hotter as the gold school rode the silver dolphin around with them, gathering and swirling about their heads until it became a virtual indoor weather system. This one would be good; everyone at whatever table they ended up on would benefit. He looked for Jürgen, to tell him to get in on it, but saw him leaving, with no hope of alerting him to the summoned money-storm these girls had defacto rain-danced into being.

Who the hell were they? This was bigger than he'd first thought.

Not a divorce; divorce parties could be decent payers but there was too much undertow. They'd usually blow it, because they didn't really want it; not entangled in the celebrations that were really commiserations. Who then?

He moved further toward the four as he saw that they were ready; their game would be roulette. Okay, now he knew; this was really going to be one of those times. Roulette payed thirty-five to one. Two numbers in a row was rare, but if you let it ride on a dollar bet, which was how most people did it, that was thirty-five times thirty-five, and you'd won just over twelve hundred bucks. Most people lost on the second, but if they were lucky enough to get that second roll, they would usually walk. Inevitably some smart arse would point out that they could parlay that on to almost forty-three thousand if they won again, but you had to be drunk, stupid or clueless to play those odds.

'Oh well, it was only a grand!'

'And you didn't have it when you walked in!'

'And you only lost a dollar!'

Commiserations.

Feel better.

Keep drinking.

'Is it still actually chance?' Barker had asked Cheryl once. 'If I'm there, do you think it changes things? Creates something that wasn't meant to be?'

'I think the energy in a casino is so dense, it's like a karmic black hole. Nothing happens in those places by accident.'

He was at the table with them now; the four of them were along one side, in pecking-order with the athlete at the end, the two sevens bookending the two sixes. The sixes knew the leader was having adult experiences with her work friend, whereas they only shared adolescent memories. But something about it was working. There was an edge to their individual tightropes, a shared light above the social abyss over which they were all perfectly balanced. Nights out like these were rare; magic nights, alchemic, when a group worked although it shouldn't, with everything unquestioned, everything a surprise, all things delighting unexpectedly.

*I never knew she was so funny.*

*I never knew she was so laid back.*

*I feel more confident when she's with us.*

*My three best friends getting along.*

Barker came up on the other side of the table, just one second ahead of a small swarm who had sensed from two other tables away that the vibe was hotter over here.

But Barker had already caught it. The vibe was burning, electric.

The leader simply couldn't believe she'd done it; they'd done it… but what?

This *was* bigger. He'd hooked onto them with something superficial, but there was more. The leader; she'd done it. She was… he scanned deeper; an engineer. She had been hailed, ordained when she had graduated. She had started a business with her best friend from college, got work, contracts and business, favour and kudos, and along the way she had hired her other two best friends. Now they had secured the contract to design a cable car that would go from the foothills to Mounty Lofty.

*Christ, are they really going to do that?*

Barker couldn't believe it.

Hot little seven couldn't believe it either, yet here it was. This would seal her reputation. If she played it right, she would never be poor again, never accept a job she didn't want to do. She would be successful forever, with her friends around her, whom she had taken with her to that success. They were like something from TV. And tonight they were all happy.

On the roulette table, the black and red number-grid on the green felt layout looked to Barker's psychic senses like a three-dimensional topographical map of the world's most extreme ocean floor, with a series of high spikes and deep trenches scattered across it that only he could see, shimmering like coral seen through the surface of the ocean as it reflected a distant sun, the tallest of which symbolized where the next roulette ball would land. The pockets around the wheel, the squares on the table, the numbers corresponding, the numbers themselves, even the amount of the bet; these were all symbols, Barker knew, that everyone decoded anyway, instantly, involuntarily. The symbols all transacted in the mind, based upon deeper symbols in the reality that occurred here, in front of everybody. It was all equation, algorithms, and then you added colours and spinning, the element of game, of luck and surprise, and good old adrenalin and alcohol; it was an astounding matrix to be playing or manipulating in any regard. But these girls were about to direct their will, and that whole energy field itself already knew it.

Barker had never seen anything like his, certainly not here and not with him in the middle of it all. Nothing could stop this kind of build. But exploiting it? He could see how you could fuck it up. He could see; sure, these women were quite capable of ruining their luck at the last minute. And he was here… to make sure they didn't?

But… where had that come from? He sensed the water motif again, but shook it away and refocussed on the quartet. He didn't want them to fuck it up. There had been something about them he had liked straight away, these four, and more importantly, he needed the money. A score this big tonight could tie the bow on everything. Pleasance, Herb, Heather, everything.

From the opposite side, Barker directed his play at the doe-eyed blonde six. Although, close-up, they were clearly sevens and eights. But then, people always went up a slot or two, once you liked them.

'I'm going for my birthday!' She cried out. 'Sixteen!'

He saw it. The coral spike was there; sixteen. This was what most people did on autopilot; one number, their birthday. Everyone was programmed with that; a lot of people won like that, randomly. Roulette was made for it. One to thirty-six. If they didn't think too hard, or get in their own way mentally, and if they had a little magical will in their blood, it was pretty simple to win thirty-five bucks off a dollar bet. The trouble was, they didn't know what to do next, and lost it again.

He scanned for the blonde woman's name; Maria. The engineer, the leader, was Rita. Rita slammed down a dollar chip on sixteen as well. The other two exchanged glances as Rita smirked a little wildly at her childhood best friend, whom she had three years ago made office manager, and just this evening doubled her salary. Barker slapped down his last two chips. Both Rita and Maria shot stunned looks across the table, and they all smiled.

'That's my last two bucks, Sixteen.'

Rita and Maria looked at each other, then back at Barker.

The croupier called out. 'Last bets!'

Rita scoffed. 'Ohmygod!'

Barker just grinned.

'No more bets!'

'…I can't believe this…' Rita guffawed as the clattering wheel spun, and whirred, and –

'Sixteen!'

Shrieks all around.

Barker didn't look up. Sometimes he could see the spirit, the deity, even the god or goddess who had sent people here to win, lurking or hovering somewhere; not always a friendly benefactor either. After a while, he had learned not to look.

But this time, he could feel her.

She wasn't here.

She wouldn't come in here. She, whoever she was, was watching, sensing, through an open window, a smoker's balcony, all the way from the lake outside. Barker looked down at the board again. The spike he had seen on sixteen had vanished, the wave had collapsed. The game might have been rigged in the casino's favour, but anyone, absolutely anyone, was free to try and change that. In these kinds of situations, none of the higher planes entities had ever seemed to mind his interference, nor him taking his cut, so long as the outcomes were the same; sometimes he'd gotten the impression he'd been sent there to help. But he'd never been warned before. He'd never been told.

*Don't let them ruin it.*

Maria cried out. 'Reets I just won thirty-five dollars!'

*It is preordained. It is unprecedented. A run of four. Do not let them lose, Barker Moon.*

Barker looked up at Rita, still grinning.

'What's your birthday?'

'May!' Rita announced. 'Twenty!'

Barker transferred all his winnings, seventy dollars, to twenty.

'Ohmygod!' Big, pretty six, whose name was Pegs, almost passed out with excitement then demanded breathlessly. 'Let me catch up!' She reached in and the croupier helped her cash thirty-five dollars into chips, then he slid them in with the others. 'We're all in this together!'

The fourth of the quartet, athletic Raylene, quickly did likewise.

Now twenty was peaking on high volume, pulsing high and sharp like a stake.

The little ball spun on the giant wheel, bouncing and clacking and ricocheting.

They won.

Jillian refused to state her birthday because she was never lucky, and Raylene's birthday was the twentieth too.

'What's your birthday!?' Rita demanded suddenly. *We're gonna win, and this guy's gunna take me home!*

'Ummm…' Barker hadn't been expecting that. He looked at the spikes. There were still two more. Where was their unconscious willing it to go?

36.

Shit.

'Ummm… I was born on the third of the sixth, but I always bet on thirty-six.'

'Why?' Maria demanded. *Who is this guy? Isn't he on Neighbours?*

'Yeah, why?' Pegs giggled. *Must be one of those gamblerholics.* 'Weren't you down to your last two bucks?' *Shit… was that rude?*

Barker's heart dropped into his bowels.

They had to win, or the entity out on the lake was going to drown him in it.

'No, no!' Rita suddenly gasped, then shrieked. 'Girls! It's meant to be! Thirty-six! Our office; that's our number, our street address!'

They won again; and several more around them had won too, following their lead. It was a genuine run, a hot streak. The casino was going to pay out. A lot. Barker's head was spinning as they decided again.

It needed to be four in a row.

But then he realized; it was going to happen anyway. The girls quickly created momentum around the number five; it was the fifth of August, but it was not just something as simple as the date; *the date they won the contract!* Rita also worked out that she had met Raylene in 2005, Pegs in 1995, and Maria in 1985; *when they were five!* Barker could see the five, but that was it, four in a row.

But… four in a row?

He hadn't stopped to think.

How much…?

Seventy times thirty-five… times… thirty-five, and again, and…

Usually, he just hit blackjack a few times, came away with a few grand.

This was a lot of money…

'Forty-two grand…' Rita was muttering to herself. 'We're all up forty-two grand…'

Only Maria heard, right next to her. Barker saw her hands start to shake. Then she saw that look in Rita's eyes. He'd seen it before. The intuition. Not the made-up one, the one that you tell yourself is intuition just because you want it to be. The real deal; she was sensing the dolphin, and the goldfish, that were still there, over the four girls like an upturned funnel.

The spike hadn't moved.

'Let it ride!' Rita shouted. Her eyes were glistening.

Silver and gold.

'Ride on five!'

Pegs and Raylene didn't have a clue how much they were risking. They had no idea of the odds, nothing. They were doing that thing; *came in with nothing, leave with nothing.* They were thinking; if it's this easy, it can't be too much we're winning, or risking, can it?

'Ride on five!' Barker shouted. 'Ride on five!'

'No more bets!'

Maria was shaking still, all over, but she hadn't protested. In fact, they were all so fired up, he didn't know how they were going to stop. There were rumblings all around; impossible, too soon, pushing their luck. Other people removed their bets. But Barker saw it; it was going to happen. He watched it happen; watched the women freak out, like, really freak out. Jumping up and down, going mental. He closed his eyes and put his hands over his face. He knew Rita would want to keep going.

'I'm out…'

He removed his hands.

'I'm out…'

He had won three million bucks. The silver and gold remained in the air, but it had dispersed, it was spread out everywhere now. It had held, held for four, then burst like it had been fired from a glitter cannon into the ceiling. He looked at the board. Nothing was clear. There was energy but its solidity had dissolved, and the coral was completely gone. It might have been any one of… three… four… five different numbers. And even those waves were shifting, fading; his ability to even read them going suddenly fuzzy.

It was over.

Everyone around him seemed coated in glitter, like the aftermath of a kindergarten's arts and crafts afternoon. Anyone who'd been at the table who placed another bet, anywhere, within the next few minutes would probably do okay. But he could no longer read this table. Nobody could.

Rita could though.

*Five again, five again, I can feel it….*

'We all just won a million bucks…' Barker said to her, as loud as he could without it seeming too crude. '…let's get a room!'

'What…?' Pegs gasped. 'We won what?'

Rita was staring at him. She didn't trust him. A guy like him. Too good-looking for the bad clothes he was in, but still… a guy like him could get anyone he wanted. There were already three girls in skimpy cocktail dresses, right behind him, lurking, hovering, about to descend. Models or actresses or strippers or hookers. Why was he…?

'One and a half…' Raylene's maths had finally kicked in. 'It's one and a half each…'

'No!' Pegs guffawed. 'You mean; this isn't *normal*?!' She looked at the other girls, assessing their faces as the realizations hit. 'Stop!' Pegs shouted. 'That's enough!'

She looked back, stared at Barker. Barker could use that. Her desire for it to halt. She had almost passed out before. Barker remembered a spell. His mind spoke to hers.

>*Shhh-hushnow-night*<

And Pegs fainted clean away.

# CHAPTER TWENTY-FIVE:
# IN INDIGO

I

There was a flurry of activity after Pegs had fainted. Members of the casino staff accompanied them to a private waiting room where Barker pretended to be in a state of stunned happiness, Pegs recovered quickly, and the girls chattered amongst themselves as though Barker wasn't there. Barker didn't listen but every now and then he would catch Rita, staring at him suspiciously, and Pegs staring at him with a look he could only interpret as quiet gratitude. But he was too deep in his own thoughts, and what he was sure would happen next, to connect with the women to any large degree.

'You okay?' Pegs asked once.

He smiled. 'Just thinking…'

'Leave him alone!' Rita smiled nervously. 'He's in shock; he won twice as much as we did!'

Complimentary champagne arrived right then, and Barker could tell from their excited conversation that this, and the contract, meant they could do all the things they'd been talking about, all the things they'd ever wanted to do, between them and individually.

Barker would do none of the things he'd been talking about.

They each provided the casino with their basic details, for tax purposes, they were told, and each opted for an instant electronic transfer. Then he watched as each of them checked their banking accounts on their phones, and drank more champagne as it became real. They took pictures on each other's phones, of each other's phones, of each other's accounts, before and after.

Barker was in even more of a daze now.

Even though he seemed to be perpetually broke these days, he had a phone, a good one that his mother had bought him for Christmas. But he didn't bring up his account; didn't even look at his phone.

The women said they were going back to the office, and Rita gave him her card, which had their address, just in case he wanted to come along later. A little later he thanked the casino staff and went back down to the bar. He didn't need to scan their thoughts to know that nobody ever reacted like this.


II


Jake the barman was younger than Barker, and over the last while they had struck up a bit of a rapport. He was sandy-haired and plainly handsome, with a blemish free, rosy pink and alabaster complexion. Drinks were cheap here, as the management liked people drunk, and Jake made strong ones, cocktails, with the smoothness of a programmed automaton and the innocent smile of a Disney child star, grown up and moved on.

'You're not a Disney child star, are you Jake?' Barker had asked once, as he'd sat and fished. 'All grown up and moved on? Settled down on the other side of the world in quiet but still convincingly metropolitan Adelaide?'

'No Mister Moon,' Jake had laughed. They genuinely liked each other for some strange reason. 'That's not me, sir.'

Barker had no idea where casino hospitality had found Jake. He spoke like some kind of Dickenisan grifter who moonlighted here after cleaning chimneys.

'Still get recognized from time to time do you Jake?' Barker had teased.

Jake should be asking Barker the same question. Barker did get recognized still, but only in Adelaide, and only by the worst types. Jake always said that Barker was good, because even though he only came in every two weeks or so, he was the only person that didn't talk about sport, or whatever cable series everyone was binge-watching right now. So Barker, who knew virtually nothing about sport but did almost nothing but binge-watch television series, had needed to work to maintain Jake's interest somehow.

One of their early conversations had gone something like this.

'Ricky Gervais said Sharks and Nazis…' Barker had offered.

'That's right sir. He did say that. You watch the documentary channels on satellite do ya sir?'

'I do Jake, I do.'

'I would extend that to Sharks, Nazis and Pyramids, sir. Can't go wrong with that combination. That's a winning combination any day sir.'

'Win you the jackpot will it Jake?'

'Can't guarantee that sir, can't do that at all. Keep the mind keen, sir, that's what it'll do.'

Barker nodded and smiled. 'I have noticed the other channel is quite fond of Crocs, Romans and Atlantis, Jake.'

'There's also Lions, Pirates and Twisters, sir. Covers all sorts that does.'

Barker nodded. 'Then there's celebrities of course.'

'World of their own sir. World and a will of their own. Menace to themselves. Fools to themselves as well, if I dare say sir.'

'I've no doubt you will dare, Jake. No doubt at all.'

'I'm afraid I must sir, I'm afraid I must insist. Who knows what madness they will perpetrate upon a willing, watching, bewitched and bewildered general population next, sir?'

III

Jake's bar was a smaller bar, almost a separate room in an alcove off to the side, and as Barker approached from the winner's suite he took his customary fourth seat along of the six well-spaced bar stools.

'What did I say Mister Moon?'

Barker had thought for a second. Jake had the habit of picking up from wherever they last left off, with no warning. He might have been referring to something Barker had said two, three, even four weeks previously. Then Barker remembered.

'You did say Jake, you did.'

'Who knows what might rain in from the mysterious, looming, leaking cloud everybody seems to trust so much these days sir, for no good reason I can tell, and no mistake sir.'

It was all over the news. A famous hacker, who called themselves LAxe, had stolen the personal photo and video libraries of several famous celebrities and posted them online; some were extremely personal, and a handful of stars had been outed as, in the very least, bisexual.

'Good point, well made Jake. I shall bear it in mind next time myself and the entirely imaginary Mrs Lady Moon embark upon digitally recording the private antics of our esteemed boudoir...' Barker caught a startled spark in Jake's eye. '...what? Too far?'

Jake's eyes had turned into saucers and his mouth had pursed. His alabaster skin had become pale alabaster. Palabaster, Barker supposed.

'Don't turn around sir, she'll see you.'

'She'll...? Who?'

'I'm doing you a favour sir. That sir is a very attractive woman sir. You're a handsome man sir but she's... ew Gawd sir, I think I might flippin' wet myself.'

'Don't wet yourself Jake.'

'She's comin' over sir.'

'Did you just call me handsome, Jake?'

'She's comin' over to my bar...'

Jake's bar was where people, Jake had informed him, often came either to compose themselves, or to play down something big. Not so much centre-stage as time-out. If Jake had seen Barker win the three million, he had been good enough not to say.

'All mighty... you should see this sir...'

'Can I turn around yet?'

'No sir! She's walking past everyone, all the tables; and just before she gets there and they see her, the whole table freezes, then as she walks past, everybody looks and their heads all simultaneously turn in the same direction. She's like an indoor weather system or something.'

'She sounds like a cop.'

But he knew enough to know; Jake's description had not been coincidental.

'Sir, I mean, your face could be on telly…'

'You really think so?'

'Hers should be on a billboard.'

Barker flinched and almost turned.

'Don't look at her sir! When she arrives; *don't look*. You're going to have a reaction and a woman like this will see that reaction all the time, every day from almost everyone they meet; look down, be Bogart, ease in with some clever remarks, and *then* look at her…' Jake gulped. '…allow her a glimpse of the real you sir, a little chat to reveal your true spirit, before she sees that look, again, for the twenty millionth time, sir.'

Christ, thought Barker. What a weird night.

'My spirit chat?'

He might have forgotten most of his mystical training, but he was pretty sure he'd never…

But really, what else did he have to lose? He'd already lost three million imaginary dollars he'd never be allowed to keep, and now here was his chance to blow it with some fantasy movie star as well. The weird night just kept giving.

'Okay, Jake. Whatever.'

'That's the spirit, Mister Moon sir! That's the very one!'

Barker felt the woman arrive, then saw her shape from the corner of his eye. Jake put something in front of him; something hard, on the rocks, that he would never otherwise drink. She was standing a few stools down, in time honoured fashion. Any other bar, she would have most likely sat way down, but Jake's didn't allow it; to sit against the wall here would give a very dark signal in a place like this.

'Best vodka rocks please'

Jake and Barker both remained silent.

Jake iced then poured.

'Weren't you on television?'

She had directed the question at Barker.

Okay.

Barker was surprised, but managed to smile to himself. He threw her a sideways glance; no eye contact but enough to see she was tall with long dark hair.

'No, I...'

'Yes. One of those they make here, and play in the daytime in England.'

Jake delivered the vodka. The woman raised and sipped immediately. Just softly, but like she needed it.

'Thank you.'

She'd purred the thanks, just a bit. Her voice was middle-register, with a faint European accent that Barker was unaccustomed to hearing in Australia; very matter-of fact and well-modulated.

'No...' Barker offered, trying the same kind of even vocal tone. 'I've never...'

'But I have seen your face on television. I am sure.'

'I can't think...'

'I used to watch a lot of television, and I have a good memory.'

Her Australian sounded Sydney, but he just couldn't quite nail the Euro-inflection. Jake had freaked him out and he was too nervous to try and skim her; if you tried it while you were nervous, especially with a sexual vibration, women found themselves walking off; even they didn't know why. It was just too creepy.

'You used to?' Barker asked, just casually enough.

'I stopped watching television.' It sounded as though she had given a slight smile. 'I found that it gave me what I needed; too much in fact.'

'Too much?'

'I have enough ideas. Time to deploy.'

She hadn't fully turned to him either. They were both looking into the mirror, which was angled back to catch only the people behind them, gambling, having fun; to get you back out there.

Barker heard Jake pipe up suddenly.

'You're… you're not on television yourself, are you ma'am?'

'No; Jake.' Politely reading his casino name tag. 'I cannot master the autocue. I cannot stop my mind and just read text. And I am a terrible actress. In real life, I am an okay liar, like; I can talk my way out of things. I can talk people into things, without being too deliberately manipulative. But I don't like doing that if I am not forced to; I am not one of those people. But in real life I can, out of necessity. Because of how I look, it helps. But on camera, on film, on digital, even in photographs, when I act, nobody believes me. They can see through me, they can tell I am lying. I know this, I have been told this, many times. I don't even believe it myself, my acting, no matter how hard I try. Truth is; I did not try very hard for very long. But I did try. Enough to know that I suck at it.' She smirked, just briefly. 'My mind keeps going. For all these things, you need to shut it off. Perhaps I should meditate more. Or – some.'

Then the three of them were silent for a few seconds, the jingle-jangle of the matrix banks suddenly seeming just a little more distant.

'I'm sorry, you were talking, I could see as I came up. I did not mean to interrupt. What were you talking about, was it personal?'

'You sound like you're looking to become a script writer…' Barker smiled. 'Watching enough movies to write one?'

'Is that how it's done?'

'It's one way.'

'No wonder there's nothing new.'

Barker was suddenly irritated. 'There's nothing new in genre by design. It's like a Rubik's Cube, there are a million permutations; people enjoy that.'

'I enjoy that. I'm just saying…'

She stopped.

'Are you okay, Ma'am?'

Barker should have looked then. How much longer was he going to keep this up? She might even have come over specifically to talk to him. Maybe he was in her league after all? He was like a comedian now, committing to a bit, but for too long. Then again, how long was too long? When did he become, not funny again, but in this case, okay again? Even cool again? Had it been cool in the first place? How old was Jake anyway? What the fuck did he know about women? Fucking chimney sweep!

'…I was just thinking.' The woman opined curiously, all of a sudden. 'Didn't they have pyramid-shaped Rubik's cubes? And… I want to say… dodecahedron cubes? With more than six colours? I'm sure I remember that from my childhood. Perhaps even my teens.'

This was ridiculous. Barker felt himself smile. He remembered them too. He kept the smile, and felt it broaden as he turned to her, being, he thought, genuinely charming.

'No, I remember them.'

She looked at him too, and smiled.

He didn't get it right away. Her face was so startling that his mind had to interpret it like a symbol, like the dolphins and the goldfish.

'Holy shit…' He wanted to say, and checked himself to ensure that he hadn't.

'I'm not mistaken then? Not dreaming?'

'No…' Barker told her. '…there were all sorts of varieties. I never solved any of them myself. My sister did. She bought them all.'

She was just like one of those variant Rubik's Cubes, because he had never seen this arrangement before. She was simply too much. Too much for him to process in just a second's glance. Even a full two.

'She solved them all…' Barker spoke, as though the dribble of his previous nonsense couldn't help but involuntarily follow though.

She was a hawk, he could see that immediately. And she had a slight Spanish aspect. That was the accent; lent from a parent, possibly a grandparent. Maybe she hadn't been born here but she'd obviously been here a while, been in Australia throughout high school most likely, at least. All the while, getting the look he was giving her now.

She'd never been normal.

She'd always been like this; her bearing gave that away. What must it have been like, to see a person adjust to the essential genetic deformity, the freak pattern, of how you looked, just as he was doing? No matter the aesthetic? Never mind that it was such beauty that the mind was forced to take a few beats to absorb it. To have that happen so many times… it must have been everyone, and yet she must always have known that it was not normal.

'Older sister?'

'Yair.'

The woman nodded. 'You were well-served by the universe. A boy with a smarter older sister – you got along I can tell – is a man who will be better served to navigate romance and sexual politics. Why aren't you married?'

She was wearing a baggy black leather jacket and a thick silk scarf with blocky, angular Aztec patterns of indigo and deep blue, with traces in white. The scarf however, and indeed her shoulders and chest, were barely visible due to her long, dark, chestnut hair, which was straight and centrally parted, all one length at least halfway down her back, resting with the impression of so much body that it was as though she wore some kind of massive fur stole.

'Line of work…' Barker responded. 'Not conducive to…'

'Oh. You travel?'

She was sitting comfortably, both leather-clad arms out loose on the bar as her long, fine fingers toyed slowly and rhythmically with the curve of the glass. She glanced at him again then, absently but almost curious, as though semi-engaged, but genuinely semi-engaged, with his reality.

'I'm Emerald by the way. Emerald Tarragon.'

She held his gaze.

Under a high and somehow noble brow, her long, precise, dark chocolate eyebrows and her low, wide, delicate cheekbones framed enormous green eyes, wide and alert with vicious black lashes. The eyes were one of the things it took extra seconds to process. They were a quantum further apart than normal, an iota wider, brighter; more open and immediately, involuntarily demanding. It was as though this suggested, somewhere deeply, unconsciously, that she could absorb more, take more, and that this made her dangerous. The extraordinary colour of Emerald's eyes was dazzling, and caught both the breath and hypnotic attention; the bright but deep emerald green irises, and the shining, demanding black pupils were simultaneously the rewards of fantasy, and the doom of the hardboiled. Between and beneath those eyes, the bridge of her nose, also a jot wider than anyone could expect, was set in a long flat ridge as though sculpted; sweeping down softly, and perfectly symmetrical as she looked at him, just for a second, dead on. Just two sharp lines, then down to a pair of lips surely bequeathed by her Moorish ancestry, just as was the light golden tone of her Spanish complexion; the lips full and lush and North African, though deep pink in tone.

'Barker.' He was responding on auto-pilot. Amazed that he was able to do even that. 'Barker Moon.'

She turned from him and looked back to the mirror, and the casino behind her, as though she knew; this was the procedure. The possessor of this kind of sharp, anomalous beauty, as well as the wise possessors of any other kind of anomalous appearance, would be quick to realize that those engaging with you would require an extra second to adjust. One would learn to pose, take a subtle pause, and without it insulting either of you, allow it to be done. You would then have to earn every second of attention, after that.

Having given him her profile, Emerald suddenly sat a little more upright.

As though, startled by her own thoughts for a second.

Barker couldn't help it; his eyes lingered a second longer at her de facto invitation. All of what she had, her sum of parts, should have been harsh, too much, but instead was fully, freakishly, compellingly beautiful. Her profile was the same; hawkish but magnetically, aesthetically attractive, her massive lips protruding at the prow of her aggressive jawline, but the cosmic, genetic geometry was unmistakeably a reflection of the Goddess herself.

Great Mother…

Emerald belonged here, in this city; geometrically sacred, line-and-angle perfect.

'Wait,' Emerald spoke. 'I do remember you…'

How many ways could she look? Barker wondered. How many angles did she have, to employ, deploy, to shift? What idea had she garnered from television and its implicit statements of expected gender roles; even in this, the Third Golden Age?

She softly jerked her head out of profile and toward him again, examining him suddenly and earnestly. As the brilliant emerald and pitiless black refocussed, it was as though she had registered, immediately, the proximity of someone who was attempting to determine something about her. He hadn't even attempted anything like a sweep but his mind had gone to the question of her personal reality; he'd attempted to see through her, and she had reacted as though he'd reached over and poked her gently in the ribs. She hadn't objected, not exactly, but this, now, was at least a minimally defensive gesture.

'You were on trial.'

He had, half, been expecting this.

'You know I was. You've come here to find me.'

She smiled big this time with the Moorish-cherry lips. You could see her jaw muscles; there was not an ounce of fat on her. He didn't look down, check her out, but he knew what he would see; tight jeans on a proper, healthy size eight. When she walked away, and she would, she would be one-eighty minimum. And painfully slender; six feet in heels. It would take a miracle, after that, if he ever saw her again, but it wasn't his looks that would keep her away; he was handsome, he knew, though more so when he was healthy, and happy. It was that he wasn't; he wasn't that. He was good-looking enough to have parlayed his looks into an upswing. But he hadn't. He was here, a psychic skimming luck to take the crumbs home. And not good enough at that to buy decent brand labels, as she no doubt had. Maybe once she would have seen a place in her life where she might have looked at him, seen something she could try and fix. But not now; Emerald Tarragon had passed that point at least a year ago. Barker was pretty sick of it too.

'I was looking for you, yes. I was looking for those who can do what we do.'

*I fucking knew it.*

She proceeded. 'Territory can be important for our kind. There seems to be plenty of room here though?'

Okay. He did a quick surface scan now. Massive walls, but...

'There are one or two others,' Barker told her. 'We keep to ourselves, but it seems to work out that if we keep it down to once a fortnight, and just a few k, it all works okay. No anomalies. Just skim what we need.'

Emerald nodded. 'Just what we need.' She looked back at him. 'Is that enough for you?'

She'd read him and realized he wasn't a grifter, or a shifter, or a schemer or a plant. So far as he could tell, over the intimidation headache she naturally inflicted, she wasn't either. How long did her friends take to get used to that? Did they ever?

'I sensed you here. But I didn't know who you were. You were on trial though, weren't you? You are *that* Barker Moon?'

'Sure.'

'Did you do it?'

'I can't remember. Probably not, is what people tell me. People I like.'

'People you trust?'

'I only trust people I like. Or is that, the other way round?'

'It can be whatever you want it to be. It's your thing. You decide.'

'I will. But thank you.'

She smirked lightly again, and waved at Jake for a second drink. She was the kind that would take the second one a lot more slowly.

'Truth be told, that's all I remember about you. Some black magic went wrong.' Emerald shrugged. 'I'm sorry now; I thought it was all bullshit, made up to get you off. I thought it was a media circus, a distraction. Now I meet you in person, I realize, it must have been real.'

'And I really don't remember.'

The boots matched the jacket, the scarf matched the jeans, the jeans looked old, but were new, looked denim but were some extra, magical shade of indigo that was…

'Oh really? You didn't see what happened over there, before, and see me come back and think…?'

She smiled at him, so he didn't finish the sentence.

'I thought that would be your next thought. Some kind of high-end grifter-psychic, and I don't blame you, but no, Barker, I'm not that. Although, I did see what happened before, but I assumed you would either be long gone, or still upstairs. You are the only other of us still here tonight; the second one left earlier. I was asked to deliver a message though, if I would, to the psychic at the bar here; I did not expect it to be the man who won, just an hour ago, nor the famously acquitted Barker Moon.'

Barker stared at her.

'But I was already here…' Emerald shrugged. '…already watching this place. You realize they have no idea? They're all numbers people and pragmatists. They already have facial recognition software in Europe and Japan, but it's no good. It's not designed for us, just to recognise people who keep winning anomalously. Walk in with any kind of basic glamour and the program thinks it's never seen you before.'

'You saw me win that money?'

'I wondered if you would be a bit shell-shocked. You don't have it, do you? They didn't catch you out being psychic, so it must have been…'

'Let's just say it hasn't come through yet.'

Emerald nodded, but this seemed to make her very angry.

Angrier than Barker had been.

'Of course I was a watching,' Emerald sighed. 'Everyone was watching, Barker. I'm the only one that saw you come back here, though. There was something out on the lake. It asked me to find you and tell you that you're not ready.'

'I know. I worked that out. It just used me to make sure those women became instant millionaires.'

Emerald frowned curiously. 'Is that so?'

'Yep.'

'I wonder who they are.'

She could find that out herself. Barker shrugged. 'I wonder who they will be. Anyway; I just got caught up in it. They would have lost it all on the fifth. When the ring leader was caught by the bug, I collapsed her best friend. Cut the loop.'

'You remember some things then?'

'A little. Things come when I need them. When I'm prompted by lake spirits.' Barker turned to Jake. 'You're not hearing any of this.'

'It's all going in the movie script I'm writing, Mister Moon. It's everything I've heard that makes no sense to me at this bar, and it's so big I just moved to a two terabyte hard drive to store the first draft. Peter Jackson's going to make it into three trilogies, and none of it will make proper sense until you've bought the extended box sets. And, I've heard stranger.'

Emerald gave a short but genuine laugh.

Barker turned back to her. 'There are some mansions here that were brought over, stone by stone, by the early settlers, to ensure continuity. So although we only go back to the 1830s, some of the houses are twice that old. He came with one of the chimneys. He secretly owns this place.'

She laughed again. 'I've heard stranger.'

'See?' Jake grinned.

'So…' She looked at Barker again. He still wasn't used to it. '…how do you feel about being policed by an ancient organization that has next to nothing to do with this country, let alone this city, or this casino, or you, for that matter? An organization that is covert, totally occult, and yet can step in and circumvent the transfer of funds, the size of which you won tonight, Mister Moon, and –'

'You can call me Barker.'

She paused. 'Emerald. I said that, didn't I?'

'Yes. Emerald, I feel pretty strange about it tonight, to be honest. I wonder what I have been used to achieve. What those four women have coming to them. I'm pretty sure you're telling me the truth. I'm pretty sure you're here on your own business and they asked to you act as a go-between. I don't think you mean me any harm. But you have…' Barker levelled with the green eyes, and the deep black. Now he was getting used to it. '…psychic shields that remind me of something. They remind me that I have seen their like before. Before I was hit, five years ago, by something so powerful it knocked me down from Dumbledore to Dobby, and that's on a good day.'

'Is that so?' There was no emotion, just calculation.

'I have seen powerful minds, Emerald, confronted and collaborated with them. The being out there, it used me, it made me become involved in something tonight. That's as may be. But the way it was done endangered our kind. I don't like that. Not profiting from that is just the lousy icing on the lousy cake. Was it London who asked you to speak to me, or further back?'

'I don't know. I've never…' She frowned more deeply. '…I didn't know there was any further back than London. At least; not that speaks to the likes of us?'

'Us? What's your story?'

'I'm the same as you.'

'You're one of the most striking women I've ever seen; you're the same as me? You still have your powers, for a start.'

'I'm still a woman. When men realize what I can do, they want to control me, even more than their world already does. But if I agree to work for them, live with them, I can do what I like.'

Barker stared at her. 'And, your ideas, the ones it's time to deploy; they're designed to get you out of this?'

'I think the whole London thing is full of shit Barker. I think London is all myth. A bureaucratic boogieman for psychics and witches. They're fright merchants; they're a company, a corporation, they always have been, just like everything else. Just like the people way back when, who colonized across the sea, and paid for cities to be built. But, they are all going to come crashing down with the new energy…'

Barker scoffed. 'You don't believe that, do you? The new energy that brings everything down? All the old systems, all the old ways?'

'I might. Truly; I don't know; but I know this. I can play the myth card and the symbol game as well as anyone. I've watched a lot of things Barker.'

Barker kept staring at her, then she turned back to face her vodka.

'Things will be different soon. This place won't be the same.'

'What are you going to do? Torch it?'

'In a way. I'm going to shine a light on it. But the next time I see you, I will make you an offer.' Emerald threw back the second vodka in one hit, as gracefully as though she'd just softly swiped her hair back over her shoulder. It seemed he'd been wrong about almost everything. She reached into her jacket and removed an envelope. The kind and shape that contained a brick of money.

'They didn't psych me. Or phone me. It wasn't London calling. It was a plain clothed cop with an Adelaide accent. Psychics are real Barker, but to run an operation the size that London says it does, or even further back, if that's even a thing, they need people. People on the ground, people who get paid to keep their mouths shut, just like any other occult organization. Tonight I'm just the messenger.'

She handed him the money. He took the envelope and for a second they were connected at either end. More than a second. She held it, just a bit longer. Not intimidating. But maybe binding?

He put the envelope in his new coat pocket.

She didn't break the gaze.

'You can't even feel that, can you?'

'No. I told you. It burned me out. If you see anything, let me know.'

'I can't see anything, Barker. There's a section in your psyche that's like petrified lightning.'

'I know. I see it, in my vision, all the time. It's like a migraine aura, always just about to flare up.'

Emerald stared at his eyes. He really could get used to that, it seemed.

'You really are a very good-looking man…'

She said it quietly, though not softly. Like it was just fact. Nothing more. Then she stood straight, and was looking down at him, like a stern but caring doctor would address a sick child.

'You will see me again, Barker. And it will not take a miracle.'

With that she turned and walked away, just a quick spin, then striding off. His heart sank a little. She could have whatever she wanted and she did not want a man, not tonight. He'd go home, thinking of all the things he should have said, and jerk off to the fantasy of what might have happened if he had said them, said them perfectly, and opened the door to something fiery and passionate. He'd add a little something, a faint spell, to exploit the expulsion of sexual energy, so that, should there truly be any chance of them crossing paths again, it would be more likely to happen. At least he could still remember the small stuff.

He watched her go; then she stopped and turned. She looked back at him.

Then she parted her leather jacket, her hands buried deep in the side-pockets, just a shrug.

'Off the rack black tee. Just like yours Barker. Painfully slender and six feet in heels. Tick, tick. You weren't wrong about everything.'

She closed the jacket again and stepped back toward him, back into the tiny archway of the tiny bar.

'Novel, album, movie, show. Bring me the thing that unites them, and we'll see.'

She didn't smile. She nodded. Then she left.


IV


Emerald walked across the casino and pretended a while to be interested. Then she saw her contact. They went to the main doorway and stood in a corner that caught a lot of echo.

'So?'

'No. He's no good to us. He's wounded. Perhaps beyond repair.'

'He comes highly recommended.'

'Five years ago maybe. You've been looking at this place that long?'

'What happened to him?'

Emerald considered. 'I think he went to war.'

'War?'

'I think he saw one of his friends get killed. And it's scarred him. Like lightning.'

'War with whom?'

Emerald sighed. Some things were too hard… too tedious to explain.

'I don't know. With whoever sorcerers go to war with.'

'Demons?'

Emerald did not like to lie.

But in this matter, she had no choice.

'Their own demons, maybe. But, something wanted him to help those women win big tonight.'

'A big win is good for business. It's factored in. It's marketing.'

'But not like that.' She looked around. This was it, now. 'Everything needs to change.'

He didn't seem completely convinced about this. And he would have to be, if her idea was going to work.

'And what about Barker Moon? Will you reassess later?'

She smiled.

'I haven't seen you smile like that before. Is there something about him you find amusing?'

'Not… no. He thinks if he solves a riddle, I'll go on a date with him.'

'Why would he think that?'

'I gave him that impression.'

'But why?'

'He needs to work some proper magic again. It will help his imagination. I threw him a bone.'

'But if he solves the riddle, you'll date him?'

'He won't.'

'How can you be so sure?'

'Because to do that, he would have to know me better than I know myself.'

And she smiled again.

*Or… he could just ask.*

# CHAPTER TWENTY-SIX: BAR

Barker never told Carlton, nor Cheryl. If they'd found out what had happened that night, there would have been hell to pay; literally, so far as at least Cheryl would be concerned. Still; August Fifth; that was a date he was not going to forget. At least, not now he had clearly remembered it again. Not quite the full two years ago he'd suspected, but close enough. It had been cold then and it was cold now. Cold when he'd watched himself bleed out on the street. Cold when Brixton had told him it was time to remember. Or someone, not of his choosing, would make him remember. Jesus. How cold was that? But now, not only was he remembering things he didn't want to, but he was remembering the *wrong* things he didn't want to. The encounter with Brixton, then the tour with Parry seemed to have caused that. It was as though he'd been stranded on a desert island, with a limited diet, and now he'd returned to the world and been shot with a vitamin booster. All the parts of himself that had been working sluggishly for the past… what? Seven years? Those parts he hadn't even realized had been sub-par, were now coming back… and his mental focus seemed to be first in line.

Emerald had worked very quickly after that night. Not long after, the casino had been bought out, and Emerald had bought herself a job along with it. An industry really, if she played her cards right. So he'd heard. So people told him.

Bought herself something, and sold him out.

Sold them all out.

And then bought most of them back again.

Now, trying not to think about Emerald, and the night she had approached him at the bar, Barker stepped inside as three office girls came staggering out, just as he pushed the door open, right past him, drunk as skunks. Barker had to pause and allow them through.

'Who cares! I only ever come here once in a Blue Moon!'

'And I get paid again on Friday! Whooo-oooo!'

'It's only money!'

'Yaaah! S'only bloody money!'

They all laughed raucously.

'Let's go to the races next week!'

They all whooped and hollered as they rolled, virtually as one, into the back seat of a white cab. The cab door closed, the vehicle roared off. They could just as well have been Rita, and Maria, and Pegs and Raylene. Then everything was silent again, cold and crisp, and the main doors swung shut behind him.

There was an apparently normal security woman inside the vestibule door, and a plain-clothed security guard just ahead. The third, a plain clothed psychic security guard, jerked his head involuntarily toward Barker as he entered the main room.

It was only Tuesday night, now into Wednesday morning, with the single chime of the Town Hall clock echoing faintly behind him, but there were still people. Not just the hardcore gamblers, wandering about. Enough tourists scattered throughout to still make it look almost like fun. He picked the larger groups easily; friends out late, like those girls he'd seen, celebrating an actual-day birthday or something; older sporty mates who'd decided to play on after a midweek indoor game at the gym down the road; younger sporty mates still out bonding after training… the usual victims. A bunch of bankers came in behind him, loosening their ties; and there was some kind of older club bash, going long; and a night out after the theatre… enough to make you realise it was late, and midweek, but not enough to make it look depressing. Until you looked deeper; at the singles, dotted here and there. They were all here tonight, as they had been most nights; a lonely one, with nothing better to do; a broken one; a frightened one; a curious one, dying to jump in, weighing the risks but already on the path to ruin; and two or three of the deadly serious, compulsive ones, dropping hundreds at a time, chasing the adrenalin rush. The real sad cases, the total addicts, were on the slot machines, the poker machines and one-armed bandits. There was an entire floor of them upstairs now; almost nothing else up there anymore. Or, they had been whisked away to the executive floor, and the VIP rooms, on the third floor, where they were slowly losing their houses while the management poured them champagne, and booked them a free room in the hotel next door so they could come right back in the morning. The electronic machines made it so easy, but so did the thrill of being included in a high stakes poker game.

Parasites on the mentally ill.

Demented, evil.

Ten times more than what it had been two years ago.

Having just thought of the old casino, and having it fresh in his mind, made the refurbishments, the bland electronic screens, the dull-toned carpets and the thin, cheap veneers over the old walls, seem even more rude than usual.

Maybe that was part of his exposure to Brixton as well?

Was he genuinely seeing clearer, or had Brixton just fired him up? Had he done it using a spell, or was it enough for Barker just to have had an experience like that, an encounter with something infinitely more powerful than himself?

His first since Bridger…

*No, don't go there.*

*Just – don't.*

The new World Casino was modern and functional now. In the old days, because the building itself was classy, they had approximated, and clearly suggested a classic casino. Almost achieved it. But this; this was nothing like the super casinos of Monte Carlo, or Singapore, or Hong Kong. This was little more than a glorified pub now, with a huge but clearly glass chandelier, and plastic fittings everywhere that looked as though they had been bought by the dozen from Ikea. Where the lighting had once been warm, golden and inviting, it was now bright, fluorescent, and was reflected garishly, everywhere, from the upward-angled digital screens. Every vacant space was lined with banks of what Australians and Adelaideans traditionally referred to, with increasing disdain, as 'the pokies'. The tables were all electronic, too. Each player with their own screen, like a personal laptop. They still had dealers on the weekends, he'd heard. But he could barely stand to go upstairs these days; what had once been a kind of party space, with room for bands and even stand-up comedians between the banks of poker machines, was now just wall-to-wall pokie-banks, with a food canteen.

The balcony smoking bars, and the barbed wire.

From here the weird but inane jingle-jangle tunes carried well down the escalators, thousands of different wanna-be cheerful, annoyingly impossible to ignore electric old-time piano riffs, competing for attention in a way that gave him the un-nerving impression of a convention of old-time western-bar piano players, all having a mass play-off, but packed into one not-big-enough saloon where the beer had been spiked with the baddest, brownest acid ever.

He'd walked through it once, but he had sworn, he would never do it again.

It was like the first curve on the first path, along the first circle down.

Barker pulled his mind back from the second floor. He saw another plain-clothed psychic guard react, but ignored it and walked on, toward the bar. He knew that the mock-glamorous world of plush carpet, marble floors, chandeliers and warm lighting was gone; that the security guard would be speaking quickly into the small mic on the collar of his shirt.

'Confirmed psychic at the main entrance. Known offender. Repeat, confirmed psychic entering the casino.'

The chocolate wheel was still there. But it was propped up against the wall, not in use on a weeknight, just leaning there; a prop, exposed as a prop, not even put away, not even the barest sense of theatre or romantic illusion maintained. It was like seeing Moriarty in his underwear. The famous two-up arena, the genuinely interactive arena of actual game-play, the style of gambling that was almost sacred in Australia, sacred especially to the ANZACs, was completely gone; just, that simple. More space for the pokies and the electronic screens. And the punters dabbling at the digital blackjack tables were all significantly less dignified for it.

He didn't try to use his moderate psychic ability on anyone or anything.

Too heavy, too angry.

He kept his screen up, but didn't look for goldfish or dolphins. He sensed a few spikes but ignored them. There were still entities here though, open and raging, alive and electric, sometimes openly incarnated, and walking the floor. Djinn, devils, spirits… and not to mention the terrible thing at the heart of such an enterprise, that was required to run it. But they were legit, it seemed. They had every right, so long as they played fair.

But Barker didn't have to be psychic, nor a sorcerer, to notice the second plain-clothed security officer receive a message via his ear-piece and look directly, menacingly, at Barker.

Jesus, Barker realised. It's Jürgen!

She's got *Jürgen* working here…

If she could convince Jürgen…

Fuck it, he thought.

He kept his cool and went to the bar.

Jake's bar was gone. Again, more space for poker machines. But Jake was still working the main bar.

'Jake.'

'Strike me pink and call me a lunatic! It's Mister Moon!'

Jake immediately picked up where their conversation had last left off by mentioning an extremely famous actor in conjunction with his most famous role, a beloved superhero, the seventh portrayal of which was about to be released with no sign of diminishing box office returns.

'You'll have seen it then, sir? Never been a run like it. No idea who they're going to cast if he leaves. He owns that role sir. Created and dominated.' Jake smiled. 'Have one on me sir!'

'Strictly business, Jake,' Barker smiled tightly. '

Jake slid the drink forward. 'Bundaberg Ginger Beer sir. Still in the bottle.'

'Well in that case…'

'Is it true what they say… Mister Moon?' Jake asked, a little more quietly.

'What's that, Jake?'

Barker gulped. He tried not to ingest pure, processed sugar anymore, especially in the amounts contained in brewed soft drinks. But damn, after a night like tonight, and handed straight to him?

'That you've got the gift…?' Jake waved his fingers over his temple. 'The psychic powers? That you used them to win all that money? I mean, I can't pretend I didn't hear the conversation between you and Miss Tarragon that night. But; was it… was it *real?*'

'That's what they're saying, is it?' Barker swigged again and raised his eyebrows. 'Mister Quaker in this evening, Jake?'

Despite the fact that there were still mirrors everywhere, he didn't need to look; he could feel Jürgen behind him.

'*Mister* Moon, would you accompany me please?'

Jürgen still had the edge of some kind of Dutch accent.

'Funny,' Barker turned around, narrowing his eyes. 'I just knew you'd turn up. You'd think I were psychic.'

Barker stood level with Jürgen's overlarge head. He had small features, the way some bodybuilders did, that made him look slightly freakish, but highly intimidating. He shook his head, stiffly and just slightly, and clenched his wide jaw, which looked like a big hexagonal block was stuck at the top of his throat, as though to indicate that this was just what he wanted tonight; the opportunity to nut someone with his enormous forehead.

'You used to be something, Moon. You could have had anything.'

Barker was shocked.

Jürgen shook his giant head. 'You don't even remember me, do you?'

'Sure I…'

Wait. When he'd seen him… he'd thought… if they could get Jürgen… and now Jürgen was angry. And he remembered Jürgen from the night he'd met Emerald, with the millionaire quartet and the lake spirit… he'd been hanging around. But he didn't know why. To save face, he attempted to cover.

'I know if they can get you working here as psychic police, they can get anyone.'

Jürgen regarded him coolly then. His anger seemed to… if not vanish, then diminish significantly.

'You blew it, Moon. If it wasn't you who killed all those people, it was her; why are you taking the – ?'

'Thank you, Jürgen.'

Barker had been about to take a swing, something he'd done only a few times in his life. The impulse had been totally involuntary. If he'd hit Jürgen, not only would Jürgen have not seen it coming, but Barker would not have seen it coming.

Then he'd caught the scent of her perfume, just before she'd arrived, and he'd momentarily forgotten everything.

Jürgen stiffened. Then he shrugged and turned away. 'It's always the great ones that disappoint…'

Jürgen's mistress had called him away.

Then, once again, Barker was left in front of Jake, trying not to turn and look at Emerald Tarragon.

# PART FOUR
## LINES AND ALLURE

# CHAPTER TWENTY-SEVEN:
# IN BLACK

I

Emerald Tarragon was not impressed.

'What happened to our arrangement?'

'I wanted to know.'

'That's always your problem Barker. You want to know.'

'If it's a problem to want to know, I assume it's the opposite of a problem to not want to know. What do you call someone who doesn't want to know?'

'I don't know Barker. The opposite of a problem is a solution. And you are not the solution to anything.'

'A punter. In the case of this place, a solution to having no money is to bring in more punters.'

'I don't make more punters come through the door Barker. In fact, in the whole scheme of things, it's my job to make sure two or three less punters come through the doors. Now what was it that you wanted to know?'

'Just…' Barker smiled again. '…if it wasn't pure luck, the last time your psychic police decided to bust me.'

Emerald smiled, wry. 'You, of all people, know that luck has nothing to do with anything. Especially here.'

Barker's smug smile dropped. 'What did you just say?'

'You heard me.'

'Where did you hear that?'

'It just came to mind. Why?'

'Someone I…' Barker felt himself becoming uneasy. '…it just sounded familiar, that's all.'

Emerald stared at him. It was a look that told him, so far as she was concerned, that he had not changed, and that this was not a good thing.

'We had an agreement that you would call me first, and come through the side entrance. Then you would wait for me in the café. If you come through the main entrance, you…'

Emerald faltered.

'I what?' Barker was surprised. There was something there. 'You just didn't want any other psychics to see me come in here; like they might think it was okay?'

'No. Yes. Of course there's that.'

He knew that wasn't the reason. The real reason was humiliation, part of his punishment. There was nothing he could read from her to prove that; her shields remained as permanent as ever, solid steel. But he knew that was it, and he wanted to hear her to say it.

He didn't know why.

'You… disrupt things when you come in the front door. You know that.'

'Do I?'

She scowled, as though he were stupid for not understanding what she was trying to say.

'Follow me Barker. And don't…' The scowl deepened.

Barker took another gulp of his ginger beer and stood.

'Don't what?'

'Don't help anyone.'

'I know, I know. He doesn't like it when I help people.'

'Least of all yourself.'

Barker's smile vanished. 'I hope you can hear *your* self.'

She turned and walked off.

He followed.

II


Ernst Quaker watched Moon and Emerald approach on his private security wall as they rode the suite elevator in silence, each staring forward at the closed steel doors. It was fast, even for just three floors, but their expressions seemed to indicate otherwise.

Moon sighed between floors two and three, long and shallow. Emerald shifted her stance a bit, just before the door opened. Quaker didn't like it. He could see it, even if they couldn't. And neither of them lacked self-awareness, not to that extent.

The doors opened and Emerald exited immediately, like she couldn't get out soon enough. Even so, she waited politely outside for Barker, who paused just a second or two longer than he should have before disembarking.

'After you,' he muttered.

Moon had been of little interest to him, initially. Just another downcast psychic on Emerald's list of potential employees.

But Emerald. She was another story entirely.

Often, Quaker found himself resisting the urge to watch her.

To just switch on the wall, for no other reason than to see what she was doing; and yes, to admire her beauty. But whenever he succumbed to the temptation, however briefly, he couldn't escape the feeling that she knew; those moments might have been brief, but they were intense, and she was psychic after all. But he was still unsure about exactly what was possible in that regard, in that… was *world* the right term? Not that he thought Emerald disapproved of his admiration necessarily. Some women, if there was an implicit, unspoken approval, liked to be watched. It was part of a game. An approach, a flirtation, a foreplay. She hadn't said anything, but neither had she acted differently.

And now, it was almost too late.

Quaker had become quite taken with her.

Not just her beauty, although that in itself was more than enough to gain his attention. Refined beauty like that, well, it didn't come along every day. And he was wealthy enough, one hundred times over, to ensure that it might. Genuine emerald green eyes, and with such an unusual shape and curve. Almost actually feline. Tall, slender, the figure of a swimsuit model beneath black tailored suits and heels. Audacious with the absurdly expensive suits he had purchased for her. He'd offered them as a launch gift, requesting it politely and given her the address, letting her know, all his staff were required to be dressed here, his private tailor, to maintain a united appearance. She could choose what she wanted, but they had to be business suits, and that was part of the deal. Quaker liked a united front; a theme. (He would not have approved of the word 'brand'.) Emerald had asked for several to be made, all different. All black; all fitted smoothly to her figure, but then she had worn them with ordinary black tees. Low cuts. Or, worn the waistcoat and jacket without a shirt; cut just so, using the gracefulness of the slender neck she otherwise hid behind those Aztec scarves to draw attention to her throat. A firm suggestion of skin, of sensuality, yet exactingly contained and unyielding. The tailor had informed him that she had worked intensively with him on each pattern, to the millimetre. He had designed lingerie for her as well.

Did she think… he would not find out?

But, no. It was not just that.

She was unique in other ways; the kind of sharp-minded, genuine psychic he'd only ever read about, heard about. Been assured by colleagues that existed, but never encountered.

And she had ideas.

Excellent ideas, exploitable ideas.

He watched her now, her thick hair tied tightly back in a simple, elegant, professional ponytail, accentuating the extraordinarily fine lines of her Latina cheekbones and jawline. He saw how uncomfortable she was, so close to Moon. And yet… undeniably, it was generated by… yes. That would not do. Upon closer inspection of the footage, Emerald seemed more aware of it. At least, from her body language, Emerald seemed… easier with it. Able to handle him. Moon was so angry, so repressed. He was clouded with delusions of grandeur, misjudging his place in the scheme of things, making stupid mistakes. He had to confess though… they would have made a handsome match.

Quaker briefly assessed some of the other monitors on the wall; the guard in the entrance lobby, Jürgen just within the front doors, Jake the jolly barman, the empty lift and the penthouse antechamber – then, once again, Emerald and Moon. He hit a remote and a panel descended over the wall, as though the monitors and the images they'd held had never existed. He liked that. It was here from the old casino, the James Bond casino. He'd kept it up here, along with a few other bits and pieces.

Quaker took a Havana cigar from his humidor, which sat on his private bar, sniffed the tightly rolled tobacco, clipped it and lit up, savouring the first pull.

Moon and Tarragon.

Sad. The beautiful, pale skinned, dark featured offspring they would no doubt produce together were destined not to find life in this world. Not if Quaker had a say in matters.

And Ernst Quaker had a say in any matter he chose.

On the ordinary desk security monitor he saw Emerald motion Moon to stop at the door of the penthouse antechamber, then spoke upward and in a slightly raised tone at the double doors.

'You asked to see Barker Moon when he arrived?'

He swiped an icon. The doors clicked.

'Will you bring him in, please Miss Tarragon?'

Moon looked around, as though he could not directly pinpoint the location of the speaker, then Emerald ushered him through.

Quaker's private office-lounge was part of the smaller, renovated fourth floor. It had started as a maintenance shed attached to the elevator engine, but the previous owners had been able to exploit a loophole, to do with a pre-existing structure, to classify executive offices under maintenance. Once they had been able to build rooms around the old shed, and the rooftop engine shaft, they had been able to expand. Eventually it had legally, and at great expense, been agreed upon that to the extent that the structure did not extend beyond the purpose of maintenance, as defined by the previous owners, and so far that it did not constitute an entirely new floor, which would have been against heritage rules and incurred a hefty fine, then Quaker could essentially build whatever he liked up here, behind the new neo-classical veneer.

Quaker had pretty much run with that.

His designers and architects and builders and masons had expanded the previous owners' four rooms to eight, the new four much larger, but they had been exacting, and Quaker had spared no expense to match the new extensions with the rest of the heritage building. Everyone had been paid appropriately, and Adelaide had barely reacted. Those who had not benefited financially to look the other way either hadn't noticed, hadn't cared, or had actually approved. The ideal result in such circumstances.

The previous interior had been nineties-functional, but Quaker's revision was classically luxurious, whilst also being reflective of his expensive contemporary tastes. He'd built himself an apartment, essentially, around the highly modified maintenance shed, and the new security section. This included a stunning light show view of the city to the south, and one half of the Adelaide plains to the north. From his illegal open rooftop garden, he could also see the shoreline.

Although he did not particularly want either right now, he made sure that he was watching the view, with his back to them as they entered, smoking the cigar and drinking the cognac, as though he were thinking of other things, far removed from the mundanity of a psychic who owed him a relatively minor financial debt.

Minor to him.

But not to Moon.

Emerald Tarragon entered.

'Good evening, Mister Quaker.'

She stopped and stood a few steps into the doorway. He didn't have to look to know that Moon was instantly annoyed. The old clichés, the classic intimidations were the best. Then Moon overtook Emerald and crossed the room to his desk, where he placed something on the side. A bunch of notes; a thousand most likely. He knew that Barker was operating as a psychic for hire around the city, but because so much of that sort of activity was done in secret, word of mouth, for cash, it was almost impossible to tell how much he was making. Not much, by the look of him. Apparently, before whatever accident had befallen him, he had been something of the smooth operator. Something akin to the cold-reading magicians, the fraudster occultists of the Depression Era, complete with the black suit and theatrical veneer. Now he looked like an Ordinary Joe. Making virtually no effort at all, on a limited income.

Quaker turned around and saw that Emerald was standing rigid, uneasy.

Always striking.

But never this nervous.

Why?

Surely she harboured no true feelings for this scruffy psychic con artist? He was handsome, that was not in question. Quaker was also handsome, and more mature. A lot wiser, smarter, and immensely wealthy. Surely Emerald was not… no, she was not swayed by looks. Or she would have been his already. Emerald demanded more. A lot more; what he had discovered of her history proved this. She had not slept around, but if you stood all of her former beaus in a line up, it would look like the cast of the last *Oceans* movie. In which Barker Moon would not be cast. But there had been some real surprises there.

'Good evening, Miss Tarragon.' Quaker nodded to Barker. 'Mister Moon, I gave you a month to repay me. While you have maintained a steady trickle, this is hardly the amount required.'

'It's all I have.'

Moon was silent as Quaker turned from him and went to his bar. Good. He'd made an impression. They were standing quite close now. Moon wasn't budging at Quaker's proximity, but standing behind Moon, Emerald's back arched slightly.

'Would you like a drink, Mister Moon? I understand you're quite partial to locally brewed soft drinks.'

'No thank you.'

'I admire a man who keeps a clear head. Especially those who genuinely require it.'

'I like to keep a clear conscience as well.'

'And yet you stole from me.'

'There are rules. I wasn't breaking any, until you...' Barker looked sideways, just a flinch at Emerald. '...changed them. Without telling anybody.'

'Those rules were not law, Mister Moon. They were simply common understandings held by a tenuous subculture. And barely that. Now, we have brought order. You are suffering the consequences, that is true. But things change; when there are changes, not everyone can benefit, but the greater number will.'

'The greater number will? What do they will, exactly? A bigger casino?'

'Barker, don't...'

Quaker looked to her; Moon did the same. He didn't catch the expression, Moon was in the way, but he would be sure to examine it later. Clearly though, Barker felt resentful that Emerald thought that she had any say over how he acted. They weren't even ex-lovers, not even close, yet they behaved as though they were recently divorced. Divorced, but still attached...

The penny dropped for Quaker, finally. He ignored it, although it bounced and rolled and clattered and spun to a slow halt in his mind. He simply ignored it.

'You have a BMW motorcycle, Mister Moon. I'm reliably informed that it is kept in exceptional condition, barely two months old. You also have three days remaining to meet the required deadline. I should hazard a guess that one might quite easily be able to rid oneself of such a fine motor vehicle within that time.'

'I'm not selling the bike, Quaker.'

He could feel Emerald twitch across the room. Not Mister Quaker. Just Quaker. As though they were equals. Quaker did not agree, but he did not allow it to bother him.

'Ah,' Quaker smiled, condescending. 'A man and his bike. I see your dilemma. What use the cowboy without his horse? A quandary for a teenager, surely Mister Moon?'

Emerald sighed, involuntarily. Quaker took note again; it was as though she found all this unnecessary. But this was important between men. That the more powerful tested the lesser, toyed and played with them, wound them up and set them off, intimidated them to discover the limits of their temper, their weaknesses, their sore points, their Achilles Heels; to find where their challengers, their rivals (though they be lesser) were raw and would snap if poked, bite if provoked, break if persisted upon. Die if pushed.

'You have three days remaining to deliver twenty-seven thousand.'

'Twenty-six.'

'Ah yes.' Quaker almost made a face, almost like "diddums", then ruffled the notes on the bar with the tip of his burning cigar, tempting the bright green plastic cash to melt. 'I almost forgot.'

Moon stood firm, even then; square jawed and handsome. He exchanged another glance with Emerald. And there, Quaker had it. How he looked in front of Emerald was important to him; but not as important to him as how Emerald saw herself. He was seeing Quaker's behaviour as childish, perhaps even pathological. Something like that; sociopathic or psychopathic; Machiavellian or narcissistic; or maybe just egomaniacal and controlling? It would be whatever the higher up social engineers had programmed as terminology buzzwords for the educated revolutionary classes for this cultural phase. Regardless, Moon saw Emerald as debasing herself, by working for the World; working for him. Betraying their kind, the psychics, having set up her company with him, as an exploiter of the weak. Moon had feelings for Emerald, and could not abide that she treated herself, in his view, so badly. He desired her, but could never be with her while she was working for him, even if she would have him.

Emerald's back arched again when Moon looked back at Quaker. Quaker didn't see it but he knew; the look Moon gave her would have been; '…see? He is a monster. A giant child, mentally ill, psychologically unstable. This is not how 'good people' behave.' One quick look from Moon would have encapsulated all of this. The look did its work; an edge of guilt spasmed across Emerald's eyes. A flicker she averted, ever so slightly, from Quaker.

Moon headed for the door without turning back.

'I know a good memory man in Geneva. Doing excellent work, making tremendous advances. Emerald wants you.'

Both of them flinched that time; ultimate proof.

'She needs a strong second on her team. She says that even though your psychic powers are diminished, you are still twice as good, your range and accuracy, even your stamina, as any of the psychics she employs here. You can start any time. I will take your debt off your salary, which will be at a weekly rate so generous you won't even notice. I will throw in a consultant's fee for my man in Geneva.'

Emerald was holding her breath.

Moon kept walking.

Quaker had expected nothing less.

He had played him perfectly; made him an offer he had no choice but to refuse, made him look arrogant, reckless and better still, stupid, in front of the woman he desired.

He did not look at Emerald as he departed, she did not look at him either.

The lift opened, perfectly in time.

Moon was gone.


III


Barker followed Emerald from the bar, throwing a look to Jake.

*Uh oh. I'm in trouble now.*

Jake smiled back, rolling his eyes and trying to pretend that he was sure it would all be fine, like Emerald Tarragon was taking convicted psychic cheats up to the billionaire boss's secret penthouse headquarters every day here. Like, it happens all the time. All the time!

Emerald led Barker silently through the casino to a nondescript staff corridor behind the café, hidden in plain sight beneath the escalators to the matrix banks. The doors opened before they got there and Emerald entered first. They didn't meet each other's eyes as Barker entered and both of them turned to face the doors.

The Ox was killing him.

He sighed, long and a little pained, but under his breath he muttered, low enough for Emerald to hear, but not for a security mic in the ceiling to pick up.

'…he's only about the money…'

Emerald didn't respond, but just as the elevator was about to open, she shifted her stance awkwardly and uttered something back in similar fashion. All Barker heard was:

'…*so bloody naïve*…'

Then she was out. Barker stood a second, thinking. Was he actually going to do this? Go in and let this egomaniac speak to him as though he were the school principal of the whole city? He supposed he was.

'..after you…'

Emerald led him down a corridor from the elevator, past a futuristic looking security station that made him feel old and out of touch, where Emerald nodded at a normal, World-uniformed guard, then they turned a corner and walked down another short corridor to some double doors. The doors clicked and she opened them manually, with both hands, one on each handle.

He tried not to place his gaze upon her, but it was very difficult.

Those hands, her figure, the simple physical act of opening the doors, and, naturally, The Ox.

She seemed insanely well-put-together now.

Barker had come back to the casino maybe six or seven times in the past eighteen months and each time walked away with a few grand. Maybe two, maybe three. Once, four. He had learned recently that since Quaker had taken over the place, it had added up to twenty-nine thousand; someone had been keeping track, even if he hadn't. He hadn't seen Emerald in all that time, and had been too busy working with Cheryl to consider Emerald in any way that was not fantasy. He hadn't thought about her challenge much, other than at least once every single day, but never seriously; never in any way he was going to act upon.

He had the answer; he'd guessed it immediately.

He dared not use it.

Despite this, every time he had come to the casino he had hoped to see her, but never had, and had never asked after her. He had sensed though, very clearly, somewhere in the back of his mind, that she was still in the city, and that if she had wanted to see him, she would have found a way; what with her pick of men, and all that.

Then one day, he had been arrested by Quaker's private police and invoiced for twenty-nine thousand dollars. Finally, his hand forced, he had demanded to see Emerald, suspecting that this, whatever it was, was part of the grand idea she had mentioned the night they'd met. Barker had been told that Emerald was out of town, and in any regard did not deal personally with thieves. He had rolled up the invoice and thrown it like dice down the one remaining craps table on his way out.

The next time he had seen Emerald, she had looked like she did now. She'd tried to call him, but he hadn't answered. So she'd tracked him down to his local café, and spoken to him on the street.

Emerald wasn't casual chic any more. She was still wearing a plain black tee, but it was underneath a business suit that made her look so stylish, so fully empowered, and so magnificently attractive that it was actually, genuinely scary.

Barker hated it.

She might as well have been driving around in an AFV, or gliding around in a Dalek shell, her armour was so impenetrable now.

She had apologized profusely; she realized that she had promised to have a conversation with him first, to offer him a job on the team, to avoid this kind of situation or at least give him fair warning. But she had been away for a couple of days and a new recruit had not been made aware of the 'no go' list. The processing had been underway for days before Emerald had returned, and now there was nothing she could do about it.

They had had words.

Right there on the street.

It had not been pleasant.

It had not gone well.

The invoice had not been revoked.

He had returned to the casino and Quaker himself had come down to the floor, and in no uncertain terms, given him terms. Barker had been so shocked at all this that he had walked out of the casino without a response. When Emerald had turned up at the door to his apartment, two days later, one week ago, Barker had just returned from a reasonably lucrative job with Cheryl. Emerald's presence had so darkened his mood that he had simply handed her two grand from the job, right then and there. He had told her; *that's all you're getting*, and slammed the door in her face.

But now he had made Bach bring him into the city, and asked Chief Inspector Parry to bring him here, right here, on a freezing Tuesday night, with a thousand dollars in his pocket. Now Quaker had summoned him up to his office. Now he was standing beside Emerald Tarragon again. Angry.

As they entered the office, Quaker was watching the city from one of his notoriously illegal windows, up here in his luxury apartment on top of his casino, that he had paid enough people to be able to buy and then build this. It was a great view. Almost an opposing view of the Adelaide valley, though no lesser, to that of the balcony at the Lion and Unicorn. He couldn't blame Quaker for wanting to spend a lot of time up here. He might do the same if he had that much money. Then again, he might not. It was just more camouflage; he had built it under cover of night, hidden it from sight by blending the veneer into the surroundings, and made bribes, so there would not be a fuss. And on top of it all; it was fine. It looked great. Like it had always been there.

Nobody cared.

Quaker was posing, that was completely obvious. He looked like something out of *Dallas*, or *Dynasty*; any one of those ridiculous shows that had been popular when he was a kid, from which Quaker, being a good generation older, had probably taken his cues. In his left hand was a cognac balloon, with just a few sips of brandy remaining, in his right, a Havana cigar. The combination delivered him, Barker suspected, a power kick that Quaker handled extremely well. The smoke was pleasant enough if you didn't hate cigars; the air conditioning was sucking up most of it anyway. Quaker himself looked terrific; traditionally great, even. He could have passed for early fifties, but Barker knew that he was a well-preserved sixty-three. He looked a bit like that Australian actor, the one who had been awfully good-looking, kind of cruelly handsome, but really terrible in just about every soap opera they had made here in the seventies and eighties. But then he had flown to Los Angeles, adopted a neutral American accent, and now he won guest-star Emmys for playing The President in just about every drama series the Americans had made in the past twenty years. One new skill and a leap of faith, and a person's career, their fortune and reputation, could change, just like that.

*I'm looking at you, Emerald Tarragon.*

Actually he was trying not to. But she had overtaken him and was now standing a few steps ahead. Like a butler. Jesus. The severe but sleek black pant suit, cut specifically for her, by someone who knew what they were doing, made her bottom look amazing… so he overtook her. But he misjudged his own stored tension, his own speed, the power of The Ox, and the size of the room, and was suddenly slamming the money down on Quaker's desk like a complete dick.

Quaker turned around and looked totally, genuinely unimpressed.

He knew what a thousand dollars was to Barker.

Now who was being a dick?

And the way Quaker looked at Emerald…

Or rather, the way he pretended not to.

But the one second his eyes passed over her they lit up like Lucifer, absorbed every pixel of her so that he could pore over them later in his imagination; that was scary. Quaker wanted her, so badly. And Emerald stood straighter when his gaze passed.

Was she nervous?

Why?

Surely she wasn't hot for the wealthy older man?

'Good evening, Miss Tarragon.' Quaker nodded to Barker. 'Mister Moon, I gave you a month to repay me. While you have maintained a steady trickle, this is hardly the amount required.'

Barker shrugged. Fuck you. 'It's all I have.'

Quaker turned from him and went to his bar.

Like… he didn't know what to make of someone who might actually take more than three weeks to raise thirty-odd-grand. And instalments, no less. What an arsehole. And now he was standing closer, trying some standover bullshit. It weirded Barker out, but he stayed put. Then, oddly, he felt something from Emerald. She was hating this. Wishing it was over; wishing she could get out of here, leave them both to it.

To what? Barker wondered. What did she think was happening here?

And why had she… let him know? Allowed the edge of a ripple of her discomfort to pulse out and inform him?

'Would you like a drink, Mister Moon? I understand you're quite partial to locally brewed soft drinks.'

'No thank you.'

'I admire a man who keeps a clear head. Especially those who genuinely require it.'

'I like to keep a clear conscience as well.'

'And yet you stole from me.'

'There are rules. I wasn't breaking any, until you…' He looked sideways, just a flinch at Emerald. '…changed them. Without telling anybody.'

'Those rules were not law, Mister Moon. They were simply common understandings held by a tenuous subculture. Barely that. We have brought order. You are suffering the consequences, that is true. But things change; when there are changes, not everyone can benefit, but the greater number will.'

'The greater number will? What do they will, exactly? For a bigger casino?'

'Barker, don't…'

Barker looked around at her. What the hell was that? Which one of them was she protecting, concerned for? The expression she returned was moderate anger, and a clearer indication of her dislike for what was going on. She didn't like any of it. Was it just that she had created it? Was that what was making her feel uncomfortable? Seeing her friends fight?

But; neither of them were her friends. A potential client and a boss, that was all.

'You have a BMW motorcycle, Mister Moon. I'm reliably informed that it is kept in exceptional condition, barely three months old. You also have three days remaining to meet the required deadline. I should hazard a guess that one might quite easily be able to rid oneself of such a fine motor vehicle within that time.'

Barker kept looking at Emerald. Even when he looked back at Quaker, barely listening to his bullshit, he was still really looking at Emerald. She was wearing less makeup, more subtle. No lipstick. And she looked even more intimidatingly unique than before; the hair straightened and tied back.

Holy crap.

She was going to get him killed.

'I'm not selling the bike, Quaker.'

Barker felt a spike; a warning from Emerald. Do not piss him off.

Barker ignored it, but Quaker had sensed something.

'Ah. A man and his bike. I see your dilemma. What use the cowboy without his horse? A quandary for a teenager, surely Mister Moon?'

But, that wasn't it.

Not at all.

Did Quaker see everything in clichés of power?

Emerald sighed, involuntarily.

Barker had given up trying to make sense of her. Did she care about him or not? Was she concerned that he wasn't going to be able to find that kind of money? That this shouldn't have been happening? That she had taken her eye off the ball, his ball, and now he was fucked? That they should have called each other eighteen months ago, the night they'd met, the next morning, that afternoon; whatever, and figured this the fuck out? But now that everything was starting up again, this was all going to get sucked into it, and become…

What?

Weaponized against him?

'You have three days remaining to deliver twenty-seven thousand.'

'Twenty-six.' Barker said it without thinking.

'Ah yes.' Barker saw him try to set the thousand dollars on fire with the tip of his cigar. *What a dick.* 'I almost forgot.'

Moon stared at the cigar tip, then turned to Emerald again.

He didn't care if the shields were up or not.

*Look at this prick. Who does he think he is?*

She responded: *He's security.*

*He's a fuckhead. I could live on that for a fortnight and he thinks he's making a point by burning it in front of me…*

*He isn't —*

*He might as fucking well be!*

Barker turned back to Quaker. He let him see how disappointed he was that Emerald was in his employ. Quaker couldn't help it and looked to Emerald. He saw something there he didn't like.

Barker had had enough. This was ridiculous. He turned to exit.

*Barker, he's security! We need security!*

*He's evil. Ordinary, exploitative, human evil.*

'I know a good memory man in Geneva. Doing excellent work, making tremendous advances. Emerald wants you.'

She flinched and he flinched at the wordless psychic anger they exchanged, left over from the previous exchange but hotter, angrier at Quaker's bait.

'She needs a strong second. She says…'

The anger remained. Barker couldn't listen to him crapping on, he tuned him out.

But Quaker had drawn them out.

And something else, too; hurt. He had brought a mutual, emotional, psychic hurt to the surface, hurt that neither would back down, so they could not mean more to each other than they did now. Inexpressible frustration at the inexpressible frustration.

'…I will throw in a consultant's fee for my man in Geneva.'

*Men like this destroy everything they touch. And he will touch you, if you stay.*

Emerald was holding her breath.

*Go. Don't say another word Barker.*

He was telling her as he walked to the elevator:

*He is sociopathic; he is keeping mental notes; he will play you and have you, and you will not know how it happened, or what hit you. Then you will be the wealthiest, emptiest psychic in the world. I'm not coming back.*

The elevator opened. He had summoned it.

*I just paid a thousand bucks to see you. He can come and get the rest himself. I'm done.*

Barker remained cool until the lift door closed.

Then he punched the wall.

Watching the monitors with Quaker, Emerald flinched.

Had they really just done that? Thrown thoughts back and forth? Like they had been shouting at each other? There was only one other person she knew who could do that with her.

She watched as Barker held his hand, then shook it, feeling no doubt like a prize idiot.

'You feel pity, Emerald?'

She knew, knew for certain, that he had not been able to do that before. Maybe even before tonight. Were his fabled psychic strengths returning?

'No.' She had responded quickly, but not too quickly. Then she amended, just as fast, but clearly considered. 'A little. I suppose.'

Quaker nodded. 'The mathematically gifted are no more allowed to come to my casino and count cards than psychics, like Moon, who are able to read the minds of my dealers, or read the vibrations in the air; or whatever it is that they do. I'll leave that to you. But he is lucky; lucky I allowed him the chance to repay the money he stole. He could work it off, fairly, a good deal, like Jürgen, but he refuses every offer. He abused the system. He is not a special case.'

'I agree.'

Although…

He turned off the monitor, apparently having no interest in watching Barker depart. Or was it that he had no desire for *her* to watch Barker depart?

To watch her watch?

Fuck; this was getting intense, and complicated.

Barker was a nice guy. He was handsome. She had liked him. But she could resist him. Even though she'd thought about him, she *had* resisted him. She had overthought it; tried to imagine a scenario where it could work. Where he could fit in. But she did not want to settle again. Maybe if he'd had his shit together, maybe if he had not invested so much of himself and his reputation in the occult, so much of which she was now sure was theatre, or plain nonsense.

She didn't mind that he had a past.

He had an edge, which was fine.

But he could not protect himself.

She had known that, right from when she'd first set eyes upon him. He was not being smart, he had no plan, no end game. He had fallen to a demon, but still had not protected himself against further incursion. And he thought she was the stupid one? No; he had to be kept at arm's length. She had made that decision. And that had been *before* she had known that he had once been one of the most powerful acolyte sorcerers in the world.

He'd blown it already.

Still. It didn't make her like him any less.

Just; it made him irresponsible, undependable.

She didn't care how it had happened; if he had saved the world from a planet-killing demon, saved a busload of orphaned children, or just made a play for power that had backfired. What mattered was; he had failed, and now he was out. Barker Moon was broken, and while he was clearly a good guy, his welfare beyond a certain point was none of her concern. Emerald Tarragon had had enough of 'good guys', 'trying to make a difference'.

'Then why the pity, Emerald?'

Emerald was stunned. Had she really confessed to that?

'Emerald, catching men like Barker Moon is the foundation of your business. This test period has been note-perfect. Because of my endorsement, casinos around the world will soon be demanding the services you provide. You are going to be very wealthy.'

'I have thanked you for that opportunity, Mister Quaker. I do feel slightly responsible for Barker's present dilemma. I considered him as a potential second, as you know. But to be completely honest with you, he does have a kind of rugged charm that appeals to me. Or, should I say, appeals to an aspect of my personality that I once allowed to dominate. I am familiar with men like Barker; not necessarily in the romantic sense but… in the business sense, certainly. He is of no… no *real* interest to me.'

Quaker was apparently satisfied. 'You grifted yourself, with a man not unlike him.'

'That's true. But it's not a path I wish to revisit.'

'You no longer indulge the delusion of being able to fix a broken man.'

That had been a statement.

Emerald's shoulders tightened. 'I prefer to fix broken roulette wheels.'

Quaker nodded, and allowed himself a satisfied smile.

'I admired the efforts you made, to restore the original mahogany. They say that wheel now works better than it ever has.'

'I know.'

'If only people responded to so much care and attention.'

Now Emerald nodded, and allowed herself a smile.

'Your point is well made. My previous attempts at fixing… people, did not end well for either of us. Those attempts led me to re-evaluate. To an epiphany, or sorts, if you will. Not just my own existence, but the lives of those like me.' She smiled tightly at Quaker. 'And now here we are."

'It's hard to believe a woman like you has never been married.'

'You are aware of my romantic history.' Emerald froze her face, and betrayed no emotion at all. 'At first it was lifestyle. Psychic grifters, even honest psychics… you can equate the lifestyle with painters, if you like. Poets if you must. There is something about us, about accepting the gifts we have, that makes us prone to refusing any other work, any other lifestyle, once we've been called. Awakened. But it pulls us onto an unreliable plane of existence. Energies there shift as readily as allegiances do. Proof is difficult, so payment is often refused.'

'But you… transcended that lifestyle?'

'With the men I cared for after that, it always ended in tragedy. Terrible tragedy, sometimes. I don't know how much you know about New York. Suffice to say; the media know nothing. Nothing at all.'

Quaker did not respond. She knew; he'd found out very little about New York.

How could he have?

'And so you came here, to a place where many of the more skilled psychics seem to have gravitated… to a place of exacting quantities, and equations, and clear illusions. You thought; if you could practice your art illegally, to make an unreliable living, why not find a way to practice legally, in a regulated fashion, and make…?'

'I wanted to break ground on proving that what we do has validity. I wanted to – I am – ensuring that there is a measurable outcome, from which we can set negotiated fees.'

He was building up to something.

He was going to make an overture.

This was the kind of man he was; this was why Emerald had come here, to this city, and approached him, and not any of the others; not the womanizer up north, nor the maniac on the east coast. Quaker was old school. He was handsome and, in context with his business, so far as she had been able to determine, he was honourable. He was, in short, and if things went as far as she was prepared to take them, an acceptable option.

She knew this was cold. She knew that she was making a calculation. But she had become cold; made herself cold. Come to yet another cold city, to be cold. If she were truly, legitimately, to exploit her abilities in an industry that wasn't already totally corrupt with her kind, this was her only option.

In the past two years, since New York, she had learned to meditate again. To shut down her emotions, her chattering mind; her desires and dreams, her biological clock, her sex drive. She had assessed, dispassionately, but with focus and intellect, how she could move forward safely, and still live with herself. And from this position of centred rationality, she had patiently awaited an opportunity, for her mind to alert her to her best possible option. She had heard mystics say that from this state, the universe, the cosmic mind, or God, would show you the nearest astral on-ramp to the path you desired to follow. Either that, or manifest the best and closest version for what it was you desired, or had planned to achieve, given where you currently stood. The drive to Montreal had shown her that.

But still, even after an experience like that, you had to be sure.

Your will had to be completely focussed.

Then you had to let go, and take action accordingly.

Through this process, and free of the thing she had referred to as Coveth, Emerald had finally learned who she was.

This was clear to her now.

Emerald was a psychic, but she was not a mystic, nor was she superstitious, or religious in any way. She was spiritual, but only in the broadest, most noncommittal sense of having a general optimism toward the possibility that there was something greater, something no human mind could ever hope to grasp, that meant that all was good, or in the very least One, and in harmony, in the end. And yet, despite her general skepticism, this had happened; the path had opened up. She had been shown the way. Of course; that was how a mystic would see it. But she knew better. She had focussed and utilized, for the first time, anything close to the full power of her own mind; her ordinary human brain, and her general consciousness. In doing that, in manifesting focus and intent within her own mind, using age-old techniques involving willpower, she had set herself to work, to provide a solution. When the clouds had parted, so to speak, and given her the idea for Wires Inc, there was no cosmic order to it, other than the reflected cosmic order of her own mind; that which she had allowed to operate, her own consciousness, and the pure focus of her will toward finding a solution.

A lot of it had been obvious, in the end.

Just a matter of facing the truth; like so much else.

And so, free of Coveth, she had made her final play.

She had headed for home; a home she could make, and be satisfied with.

Plenty of beautiful women had gained security, and position, even independent wealth, by marrying a millionaire or billionaire, sometimes a trillionaire these days, and and becoming his… trophy wife?

She still smiled at that expression.

Although she had to wonder; was that still the tabloid expression?

She dipped into that world so infrequently these days.

And in turn, plenty of psychic women had manipulated those wealthy men, in order to have them part with their wealth. Many women, both psychics and the physically beautiful, had used one or both of those factors to manipulate themselves into a position of protection; legally, illegally, charmingly, and with guile and-or cunning. Emerald had never done this. Coveth had never allowed it; not with any of her five previous….

How much *did* Quaker know?

It didn't matter.

He was in.

But regardless, her studies into these relationships, if not exactly cold arrangements, had also revealed to her that there was always risk; just as brazenly, those relationships, those schemes, often failed, and the women were left broke, if not broken, sometimes even publicly humiliated and more often than not ostracized from their peers.

By the same means however, many did secure a business of their own. But then again, after a separation or divorce, the business could go down, and they were back out again. Or, by the same token, their business could be brought down. With money, through spite. Especially if the said business's client-base was essentially filled with friends of the husband. People, ex-wives, could be brought down, brought low, through all sorts of means. But that was not for Emerald. What Emerald desired, if not demanded now, was security. She would have her looks forever; she was that sort. She would not become fat or masculine as she grew older. Her mother hadn't, nor had her grandmother. But even as she would retain her slim figure and bone structure, she would not be young, and vital, and sexually viable. She would not be fertile, nor as determined. She would fade, as we all did, and want it least when she needed it the most.

Casino to casino, grift to grift, she had been all over. Not the entire world, but enough of each country to know. Pursued by men she loathed, exploited by men she loved. Quaker must have known this, known she had been with Manny, even if he hadn't known how it had ended. He would know their type; the men she had been with, as well as she knew it herself; he would have… done the math, as the Americans say. Done his homework, done some digging. That didn't matter. She had come up with the idea of the business and offered it to the person best-suited to its use, at the same time knowing that any wealthy man in that position, having been made that proposition, would want to possess her as well.

It was a foregone conclusion, a part of the equation.

Without Coveth, it would work.

But there could be no pretending otherwise in this world; he would want her. This was not a world where the social justice of sexual equality had any real meaning. This was a world where everything, down to the last cent, was calculated. Everything was currency, and for a woman that included age, beauty and sexual viability. All was commoditized, all was negotiable, but all of it went, at one time or another, to someone.

Two years ago, in the space of a few hours, Emerald had almost lost everything.

People had tried to kill her.

Not for the first time, people had tried to disfigure her.

There had been blood, and tragedy.

There had even been a few days where her powers had not functioned, something she had not believed possible.

She had turned thirty-five.

She had barely survived, but she had found the cold. Not the cold of Central Park in winter, nor Canada in January; not even the nineteenth story of a mystical parkade. A different cold. Found it, ushered it, fed it, nurtured it, befriended it, and picked its brains for all it was worth. She had hidden from the world for weeks, then on the day she had emerged, she had seen Ernst Quaker on the street. Coming out of a building, getting into a private car. Exposed to the elements for less than a second.

And the dominos had fallen.

This was her way in.

This was her sign, from whatever source.

And yes, she would allow herself. He was handsome. Not everyone's handsome, but close enough to hers to be more than acceptable. His body was as healthy as money could keep it. She had heard that he knew what he was doing; how to read and respond to a woman, and so she was prepared to be surprised, to be properly seduced and perhaps even swept up. Even to believe it. She had not had to convince herself to like him. He was older, by a quarter century, and old-school, but he had old-fashioned manners, and some natural grace. He possessed no natural wit but he had shown her some kindness, and wisdom. He was masculine; she had seen an edge of brutality in his business dealings, that had also revealed a cruel streak; in competition at least. She had not liked or enjoyed that. It did not excite her. But she had expected that; it was the price of her newfound coldness, her new rationality. Cruelty was a part of power, and power protected. She would deal. Compartmentalize. Appreciate the percentages; only this slice of him was…

An acceptable loss for a much greater gain.

She would not be Kay Corleone; she would not ask.

Rather, she would tend to her own business, and be safe.

And from there, she could build a home.

V

Emerald had met one of Quaker's ex-wives, his second, an Italian film star only a few years her senior, the mother of his only son. He was only twenty-two, but his father had bought him a shoe store in his mother's home city, and the son had turned it into an international footwear franchise that fashion magazines liked to use in photoshoots with guesting film stars. She had been on the east coast, out here, filming a cameo in an American science fiction spectacular when she had flown over to Adelaide for the day to see him. She had at first, quite innocently and very politely, mistaken Emerald for the hostess, then as his current mistress, but then been informed by Quaker in no uncertain terms that Emerald was the Head Supervisor of Casino Security and a business colleague – despite his best efforts to take her to dinner.

There had been no such overture; Quaker had seen that last quip, hitherto his most advanced level of humour, as helping Emerald save face. And, in the eyes of the film star, it had. Emerald had appreciated that.

Before the film star had departed, she had found Emerald outside, smoking the second of her three daily cigarettes. She didn't like to smoke up with the punters; it was too depressing. That was a slice of the pie she was learning to remove, and freeze.

'He admires you. He respects you.'

Emerald had been away with the pixies, staring out over the Torrens Lake. The European film star had been wearing huge dark glasses and a dark gown, like a sixties screen icon desperate to be seen trying not to be seen.

'His needs are simple; his routine is nothing special...' The Italian had told her. '...but I found his predictability part of his charm. Staying with what he knows; what he has perfected; that is part of his wisdom, his strength, his power. He has stamina, but you will always be on top, where he can admire you while he is inside you.'

Emerald's newfound coldness had set in by then.

'I simply present myself. I will accept what he offers.'

The film star had nodded. It had actually been like some classic European movie; outside in last winter's core, the two of them standing side-by-side on the rise above the lake, just before the bridge, staring out with the wind blowing up, right onto their chests, speaking without looking at each other.

'Not everyone can make this decision. You are beautiful enough. But making yourself available to a man you might not love. Might not ever love. May not even like by the time you are done...'

'Done?'

'Ten years and a child. It doesn't matter who or what you are; you have your arrangement with yourself, and that is his. You do not know this?'

'I knew he'd been married... three times.'

'For ten years each. With one child in each. He will want another child. Do you have another cigarette?'

She gave her one, and lit another herself. It was a rare day she smoked four, but she always needed a last one, before she slept, so this would be one of those days.

'Can you have children?'

'With him. Yes.'

'With money, you mean? Is there a problem?'

'If there is a problem, it might require money. But it should be okay.'

'He will expect you to have thought everything through. He will not ask; if you have not, he will see it as a betrayal.'

Emerald lit the cigarette and passed the famous actress the lighter.

'Without him, I will be dead in a few years.'

'Yes. I thought the same.'

She lit her cigarette, inhaled, then waved it casually at her.

'Of me, not yourself. Men have already tried to take your life?'

'More.'

'I see. Your strange world. I had a great grandfather…' She exhaled. 'Never mind. Ernst has already convinced me.'

'Convinced you?'

'That your powers are true, your business is real; he will observe you, at length. Then he will seduce you. Are you able?'

'I can't act. I'm terrible. The one time I managed anything passable, they had to make me better with computers. People told me I was better than I was, because… well, I don't have to explain how that works. You must have seen a million of me.'

'No. A few.'

'They've replaced me now. Nobody noticed.'

'I don't think you are so terrible. Are you open to seduction? Can you play?'

'I… could. We'll see. I think so.'

'You have done well, to bind him to your strange world. There is no better challenge to a man like Ernst Quaker than a frontier unchallenged. If he can protect you from it, he will. If he can claim territory as he does, he will reward you for being the reason.'

'I'd considered that. But not seriously. I don't think the two worlds cross-over well. Some manage, but it goes back centuries. Quaker is all… real. Material. If he tries to blend that world with his, I don't think he will thank me. I need to make sure he understands that. My offer is to define it, and keep it at bay. That is all.'

The actress nodded. 'He should know that. You should force him to understand that, if you can. I never knew it was real.'

Emerald exhaled. 'It is.'

'Then, if I may ask; the first thing I wondered was, why have your kind not taken over?'

Emerald shrugged lightly. 'Why have his kind not taken over?'

'His kind?'

'Sociopathic materialists.'

'You believe him to be that?'

'He is that. There is no question.'

'Psychopathic?'

'Sociopathic. There's a spectrum.'

'I see. Sociopathic materialist…' She huffed. "I suppose I can see that. I still don't know if he ever truly loved me. He did in his way, but… not as the peasant classes do.'

'The peasant classes?'

'Drinking and fighting and fucking. Love is a stress they exorcise with sex, because they know they will never escape their socio-economic class, to be happy any other way. They fight to fall out, to be angry, for the adrenalin; then they fuck to be friends again. They call that love. They fuck so much to begin with that they all have more children than they can afford. Then the fighting becomes too real. The problems too big. They still fight and make up. But it takes longer to make up. Then they are older, and more exhausted, and the makeup sex is no good. Soon, there is no sex. Only fighting. And too many children.'

Emerald smiled, tightly. 'That sounds like my sister.'

'She is not a witch, like you?'

'I'm not a witch.' Emerald inhaled. 'Witches are different.' She exhaled. 'My sister is a witch though; just, different again to the ones you mean.'

This amused the movie star.

'You have not answered my question, Emerald. I may call you Emerald.'

Emerald shrugged. 'Why don't we take over? Because we fight. Like the businessmen. Like lovers and families. Like everyone. People say, if only we were all rational, things would be better; but we are not. Passion is the most powerful. Those who truly realize that exploit it. Rationality is just another negotiation method around passion; it essentially ignores it. Logic might describe base reality, but it is always destroyed by passion. Psychics who are ruled by passion fight and fuck, and come undone, just like anyone else. Mostly.'

'Not you? You will exploit that reality?'

'There is no single reality; just different ways of describing different ways of negotiating different levels of the reality matrix.'

'They offered me a part in that film. I didn't understand the script, so I turned it down.'

'Are you trying to illustrate my point? Or is the matrix listening?'

The actress smirked.

'Don't think I am unaware of your position. Powerful men want to possess women like us, and when you will not let them, they will want to destroy you. From within; so it shows on the outside. If we wish to remain as we were made, if we wish to learn what the Gods intended, we must find sanctuary, with the best of them. We must find protection, we must find the quiet, and the cold, until we grow accustomed to the chill, and the silence, and then we must listen for what we tell ourselves, from deep within; frozen, alone and naked. Great beauty is power, and power must be wielded, for a purpose. That purpose can only be learned then, in that moment. Then, how. How to wield it. Everyone will try and prevent you. But, I think you will succeed. With or without my husband.'

She exhaled then, and stomped the cigarette under her shoe, not quite half finished.

'I go back to when nobody cared. People smoked. My first director gave me the best advice about smoking.'

'Okay...'

'Never more than half.'

'What? Is the second half more carcinogenic?'

The actress laughed. 'No. Only the first half is cool. The first two fifths. After that, it makes you look like you need it. Unclean, like a junkie. Put it out, light another.'

'Expensive.'

'You won't care.'

She looked past Emerald then, up to the fourth floor.

'Money cannot buy happiness. But it can buy an amicable separation out of sadness, so one can resume, and begin the search for happiness once again.'

Now here Emerald was, up on that fourth floor; her plan playing out as she had hoped, the prediction of the actress coming true.

He had waited a year. He had allowed her to prove herself, allowed her business to prove itself. He had allowed her to keep it, and had endorsed her.

And… now here she was.

Quaker walked back to his bar. It seemed he required a second cognac. He wasn't really a drinker. Sometimes she felt he did it just because he was supposed to; a cognac and a cigar in the evening. She hadn't realized until now how much of his private pad was left over from the old casino. Gold and scarlet. Shining. Over the plush carpet, the shoes that would, only months before, have been the equivalent to a week's psychic grifting for her, hardly made a sound. For a second, the notion of stalking came to mind.

She wondered if she should pay attention to that.

It felt resonant, not just an association.

How much did he really see up here?

How many agents did he have, watching?

She decided not to pay attention. She returned instead to the previous thought. He'd had a lot of the décor repurposed, but it had been appropriated from downstairs, before the five-million-dollar facelift, that was for sure. She realized; this was his era. This was where he felt at home; these were his symbols, his trappings of power. Why had he changed it, downstairs?

'Yes. You have thanked me, Emerald. You thanked me by coming to me with Wires Inc. first. But I would like to discuss the matter further.'

Quaker poured a splash more brandy into his balloon.

'…Emerald, would you be available for dinner? Tomorrow?'

There was an uneasiness within her own response that annoyed Emerald.

'I would...' She placed her hands behind her back and arched her shoulders deliberately. 'I would look forward to it.'

Quaker swirled the brandy, the auburn elixir licking the glass globe as it swirled within its own private maelstrom, a whirlpool he controlled completely.

'I'll make some reservations and text you where to meet. Unless that's...?'

'Wherever you choose, I'm sure it will be... I'll look forward to it.'

There was a moment, then. Neither was really sure where they stood. Emerald was sure that Quaker was becoming uncomfortable, and that he was entirely unused to feeling that way. So she left with a curt nod, without another word, feeling initially awkward, then angry for that.

This was what she had wanted. Her own business. Quaker offered protection, and wealth. There was no question; this was the smart move. So what if Quaker was old school? He knew her past. She had made it plain to him, when she had made her proposal, that her past was open to him. He could investigate any area he liked. So long as it remained private, between them and his investigator, that was on the table.

So, here she was.

She had made it, another step.

Quaker had observed her for a year, watched and approved.

Apparently, the investment had been worthwhile.

# CHAPTER TWENTY-EIGHT: BROAD MOONLIGHT

The second Barker stepped outside of the casino, he realized that something was terribly wrong. It was as though his powers had returned; and yet he knew they hadn't. It hadn't been the shock of the cold either; merely stepping out of the air-conditioning. There was genuinely something inside the place that dampened the mind's natural senses, and almost completely blocked his, or he assumed, anyone's psychic abilities. He almost reeled as he stepped out through the central of the three arches and out, onto the road outside.

*What had happened here?*

There was no civilian traffic, but a trio of parked cab drivers on the rank looked up simultaneously to see whether he was a fare. He wasn't and, standing out in the middle of the road, they picked it just by looking at him. Tagged him as a broke loser in under a second.

He looked back, behind him, into the brightly-lit marble lobby. The triple-arch was deep, and had probably been a proper porte-cochère at one time, superseded now by the sort of basic, no-nonsense, pick-up and drop-off stretch of pavement that almost all hotels and airports now had; the higgledy-piggledy cul-de-sac roundabout that functioned purely upon the common understanding that, whether you were coming or going; late, on time or early, everyone was expected to be in a hurry.

The cul-de-sac before him went straight up to the end of the casino building before turning back in a tight but longish teardrop, out again to North Terrace, with the point of the teardrop facing back out. Barker walked over and looked down into the hollow center of the teardrop, which was foot-pathed right around, encircled with five gold-glowing ye-olde colonial street lamps, and barred with a low concrete wall. The drop beyond, through the centre of the tear, was steep; a full floor.

A second lane came in from North Terrace, tightly parallel with the teardrop cul-de-sac, and through the eye, looking down to the other side, you could see it descend, ramping down at forty-five degrees and curving in, under the casino to the carpark, forming a second teardrop. That road also led out to the bridge, and across to the alien mothership.

Also along the other side were the basement trade-entrances to the lower floors of Parliament House, the oldest rear walls of which faced the casino, and complemented the fake golden street lamps. Barker's eyes traced the path fully, bringing him back to where he stood, at the tip of the teardrop, outside the triple arch.

Thunder rumbled.

He thought of the lake, just through, down there.

The bridge that ran across it.

The weir, just a little further down, that formed it.

The thing there, that had wanted the four girls, two years ago, to have no barrier between their company and the cable car to the Hills.

*Why?*

He walked around a bit. The Festival Centre blocked the view of the river, and the lake straight ahead, but he walked toward it anyway, just to get further away from the feeling of void; the spiritual and magical void at the heart of the casino, and think through the incident once more.

The further away he walked, the more he felt his mind return.

Then he stopped.

'What the…?'

How could that be?

He'd zapped Emerald, tonight, *in there*; they'd snapped at each other telepathically.

*How?*

If there was something, a force, in there, blocking all supernatural ability other than its own ability to block everything else, then…. *how?*

And; was that what it was? Was that the feeling he'd had coming out?

A series of thoughts came together, a series of… not memories, but things he'd missed, started coming together. He'd seen Cheryl; known she was at the casino, earlier. He'd opened the portal at The Lion. He'd fought and survived some kind of supernatural battle, and now he was piercing a veil around the casino that was designed to prevent all psychic activity.

And…*so was Emerald.*

Jesus Christ.

*What had she done?*

Then he remembered.

Right now, it didn't matter.

He'd forgotten about Cheryl.

He pulled his phone from his breast-coat-pocket as he strolled further down the teardrop, seeing a sign; Railway Road. They had even named it, the literal hook-in from the road. He slipped on his Bluetooth and checked the screen.

Nothing. No more messages.

He called her.

Nothing, it rang out. No message bank.

Had she gone back to the apartment? Phone dead, recharging? Was she asleep? Maybe she was right here, in there, in the casino, gambling, managing to hide her tricks from Emerald; having the time of her life?

Stupid.

No, there was something happening. Hopefully not to Cheryl, but it was something big, and he was still too magically repressed to understand what it was. He felt impotent, not being able to know; as though before, he would have known, immediately.

The phone rang.

Barker answered.

'Chief Inspector.'

'Anything?'

That was curious.

Was it just the way a cop started a conversation? That was, to all intents and purposes, professional? But no; it said something. His finding, or not finding Cheryl was not the only thing Parry was waiting for.

'No sign of her. I was in there…' Barker paused and considered a second. '…Parry, I had a secondary purpose. Another… comrade. I think there's something very weird, maybe very bad happening here. Cheryl would usually keep low and just pop out when she saw me, and we'd be gone. Cheryl's absence, and my other friend… whatever she might be doing… they might be connected.'

'Do you want to tell me who that other friend is?'

'Cheryl getting fed up waiting, going on ahead; that would be fine, obviously, any other night. Look, maybe her phone *is* dead? Maybe she's flirting and I would have cramped her style? But on a night like this… if she's still there…? Whatever reason it takes for that to happen, that's trouble.'

Barker kept walking along the Railway Road, away from the main street, toward the Festival Centre and the Torrens Lake, away from Parry, or at least where Barker assumed Parry to be. He reached the end of Railway and saw that there was now a secondary bridge, just around the corner. It led over the road below to the main, iconic, rough-white-concrete concourse, and main entrances and exits of the Festival Centre. He walked half way, amazed. So that the theatre people, the opera people, the lonely old wealthy people, could wander directly over here too, directly into the casino. What had Quaker paid the City Council, or whoever, for the savage advantage of that kind of outright parasitic interconnectedness?

He stopped in the middle and looked down.

The bridge was also a one-floor dead drop onto asphalt, like the inner teardrop.

But from here, to his left, he could see the start of the lower, much larger bridge, around the side of the Centre, and a hint of the Torrens Lake itself.

He heard a metal crunch; the push-bar on an emergency door, and through the darkness there was a brief glow of fluorescent light across the road below. Then it was gone. His eyes couldn't adjust, then he heard a strange clicking sound. He smiled as he realized what had happened; obviously, not all of the emergency doors had been fool-proofed by the casino. It was the same one he had used, back in the day, on the night he had hung around.

The lighter had been like a gun being cocked, in a western.

The woman who had found her way out walked into the open. She was slender and beautiful, with long flowing hair. She walked straight across the road and turned, toward the main bridge. Christ, she was stunning. She went to the start of the bridge and stopped at the top of the stairs that led down to the water, under the bridge, and leaned against the guard rail.

She walked as though she owned the place, inhaling and exhaling twice on her graceful stride to her position of tranquil repose. After another few slow, elegant draws of her cigarette, moving and posing like a forties film star, she put it out on the public ashtray nearby and stood with her arms braced apart, her hands on the rail.

She was exquisite.

She stared out at the lake, and the cold wind blew her hair back.

Barker just stared.

He dared not make a sound.

After what was perhaps another minute or two, she took out another cigarette, and lit up. She took a drag through thick lips, and held it, this one not casual, but like she meant it, like it was her first one for hours, maybe for the whole day; her breasts perked as her shoulders arched, then she exhaled the smoke in a cool, jetting plume, her jaw angled up, her shoulders relaxing.

Seeing something like that was one of the few things remaining that could possibly be sexy about smoking.

Then suddenly, she turned and looked up at him. She had not been looking for him; it had just been casual, as the next part of the common ritual for smokers. He felt her vision lock, felt her immediate sexual attraction, as strong as his was to her. Innocent and out of nowhere, but as real as it got. Lust; at least at first sight. They realized they were looking at each other like that, with pure animal magnetism, seeing each other close, but from a distance, just a mere instant before they actually recognized each other.

There could be no denying it.

He could feel himself tremble and she felt it within herself.

Anger and desire.

Betrayal and resentment.

And again, a shockingly powerful blast of white-hot lust, like nothing either of them had ever felt before.

'*She doesn't need you.*'

The voice had come from the end of the bridge, behind him.

It startled him so thoroughly that it broke the spell and he turned.

There was a woman at the end, blocking his path back to the casino.

He looked back down to where *she* had been, but she was gone; perhaps back to the casino, or maybe down the steps to the river, beneath the bridge to the walk paths and bike lanes, along the deep riverbank where only secret lovers, perverts and depressives lurked this time of night. Regardless; gone.

He turned back.

'Who are you? What are you talking about?'

'Men like you have been stalking her, her whole life. Get out of here and never come back, or I will throw you over, right this second.'

'Who *are* you?'

'I am not fucking around!'

Barker spread his arms. 'I am on my way home; I'm just looking for a friend; she's about five-five and sort of quite attractive –'

'You'd better get out of here and leave her alone. Last warning.'

Barker stared at her.

'Look, I really...'

The woman started forward and Barker really thought he was going to have to do something; defend himself, or even turn and run. She was short, but she was clearly tough, and her attire, now she came closer, suggested she was something to do with casino security. The look in her eyes was lethal; *who the hell was she?*

Then his phone rang, and her phone rang, simultaneously.

Both of them jolted, physically and visibly.

They froze.

She was as hard as nails, Barker could see; tell. She stared at him, then abruptly pulled the phone from her pocket, turned and walked off in the other direction.

Barker heard her speak one word upon answering.

'Dash.'

Then she was gone, walking toward the casino and into the shadows, and he was left holding his phone in his hand with the last name he expected to see, coming up onscreen.

'Moon; what the hell was that?'

Parry was still on the line as well.

'That's what I want to know...'

'Have you found your friend?'

'I don't...' Barker felt paralyzed. His phone vibrated to let him know that there was still another call coming in. But he was distracted yet again; he could see something, an energy form, shifting on the other side of the lake.

'Parry, where are you?'

'In my car.'

'Are you watching me? Can you see the lake?'

'No. I'm watching the exits. What are you doing on the lake?'

'There's something...'

'Something...?'

He was startled to realize that he found it somewhat familiar. 'Something about the lake…'

It was the entity; from the night with the girls. Raylene and Rita… it was the same one that had wanted them to win the money. He recognized its psychic signature, the mystical sense of it.

'Listen, Moon, not to put it too delicately but a few minutes ago I was here in the car, half asleep, waiting for you, I heard you grunt and now I have a savage case of instant blue-balls…! If you're doing that screwed-up sex magic stuff, with me on an open line…'

'What?'

The lake entity had been *watching them.*

Them? *Or her?*

'I said …'

'Chief Inspector, I'm sorry but… just, keep an eye out. You're watching the exits, but someone, maybe some-*thing*, is watching us.'

The other call was still signaling on the screen, still coming in, but it would soon ring out.

'I'm sorry; I have to take this call!'

He quickly switched over, in such a panic that for a second he thought he'd accidentally rejected it.

'Carlton?'

'No, no Barker, it's me, it's; you remember me? I was Fiona Pitcher in high school…?'

'Who? Fiona Pitcher?'

'Yes, Barker; it's Carlton I'm calling about, I'm calling from his phone, he's here, with me –'

'Fiona Pitcher?'

'I'm with Carlton! He's here, Barker! Listen, *please* –'

'He is? Where? *Where* is he with you?'

'I…' She sounded choked up.

'Fiona? What? Has something happened?'

'Barker, you have to help us; I think the things, the little children, I think they're going to kill us…'

'The little…?'

'Barker, I can hear them…'

'Where are you?'

'A town that shouldn't be here. A place called Argent. Out in the Hills, out past…'

'I know where it is!' Barker snapped. 'Where it *isn't*! Jesus, Carlton, how the hell did you – ?'

'A long story, and a long walk; I think it's a trap, I think…'

Now Barker was choking up.

Argent.

There was almost no worse a fate.

'Barker, I think he's…'

'Fiona, where's Carlton? Where is he now?'

'Barker… I think he's already dead.'

# CHAPTER TWENTY-NINE:
# ARGENT MESSAGES

'Barker?'

She could hear running. Panting.

'Why does she have bags in her boobies?'

Fiif immediately understood the exact meaning of a chill down the spine.

'Bags in her boobies?'

Two little girls, talking in the dark nearby.

'Look, see through her skin. Bags of watery goo in her boobies, to make them bigger.'

'Is that why she has them? To make them bigger?'

'So the boys will like her better. So they will give her more babies, because she has bigger boobies to feed them.'

'Ewwwwww.'

There was giggling.

There had been these two, then another, then five or six from all over, all at once from all through the dark. Surrounded. Everything, the town, everything, was pitch black outside the low glow of the street light. Even the one at the other end of the street seemed not actually to illuminate anything. If she hadn't known there was a park, just outside the light, on either side of the road, it could have been anything.

'She loves him…' The little girl giggled sweetly. 'She thinks about how she will never fuck him again. She's thinking; they never fucked while they knew they loved each other. Just silly sport. Just silly sport fucking. Wasting more time, when you could of had love! Boo hoo! Wah wah! Never have his pee pee inside her woo woo again! Ha ha! Ha ha!'

*Ha ha! Ha ha!*

In full surround, over and over.

Just a minute ago he had looked like he was going to come around. Something about him had stirred, something about his changing expression had shifted to determination, like he was done with whatever he'd been doing, wherever he'd gone, wherever he'd been all this time. Then he had gasped, as though in shock, sneered and pulled back with his whole body. She wasn't stupid, she could tell; he'd been trying to return. But something hadn't let him. Now he was trapped there. But, if he got out, and his mind or spirit or whatever came back, and he woke up; then, they were still *trapped here*. The whole thing was one big bloody trap and Amanda was dead, just to bait the trap, just to lure her, and to catch him, and all that just to catch Barker Moon.

*She swallowed the spider to catch the fly.*

Fucking Barker Moon.

*I don't know why she swallowed the fly…*

And she'd thought that his heart had stopped.

*Perhaps he's died.*

Checking his heart as best she could, she'd felt his phone in his inner breast pocket and realized, like a bolt out of the blue, that he knew the one person that could save them. That maybe his fucking stupid name had come into her mind for a reason; maybe her stupid fucking mind had led her there, to his name…?

The children had been silent since then.

And then, the call had gone through.

She was still listening.

She listened again, the line still holding somehow.

How?

He was definitely running. Upstairs now. There were sounds all around. Music and weirdness. A mad cacophony.

'Barker?'

One of the children spoke again.

'He doesn't like you. He remembers you, but he thinks you're a snob. You never used to talk to him. He thinks you're a bitch. But now you want his help. Oh, now you do. Well, that's all very well and good isn't it? But where were you when he wanted a good word put in with Marianne Herbert? Didn't think they were right for each other, did you? Couldn't find a good word for poor little Barky back then, could you? And now, all these years later, you want his help…! Now. *Now* you want *him*, to help *you*.'

Fiif wasn't going to let these demon kids, or whatever the fuck they were, make her afraid, right before they killed her.

'We're not demons.'

'I don't care. Stop playing my thoughts back to me. I'm not a bloody idiot. I know you can read my mind. I know you're… picking at my insecurities!'

'We're not! We're not demons!'

A small rock flew out and hit her shoulder. She flinched at the impact.

*Petulant little… that fucking hurt.*

'Good!'

'Well what are you then?!' Fiif shouted. 'What is this place?! Why is everyone so fucking scared of you?!'

Titters in the darkness. They seemed to like that. Reports from the outside that people were still scared of them.

'We like you. We might leave you alive a long time before we kill you.'

A voice came through the phone.

'God dammit this is all my fault!'

'Barker?'

But no… there was talking, muffled shouting.

Barker had put the phone in his pocket.

'Fiona?'

'Who is that?'

'Fiona, it's me. Moon was talking to me. He was talking to me and he added you to the conversation instead of switching over.'

Fiona's chest was tighter than she could remember.

'Oh no, oh no. I'm sorry. I'm sorry; please hang up, please, just end the call! It's not your fault, it's my fault, I asked for this, I came to you…'

'Don't be sorry Fiona. Tell me how to get where you are. I'll come. I'll come right now.'

'I've screwed up so much. I'm so sorry…'

'Fiona, tell me where you are, and when Moon gets here, we'll come –'

'I'm sorry, Uncle Parry. You tried. I let you down.' She was crying now, she couldn't help it. The children had started up a chorus. 'I came to you…'

*Cry baby cry.*

*Cry baby cry.*

*Cry baby cry.*

'I'm so, so sorry.'

Carlton's breathing was so very shallow.

She looked at his face in her lap. His coarse, thick brown hair, his stupid unshaven jawline that seemed to stay in her mind, linger with those dumb, hard lips. She raised her hand and placed her fingertips there, quivering. They felt soft but hard at the same time. He was dehydrated; there were little shards of dry skin all along. Stupid thoughts in the dark, as he lay dying in her lap. A stupid death, a stupid way to go. A teardrop fell and splashed onto his lower lip. As she sniffed her sad, runny nose away, she wondered; if magic really worked, why didn't that kind of thing break the spell? She leaned down and her long blonde hair fell over his face, and she brushed it aside as she kissed him. First softly, then harder, weirdly, sideways and craning down, but passionately, the way she had wanted to all night.

'Carlton…' She whispered low into his mouth. 'Carlton… it should have been us. I'm sorry.'

She was aware that when she looked up, they would be surrounded by the children.

'What is she doing?'

'Making babies.'

It was the girls again, the same two that had started the talking tormenting.

'Do we want more babies?'

'We don't have any.'

'Aren't we babies?'

'No. We're older.'

'But my stupid Mummy cries all the time and says we're still just babies. She's been doing that every night for forty years, every time we drink...'

'Maybe Pee-Pee Fee-Fee is drinking the empty-man...?'

'I want to drink the empty-man too.'

Fiif held her breath, and kept low, crouched over Carlton, her long hair draped over his face, around both their faces, like a net.

A tiny hand touched the back of her head. She jolted but the hand didn't react. It just started patting her, down the back of her head, just like a little child would pet the side of a dog. Flat-handed, and a little nervous.

'Her hair is so pretty.'

'Can we cut it off and wear it?'

'And keep her to drink?'

'If we keep her, we can have another Mummy to share! We'll both have two Mummies!'

'One and a half...'

The child's hand was still petting her.

'Oh... I suppose. Maybe we should just let them make the baby, and we can feed on that, and have a new flavor! And just, make them keep having them, and feed and feed. We can have a *new* new baby to feed on every year!'

The hand stopped petting.

*'What is she doing here?'*

Fiif felt the kids back away.

She couldn't understand.

Then suddenly there was a terrible pain as one of the children yanked, improbably hard, and a chunk of hair came away from the back of her neck.

She shrieked, she couldn't help it. Then she looked up.

There was nobody close. No children. But there was someone, a woman, under the other street light. Even from down there, maybe three or four hundred meters away, she looked unusually tall.

Where had the children gone?

Back into the bushes? The shadows?

There were enough strands of her own hair on the grass around them for her to know.

It had happened, it had been real.

The tall woman under the street light had very long and thick dark hair, and was dressed in a sleeveless black dress, tailored specifically it seemed to highlight a very dense pattern of tattoos along her inner arms, which were open wide and slightly raised toward them in a faintly messianic and yet utterly mesmeric pose as she approached in a manner that, nevertheless, made you want to stay as far from her as possible.

As she drew closer, Fiif saw under the streetlights that the patterns seemed to be roses, twisted through lace perhaps. They almost shone under the street light, and glinted with the angles that she tilted them, as though it might matter, as though the movements might control something.

Fiif heard herself whisper. 'Where have they gone…?'

It was so quiet.

'Who are you?' Fiif asked, as loud as she dared. The sound carried; this strange valley seemed to amplify every sound, every thing. 'How did you get here?'

Still nothing. She was about half way to them now. It occurred to her that she had only taken people's word that there was no escape from this place. But it was Carlton's word, and that was good enough; plus, Barker's response on the phone… that had seemed to confirm it.

'Can you get out? Can you help us get out? Did someone send you? Is that why you're here?'

'The bait speaks.'

Fiif's heart sank.

'You won't kiss him into third dimensional consciousness, darling. Unless you get your tits out. Rub them in his face…'

Fiif felt a little hatred well within her. She could feel her heart growing darker, her hands curling into tense fists.

'Jerk him off with that fist, that might help too!'

Fiif's throat was caught; she couldn't think of anything as the woman laughed to herself, filled with mockery.

'You're the youngest person here, in this dimension. You call them children; they have been here since before your people ever knew it existed.'

Fiif thought that was bullshit. 'Mythology! Bullshit! They talk like children! Traumatized children – who've seen too much that they don't understand! They've been witness to something fucked up, and you've created some story around it to keep people away!'

The woman laughed. Fiif was guessing; but she figured if lanky-hood-lady was not here to help, it was only a matter of time before she attempted to actively hinder.

'They are that, too.'

Fiif growled at her. 'What have you done to Carlton?'

'Nothing. Your friend followed the trail, of a few nights ago. Very good to have done that; so skilled. He found us but he hid from us, then when we found him, he put up an excellent fight. But, he doesn't need you. Doesn't need your help. He found his own way back. Eventually. He'll be back soon, from then. Back to now. You see, before he fled, we got the scent. The scent of *this*, here and now; the scent of a Tuesday night into Wednesday morning. And sure enough, all we had to do was wait a few days, and search a few places.'

Fiif did the math.

'Where's Amanda!?'

'Amanda?'

Fiif waited.

'Oh, Amanda! Oh, she's fine; she's getting the hang of things *very quickly*.'

*Things?*

'Well, it's only been a few days. But they tell me, the more she has inside her, the easier it is for her to lose herself in the moment. If you see what I mean. But of course, you soon will. Won't you?'

*Christ. Jesus Christ.*

*Amanda. Little innocent Amanda.*

*Maybe it would have been better if they had killed her.*

'No. No, I don't think she would agree with that. That's, if she could find her way back to remembering where she'd come from in order to have some kind of perspective as to there, from here. A lot of that going on at the moment, isn't there?' The lanky-hood-lady suddenly adopted a series of poses, and different tones of voice, that Fiif assumed were supposed to be funny. 'There? Here? Then? When? Now? Why? Why not?!'

Fiif gazed down the road at her, where she'd stopped, and sneered.

'You must be 'the funny one' in your crowd.'

'Lanky Hood Lady. That won't do. For the short time we shall be required to endure each other, you may call me; no, you may bow down in my presence and think of me as, *Echidna.*'

'…yer spikes…?'

Fiif jolted.

Carlton's eyes were still closed. But had he spoken?

'*I told you…*' Echidna sneered now.

Carlton's eyelids fluttered, and as he opened them and saw Fiif, she swore they seemed to shine from within.

'Oh, g'day…' Carlton croaked. '…did we…?'

'Carlton, we're –'

'We didn't… again… and I missed it? Did we?'

'No! Carlton! Wake up!'

His eyes suddenly bulged.

'Oh right! Sorry!' He tried to get up, but it was as though he hadn't quite yet regained any control over his body. 'But we will though, won't we?'

Fiif nudged her head sharply down the street.

'If we can get out of here, yes! Yes, that would certainly be one of the first things on the general agenda at this point in time, should we survive! Okay?'

'Great, great, all I needed to know, just checking.' He gritted his teeth and as though through an immense force of will propped himself up on his elbows. 'I said, Echidna; where's yer spikes?' He looked back at Fiif. 'Where are the kids?'

'They're not kids. They might be *children*, but they're definitely not kids…'

'Y've *seen them*?'

'They were here, until she turned up.'

'And y're alive?'

'Well, yes.'

'Doesn't make sense.'

'I think I flattered them. I kind of told them everyone out there is terrified of them.'

'*Are we…*!' Echidna cried out. '…*quite* caught up with recent events for now?'

Carlton groaned a little. 'We need to get up…' But he didn't move. 'Or do we stay down, look more vulnerable?'

'Carlton, we are vulnerable!'

'Oh yeah. Right. Then; why hasn't she killed us yet? Why haven't *they*?'

One of the girl's voices came from the bushes nearby. 'We like her…'

Then the second girl, creepily familiar to Fiif, chimed in.

'We want her to stay and be an extra Mummy…'

Fiif took a sharp breath. 'But I can only stay if he does, too.'

'We don't want an extra Daddy.'

'But…' Fiif gulped. '…that's the only way I can stay…'

'We don't like you *that much*…'

Echidna was moving slowly, at a deliberate pace, up the street toward them again, but Carlton was staring at Fiif as though she'd sprouted horns.

'You will not keep them!' Echidna insisted. 'Neither will you kill them! Do you understand! They are useful to me; I told you! I will find you other new Mummies.'

Carlton looked back from the shadows to Echidna.

'Why the hell are they doing what she says?'

'I don't understand… who are they? What's wrong with them? What happened here?'

'People made choices.' Echidna sounded colder than ever. 'They made a place for themselves with those choices.'

Barker's voice suddenly came through the air, over the phone. 'Fiona? How's Carlton?'

'Barker?'

Carlton's hand scrambled for the phone on the grass beside him. He grasped it and held it to his ear as he sat upright.

'Barko; is that you?'

'Craven? Where the hell are you?'

'Bit of a story, mate. We've ended up in Argent with the evil little kiddies and Fenner Shilling's new mistress.'

Echidna made no response to that.

Barker was silent.

Carlton could tell; that had not gone down well.

Not well, at all.

'I'm sorry mate. Shilling's alive. Hate to be the one to tell you, after all that shit we went through, but he is. At least he was, three days ago. He's reactivating Bridger Mansion, mate. Cranking it up in his own image.'

Barker was still silent.

Carlton grumbled. 'I told you we should have burned that fucking place to the ground.'

'Carlton…'

Barker sounded sad, desperate and exasperated all at the same time.

'Yes mate? Good to hear your voice by the way.'

'Yours too. Hang tight. Don't get killed.' Barker sighed. 'I'll be there in a minute.'

# CHAPTER THIRTY:
# WITH AND WITHIN

'Fiona, where's Carlton? Where is he now?'

'Barker… I think he's already dead.'

There was no time. He had to speak to her. He knew how. It was possible but risky; but he had to know. Barker shoved the phone back in the deep breast pocket of his torn black coat and ran, back toward North Terrace. Everything was on the line now; his life, Carlton's life, their city and everyone in it. He suspected that the last seven years had been a lie, a fool's sacrifice; or worse, a coward's gambit, but he blocked that out, along with everything else. Because of his supernaturally fit body he could run like the wind on a decent meal, and as he powered up with three, four, five strong strides, he was making excellent speed.

Time was vital, nothing could stop him now, nothing.

Just as he was about to truly bolt around the corner, just as the new spring in his step was going to catapult him onto North terrace and down, around the corner, she called his name.

'Barker!'

His feet skidded as he halted, like a dog that had been pulled back on a chain. He was just on the corner of Railway Terrace, past the ramp tunnel down to the station. She was walking toward him, past the arches of the casino entrance.

'Why are you still here?'

The Ox. He couldn't move.

There was so much of it; she had the power. But he saw something; he was right by the ramp, down into the station. It was wide and tall, descending steeply, darkly in these hours, from beneath the corner frontage of the glorious old building, down from under its distinctive brownstone, pillared canopy, and the distinctive Adelaide Railway Station sign that was, these days, crudely overwhelmed by the banners for The World Casino. The ramp tunnel came out on the long concourse inside the station below, but it was shuttered-closed now, with an old-fashioned iron concertina that was still part of the original station…

'Barker? Security said you were still out here…?'

The iron concertina was eight metres wide, and three high; installed to cover the whole of the descending ramp, heavy as a wrecking ball.

Barker was momentarily caught, and utterly attracted to, then puzzled by it.

Then Emerald was upon him.

He turned; she had halted stiffly, just a few steps away.

'You know I was…' Barker gasped the words impatiently. 'We just saw each other back there on the bridge like bloody Romeo and Juliet in reverse.'

It was as though he'd slapped her.

'*What?*'

'Just then.'

'No we…'

That seemed to be the final straw for him. Her capacity for denial seemed colossal. For a second then, he even entertained the idea that she must have had some kind of doppelganger, or secret twin sister. He couldn't repress one more emotion.

'Listen, Tarragon, it's all about to kick off. If you haven't truly picked a side –'

'What is? What are you talking about?'

' – and I don't think you have, you've got about five, maybe ten minutes before the last seven years come thundering back like a supernatural meteor shot from a demigod's slingshot –'

'Side? Barker, was that *really you* over there on the bridge just then?'

'You know it was, we both knew, at the last second there, *we both knew*. And before you ask, I don't know. I don't know what it means that we didn't recognize each other. But my friend is going to die unless I do something right now to save him, and when I do that Tarragon, when I do that, you can run, or heaven forbid you can help, but whatever you do, please, *please* don't just stand there and pretend it isn't happening; because it will be happening *right under your stupid bloody nose; your stupid bloody-beautiful, beguiling nose!*

He wanted to kiss her before he turned and ran again.

She was incredibly tense. He could see her chest pounding with outraged breaths beneath her tight black tee, as she stared fiercely out at him. He could clearly see the outline of – *fucking pull yourself together* – her *emerald eyes*, shining bright, so bright with reflected neon, but also from something behind, from *somewhere else*, as was the way with sorcerers. That light was bright, so bright, but reflected softly under her eyebrows, and glanced off the top curves of her cheeks, highlighting all the shades of her luminous skin. If he stepped forward and reached out now he would be able to touch the energy, not practically or metaphorically but actually reach out and touch the powers of sorcery that were dancing over her every pore; the essence of the sorceress within her, emanating a shell of magical-electrical energy around her body. He could pull her to him, they would kiss and stagger down the ramp and fuck, half-clothed, fast but with true, animal, sensual, mystic passion against the iron –

It took him everything not to.

Not to simply step forward and just kiss her, gently on the lips.

She whispered, loudly. 'You don't even know, do you?'

He turned and ran.

'Barker!'

Again, she practically reached out and grabbed him by the scruff of the neck. He jolted again to a stop, his back arching like he'd been shot between the shoulder blades, again, *almost* with one foot back on North Terrace.

He paused and turned slowly.

'No.'

He didn't even know to what.

'Barker!'

He'd had enough of her. He took two steps back toward her and he saw her gasp, recoil, shocked that he would; would what? Dare? Call her bluff? Move aggressively?

'Go or stay, Emerald? Which is it?'

She was so tense she was trembling. They must have been fifteen paces apart, but Barker could see it. She was going to act. Big. But he couldn't figure it. Was she going to zap him? Fry him, burn him? What? What was she willing to do to maintain this denial, maintain her position, maintain the security of the casino?

She stepped forward.

One foot.

He could have fallen on his arse.

He didn't.

Then she closed her eyes and shouted.

And the top, terrible layer of tension totally evaporated.

'Go!' Emerald cried out; a demand but also a plea. 'Go you bloody idiot!' It was a tone of pleading that told Barker; she understood. She *absolutely understood*. 'Go!'

One did not disobey such an order

Not from a sorceress.

# CHAPTER THIRTY-ONE: LONDON CONNECT

Since the wild proliferation of smartphones, the Australian government had been slowly but surely decreasing the number of free-standing, outdoor public telephone stands throughout the country. There had been booths once, proper glass cabinets that people could stand inside, with single-bend concertina doors, relative sound-proofing and privacy. Barker could remember far enough back to when, in busy times, people would be queued up behind the public phones in the city, and banks of them in Rundle Mall, waiting to make a call. There had been dozens of them back then, but now there were almost none; and famously, nobody had seriously predicted their demise. Not in time, anyway. Not even the sorcerers.

There had always been sorcerers.

And the sorcerers had always had their own clandestine parallel to whatever major communications network was going. Barker had been told about the phone lines at some point, how the copper wires allowed for strong magic, how London had set up an exchange that would always be available and could not be circumvented.

All you had to do was pick up a payphone and speak your name whilst simultaneously sending an image of your surroundings down the line on any telepathic frequency you liked. It had seemed like a foolproof system that would last for eternity – at least, it had seemed that way in the second half of the twentieth century.

There was still one though, this end of North Terrace.

He ran on, downhill past the casino café, closed tight this time on a too-early Wednesday; past the second railway entrance, a long line of glass-paneled doors that led directly into the main station hallway; and on again past the adjoining, towering corporate hotel, set back from the road with a traditional roundabout entrance.

And there it was.

The most modern iteration of an old fashioned phone booth.

An oval shell on a stand, bright pink for visibility, so it would seem friendly to 'the kids'.

Barker grasped the receiver, held it to his ear, and telepathically absorbed the vision of the empty North Terrace tram stop right before him in the middle of the street; the one with that hairdresser's behind it that Freyanna had owned for decades.

'This is Barker Moon. I need –'

There was no dial tone.

Friendly to 'the kids', or make 'the kids' want to vandalize it.

Your call.

'Just my luck.'

A terrible, cold wind shot up North Terrace.

It was all coming together now, he knew.

But… did evil win, if he kept his two closest friends safe?

Did evil win, necessarily, if the most evil sorcerer on this continent (and pretty much permanently competing for the world title) got what he wanted? Would there be another chance to stop him? Or did Carlton and…

*Carlton and Fiona Pitcher?*

*Really?*

*Hadn't she gotten married, like, seven years ago to the head of the hills footy nerds or something?*

He heard an old fashioned phone ring.

Brring, brrring.

Echoing?

*…married, seven years ago…*

Brring, brrring.

*Seven years… could Fiona Pitcher be in on it?*

Brring, brrring.

Wait, was that real? That ringing?

Was London calling…?

Was London… *calling back*?

In his *mind*?

He crashed the receiver back into the cradle of the dead phone and ran back up in the direction of the ringing, certain it was coming from within Adelaide Railway Station. There were two glass sliding double doors on the North Terrace entrance, both of which were locked closed not long after the last train had departed; about half-midnight. Locked. But yes; the echoing ringing that he thought was being muffled in his mind, suppressed by the ether, or *something*, was, in fact, coming from down in there; somewhere along the high-arched hall of the station's central thoroughfare.

He stood outside on the footpath and pressed his hands against the glass. The street here was level with the higher of the station's two-storey concourse, a giant open space that was punctuated with huge arched windows on the western-sunset side to his right, and a sheer wall of massive sandstone bricks dividing the concourse from the casino on the other side. A descending line of large lamps hung down, one third deep, along the whole chamber from the panel-arched ceiling, the first of which was hanging pretty much right in front of where he stood. Interrupting the line of inactivated lamps was a centrally-dissecting indoor walk-bridge that connected the casino on his right with the lobby of the towering corporate hotel on his left.

In there, somewhere.

Brring, brrring.

Brring, brrring.

From outside it was difficult to see over or around the massive, descending staircase that was just a few steps in past the glass, as to where below, on the long concourse, any phone might be located in this day and age. But the sound of an old-style public phone, continuing to ring the distinctive double-bell, was definitely carrying up, into the ceiling and reverberating on the glass right before him.

He had to get in.

*How?*

The spell, how to safely bend and split glass, came quickly, before he had even seriously considered any attempt at a violent entry. The words and the mental signature and frequency to project; the spell; came to him like the name of an old friend he had been trying to remember since a conversation with another old friend he'd had earlier that day *>see-me-see-through-slip-through<* and he stepped forward, through the slit that the spell created, and stepped into the station without hesitation.

It was exciting.

Holy shit.

Here he was.

He'd just *done that*.

Just *done it*.

Brring, brrring.

Brring, brrring.

No doubt there were security cameras, and they were recording him. He didn't care; he would deal with that. He moved quickly, pumped with adrenalin. The only person in there. Not supposed to be in there. Like a naughty school boy playing explorers, like a mystic in a sacred temple.

He ran down the forty-odd marble steps, trying to listen, but his feet were practically crackling with the echoing speed of his pace; that and the echo of the empty, cavernous sandstone hall were totally obscuring his sonar. He reached the floor of the station and stopped sharply, listening keenly. Ahead, to his left, there were the four pillars that led through to the nine domestic passenger train platforms. Access was locked away, again behind massive, heavy iron concertinas, only here they were the old-fashioned diamond-patterned kind that opened and closed sideways, and looked as though any one of them could snatch a careless person's fingers off.

He was pretty sure there were no phones out there on the platforms.

To his right there was a kiosk and a newsagent, closed away and dark, but light came from a Coke machine between the two. Illumination also entered from the city, through the huge line of arched windows above to his left, and from the other end of the concourse, where the teardrop road trickled down and passed along, and with it the well-lit pedestrian access through to the Torrens footbridge where he had seen Emerald smoke her cigarettes.

And then again, there to his right was the internal entrance to the ramp-tunnel.

What was so important about that?

Brring, brrring.

Brring, brrring.

All these access points were locked, shuttered and blocked. But it was possible someone could cross the bridge up there, from the casino to the conference centre? Perhaps a weary midweek gambler on their way back to the hotel, and eyeball him?

He had to move.

He turned one-eighty, back to the stairs. Someone was moving up there, outside. Maybe someone had seen him walk in, from a distance, and thought the station would be open. But his eye was caught by the sign that had been up there, over the stairs, since he could remember.

Steppell's.

One of the great South Australian wine companies that had started here, started with the colony, and… gone global.

It triggered something.

From memory, from childhood, maybe even early teen years…

Hadn't there always been…?

Brring, brrring.

Brring, brrring.

Barker spun about to his right. Between the side of the huge staircase and the wall was a rest and child-changing area, and opposite that, he was sure, a small room, an antechamber almost, that had, at least at one time, contained public phones. The minute he remembered that, it was as though his hearing zoned in through the echo and locked.

Brring, brrring.

Brring, brrring.

Barker followed the ringing around, saw the room, pushed the door and went inside.

He was astounded; they were freestanding but squat and solid, silver-gray, barely upgraded with almost mechanical, hard-press keypads, the first kind that had been upgraded from rotary dials, decades ago. But they would have seemed like H.G. Wells science fiction to the people who had first used this room; a private room for making telephone calls upon arriving by carriage engine into the barely half-centennial Adelaide.

Brring, brrring.

It seemed ludicrously loud in the small room.

The receiver was a heavy and black, and very serious. He lifted the furthest to the right.

Brring, brrri –

 Freed from the solid plastic receiver's weight, the metal cradle clunked up and engaged the call via some other clunking mechanism within.

Barker lifted the obsolete device to the side of his face, and gave it a go.

'Adelaide Railway Station?'

The tone that come forth was old-school bureaucratic, but apologetic.

'We're very sorry; we do generally aim to be efficient.'

If Barker's life was ever written up, and if whatever it was written up as ever became a movie, you could get any one of dozens of tremendous British character actors to play this role, Barker realized. Indeed, this was real; this was actually happening, and it *still* felt like it was a famous British character actor, one you knew but just couldn't quite pick, speaking on the other end.

'That's okay. I'm glad you called back.'

'The wireless network is so dense, you see. We haven't quite worked out any stable method of penetrating it. Not securely, and certainly not to the standards we require.'

'London?'

'You did call.'

'I did. Thank you for tracking me down.'

'Barker Moon you are registered with London as an entity and known quantity of serious regard. To whom within our community do you wish to speak?'

'I need to speak to Heather Holden. Urgently.'

There was a very slight pause.

'Heather Holden currently resides in the Pleasance Institute. You are aware her counsel is possibly compromised by an unstable mental condition?'

'I am.'

Then, there was a very heavy silence. Barker had to ask.

'Do you know what's happening here?'

The heavy silence seemed to increase in substance.

'Do you, Barker Moon?'

'I think that I do. And I think that you do as well. I think that's why you went the extra booth, as it were, to contact me.'

'Indeed. But it was you, after all, who contacted us.'

Barker accepted that. 'I'm sure you're correct.'

Silence, less dense.

'Provided that is understood; the answer is yes. Yes. We are aware of what is happening there. We have agents present but they are not sorcerers and they do not understand the full picture. We need somebody in the eye, when the storm hits.'

'He's summoned something massive, hasn't he?'

'More than that. He intends to channel something massive. Become it; or at least the closest thing to it, in physical form. He will be its avatar, and there will be no stopping him.'

'How do you know?'

'We have retrieved one of our agents who was compromised.'

'One of your agents… joined Shilling?'

'We are an informal organization, Master Moon, as you know. It might be more correct to say that a member of our community…?'

'I see…'

'…did indeed, it seems, fall for the lure that Master Shilling currently has to offer. However, we were able to extract him, in rather short order, once we had wind.'

'Are there others?'

'Others compromised? Undoubtedly. From our community…? Unsure at this point.'

'Who isn't compromised? Who from the old days?'

'The old days? Surely you don't mean what I think you mean?'

Barker stopped for a second. He didn't. But; that had put an idea in his head.

'I mean, that I know. From seven years ago and before, when I was last active? Is there anyone from that time I can call on, who isn't compromised?'

'Anyone who can help you?' There was a slight grumbling, as though this had given his contact real pause for thought. Then, the sound of a hand over the receiver, and some quiet, but indeed very serious conversation going on behind it. Then the hand was removed, and his throat cleared.

'Apologies. We cannot be sure. Not sure enough to make a formal recommendation.'

'Make an informal one. There's a storm coming.'

'Point taken. Quite the sticky wicket. Oh, and – save the grounds, if you can.'

'The… cricket grounds? Adelaide Oval?'

There was an interesting pause.

'Do I need to remind you of whereabouts this call was placed, old chap? As we understand it, ground zero for the storm is right beside those picturesque playing grounds, not to mention that wonderful cathedral. It's a pity about that spaceship monstrosity, but never mind. If there's anything you can do, it would be greatly appreciated, by a great many in the organization. I'm sure you understand.'

'Right. Okay. Righto. Look; I broke in here.'

'Ah, yes. Quite. Very well. On with the show. Now, where were we? Let's see… Bridger Mansion Report. Abstract; yes, that's just the ticket.' He heard paper rustling. As though the men were removing papers from a manila folder. 'Here we are. Ah, yes. The very man, as they say. Well; it seems, Master Moon, that after all that business at Bridger Mansion in which you performed so admirably, the City of Churches in The Festival State was very heavily monitored for a full three years. However, given the almost total lack of supernatural, occult or spiritual activity occurring there during that time, it was assumed that whatever energy had been present and active in the city, prior to the incident at Bridger Mansion, had virtually and totally dissipated. The assessment suggested that said energy would be totally absent for another full generation, before slowly replenishing itself, based around the Victoria Square energy source, now called… dear me, how does one pronounce…?'

'Never mind, I get it.'

'Yes. Quite. As you will have gathered for yourself, Master Moon, it appears now, sadly, that it was not the case. It appears now, that it was quite likely that the assessment was filed, if not by Master Shilling himself, then by…'

The Ox was boiling within him.

'I get it.'

'…yes. I see your dilemma. It has been pointed out, in no official capacity, you understand…?'

'…yes…'

'…and, only in light of the very recent reopening of some of the cases that, until very recently, had been considered closed or at the very least inactive over the past six or seven years…?'

'You mean… so far as your man on the ground, who probably just came here a few hours ago, tonight, can ascertain?'

'We believe that… Freyanna…?'

'Yes?'

'*May have* managed to maintain a lightworker power base during that time? At least, until now. It has been reported to us that, given that we have also been made aware that she is dying, and that one of her protégées, perhaps more than one, are working to undermine whatever choices she may or may not be making as to the division of her… 'company' after her aforementioned passing on, that the hitherto mentioned protégée may or may not be working in conjunction, temporarily or otherwise, with Master Shilling, in the endeavor of his most foolhardy summoning.'

'One of Freyanna's girls is working with Shilling so she can step directly into Freyanna's power base when she dies?'

'Is that not what I just said, Master Moon?'

'Names?'

'We don't have the names of all five contenders for the crown, as it were. But Freyanna, and her organization… we believe you can call on them, through one of two women; either Shirley Swansong, or Karri Cork. However, it must be stressed, the veracity of their testimonials, as to their allegiance to Freyanna, and to The Side of The Angels, as it were, and, as it were indeed, always shall be… sadly cannot be verified.'

'I remember them. But only in passing. I think Karri cut my hair once.'

'That could very well be the case. However, Master Moon; it is possible for us to register when a powerful magical awakening occurs. There has been one in your direct vicinity already tonight. Not an hour ago.'

'Where?'

'That is why we mention it. Our agent was on the case but has become preoccupied. However, we believe, the event itself may have occurred very close to the proximity of the telephone booth at which you initially attempted contact. The nature of the energy under speculation was reportedly *white*, and *feminine* in nature. Perhaps a witch? Having a great spiritual boon bestowed?'

'Cheryl...' Barker uttered under his breath.

'It is... possible. We thought perhaps Shirley Swansong. She was known to have been in the area. Perhaps Freyanna making bequest of her realm and dispensing her powers early? Preparing for trouble on her way out by beating them to the punch? Given the aforementioned defection? But regardless; we can also ascertain, the boons were overdue by a factor of years. Seven years, in fact.'

'Is that a fact?'

'Part of what might be called a configuration. There are definitely great shifts, and powerful energies being *released*, all in your direct vicinity Master Moon. I cannot underestimate the importance of caution in moving forward.'

'Thank you. I appreciate this. Do you have a name?'

'I do.'

'Can I call on you in future, given you're up to speed?'

'Oh, Master Moon; do not be under any misapprehensions. Whomsoever you make contact with in London will be extremely well-versed in matters to do with your fair southern metropolitan grid. This matter is being overseen at the most highest of levels, Master Moon. The most highest.'

'Like?'

'That we know of? The Vatican is all we know for certain. But; they are always everywhere. You are speaking with London, obviously. Montreal may have a hand; but that is unsubstantiated. There is a time lag; many things may have happened in the past four to five years. Perhaps New York is involved in some way. And there is always Babylon, of course. But regarding Montreal...' There was a shuffling of papers. '...a report just in... it is affecting things. And those things are at play. It seems there is much at play, Master Moon; quite the centre ring.'

Barker wasn't quite sure what to say.

'Thank you for your help.'

'Pleased to be of service Master Moon.'

'Can you put me through to Heather please?'

'One more thing, Master Moon. Regarding the eye of the storm I mentioned earlier? The need for London to have eyes, within the eye itself. Might be useful for you to know that while the three-system storm that is currently encircling and enclosing upon fair Adelaide is a natural storm, it has not, so far as we can ascertain, occurred naturally.'

'It's a meta-tsunami.'

'A what was that now? Oh! I see! Yes, Master Moon; very good. A meta tsunami. Yes, I shall write that down; we shall all use it here at Systems. Very good indeed.'

'Really?'

'Oh yes. We do love a good coining; the franking of a new phrase. Very good. Now, it will come in three waves, Master Moon. You must be ready. The first will be duh –'

Silence.

'Hello? Systems?'

'Hello? Barker?'

She sounded exactly the same.

'Heather. Thank God.'

'I taught you better than that.'

'The real God not the fake one.'

'If you must. You're here?'

'Yes.'

'You're in the city?'

'Yes.'

'My city?'

'Our city.'

'Yet you came through London?'

'No choice. But they'll be listening.'

'Let them listen. They're the reason I am safe here. They're the reason you gambled up all that money, to keep me here. Little did we know.'

'You can feel it?'

'Of course. That is a stupid question, my hound. You must be very flighty. You know it's him, don't you?'

'He's alive. Or; he's here, anyway…'

'He was never dead. That is the only explanation. He never left that bloody house. His energy, our energy, it never dissipated, we never truly defeated him, and now here he is; returned, replenished and well-rested. On the attack. Who got the boon, do we know?'

'Cheryl. I think. I hope.'

'*Cheryl?*' Heather hummed. 'Nice. Nice it's one of yours. But I would have thought Karri Cork. The higher realms tend to go for chirpy and polite in these cases.'

'Heather; Shilling has Carlton trapped in Argent.'

He could feel her emotional response. Horror, sadness. Regret.

'Argent…' Heather let out a low breath. '…poor Carlton.'

'Is there any way I can get him out?'

'No. No, I don't know. Maybe, if *I'd* trained him…'

'Heather this is no time for…'

'You can't do it, Barker.'

'Can't do what?'

'Don't be coy. And don't be facetious. I felt it this evening when you opened that portal. You are connected to this city, to this continent, in ways you don't understand. In ways I didn't understand until tonight. You've spoken to London. You know there is a storm closing in on three fronts, you know that higher powers are deploying; energies are shifting, boons that have been blocked have become dislodged from where they were stuck, and are landing on our friends…'

'I don't know where she is.'

'She will find you. My concern now is that Shilling has become so powerful that I am not sure anything can defeat him; not tonight. Maybe not ever. We were all warned Barker. We were all warned, seven years ago; you were there. The cosmos is shifting, the planets realigning. This is a new age, a new time, for new energies; but the dark energies that have ruled this dimension for three ages now will try to come over with the new energies, and they will try to have dominion once again. This planet cannot sustain another two and a half thousand years of demonic rule. It simply – *cannot.*'

'You sound like him. That's what he told me.'

'Who?'

'The Rock Icon.'

'You've seen him again?'

'Again?'

Heather was becoming frustrated.

'Barker; be clear. The immensely powerful deity who works with musical frequencies. He dresses like a rock and roll dude.'

'You know him? Who is he? Pan?'

'An aspect of, probably. And you've seen him?'

'I nearly crashed my bike. Or maybe I did; but he took me to the astral and made sure –'

'Barker; he was the one! He was the one we were talking to, seven years ago; he was telling us back then that all this was going to happen!'

'He…?'

'This is the start, Barker. Back then; Shilling might not have expected us to resist when he made his – *monumentally idiotic and irresponsible move.*'

Barker gave her a few seconds to cool.

'…but like every great homicidal, Machiavellian, narcissistic, psychopathic manipulator, he knew, if not how to create a disaster, then certainly how to turn a disaster to his advantage when his insane meddling created one!'

'I don't care about any of that. Not tonight, not now. I need to know, Heather.'

'You already know. Listen to me Barker; we need to learn how to turn the tables, how to do the same. Shilling is going to cause a calamity. An almighty calamity. And we must be wise enough, to learn to use that, as he did, to our advantage. We must defeat him under the cover of the storm he is summoning in order to claim victory.'

'Heather; I still don't remember.'

'Of course you don't! Only I can remove that block; and only if you truly desire it, deep down in your brave heart, and fine mind, and magnificent balls.'

'You?'

'You begged me, Barker. Begged me to block you. You were inconsolable. So many of your friends, our friends, so many dead. For *our curiosity*. You couldn't live with yourself. You begged me to remove your magic. Remove any trace of it. And with it, the memory of what Shilling did to you. To us.'

'I asked for this?'

'I have an iPod here. With you on it, swearing as much.'

'But…'

'You can't do it, Barker. You understand that, don't you? He's summoned you. He's summoned you, in order to use you. He knew that eventually Carlton, or Cheryl, or someone you knew, someone you cared about, would stumble on to his trap, and stumble into Argent. He's been waiting for it.'

'Fiona Pitcher…'

'Fiona…?'

'She's with Carlton.'

'Didn't she marry some kind of local amateur athlete? The local rugby captain?'

'Football.'

'There's a difference?'

'There is to them. A big one.'

'A local sports cult. You think that has something to do with it?'

Barker had seen it before. 'Sports clubs can be as effective as the Freemasons or the Mormons or the Catholics when you want to infiltrate a community. It's starting to add up.'

'And what do you think *she* will do, Barker? If you do what you intend?'

'I thought you'd forbidden that?'

'No; but I will answer your question, so that you won't have to. You want to know; did your powers get your friends killed? The answer is yes. Yes, they did, to an extent. Without you, the portal would not have been opened. Shilling would not have been able to do what he did, and your friends, our friends, would be alive today. Adelaide would not be activating into darkness, and would not be under siege. The lives of every lightworker in the city would not be in danger, and there would not be demons making plays they have waited hundreds of years to make!'

Barker trembled, from head to toe.

'…demons again…'

'And they are not the end, or the least of it. So yes, Barker, every time you use those magnificent powers of yours, there is a risk that people will die. Tonight, because you did, seven years ago, your friend Carlton, and his delightful, I'm sure, paramour, will die, and all Hell will be unleashed upon this city.'

'I don't care…' Barker held his breath a second. 'If I use my powers, I can save them. That's true, isn't it?'

'Tonight that is true; perhaps. But if the situation you allow to arise, by using those powers, by allowing Shilling to spring his trap, and release his beast…?'

'But…'

'If you open the portal to Argent to save Carlton, you will be doing the same as when you opened that portal in Bridger Mansion the night he was waiting, and wanted you to do exactly that; you will be opening a portal for Shilling, because Shilling wants you to, in order to do Shilling's work.'

'I can save them.'

'But will you be able to save them when the city falls?'

'Will I be able to save… anyone?'

'Will you be able to prevent the city from falling?'

'What?'

'Is the question you should be asking.'

'I can't let Carlton die.'

'You save your friend; Shilling gets his portal to Argent. What is in Argent?'

'Evil. Does anybody truly know?'

'Evil Shilling apparently now controls. What is beyond Argent?'

'The place where Shilling actually wants the portal open to…'

'At a guess?'

'Bridger Mansion.' Suddenly Barker twigged. 'I have to save Carlton; and then together we can retake Bridger Mansion, and put a stop to all of this, for good.'

'You were planning that anyway; all your friends gathering at the hotel tomorrow.'

'You bloody-well *are* watching!'

'That's how you turn the tables. He will see it coming; but he won't see this.'

'What?'

'…me.'

Barker smiled.

'I have been watching, Barker. Of course. From afar. But now I must return; the price of greater perspective is inaction, and I have been inactive too long. But don't wait for me Barker. Shilling thinks I am insane. It will take me… time, much time, to unbind those illusions.'

'We have to save them, Heather.'

'After tonight; attack Bridger immediately. If you do not, if you do not press the advantage of his weakness, press the fact that he will not expect this; he will expect you to gather forces over time; then you will have lost your advantage, and the city will fall.'

'I need to find Cheryl.'

'I agree. Do what you must. But watch the Pitcher girl; and beware of Freyanna's people. Any one of them could make a move at any time. Come and see me when it's done. If you survive. Good luck, my lost pup. Beware the storm.'

'You could just say; a storm's…'

'I don't quote movies, Barker. You know that. And beware the Montreal-New York connection that Master Systems mentioned. You may be able to resist that woman, but that does not mean that she is not holding something back from you.'

'You were listening to my conversation with London?'

'You may never be allowed to love her, Barker. Such a union; they may forbid it.'

'They?'

'Wipe the darkness out, Barker. Nuke it from orbit. It's the only way to be certain.'

And then, she was gone; but, Barker smiled…

She was still the same.

She hadn't changed.

Sometimes, amid the chaos, that was all you needed.

# CHAPTER THIRTY-TWO:
# BOTH ENDS

Cheryl's rage was irrepressible.

'*Fenner…*' She guffawed, astonished and horrified. '…*Shilling?*'

'Yes…' Feather was almost pleased. '…do you *know* him?'

But Candle knew, and could see it coming. She was already starting to back away. The walls had started to tremble. Cheryl could feel the water down there; down below… down in the sewers, in the crafted storm drains that had once been some of the smaller creeks that had fed the Torrens, but which had been caressed then directed under here specifically, to serve the city and the railways in the tunnels. But she could also feel the waters below that; the smaller and lower creeks and tributaries that ran all through the rock, beneath the streets, beneath all the Man-made stuff; directly below the flows that Man had claimed. And there was water there, deep and dark for which she was not ready, powerful water, and yet she called it regardless, called it up for the servants of the man who had put a wedge in her life, in her life's true path, where she and this heat-girl, fire-woman, whatever the fuck she had self-styled herself as, would have been friends, as fire and water, elemental and complimentary, not here meeting for the first time in total animosity, but –

*As it should have been.*

And she couldn't help it, just couldn't help it; she wanted that gone, that timeline gone, to end here, no evidence of the life that should have been, nothing of that remaining to cause her pain. She would erase it with her new power; *because she could*, and that was what she was going to do with it; end that timeline here, stillborn, as it should never have begun.

And the powerful water began to rise, just a few droplets but fast; the deep and dark and powerful Earth water that she was not ready for, and knew that she was not ready for; one drop came up fast, against the flow, against the path of least resistance that was natural to water, against gravity itself. That water had been made powerful by her calling it, and more powerful still by her enabling it to be called; and that again allowed the water to be wielded in the fashion she desired; here, now, she was making the dark and powerful water rise, against the natural order, something even the most powerful sorcerers undertook only under strictest precautions, at their own risk; and this was her will, her own will, doing this, without a thought of care or caution…

And the drop came slithering up the shaft, ready to obey because it was so powerful, so old and neglected and ready to be wielded without restriction, from so deep, uncalled for centuries; and she was ready to call more after it, a whole torrential rage. And the old water, lightless and oblivious, was eager to please and to bond and to nourish a new host, a new growth, a new creation, to be absorbed and integrated; and the first drop was ready to bring more as it rolled up, onto the edge of the wood and along, the wood screeching and groaning, seeking out her padded foot.

Candle saw it.

'The dark magic! She brings it! She is one of us! She is with us and so much more!'

Cheryl fell to her knees.

The droplet stopped and rolled backwards.

It fell back and was gone.

She looked up though her dark, sunken, white eyes.

'Fenner… *fucking*… Shilling… *is alive?*'

Pitt came from behind Feather and grasped her in a bear hug. He was white and shining, pale as a ghost and yet somehow vital and alive. He was younger as well, or in the very least, with what Cheryl could see, seemed more virile and spry.

Feather, who worked for Fenner Shilling, who had not died, despite all their efforts and sacrifices at Bridger Mansion seven years ago, screamed blue murder as she was dragged off, but Cheryl didn't care.

She had almost fallen, just in that second, literally, figuratively, and spiritually.

Should she have been grateful, though? For the reminder of that evil, the gleeful celebration of true wickedness, there in that second? For the man who had…

She didn't care about that either.

Candle looked back and forth, stunned and appalled.

'They're supposed to do what we say!'

Cheryl barely listened; she was putting it together, as best she could, in a hurry. Water flowed down, with gravity. She would have to learn to do that also. To fall and rest and gather and pool and then condense, and rise and fall again.

To call it up only…

…only when. There would be whens, and possibilities, but that was not now.

'Or something…' Cheryl uttered. '…whatever. I'll pick it up as I go…'

'What!?' Candle spat. 'Fuck you, new girl! Come and help me find her before those things…'

Her face contorted at whatever thought she'd had of what those things could do to her fellow practitioner; whatever that meant. Practitioner. Cheryl didn't like that word.

She was a sorceress. A water sorceress.

A water witch, okay.

Practitioner?

Fuck you.

Regardless; she still didn't care. This was her new reality, her new shape, her new form and function, her new law, the law of herself; she wasn't taking another step until…

Candle raised both her hands, like some kind of badass superhero.

They were shimmering with heat.

'Come and help me find her – and I won't boil your skin!'

Cheryl could feel it; the heat. This woman had an idea; she knew that the shimmering, silvery wetsuit was just willed-water.

Water could boil; and she could do it.

She was fire.

As Cheryl summoned the water down, from the gutters above, from the pipes along the higher floor level, and the one above, as they cracked, as the water obeyed the command to come to her, down, to obey her, down, to flow through her like a channel, she knew that she was something akin to at-one with it now, and that she had entered the fight.

The water came off the side of something above her, a ledge in the thin section between the shaft and the outer wall maybe, but it came, it flowed hard and pounded, down onto her shoulders before Candle could even consider attacking with whatever kind of heat-projection ability she possessed. It was so keen; it must have been there, pooling in the blocked gutters, puddles on sagging rooves, in forgotten water collections, right up there and all around. There were a few sharp cracks above and it was more, more powerful within seconds. It exploded around her. It went as she commanded, following the direction of her arms as they extended outward with the spell, the spell of pure will; to put this fire-woman out, before she could even conquer her shock and fear and dampen her own terror, before she could summon anything like the fire that Cheryl supposed she probably could.

And the water put out the spark, and slammed Candle backward into the brick wall.

Candle was pummeled for a few seconds as the water hit her like a fire hose, a brutal scouring, a sterilizing cleanse upon entering a savage prison; she cried out in shock and horror, then she fell to her knees and cried out in pain. Cheryl was going to let her fall off the edge but somehow in the water-cannon chaos, which she quickly realized was unstoppable, as the flow from the roof kept coming and coming, over her shoulders and around her head, over and past her like she was an unfeeling slab of bedrock and continuing into Candle, Cheryl watched as the extinguished fire-woman grabbed hold of the power line for the one bulb and held on as it came away from the wall, as the clips puffed out of the bricks where they'd been stapled and the cord swung loose. Then she caught the rail and allowed herself purchase, winded, gasping, and probably wounded as the waterfall continued to smash into her, and left her desperately clutching the power cord as she fell toward the edge.

She would have fallen but Cheryl grabbed her, shifted Candle's weight, and she fell sideways onto the wooden walkway.

Cheryl was exhausted. She was dehydrated and painfully thirsty.

Wielding water: took water.

She took Candle under her arms. Candle coughed and spluttered and squealed, and Cheryl propped her up to a sit against the wall.

'Those sex-pests… what the fuck are they?'

Candle was panting, looking up at Cheryl with absolutely no idea what to make of her, other than that she hated her fucking guts.

'This isn't the end, right here, Candle. This is the start. Believe me.'

Then the rafters smashed and the light crashed and it was dark. The wood fell and Cheryl grabbed the cord and felt the weight of the bulb drop, but that was just a tiny register as the spirits raced out.

Something about what she had done; something about her rage and her vengeance had unlocked them.

They roared around her, indistinct and screeching, and Cheryl found that she was clutching Candle, who was shivering worse than she was.

Then they were gone, and Cheryl knew it had been her fault.

The old woman and the little girl remained, distinct phantoms just in front of her, by the door. The old woman put her hand on the little girl's shoulder.

'Someone will pay.'

Then they too were gone.

Candle, her bright orange hair just a sheer bedraggle upon the shoulders of her drenched, candy-stripe clothes, looked up at her, unable to move as Cheryl cradled her in her lap, and spoke angrily through chattering teeth.

'You let them out...'

'I...'

'You released a thousand ghouls into a mystical tsunami...'

'But, I...'

'You... just made... everything... *a thousand times worse...!*'

# CHAPTER THIRTY-THREE: THE PERSUADER

Barker walked back out into the long, tall, hallway concourse of the Adelaide Railway Station Terminus.

He reconsidered the shape of the place, trying to see what he had missed.

He passed the base of the stairs and walked out toward the four pillars in the middle of the western side of the concourse, and stared out, past the turnstiles and security stations, through and into the low cavern beyond. He peered through the pitch-blackness, along the nine platforms and down the nine train lines, out, under a long, dark stretch into the sheer blackness of night, into the wide cavern of tunnels that extended beneath the conference centre, beneath the convention centre, running more than three hundred meters beneath them. The other end of the railway cavern opened into the night, beside the eerie, distant glow of the newly build hospital complex at the end of the cavern's open maw. The railway lines then led past the western edge of the Torrens Lake, past the weir, where behind and beyond the hospital the main lines were channeled through an urban wasteland of twisted train tracks and junctions, abandoned carriages and work sheds, past the horror of the haunted Old Adelaide Gaol, and eventually splitting, one line intersecting with Port Road, and running back down, to where the early settler horse and carts had begun their corruption of the city grid almost two centuries earlier.

He was seeing it now; the perspective.

The long game that angels and demons played.

Ports, railways, terminals.

Corporations, churches, casinos.

Here in the middle, he could see it.

Here at the terminus heart.

He could feel the threads, stretching beneath the city, in all directions.

He pulled the phone back out of his pocket.

'Fiona? How's Carlton?'

'Barker?'

Barker felt huge relief as he heard the phone juggling in his old mate's hand.

'Barko; is that you?'

'Carlton? Where the hell are you?'

'Bit of a story, mate. We've ended up in Argent with the evil little kiddies and Fenner Shilling's new mistress.'

Barker didn't know what to say. He knew what was happening; he knew that Carlton had been made bait, been placed in one of the most deadly occult lairs, of this city's several such places, simply because…

No. Not because of him. Not because he had used his powers.

No. That was done.

It was time.

'Shilling's alive, mate…'

Barker was still silent, but listened.

This was all down to Shilling.

Nothing and nobody else.

Fenner Shilling.

Carlton grumbled. 'I told you we should have burned that fucking place to the ground.'

'Carlton…'

He stopped himself. He'd sounded sad, and desperate and exasperated.

He was all those things; but not in the way he sounded.

'Yes mate? Good to hear your voice by the way.'

'Yours too. Hang tight. Don't get killed. I'll be there in a minute.'

He hung up.

But the call was still going somehow.

He checked it.

'Parry?'

'Chief Inspector to you, son.'

'You heard all that?'

'Not only heard it. I saw it. Look up.'

Barker looked up to the top of the stairs.

There he was. The poor, tall, mustachioed inspector in the decent suit and good tie. He was standing outside, but under the Steppell's sign.

'I saw you slip through the glass. I totally believe all this shit, at least in my mind, but seeing it, when you do see it, is another thing. Are you coming out again?'

'I think so. I think I have a spell… but if I forget again, can you do something about the security cameras in the morning?'

'Why? You didn't break anything. They don't check unless something's damaged. What about your mate?'

'What mate?'

'The bloke standing behind you. From this angle, I can just see his shiny shoes.'

'Stay on the line, Chief Inspector, if you wouldn't mind.'

'No other plans currently, Mister Moon.'

Barker turned around.

There was indeed a man there, and he spoke.

'It's always better if the people working for us have no idea.'

Barker knew who he was, immediately. This was a demon. Everything about him made Barker want to run. But everything about Barker, who was very-nearly completely Barker again, made him want to stay.

'You're not going to try and pull that one where you say I have been working for you all along?'

The demon smiled. 'You know that in this dimension, there is no way you can avoid working for us. Or at the very least, going along. Getting along. Playing the game. You've got to play the game. It's simply a matter of; for you, anyway, how much energy you can muster to circumvent our traps, to warn others, while you are doing it. That is all you have, your only loophole, your only option for salvation while you are here.'

The demon was tall, and good-looking.

'You're one of Them, aren't you?'

'One of…?'

'The Establishment.'

'Oh Them. Uh huh. I understand that you, and your glamorous friend, had a brush with The Land Lord and The Creditor earlier. We are all well acquainted, of course. We've all been here a long time, Barker.'

Barker nodded. 'I know. Thanks for The Bible, by the way.'

The demon smiled. 'Just enough knowledge to be dangerous.'

Barker smiled back. 'I'm sure you do what you can.'

'The immoveable rock of unshakeable truth, within the gigantic, unstoppable lie, that allows us to endure; every psychopath knows that one. Heaven knows, that book has helped to encourage enough of them!' The smile widened. He wasn't trying to joke or make friends. He simply had a sense of humour about his work. Barker liked him; but it was impossible not to. This was a creature that had been created to be liked.

'Yes…' The demon saw Barker come to that realization.

He was old, and had done this time and time again. He was considering Barker as an adult would consider a child. Every thought was a tell; every second, every movement self-betrayal. But Barker had no choice. This was what this thing did; it existed to analyze human souls in this way. 'Yes… we are starting to see each other, aren't we?'

The demon took form.

'This is, of course, how you believe I should look. But as you are several steps removed from normal human consciousness, it is how you believe I should look, given that you know that, and I know that, and you know that I know that. There is nothing you can do; I will always be a product of your mind. I have no actual appearance you could register with human senses; no matter how sorcerously enhanced.'

The various levels of resistance in Barker's mind had projected and conjured the demon's physical form as a man, perhaps Barker's age, who was immaculately groomed in every sense. Perfectly styled golden hair, skin, teeth. Crystal clear blue eyes, manicured nails and a suit that was so well fitted that it didn't need to look expensive. Just neat, unobtrusive; but of course, vastly expensive.

There was nothing in fact about this man you could not see yourself having, doing or being; and yet that, in itself, was a complete lie. He was designed to seem to be… just another you. Just another bloke. An ordinary guy who'd done quite well and had a bit of self-confidence about him. Although, a bit more than you, maybe. Maybe this bloke, this lovely bloke, this great guy, maybe he knew a bit more, had a bit more inside knowledge. But; nothing you, yourself couldn't achieve, if you just had that little bit of… what? What was it now, that you were missing? You know; that thing, that spark, that was missing from you. Some people had it naturally, didn't they? But you could get it. It could be learned. And, here he was. The man who had it. Had it in spades, as they say. And yet, just an ordinary bloke really. So ordinary, and yet so special, this man was going to help you get it; because clearly he had gotten it, and knew how to get it, and could tell you how.

All you had to do… was play his game.

He might have been a game show host, he might have been a local politician. He might have sold you a computer, a good one; better than you needed, actually. He might have sold you a car; a really good car, or shares; that would do well. Like, really okay, just like he said.

But never…

Barker smiled. 'You're here to make me an offer.'

'I think I can persuade you.'

'You're… The Persuader.'

'And I have been here a very long time, Barker Moon.'

Barker looked around again. The demon watched him. Here. A long time. Port Road to North Terrace. Everything right here. Around the Terminus.

All the cultural processing you could ask for; from the Astral Gate right through to the new Hospital. Birth to death. East to West.

'You have, haven't you? You have been here a very long time…'

'Yes. I have.'

'I mean, here. At the Terminus.'

He smiled. Effortless charm.

'And I mean…' Barker pursued. '…not by demon standards. There is no point in discussing 'a long time' with you guys. I mean, a long time, by our standards, human standards. By the standards of… the generations of this city…?'

The demon made a face. Mildly impressed.

Still a trillion eons from displeased.

He started to move a little, pacing to Barker's left, as though, in his mind, he was building up his game.

'And…' Barker nodded. '…down this end, too. You… have some kind of dominion here, over the north-west quadrant, don't you? The corner, at least?'

But then Barker saw it. The Persuader was directing him to the sign.

Steppell's.

'So many levels. So many spells, so many steps.'

'It's a terminus. So to leave, to enter the city, everyone must be made aware of what it is.'

'The rules is the rules, as they say.' He grinned a really spectacular primetime game-show grin. 'I know what you must be asking yourself. What you must be trying to recall. What is the symbolic and mystical meaning of north? Or west? Or a corner? A city corner on a grid city? West is negative, north is enlightenment, isn't it? But north-west? What is that? Ninety-degree angle? Is that Freemasonic? But what is that anyway? Hasn't it been established by now; they're just as much to blame, just as blameless, just as much a manipulatable infrastructure-slash-bureaucracy as anything else that has emerged and evolved out of human society? Can all the ninety degrees, in all the cities, on all the corners, on all the streets, in all the rooms, on all the doors, in all the world… but; why are we standing in a massive arched hall? Why did she walk into mine? Sorry, I just had to finish that thought. But wait; is north truly positive enlightenment, or is it just the highpoint of the sun? Brightest part of the lovely old summer? Or is it the upward momentum of universal energy. Or…? Does the universe actually have an 'up'? And; west? I mean, what is that? Gunslingers? A northern sunshine gunfight at noon? Is that north-west? Is it; where we fight? Or, just the primitive notion that the sun sets in the west; light dies, darkness comes and fear, fear of the tiger in the night? But the tiger protects the west in Chinese mythology. The most western-based football team in this town is called The Tigers. Coincidence? Unconscious? Part of clever old Colonel Light's plan? But what of… actual Indian mythology? Hindu mysticism; the oldest still-intact mystical system in the world? What of the mysticism of the Indigenous Peoples that were here, that gathered here before they even had the misfortune of knowing that your ancestors existed? Not your fault of course; you weren't there.' He smiled. 'Or were you? Maybe you were one of them? Do their laws, does the powerful Dreamtime magic that was laid down by beings older, stronger, more complex yet more simple and way more bizarre than the likes of you can ever get your third-density minds around, outside of the Astral, still hold? Are those energies still here? Do those Dreamtimers *still remain*? Before this was a 'Railway Terminus' and a 'House of Parliament' and a…'

'Crossroads…'

The demon narrowed his eyes. 'Ah, yes. Well may you say. But how could that ever be managed? A place like that? If you *had been here*? What if reincarnation is real and every Australian city, *every city in the entire world*, is populated with the reincarnated Indigenous People their ancestors treated so horribly; what if the

Indigenous survivors of today, who are being treated so callously, are the reincarnated Imperialists who caused their physical, but not spiritual ancestors, so much pain? To put it plainly; what if today's tortured, tormented, alcoholic and drug-addled Indigenous leftovers – *or, on any continent, for that matter* – but because we're here, let's stick with here; are reincarnated British immigrants? The immigrants and troops and convicts who tortured the Indigenous populations for centuries? And what if the people still doing that torture today, in lots and lots of evil little ways, are the reincarnated Indigenous who were, themselves, the murdered, and raped, and tortured, and tormented, all those generations ago?'

Barker let out a breath, but did not respond.

'Because, if that's how it works...' The Persuader put a showman's backward-facing hand beside his mouth and mimicked an aside. '...and between you and me kid, *it is how it works....*' He lowered his hand and spread his arms sympathetically. '...how could that ever be arbitrated upon? Even if there was anybody left in this third density dimension who could still understand it? Who would still be willing to admit they understand it? Even if there was anybody left who could, who would – and let's face it; *who – would?* – still accept it as a reality? Where would you set up the courts? In the Dreamtime? In the Astral? Same thing? Or just – *within*. Were such things to be established as real, as fact (and many believe of course that they are not; even some of those who know that we immortal imps are, absolutely, as real as it gets, and believe we have made up... *all that other stuff...* to confound you) ...where was I? Oh yes; if we, me and my kind and sub-kinds and all sorts of demonic-type *kindnesses*, were to be established as *fact* – I mean to say; what if it – all of it; *were true...?* Is it true? That the sad truth is... the spiritual arbitration and reincarnation distribution of the cosmos is, simply, on autopilot? Or, just innate? Or overseen? By angels who know better? Heavenly court, divine judgement, give 'em the handbook, but edit out all the bits about reincarnation?'

'Your time is coming to an end.'

'Just the same as adults know better, and edit, for their children, even though the children weep and call out in protest? And, who, up above, will manage all of that when the guard changes, *and this time comes to an end?*'

He smiled. Just plain. Making his point. Making… his case.

'Who, Barker? When the energies roll over and shift and new rules have to be determined for the new energies? Just like after an enormous environmental disaster, or a consciousness-altering scientific discovery? Or after – the internet? All that knowledge about us! Me and you and us and our kinds. Free! Free, if you know where to look. Hidden for thousands of years, then; ping! All there. Joe and Mary Beer-Can reading The Book of Enoch. *New rules.* Get them through; catch them up; make them play, or they fall by the way. And, yes, the guard *is changing* Barker Moon. This time *is ending*. Make no mistake. As above, so below. Your silly systems are but an echo of the great many-thousand year cycles and…'

'And the Celts?' Barker offered. 'What about their system? I mean; my genes, surely, respond to those mystical systems from whence they hail? And my blood is German and Irish and Anglo and Saxon. But wait; are we talking northern sea energies? Or, North Sea energies? Or sky; wind specifically? Western what, exactly? Western where? Western facing or the whole western mélange in general? The dying of the day's light is negative in many systems; and yet, the sunset is so beautiful, particularly so here in this city, that many people draw warmth and hope and solace from it. More than the sunrise, some of them, which represents the horror of a new day of pains and challenges in a life made solid by poor choices, congealing and setting around them like a straitjacket. So what is it that you want, demon? Who, despite all that, has turned the natural energies of the land here in on this city itself, made some crossroads, and created a…'

Barker stopped himself.

'…you said; it's better if we don't know we are working for you.'

'Yes, always better. Useful idiots, is a term I believe that was coined by one of your more useful people. Or one of ours. I can't remember, there are so many phrases, so many coins and so very many idiots.'

'Quaker doesn't know, does he?'

'Virtually none of the money people do. Some get an inkling, later in life, and try to make amends. The Creditor and his comrades are very selective as to which of the mortals become aware they are working in a parasitic system of financial exploitation designed to create pain and turn people away from…' The Persuader turned to his left and looked at the giant eastern-facing wall, behind which was the World Casino. '…well, *toward me*, really. Here. The object of the game of course is to take it all.'

'Your game. On your board. That you made.'

'Well, yes. But, yours as well. Take it all from us; that's what we tell you. And it's no lie. We made it all; all the stuff you want. And the object of the game is; you take it from us. We give you a starter; we tell you the rules. And you have youth on your side, to begin with. We are so old; sometimes we slip or get bored, or someone runs a good diversion; we're not invincible. Sometimes you just get a good head start; luck, divine intervention, law of large numbers, and you end well ahead. Sometimes, if you work out the rules very cleverly, you can make a late play, be wise, and end well. Sometimes very, even extraordinary well; we're not resentful. We like it when that happens. Keeps it interesting. But, we can't help it. We're just… clever.'

'And old.'

'I said that. Many of you are all old, also. But you forget. We – do not.'

Barker was really trying to piece it together; he knew this bit. The demon had talked a lot. Within it, within all the confounding questions, he had told Barker what was happening. Or in the least, given him the information he required.

'So…' Barker looked up at the sign. He had been born to this City Of Spells. He had fled and returned of his own free will. '… what is the deal you are offering me?'

'Thank you for asking. It's better for us if you ask.'

'We're more desperate, you mean?'

'No, it's better for the light beings as well; the angels and all. Better for you, better for everyone. We are here to serve you, to play the game, Barker. We've always been here to do that; it is our place, in the scheme of things. Tell us what you want, and we will tell you whether or not that is something that interests us in helping you achieve it. How could it be more simple? And yet…'

Barker looked up at the sign again. 'That's really how you see it, isn't it?'

Once more, The Persuader spread his open palms toward Barker. 'Yes. Because that's how it is. Barker; allow me to bring something to your attention. The girl. Woman. The Emerald. She is yours. We want you to know that.'

Barker was quite affronted at the notion. 'You control her? No; you *think* you control her?'

'No, no. You misunderstand. You can have her.'

The demon was winding him up. He had to calm down.

'No extra cost, Barker.'

Barker took a breath. 'What you mean is; all I have to do is tell her how I feel and she will be mine. You're giving me this information, as though it might be something I don't already know.'

'You did know that? That's all she wants. For you to believe that she is not unworthy. And all that would take would be for you to make some kind of concession toward her, that you accept her as she is.'

'But I don't. Not working for Quaker.'

'Of course; but we thought you should know. You could take that hot, Ox-charged body of yours, and take her with it, right after we're done here if you want. You have a perfect, aesthetically pleasant-looking, respectably above-average sized member that has more than adequately satisfied many women in your time; well, in your pre-Bridger Mansion incarnation, shall we say, but there is no reason to expect, now that you are coming back into your own so rapidly, right here before me, that a woman  such as Emerald, who has limited her sexual adventures to only a handful of the most handsome and sportsmanlike lovers of Europe over the past decade, should be by any stretch of the imagination disappointed.'

'Not going to happen.'

No matter how much he wanted it, not matter how much The Persuader knew he wanted it, and no matter how much toxic demon dust he had just blown up Barker's arse, he had to ditch that idea; her, all of that. Focus. Focus on the…

'That's just a starter. If you ask her to be yours, she will be yours. That is simply – fact. Quaker is no problem. If you don't want him to be. The casino; yours. She'll be working for you.'

So, whatever they wanted from him for, or even… *for him?* Whatever that was; they were prepared to lose Quaker. Somebody who – may or may not have known he was working for demons, but – somebody whom they had no doubt maneuvered here and wanted to remain.

'I don't want a casino.'

'Close it. Turn it into a children's amusement park where they win prizes of healthy snacks and gift certificates to higher education. The government can make its taxes elsewhere; we'll make cigarettes even more expensive. Improve people's health, remove the burden from the lovely new hospital.'

'Tell me what it is you need the city for.'

'Okay; so, I can make you Vice Chancellor at the University. As well as shutting down the casino.'

'You will close down the casino and open another one. It might take ten years to buy a high-rise on the other side, bribe everyone who needs it, work the right magic on another corner with a south-facing entrance. But ten years is nothing to you.

And I have no interest in joining the Illuminati. One member in the family is quite enough.'

'Does she know you know?'

'I don't know.'

'Oh.'

Barker wasn't sure what the demon would do when it became clear that Barker could not be bargained with. He might have already known; perhaps this was just going through the motions, perhaps this was simply theatre, and had to be performed to run out the contract.

'Then, tell me what you want. To make the city better? This is the third density of reality, Barker. The city cannot be made better. You could try; you might even succeed in running all the demons and devils and psychopaths and sociopaths and djinns and Satanists and Black Luciferians and Blood-Magic Illuminati and even all the ordinary arse-holes out of town. But it will not last. Human nature is infinitely corruptible; it will fall from within, or it will be conquered from without by all the other cities who will find your silly little City of Light intolerable. You will be the Serpico City; the one city that does not play ball, that must be crushed by all the other cities so that their corrupt but perfectly balanced way of life can be maintained.'

'I just want people to know.'

'What?'

'I want people to know. Not in code, not in symbol, not in allegory, not in metaphor or illusion or allusion or…'

'Stop!'

The demon huffed.

He considered.

This was not a game show. Not now.

Suddenly, this was negotiations, business, and Barker felt a tremendous weight as the fluid energies of the cosmos; those that could bind a new course of momentum for third density reality, flooded the concourse around him.

'We will leave you alone. We will allow you to show your side of things to as many people as you desire, and you may proceed, unhindered, until you die. I will not interfere.'

For a second, Barker's mind sparked. He could do that. He was strong enough. His friends were strong enough.

'You won't harm the people I… awaken?'

'No. That would seem implicit.'

'And the people they awaken, after I die?'

'You don't know what you're asking. But yes. I will leave them alone.'

Barker held, and focused.

'I know you are not Lucifer. Not any of the others. But you were saying 'we'. But then, you said 'I'. So… you may have had another name once, but what that means, is that this is not a promise for all demon-kind to leave me alone. Just you, and the others who are maintaining this city the way it is, for you, or on your behalf. The ones here now.'

'That is true; but that will make a huge difference. More influence than almost anybody has on this planet. The absence of my influence, of those such as The Land Lord and The Creditor, does not *necessarily* increase the influence of others; but it does make room. But that is not the same.'

Barker kept holding.

He remembered doing this at Bridger; but not with demons. *Not with demons.*

Heather hadn't lied.

Barker could not help but ask now; he needed to know. If he were going to get out of the Terminus alive, he needed to know.

'What do you want in return?'

The demon Persuader raised an eyebrow.

'You don't know?'

'I need to ask, don't I?'

'For the girl, the casino, the chair, and for your opportunity to be the Aquarian Christ?'

Barker did not respond.

The Persuader smiled.

'Leave town.'

# CHAPTER THIRTY-FOUR: BACK

Carlton stared at the phone as though it was the phone itself that were mad.

'He'll be here in a minute? What the fuck does he mean by that? We don't even know how the hell *we* got here?' He considered the smartphone again, somewhat flustered. 'How the fuck did that call even get through?'

He frowned at Fiif, although he was still frowning at Barker, and spoke low.

'This is where we stand up.'

And with that he attempted a stand, almost springing to his feet with brash confidence. It would have looked great if he had, but just the fact he had tried was, he was sure that Fiif would have to confess, pretty damned impressive. He went forward a bit and balanced on his arm, on the grass, then brushed some grass and dirt off the arms of his long leather jacket, alternately with each arm as he stood fully, more slowly, then offered Fiif his hand, finally upright again.

He felt awful as he absorbed the scene before him, dizzy and weird; not quite all the way back into his skull, truth be told. Scared, too. This was Argent. Not Greyside or Greencliff. Fucking *Argent*. But Fiif was clearly a lot more terrified… and something had to be done to stop all this.

Fiif grasped his hand; her slender fingers were freezing cold, but there was a rock there, also freezing cold, in her hand. He squeezed tight around it, to reassure her.

'Get as many as you can…'

'There's no point in whispering…' Fiif said this, despite the fact that she was whispering herself. He liked that; it showed that she had faith in him, even unconsciously. '…they can read our minds…'

'Not anymore; I just came back online.'

'You… what?'

'I think I have, anyway. Maybe.'

'Online? Literally?'

He wasn't… completely sure. He was still processing all that weird shit he'd seen via his astral trip to Bridger Mansion.

'It's a bit like…' Again, he was doing his best to explain. '…there are spells… like shielding, and localized weirdness checks, or big shift pings, that kick in, on auto, when you wake up.'

'There are?'

'Like, in the split second when you wake up and your awareness kicks in, you remember who you are; what your life is, who you're sleeping beside; the room, the house, the people in your life and what you have to do today. You check the clock by the bed, and the start gun goes off. For a sorcerer, there's a whole bunch of other stuff that goes off too. Extra awareness; so, the kids, and the tall one over there, they can't read you now.'

She huffed. 'So you'll teach me all this, right?'

'Sure.' He kept staring. He let go of her hand and dug around in his coat pockets. 'Sure, no worries. Just as soon as I…'

It didn't need to be taught, not really; why hadn't she just picked it up? Intuited it? To most people who had their talents, it was just innate. Had Zinco's tattoos, all those retrees and eshexes, prevented her from that as well?

'Like… like a soldier, I suppose.'

'Huh? A soldier?'

'Like… anyone whose life involves the possibility of waking up with someone trying to kill them. You're immediately defensive, shielding right away.'

Carlton stared at her. He'd never really seen it that way. But that was true; and more of that was coming. If they could get out of here, somehow, the life that he, that they, had waiting for them, would be war.

He suddenly noticed that Echidna was still staring at them, her inner-tattooed arms firmly folded. She had advanced a few more steps through, and was standing closer now. She sneered and turned away from them at a slight angle, as though in disdain.

'You don't even understand why you're here, do you?'

'We're bait…' Carlton snarled. 'But you forgot; bait attracts things. Sometimes things that are bigger and badder than you had planned.'

'Barker Moon? Bigger and badder?' She looked back. He knew her, almost recognized her from somewhere. 'Don't be absurd. He's a big bad little boy, who's been playing outside of his home patch. He strayed, too wide and too far, like you Carlton.' *Was she from the telly? Or; were there lines? On her face? Was her face a glamour?* 'You should have stayed inside your miserable little dive pub, Craven, getting maggoted thrice weekly. But no; you had to go looking. Like all the other little lost psychics out here, wandering the hills and dales, with nobody to train them. You and him and the witch were supposed to do that; but he stopped you, didn't he? Master Shilling. Little lost pups and pussies. Cold and wet and sad and alone and *dead*.'

She let that hang.

'Is that true?' Fiif asked quietly. 'Are they all dead?'

*Is Amanda dead?*

'I told you, idiot tits. She's still there. She's a battery now. A tool, with a function.'

'Who are you?' Fiif sneered. 'What made you like this?'

Echidna sneered back, but pressed on. 'And don't get ideas above your station, Craven Fuck. It doesn't matter what you've seen. You're a hostage here. Not bait. Hostage. We will kill you, if Moon does not do what we require of him.'

Carlton could feel his eyes narrow, his jaw clench, his shoulders tense and his fists balling as she spoke. '…then you'll kill us all, I suppose.' He turned to Fiif. She was pretending to search through the bag, dumping food out, but was surreptitiously filling it with small rocks and pebbles from the side of the road. 'Remember what I told you? The higher perspective some of these demonic things have? This demon told them; take us out. It saw that me and the others were supposed to – '

'What is she doing?' Echidna suddenly demanded. Then she took another few strides forward. 'What is in that bag?'

'She's looking for my water.'

'Tell her to stop!'

Carlton stepped toward her, and she jolted, as though startled.

'It saw that Barker was the key, didn't it? The demon behind all this? It crippled him; and made the rest of us irrelevant. Made Cheryl his doting sibling and took away my confidence. Sent a base creep and his goons out to mop up the others; control Fiona so she couldn't emerge, kept her under its wing in case it needed her. Send the coven to the four winds and everyone else off in other directions. Managed it all from behind the scenes. We didn't even know. We didn't even know we had that path to take, if we wanted.'

'I did…' Fiif uttered. '…deep down.'

'That's the way they work, isn't it? These ancient malevolents? Managing, consuming potential; just allowing the potentials they want to exhaust themselves, in the direction they want. The dark entities control things here, and in the same way, they intercede to stop anything getting in their way.'

'Shilling wanted to kill you all; he doesn't believe in allowing randoms to remain loose. But the house wants you all back; it knows better.'

'You agree with the house?' Carlton grinned. There was a spark in his eyes. 'Disagree with Shilling?' Carlton suddenly saw it. 'Shilling must have known that; he must have thought that the house would call us all back, and he could pick us all off, one by one…'

Echidna scoffed. 'I want to kill you; kill you all; hunt down the others, kill them for him!'

'For Shilling, or for the house?' Carlton's eyes glinted again; cheek and smarts. 'Wait; hunt down the others? So; there are others, not just us? From the last time? Were you there the last time, Echidna? What was your name before this? Did you know our friend? Did you know our friend, Heather Holden?'

'I want to kill you, but I will kill her; you can still be made to do what we want, with all our other *bargaining chips*; Amanda is alive, her man is alive, barely; if I kill this bleach blonde witch bimbo, will it convince you that I will kill the other two?'

'Carlton…'

'Don't worry. She's only trying to get me angry, so I'll make a mistake and attack. Give her an excuse to hurt us.'

One of the little girls chimed in again. 'She won't need to. Fight on the light, fight on the dark, fight in the night, fight in the dark; play in the day, play and away; we know Our Lord from the checkerboard.'

Carlton stared past Fiif, into the darkness.

What… what if they weren't all powerful? What if it were just myth?

'We're not myth, Carlton Craven. We hear your thoughts; you have no protection.'

He gulped.

'Is it true, then?' He thought he might as well ask. 'The story I have in my head? About what happened here?'

'Parts,' the first girl said.

That was awful enough; if any of it were true.

'The worst parts,' the second girl said.

'But why do you answer to *her*?'

'I know…' Fiif hissed. 'I know… it must be…'

'Logical…' Carlton nodded.

'Where is he!?' Echidna suddenly demanded. 'He said he was coming! In a minute!' She spun around to Carlton. 'Call him back! Call him on your stupid phone!'

She returned her attention to Fiif, standing there with Carlton's bag.

'Why is she filling that bag with rocks?'

Fiif pulled out the sticks.

'Use your sticks…?'

'What are they?' Echidna demanded.

Carlton spoke quickly. 'It's not that simple; here, there's massive magic. Like, huge, fuck off magic as old as time, just enabling this place, just to allow it…'

'Bring them to me!'

'It must be some kind of curse going back to the First Indigenous; perhaps before, or; in the astral beyond that, maybe? I mean… I start using those things here, we get Gladiator; we get echoes through eternity.'

'What about just the hitting one?'

'What?'

'Well, one's for commanding, right? Nothing you aren't willing to do yourself? But the other one, it's for defense; it's the instant-karma, do unto others weapon, right?'

'You have until the count of three to stop talking and bring those sticks to me!'

'Carlton, when you don't give her those sticks, she's either going to kill me, or order those kids to kill me.'

'Three, two, one; right, children – kill the blonde!'

# CHAPTER THIRTY-FIVE: TERMINUS

I

'Leave town?'

'Do not open the portal.'

'But…'

The Persuader looked at Barker, nonplussed. 'But what?'

Barker couldn't help but think; but since when does a demon want to stop what Fenner Shilling wants?

The demon kept staring at him.

'What more can I offer you?'

'Can you pull Carlton out of there? And Fiona?'

'Ah.'

'Is that a no?'

'Huh. Well, Barker, as I am sure you have realized, the price of whatever it is you want on – this – mortal plane, is not to open the portal, which sadly equates to any opportunity you might have, however slim, and believe me, it is – very – slim, of saving the souls of your best friend and his sometime girlfriend.'

'They're *actually* together now?'

'Barker; they have always been together. They just didn't know it.'

'Because you stopped them knowing?'

'No; there are several here on the grid vying for power, yourself included, and one of the others is taking the risk to engineer things that way, but; no. Besides, sometimes the landscape simply does not allow the roads to intercept until they have negotiated that which is immoveable. Even for us. Mankind cannot yet detonate celestial bodies, to clear the way to create better eras, can He? The way He destroys mountains to create faster thoroughfares?'

'Yet? That's a thing?'

'Planets, stars; they are made; they can be unmade. A million millennia hence, someone within humankind will attempt it. But for now we prefer to create an attraction, out of what is already there, and make an offer. So much simpler. So much easier to get your mind around.'

Barker's mind was reeling from the notion of angels and demons, god and satans, far in the future, far in the past, so powerful they could forge or burn solar systems in order to influence an entire planetary civilization. But that was what the demon wanted; distractions, tangents. The Persuader turned and looked up to the bridge. A woman walked along it, from the hotel to the casino. It only took a few seconds. Her footsteps echoed lightly and she did not look down, did not see either Barker or the demon.

'Allow me to demonstrate; that woman has been persuaded to come here. Tonight she will be here for one of three or possibly five nights, depending upon how long she wishes to delay her gratification. During that time, the casino will take her money. All of it. The casino will take the money she should pay her bills with this week, we will take the nest egg she has for her holiday that she and her husband have been looking forward to for two years now, and it will take a large portion of a second mortgage that she and her husband took out on their home, in order to build a larger home out of it, because they want to have a third child.'

'You're disgusting.'

'He leaves her, is the gist.'

'That... is why I – '

'The higher forces of light – ' The Persuader spoke sharply now, and proceeded very clearly, annunciating with cutthroat precision. ' – by now, have given her all the information she requires, in order to focus, and become less unhappy, something more, than she is. She has a terrible diet and it addles her brain; too much processed and refined foods, and she drinks too much alcohol. She spends too much time in a peer group who support each other's shortcomings by complaining, and blaming outside influences (those they all agree upon) as the cause of their collective dissatisfactions. All of it makes her sad, and weak, and tired. She's taking drugs and vitamins and supplements that she buys from the supermarket, to counteract the effects of the nutritionless foods she buys; from those same supermarkets. It makes her unable to think clearly. Her body is running to stand still, from the lack of proper nutrition, and cannot repair itself in simple ways; the aches and pains, everyday aches and pains people call them, keep her awake longer at night than she should be, because they prevent her getting to sleep. She blames age, and getting older, but she is only thirty-six; barely an adult in this era. This, and the worry over it, and the time laying still with no distraction to allow her mind to drift, and she makes more of all the dramas in her life, even the miniscule and inconsequential, into nightmare scenarios from which she is unable to awaken. Her sleep was shallow, and restless, but now she is plagued by insomnia. Lack of sleep is the Holy Grail for manipulators and tricksters. People make decisions in anger or resentment, out of spite, or out of impulse, without proper consideration. She does this a lot, all of it.'

'You've constructed this world, slowly, over time…'

The Persuader turned suddenly, shortly, and spoke as close to angrily as he had so far.

'You've allowed it, slowly, over time, to become this.'

Barker growled, just a little, but remained silent as The Persuader went on.

'All of this weariness in her… all this confusion, and dissatisfaction, as her impulse purchases fail to please her, means that she has only a slender thread remaining that is attached to anything truly greater, or spiritually higher, or more holy, than the part of herself that is trapped and weakened here, on this plane. In the broad terms of this era, she has nothing left but her old dial-up modem, running on a neglected, rusty-line-connection from a previous, bygone era, connecting to the lowest level of a higher force that she neither truly understands, nor understands why it seems to have abandoned her. Nothing has abandoned her, of course; but they, we, anything or anyone, from any resonance, simply have so much trouble now, merely getting through to her, given the meager processes the world has shown her as to how to get through to us, that there is almost no point in her trying at all. And, when she does get through, which is seldom, and weakly, the lowest of the higher forces of light have told her, repeatedly and necessarily as quickly and sharply as they can; stop. Just, stop. Limit and minimize the drug-taking. Meditate. Go for walks. Just short ones. Chill. Eat more fresh food. Clean up your diet. Just a bit. *Just a bit.* Stop sharing your dreams with people who make you feel they are not possible to reach. She has the time to do this, and recover her best path toward the divine in this realm, but she would rather binge-view competitive cooking programmes, or competitive renovation programmes, or competitive singing programmes, that make her feel at once hungry, and inadequate; physically, spiritually, intellectually and selfishly. It is a vicious cycle, I grant you; but there is a way out and it has been shown to her many, many times; almost every time she prays for help or guidance, or to be shown the way out, she is given directions to the closest and most convenient exit route that is instantly available to her. The basic idea is; she opens a path, just a small one, to the light, and her spirit becomes just slightly more enabled. It grows, just a bit. The first tiny watering on a long-winter seed. But, even when she does manage to accomplish this, on the few times she has tried, it shows her things she doesn't want to know, and cannot face. The connection is so short, the divine does what it can; stop! Breathe! Get fit! Chill out! It comes through fast, and urgent, because the divine doesn't know when it will get through again; and it's often such a low-level agent, barely above a Ouija board imp, that it just – jabs, stabs through whatever it can. That is the great trouble with the light, and how it reaches third density reality.

Most people avoid it for so long that it seems harsh, when they first see it here, after so long. Like being woken from a deep sleep by a naked bulb, blasting to life over your head. Nobody wants that. Turn it off! Go back to sleep!'

Barker could not help but show, on his features, that he knew this to be true.

'Yes. You know; we all know. What the light first illuminates for her is the great fear that resides, always, just under the surface. It is often different for different people, this first great fear that is always just under the surface, but for her it is the same as it is for many; that she married too soon. That leads directly to the second; that she had children too soon. And again; that she had another destiny once, that it is still not too late to unfold. But it will be harder now, this time; and the reason for that is because the last time, she was offered the path of least resistance, of the covetousness of diamond rings, white wedding dresses and adorable pink infants.'

'You did that...' Barker scowled. '...you and your kind.'

The Persuader spread his arms. 'We offer the path of least resistance, yes. We did that; we, as you see it, set the bait and laid the trap. But it is not as though there is not the knowledge within society for people to see; you know that is part of the rules of the game! They must be told; they must be shown!'

He moved slightly more toward Barker then, as though, quite earnestly, there was some level of relief in speaking to him; as though it was very enjoyable speaking to somebody who, for once, might actually understand what he was talking about, warts and all.

'Is there not, Barker? Is there not enough, at the age of nineteen, or twenty-three, or whatever age is too early for whatever human to be accepting the path of least resistance, and committing to the heavy burdens of chore and sacrifice entirely too early for this day and age; is there not enough of a story in place? Is there not enough of a warning narrative, they cannot see the path of least resistance, and what it brings? In culture, in music, in everything?'

'But you advertise, just as heavily, in the other direction. That *persuasion* magic, those symbols, are immense; they generate a pressure that the human psyche simply cannot resist. We crumble and beg for comfort. Even for sorcerers, even for shamans and seers, it is simply a matter of what degree one is able to resist.'

The Persuader had appreciated that comment. He spread his arms again and smiled broadly. 'We confess! And that is what here is; that is what the game is. But surely you must see the other? It is harder to read, harder to create, harder to manifest in culture, in art and music and narrative, because it is not the path of least resistance. It is more complex, harder, more demanding. That is why they all ignore it. Even when they do recognize it, they spurn it; they band together in gangs to spurn it. Willingly. They beg for the power to ignore it even more. But when they awaken from that, this is what they find.'

The Persuader looked back up to the bridge, where the woman was long gone.

But Chief Inspector Parry was there.

The Persuader smiled and made a London accent.

'Evenin' oll.'

Parry nodded, just so they could see it.

'Carry on; I'm enjoying the performance.'

The Persuader clasped his hands behind him and leaned back, directing his performance right up to the Chief Inspector.

'I really do shine, don't I? Right up there to the cheap seats! They say it has to do with projecting a natural charisma!'

'You have that. In spades.'

The Persuader nodded, beamed a smile back up to Parry, then resumed his performance alongside Barker.

'He's been watching us a while...' The Persuader uttered. '... but of course you knew that...'

Barker hadn't. But he had not been distracted by Parry. The demon had given him another hint.

'Nobody goes to the theatre.'

Barker might have done it with that; with a quick, smart comment that offered the demon a place to resume his, really quite tremendous, performance, without realizing that Barker had received one of his hints. He might have, it may have been worth trying to disguise, but he doubted it.

'Yes! The theatre! Too demanding! Too confronting! Not only in both creation and performance, but in reception as well. The path to the light is too harsh now. Theatre is angry and sad and witty and biting; filled with truth; nobody wants it anymore. Those who do; well, down there in the theatre complex, they are controlled by subsidies. That way, we get to keep an eye on those who are mad enough to rebel in public. That's why arts grants still exist. We like to know who wants them. What for. And, those who go, who are attracted, those who want the arts money, those who go and see what comes from arts money; we target them.'

'All in one place…'

'Essentially. It is the perfect city, in many respects.'

'Since… the 1830's, you were here? Did you come from Empire? Or were you here already?'

The demon's eyes flinched.

Up to the top of the stairs, near where Parry had stood.

He instantly resumed the performance.

'They are sleepy, Barker! And lazy, and want to stay in bed! Even though bed hurts them, even though it hurts their hearts and souls. It is not their children; they are not the cause. They love their children; and all humans know, instinctively, Lord Cherish Them, that children deserve to be loved. It is the knowledge that they had them too early, or too many, or with the wrong person, for the wrong reasons, or with the lesser person; that there was a second choice, another choice, that they did not know was the second choice, because they did not wait long enough to know there was another choice, a better choice.'

'This is not wisdom.'

'It is to some and it is truth to many; the harsh truth of light. I married the wrong person, I had children with them too early in life, I abandoned myself to a cycle of birth and death and rebirth that is endless and pitiless and leads to nothing but the self-propagation of the life cycle, and I want out!'

'What if I go up there and stop her? I mean; we *are* still talking about that woman you somehow lured here, aren't we? What if I go up to tell her, to her face, that there is another way?'

The Persuader was totally nonplussed. 'Do it. Be my guest. She will be back, in an hour, in a day. You could go up there and seduce her, as you used to do with vulnerable women, in your previous incarnation. Take her out of there, take her home, make love to her. *See her*, as they say. Keep her away. A week or two, maybe longer; but she will be back, because you do not love her, because if you did that, you would be *trying to save her.*'

'Maybe it would be worth it. Maybe something would take.'

*She needs to find it herself, save herself. Creating a lie out of her life with sex would not...*

'And what about the next one, Barker? Or the next one, or the next one? They come through like androids from the future, programmed to come here on autopilot, when their circuits are so dead, and they no longer remember how to function correctly, to be wiped and thrown out to start a second-hand existence, and resume their search for purpose. Will you stop them, fix them, repair them one by one?'

'If that's the only way, perhaps I will.'

'You're not a Salvation Man, Barker Moon. She wants to destroy her life. She wants to. It is *what she wants*, and it is *all she wants*. She wants her husband to hate her, she wants her children taken away, she wants to hit self-destruct and start all over again. She wants to move, to get away from her mother, who she feels never endorsed her life choices as a young student, and her father, who wanted another boy and is totally disinterested in his own granddaughters. These are some of the reasons she married too early; because her mother too, married too early, and before her, and so on. Because she was looking for another Daddy; this one who paid attention, and was interested. She wants her children to understand that there are other choices, that you can change your mind and begin again, and that mistakes can be forgiven; Great Lord, how she hopes that she will be forgiven for what she is about to do. But she has not the tools, nor the wherewithal, or in the very least, the developed intellect, to articulate any of this. She does, at least, possess the base instinct to comprehend that, even if she did, even if she could articulate her pain to them, they would not listen; they would chastise and reprocess and eventually medicate her, and then she would never again escape their cult. But even so; she herself is afraid that if she seeks help that she will be called crazy. That her second great fear that lies just under the surface will be made real, and revealed in the harsh light; that she is crazy, that she has become unstable and no longer sees reality, her life, the way it is. That she is unhinged, unnatural, and ungrateful. Oh; the third level she fears most of all; that she is spoiled and ungrateful for being unhappy when she has so, so much. And make no mistake; she has sought the help of mediums and new age gurus, but they were all charlatans...'

'Who work for you...'

'...who are encouraged and inspired by us, but in turn are unaware of how to use their own true otherworldly skills, despite the great many instruction manuals available, and so they took her money accordingly, in exchange for some hopelessly worthless or inappropriate magic, or some short-term pick-me-up platitudes. She does not know any other way to make her point, other than to go in here and destroy her financial life. She knows her husband will not forgive her; she knows he loves her, but will not stay with her after this; that is how he is; money is more important than anything, and that is why she no longer loves him; not as she once did. And that is just one person, Barker Moon, one person, that has incarnated into this world and fallen into our traps, without even realizing that they have been born, as they say, but furthermore without even knowing that there is such a thing as an incarnation, and that they may have come here as a smaller spark of a greater illumination, with a mission in mind, no matter how humble, and become lost, without knowledge or direction or hope.'

He thought of Party Girl, lost in the astral parklands for half a century.

How many Party Girls had he seen?

How many people?

And all of them, with their secret psychological agonies.

Trapped in a world of lies, run by demons.

According to this arsehole, anyway.

'And you seek to somehow turn the tide, Barker Moon? There are one million, four hundred thousand people in this jurisdiction of southern Australia. By the time this new supernatural war ends, there will be thirty million people in this country and eight billion on this plane, on this planet. And these, Barker Moon, these who think as that woman does, who have caught themselves in a situation where they would rather painfully self-destruct than take any other route, are the entitled ones. The first-worlders; the ones that the vast majority of the world would kill, and kill and kill and kill, to be part of. They are the wealthy, or the upper-middle wealthy, or the middle, or even the upper-working classes, who live like gods in the eyes of most of those who are unawakened incarnates to the underdeveloped third density plane; the supreme irony is that it is so often the highest and most privileged that seek to self-destruct everything those higher tiers of physical wealth and satisfaction have provided them.'

The Persuader stopped then, and put his hands in his pockets. He looked up at the western-facing windows. Barker understood, at least, the point that the thing was trying to make.

'So this poor woman does this...' Barker uttered. '...self-destructs in this Temple of Self-Destruction, and it's like, what? Tearing up the contract? She starts a new game, clean slate? Dump and wipe and reboot?'

The Persuader shrugged. 'Seems fair?'

Barker just shook his head in disgust.

The Persuader took note.

'So, you will not save her. You were never going to. But; you seek to save your friend, from the clutches of the little children in Argent. I understand that. But then what? Somehow… do what? Stop all this? I have made you a good offer.'

'No.'

'Then, what?'

Barker took a moment. He'd learned as much as he could, without immediately risking his life.

'Well, I can take Fenner Shilling. But he wants the portal open, and you want that stopped; so if I open the portal, I, at the very least, create trouble for you. If I open this portal, causing whatever small amount of inconvenience this will cause for you, I can then go through, kill Shilling, and save my friend. You are a demon, but you can't kill me. Not here like this; that is against your rules. I don't think you can get a minion here either, in the time it will take for me to open the portal, even if that was your plan. But if you can, I can take them.'

'You think you can, Barker Moon?'

'After your little performance?'

The Persuader chuckled. 'I see.'

'Yeah. You do. You probably do. But; what you just told me is true from a perspective. Here's mine; if people knew that you existed; your kind, your race, the way they're supposed to; not through this coded so-called Illuminati secret knowledge bullshit, but if they could *actually know*, they would stand up and rebel in a New York minute. Nothing would stop them, and it would be over in a cosmic heartbeat. But somehow, you have gotten everyone to accept a world that – nobody wants. Everybody wants to live, sure; but nobody *really* wants the world this way. Except; you, and the people you train and endorse, and support, who know how to exploit it the way it is. Who are – *the only ones who know how to exploit it the way it is.*'

'Intriguing…'

'You can be stopped, and it will take some doing. But it will not start by me accepting a deal from a demon for something that, if I wanted, I could already have. But that's your secret, isn't it? You offer people what they already have within them, but twist it so it sounds like you're the one who's enabling them to have it. That is, pretty much, your whole deal. Is it not?'

'Not to be, then....' The Persuader uttered, apparently to himself.

'So; no, Persuader. I'm opening the portal.'

The Persuader shrugged.

'I told them, they said it was worth a try.'

He bowed.

'You are an imbecile, Barker Moon. But some small part of me respects the heightened level of idiocy upon which you operate. I doubt we'll meet again.'

With that, he turned and walked away, vanishing into a translucent fog.


II


Barker looked up. Parry was still there on the walk-bridge.

'I didn't think he'd just give up like that...'

'He didn't scare you?'

'No. At least, not in the way I think you're asking me.'

'That's very interesting.'

'I'm a very interesting person, if you'd bothered to ask.'

'Remind me to ask some time.'

'Well, I shouldn't have to. But just this one time, I will make a note to do that.'

Barker looked up at his new ally.

'It's all levels and perspectives, Chief Inspector. What happens when you are very powerful, and you want something, but the polite negotiations fall through?'

'Some kind of psychological intimidation? That fails; strong physical violence?'

'So; if it comes from your direction, get down here as quickly as you can.'

'That would be jumping.'

'Not that quick. I can't actually trust that my magic's up and running that well just yet.'

'Can't you just fly up here or something?'

'No. For good or bad I am right where I need to be. I think I might have to open the portal from here. Chief Inspector can you remember three things for me?'

'I thought your memories were returning?'

'Not all of them; but all of my power, somehow. Which is nowhere near as safe as it sounds. But talking to one of those things is like being up in that room filled with poker machines; there's so much constant noise and nonsense that it's difficult to concentrate. But they have to tell you what's happening; they have to let you know if you ask them. The babble and obfuscation and bullshit is a technique they developed over centuries; they used to just scare the shit out of you, but, like they keep saying… something must have changed, energies shifted or… anyway; Dreamtime Arbitration.'

'That's it?'

'That's one.'

Parry took out a Galaxy Note and started writing.

'Cheryl has one of them.'

'I know.'

'Oh.' Barker pondered a second. 'You think I should get one?'

'They're very good. Then you could write things down yourself. What's the next thing?'

Barker looked back and forth. Four exits. Reinforced glass doors up on the Spell Steps, reinforced glass down on the opposing doors, on the way through to the Festival Centre.

'Imbecile's Theatre.'

'That's the second one?'

'Yep.'

'You're really going to open it?'

'I am.'

'Maybe you are an imbecile?'

'Almost certainly.'

'I prefer imbeciles to arse-holes.'

'I'd rather not deal with either, Chief Inspector…'

'Indeed. And the third?'

'Gunslinger's Arch.'

'Dramatic. Is that where we are?'

So, Parry caught that. To anyone mystically unenlightened, or magically unawakened, someone who had never seen or heard an evil supernatural entity speak in that way, it should all have sounded like jargon gibberish.

*He's been watching us a while… but of course you knew that?*

'You caught what he said?'

'I might not catch a lot of things, Mister Moon, but the thing about gunslingers? Maybe because I'm a cop. It stood out. And, you just put it together with the arch.'

Barker nodded. 'You see, then? It was like he wanted me to get it. Or; he had to tell me. He had to make it clear, at least on some level.'

Parry gave one chuckle. 'As clear as he couldn't.'

'Huh. Write that down, too.' Barker looked around again. 'I think this is a terminus because symbolically, people need to register that it is the end of one thing, and the start of something else. There's some kind of mystical energy field…'

'Gunslingers. He made it sound like…'

'Him and everyone I talk to make it sound like… a combat field. The grid, and the energy lines…'

'Listen, Moon; you make it sound like some kind of organized spiritual warfare…' Parry put his phone back in his breast pocket. 'What should we be getting ready for here?'

'Set up this way, since the colonists arrived, to tap into the new people, with the new energies. Originally for… well, at least *neutral* purposes. But in the first few decades, completely usurped and corrupted…'

'It should be a City of Light, an Illuminated City... but instead, it's...'

Barker glanced back up to the top of the stairs.

Where the demon's eyes had flicked, just a millisecond.

'All through the nineteenth century...'

The whole time.

Barker walked back toward the middle of the concourse and looked up the curved ramp. 'There are iron gates, both here and there...' He looked back down to the scissor-like diamond-concertina that blocked him from the train platforms. 'To stop what?'

'Well, people. Pedestrians. Non-sorcery people. On ordinary nights.'

'Iron.'

'Sometimes iron is just iron.'

'Iron is never an accident. It blocks, or at the very least, interferes with sorcery. It's usually used to protect against dark sorcery, but it repels almost any magical energy and is poisonous to most mystical creatures.' He looked up at Parry. 'I had iron weapons. You didn't find them when you found me at Bridger did you?'

'We found a lot of things. We had to assume they were weapons. Anything specific?'

But Barker was lost in thought, looking back and forth.

'Maybe they were used to stop sorcerers coming into the city?' Parry suggested. 'Did they even believe there were good sorcerers in those days? Surely if this Tarndanyangga power source is so special, there must have been people like you coming from all over once this colony was founded. Maybe even before? Weren't the Dutch here in the sixteen-hundreds? The Portuguese, the Spanish?'

'Probably. But when it came to sorcerers...' Barker looked around, still trying to piece it together. 'Depends on the country, the century, the church; but more often than not, no. No they didn't believe in good sorcerers, or benevolent witches. And to be honest, there probably weren't, back then, very many good ones.'

Barker thought on.

The Persuader ran this place. He was a demon, and demons were immortal, but their power was not instantaneous. But they had to travel, find victims, and willing helpers, to help build their power through deals and influence. Most people would never have met The Persuader, they would just have felt his influence. But he would have to have had a point of first contact; he had to have people, now, probably lots of people all over the city. But in order to have them, now, he would have to have met at least one or two, back then.

He would have started *here*.

This was where he lived; where his power base had begun, and still thrived.

The terminus.

This was his foundation.

Parry was staring down at him still.

'Penny? Maybe I can help?'

Barker didn't answer.

Everyone came through here.

But… there were the other roads, by which people came to the city. Were there other demons, waiting, making offers? Had there been, at all the main thoroughfares in? Was that part of the grid's function?

No time; The Persuader may have been one of many, he may have been the leader, the central demon of his hierarchy, but he had been here nearly two hundred years, and there would be those who would know him, those who would recognize him, and remember him.

Remember him – at the top of those stairs.

The Spell Steps.

And if there had been those who had known he was here, there would have been those who had taken measures. Hopefully to stop him, but just as likely to contain and control him.

'Maybe, the iron gates are to stop magical energies…' He pointed up the ramp, into the curved tunnel. '…escaping out onto the street.' He pointed to the nine platforms, past the sideways iron gates. '…or out, into the tunnels…'

Parry was leaning down still, staring.

Barker kept thinking. 'To stop? Corral, contain?'

Parry looked back and forth.

'Moon, what about directing? I mean, what about the other way? I mean, in my experience, electrified gates are employed to make sure cattle move in one direction. If someone was coming through the station… and they were allergic to iron…?'

'You could stop them coming in by train, at least to this station, you could stop them leaving. You could block them so they could only leave up the stairs, or out to the… the lake.'

'The lake?'

'Parry; I know what's going on!'

'Just here or everywhere?'

'Just here, but – that's a start, right?'

A security guard walked in from the casino side; he was dressed in a white shirt and unassuming pale blue suit-waistcoat and pants, but wore the unmistakable badge and cop-like hat of a security fellow.

'Can I please ask what your business is here, sir? We ask that patrons don't delay on the footbridge. There are signs at either end… what's he doing down there?'

Parry flashed a badge. 'C.I. Parry; S.A. We're investigating –'

'You're cops?'

Barker appeared not to have noticed the new arrival.

'Don't you see, Parry!?' Barker was speaking loudly, as he had been all through the conversation, to clearly reach Parry's ears. 'Both gates; the one on the tunnel and the one leading to the platforms, are original. They've been here since the twenties, at least!'

The guard looked down, quite oddly. 'The original was rebuilt around then, but the iron fixtures and clocks, and the various other items thought to be of value, or of historical significance or strong local character, were preserved and reincorporated into the new design and décor.'

Barker had taken note, and was listening now.

'Since the 1840's? That's when the first station was built, wasn't it?'

'That's correct, sir.' Strangely, Barker had the distinct impression that the guard seemed to be speaking from a perspective of experience, rather than learned historical knowledge. 'Before the casino, it was like an enormous, luxury departure lounge.'

Barker walked up more closely, craning his neck a bit more to speak more directly.

'And who told you that?'

'Nobody told me that, sir. It's history.'

'History?'

'You could chat to anyone here then, sir. Back in the twenties. It was a very wealthy state. All sorts coming through, coming and going. Wheelers and dealers. Investors. Lots of investors. You would have a drink in the lounge before coming, a drink in the lounge before going. Enough time for anyone to have a good chat with you; make an offer, seal a deal. Coming and going.'

Barker stepped back suddenly and turned ninety degrees from the bridge, toward the open ramp-tunnel. He looked down and arched his shoulders, spread his arms wide and splaying his fingers tightly, to face the opening to the tunnel.

'Parry! Jump!'

'What?!'

Massive brown wings sprouted violently sideways, as though on tight springs, from the security guard's back, spread high over the rails of the bridge. Talons, as long as his fingers, sluiced from the tips of his hands.

'Now Parry!'

Barker opened the portal.

# CHAPTER THIRTY-SIX:
# FIRE AND WATER AND
# WHATEVER ELSE

Cheryl dragged Candle, tied and bound by the electrical cord that had once held the bulb in the middle of the haunted shaft, into the ruined section of the salon. She sneered at the second of the snowman cocoons and looked up at the crumbled mezzanine.

'Get us down from here!' Karri cried out.

'Not 'til it's safe! Where did Pitt go?'

'Who?!'

'The cum-creature; the sex-pest! Where'd he go?'

'That shell thing just vanished and there he was again – thirty years younger!' Shirley confirmed. 'And a lot keener, if you know what I mean!'

'Was this the other boon?' Cheryl asked up. 'Was this, the second part – their boon? Is it possible you've been sensing – negative boons, not just from our side?'

'Our side? I don't know. I suppose…?'

Karri pointed at the exit corridor, past the remaining snowman cocoon. 'He dragged Feather down the front…' There wasn't even a trace of the other cocoon. 'I didn't hear the door, or any glass…'

'Jesus…' Cheryl breathed. 'What the creeping heebie-jeebies are they doing down there?'

'Let me go!' Candle demanded. 'What the hell do you know of Fenner Shilling anyway? He is the most powerful, the most feared sorcerer –'

Cheryl threw Candle against the wall and shouted in her face.

'Yes, Candy! He is!  – the greatest! – one of! – *thuhgreatest* – sorcerers of all time! And probably the most feared!' She must have looked pretty fearsome herself with her sleek silver body and pure white eyes. 'But he is also totally immoral, utterly corrupt and blatantly evil; being just once in his very proximity is cause enough to reassess every decision you have made, and will make, five years in either direction and always, always, to sleep with one eye open – and change all your passwords! Or don't, because it's just as likely you are doing it because he wants you to; do you understand me Candy?'

Candle suddenly sounded a lot less sure of herself.

'You don't know what you're talking abou – ...'

'He tried to kill me three times – that I know about, so; that, I know about!'

Cheryl could practically see the sharp, fearful shiver as it ran down Candle's spine, as Cheryl held her gaze. Cheryl could see now; Candace, Candy, Candle... not grey and Polish but alabaster Irish... not sunken sockets, but freckles, everywhere. Before, as she'd dragged her to her feet and bound her, she had seen, and could imagine, what she thought of as her wench's figure; booby and hippy enough for flirting but too much of a potato farmer's descendant to be... what?

Exactly.

To be; what?

Just like Cheryl. Nobody had ever told her who she was or how she was supposed to be, nor what she had, or how to use it; how to get what she wanted, even if she knew what it was she wanted. What she actually did, or was supposed to want; let alone whether those two things should coincide.

But, if they'd been together...? Allied as a coven...?

'What?' Candle snarled, half-heartedly. 'You gonna *kiss me now?*'

She must have been looking at her funny.

'No...' Cheryl uttered. 'I don't want to kiss anyone.'

I want to kill.

Kill Fenner Shilling.

Huh. That would be like; get in line.

'There's a ladder…' Shirley offered by way of polite but urgent interjection, seeming to detect that Cheryl was just a little more than a bit cross. '…at the far corner in the tea room…?'

Cheryl flicked her eyes up from Candle to Shirley.

'I've never been like this, Shirley. I've never been this… demonstrably angry.'

Shirley stared down over her nose and huffed thoughtfully, but said nothing.

'Is that the light cord? What happened to the light bulb?' Karri asked sheepishly.

'All those ghouls got out,' Cheryl snapped up at them. 'My fault, apparently, and now I've made everything a thousand times worse…' She snapped her gaze back at Candle. '…according to the woman who *works for Fenner Fucking Shilling*.'

'Stupid witch.'

Cheryl screwed up her face.

'To think; we were supposed to have been friends…'

All three asked at once. '*What?*'

Cheryl wasn't sure, but it was worth a shot.

'Shilling's been ahead of Barker and me for…' She gulped. Maybe she could sway this. Or, maybe she would just make herself cry. '…a decade, probably. Maybe more. He's known us… known of us… Jesus…' Don't. Don't cry. Don't even think, just tell her. 'Look; it's like… some people can do that. Right? They shouldn't be able to but they can; they can see three, five, ten steps ahead, they can see what people are thinking, understand their motives, where their potential can take them. Some people are just born that way; small timers. Sociopaths, psychopaths, whatever; you know the score. But others… aren't. Some people, some of them psychos but some of them not, use magic to see ahead. And some of *them*… they summon things. Things that can give them… greater perspective. Some just want to make the world better, or just, make themselves better,. Just knowledge; that's all they want. They're guided by… their enlightened selves, their better natures; the better angels of their natures, someone once said; or spirits of light, or ascended masters, benevolent spirits; guides, guardians, Pleiadeans, Andromedans, *whatever* - angels! Angels, let's say! But others become *allied with demons*. They bargain with spirits, darker spirits who enjoy manipulating, and gaining power through mortals, who get off on it, vicariously… and they merge, and the person, the psychopathic-sorcerer… it works the Moxic, and the Togic, and they become psychorers, or sorcerpaths…'

'…you're making this up…'

Cheryl snarled at her, spitting furiously. '*I made up these names because there are no real names for these things!* Toxic magic, and psychopathic sorcerers…it's the old ways blended into the new ways; spells and sigils and potions and summonings; mixed with marketing and psychology and demographic manipulation; micro-expressions and genetic modification; *it's so much more powerful now*. Shilling used it all to alter our life paths; Barker, Carlton and me; *my life path*, was diverted; by your evil, arsehole boss. Which means; yours was too, *Candace*. I was supposed to join your coven six or seven years ago.'

There was silence for a second.

'Ohhhhh…' Karri nodded. 'That explains Narelle.'

'What makes you think any of this is true?' Candle demanded, upward at Karri.

Cheryl didn't respond. She'd done what she could.

And she had not cried. She was, however, shivering.

'I'm fucking freezing with this layer of water over me… I can't think straight after that. I can't *think* any more.'

Shirley was staying calm. 'Switch it off, darling heart; then put the clothes on. It must be taking up so much energy; you're always thirsty and you already look thinner than you did an hour ago.'

'Not…' She shivered some more. '…so sure I can…'

'Just try, darling heart; the water doesn't want you to die. It's you; you and the water are one. Will it, command it; that's what you have; the properties of water and the command over water; that's what it'll be, when you figure it out. But for now, losing your water-skin should be as easy as opening and closing your eyes, or, maybe, like, you know; like whizzing?'

'Ewww!'

'That's a perfectly natural water function, Karri! That's what we're looking for! Try to be scientific, child!' She looked down at Cheryl again. 'Does your water-skin come out of the pores? Or does it squirt out of a hole and spread?'

'Shirleee!'

'I'm only interested!

'Not water-skin...' Cheryl understood. 'I prefer...' The shimmering wetsuit vanished, and she was naked again.

'Oh!'

So far as she could tell, almost everyone had exclaimed that, including herself. But it was equally because she now held a pool of water, still in her hand, like a discus.

'...just *wetsuit*, for now.'

'Stop looking at her like that!' Karri yelled down, almost instantly at Candle.

'She's naked right in front of me!'

'The chest, darling heart; the clothes you picked, get them out, before you die your death of pneumonia! Is your still skin wet?'

'Is that really important?' Candle demanded.

'It is if she doesn't want to go about town with the nickname Missus Soggy Britches!'

Karri laughed to herself. '...or Wet Cheryl!'

'*Thank-you!*' Cheryl spotted the clothes chest against the wall, and moved quickly. It opened easily, and was filled to the brim.

'Cheryl, love; if your skin's dry, it means you can wear clothes and still use the magic...'

'Yes, it is, just my hand that's wet; I think the water sort of... bonds. Molecules, or something. Binding it. It's like it knows I can't walk around in soggy britches...' She looked up a second. '...just in case that's what anybody was thinking.'

She held the water discus out a few seconds more, then lowered it to her side, where it held stable in her hand, as though she were holding a Frisbee. Then she raised it again, higher, then a little higher, until it lost integrity as it reached shoulder-height, just splashing to the floor; a tall glass worth of water.

'It likes to flow down; doesn't like to go up.'

'I hope that's not so when it's attached to you!' Shirley offered. 'Stay out of elevators for the time being.'

Karri giggled.

'You'll get better at it. Now get dressed!'

Cheryl bent over and started sorting through the clothes, but it was half-hearted.

'I'm… losing my focus…'

She picked out a white shirt and started wiping her wet hand on it.

'Hey! Wet Cheryl! Stay with us; you picked all this remember! In the van, after the light hit you, you were talking, you said you would need to stay warm, no matter what!'

Cheryl tried again. She pulled out a pair of thermal leggings and held them up.

'Why is it all white? I don't feel like white at all…'

'Best brand…' Shirley assured her. '…feel good, stay warm, flexible…'

'Not white…' Cheryl insisted. 'At least… no; not black, not white… not now, not tonight. I'm done with…' She was still shivering, but knew she had to get this right. 'I'm always second-guessing. What was the first thing…? The first thing I picked?'

'At the bottom… pull all the other things out!'

Cheryl did; like a child looking for her favourite forgotten toy, she dug furiously as she cast aside anything that wasn't the very thing she wanted.

'Yes!'

There was a pair of dark-blue demin jeans. Rich blue, deep but vibrant. She held them up with a silly grin, then immediately pulled them on, sans underwear, zipped and buttoned, then stood, not looking into the mirror but assessing the rest of the contents. The jeans were a good fit, and she felt instantly better, but she still wasn't entirely sure what she was going for; but then, as though suddenly reminded, it came to her, and for the first time in her life, she knew. She knew exactly what she had been and was now going for.

*I command water. I am water. We are all water.*

*I should* reflect *that.*

'Where…?'

She saw it.

There had been an oversized shirt, almost the same colour; that deep indigo-blue that was just right, the real thing, but difficult to find. It looked old, looked timeless, tough and durable but feminine and chic. The long shirt went on immediately; it went down past her thighs, but when she pulled a belt out, a thick black leather one with a silver buckle and studs, and fastened it around her waist, the shirt rose up a bit and became devastatingly cute… she even let herself acknowledge that.

Karri squealed. 'Shirley… look!'

Things were changing; she could feel it. But she didn't know which part of what was happening exactly that Karri was so excited about. She didn't want to yet. The deep-navy leather vest that had lain beneath went immediately over her shoulders, and pushed up the collar of the indigo-blue shirt. It was fitted, it would enhance her figure, and it did right up the front with dark-navy laces over midnight-blue eyelets. She left the threads loose for the minute however, while she searched for something else.

'The boots, the long boots, darling heart; they're not rubbish, they're tough. Durable and flexible.'

They were black, but that was okay; the laces and eyelets clearly went with the belt and vest. Cheryl pulled up a chair and pulled them on, hard and fast. They were already laced and she only had to pull and tighten them. Then she stood and wobbled a bit. They had heels, but they were solid, and she easily walked a circle back to the chest.

'Remember, darling heart, if you command water, then…'

How did she know that? Had she said something in the van? It didn't matter. She pulled out a frock coat, with some kind of Celtic-knot silver brocade up along the sleeve.

'Sorry if it's a bit Penzance, darling heart…!?'

If the outfit seemed buccaneerish up to now, this was suddenly more like admiralty; but altogether, slightly, more stylish and more feminine; elaborate, but perhaps definitive somehow…

'No!' She put it on. 'This is me now! This is me!'

Shirley bowed. 'It's merely my divinely designated task!'

Karri was still excited. 'But look Shirley, can't you see?'

Shirley called down. 'Look closer at yourself darling! Use the mirror now!'

Cheryl looked at herself.

She looked serious.

More serious than she could ever remember herself looking. She looked like someone who would have been commanding a fleet; not just in the olden days (although with some caveats, obviously) but now, or in some wild version of the badass future. She looked like an admiral-pirate rockstar-gunslinger babe you did not fuck with and to whom you gave absolutely no shit whatsoever; but at the same time, at the same time, so very deeply, she absolutely also looked exactly like someone you absolutely, absolutely, wanted on your side.

Despite that, though, despite the outfit, the most striking thing was her; her eyes, her hair, and her complexion. They had taken on the tones of her clothes, and she looked like the ocean; the blue, storybook ocean from fairy-tale star-lit nights. Her hair remained ethereal, but it was a deep blue; a luscious dark-sapphire with navy depth so rich to be almost black underneath, the brightest of the blue, almost like an aura.

But also, strikingly, where before the skin around her sunken eyes (her beautiful eyes she realized now) had once, and almost always, been darkly pigmented, but had then been watered-down, as it were, by the almost invisible, watery luminosity of her boon, now those luminous, but hitherto transparent spaces reflected the rich, brilliant blue of her sartorial choices; the whole of her eyelids had transformed into a deep, lush cobalt blue, her eyelashes a dark black-blue, and her deep sockets now carried pigments not of brown-pink, but rich, violet-blue. In a way her eye-sockets were darker, and more outcast than ever, and surely would have been deeply menacing to many, if it were not for the deepest crystal-cobalt of her irises that seemed to project a light-filled, powerful spirit from way back within.

'…what have I become?'

Karri sighed. '…absolutely…!' Then she gasped with joy. '…you're like the ocean…! You're taking on the colors that you bring to yourself!'

Cheryl touched her lips, her eyebrows. They too were blue; the same dark, rich cobalt blue of her eyelids, and of the most resplendent locks of her hair. She looked closer, stepped closer, and saw that she was still shivering. No, not shivering any longer; she was quivering, quivering now. She looked at her hands, her real hands; her nails were the same, deep cobalt. Her all-over skin however was actually milky white, but enhanced with a lighter sapphire-blue, some lightly silver-blue reflection of the ensemble, where others, other humans (if indeed she still was completely human) and those from her same genetic pool might have been pink or red.

'You could wear pink, or red, or browns, or… whatever you liked; and look completely normal.'

'Do I look… dead? Like a… frozen blue corpse?'

'No!'

Cheryl could have sworn they all shouted that at once as well; even Candle.

'…you look radiant, like the moonlit ocean.'

Cheryl looked at herself again.

'But you are now a queen on the board…' Candle growled. '…one queen on a multi-dimensional board with more than one queen; but a queen on the board.'

Cheryl turned to her.

'So you knew? You know?'

'Know what?'

'What I was talking about; the game they play. The board, the multi-dimensional board.'

Candle frowned. Then her lower lip started quivering.

'That's...' She scoffed; not at Cheryl, but at some sudden realization. 'That's what it is? That's what... they're the same?' Candle was crying now. 'What I wanted to be; what we all wanted to be; a player; a princess; *a queen*! What Shilling *promised us* we could be... but you did it...' There was a terrible, heartbroken gurgle in her throat. '...without even trying.'

'Put away those bitter tears!' Shirley snapped.

*'They're not bitter you fucking old hag!'*

Cheryl looked back at Candle, and saw that, bizarrely, and perhaps conversely, she was telling the truth. She knew that she had to make a move with this one, that it was not too late, but it had to be done here, immediately, while the break from Shilling's influence was fresh.

'Candle... Candace...'

The second cocoon made a sucking sound and seemed to implode; the mass of it reducing back, incredibly fast, onto Cruise. He stood there now, covered in thick and sinewy white slime, but still wore the same suit, drenched and covered with goo, but whole.

Cheryl held out her upward facing palms toward him. Cruise saw this and it seemed to give him pause for concern, then he snarled. He looked a lot more handsome now; devilishly so. You'd place him somewhere around forty, but the cocoon and the white goo seemed to have de-aged him (or it; Cheryl still wasn't truly sure) whilst also giving him a DNA makeover, so that he now looked like a rugged movie star from the seventies; as though the collective he'd been hatched from had telepathically...

She suddenly saw it; this was a parasite creature who registered telepathic imprints. She'd heard of such things, never seen one.

Cheryl stopped thinking about it.

'Stay there! Stay there, sex pest – don't move – don't touch anything!'

Cheryl looked up at Shirley and spoke quickly. 'Is there anyone else? Like me or her? Air or earth or ether?'

She spun about to Candle.

'I'm water; you're fire – we've all read about this stuff. We travel in packs of five, right? Do you have an air channel in your coven? An earth channel? Or did Shilling send them off on wild tangents as well?'

'I don't know. Feather's just… psychic…'

Candle seemed to be thinking; taking the suggestion seriously.

'Feather's a weak link!' Karri shouted. 'So's Narelle! There's a gap there, a big gap!'

Cheryl had put it together though. 'These sex pests, they read minds, they know what we like on a basic level, then they manifest it to gain sympathy and get closer; he's come out looking even more like fucking Paul Newman than Tom Cruise does, and that's exactly what I was thinking; it's too much of a coincidence.'

'Bastards!' Shirley cried out. 'They've taken a passing thought chain from your mind! Darling heart; someone with real psychic ability could probably exert some kind of actual control over them!'

Candle looked sheepish, then she lashed out to prevent them from seeing the truth about what she had intended to do with them.

'Enough! We have to get Feather back!' Candle decried. 'She's one of us! And that thing! What's it doing to her!'

Cheryl barked back. 'You didn't seem to care what it was gonna do to us! And I can tell you now, she's not one of you – but you *are*! You are one of *us* Candle, no matter what bullshit they've fed you! Feather is a plant, she's a classic Shilling… well; Shill! Did Feather introduce you to him? Pump him up in your eyes for weeks before?'

'Yes, but…'

'And when you met Shilling, he was like a long lost uncle, right? And this coven, Shirley and Karri's coven; *your coven*, was – beneath you? Not suited to your talents? You needed someone who could nurture you, not limit you; you needed to be set free, to find your own way under the guidance of someone… am I getting it even half right?'

'Sounds…' Candle gulped. '…sounds… kind of shallow and obvious when you say it…'

Cheryl threw her hands up.

'I fucking knew it! You didn't sleep with him, did you?'

'No! That was supposed to be – ' Candle caught her breath. 'Tonight – after!'

'After what!?' Shirley demanded.

'After we…' Candle looked Cheryl in the eye. '…after we locked you two in there with the vengeful spirits and got her to fight these things!'

Cruise turned to Cheryl. 'Did you tie her up for me? Are you with us now? Is that what the blue is?'

'No! Why would it be?'

Cruise shrugged. 'I don't know! Why *would* it be *anything*?' He was kind of like a fugly Paul Newman, a scrawny Tom Cruise; not the exact equation, but almost enough. Tall Crewman. 'I need to make wet with someone! You look like the sea, Blue Girl! Let's make wet!'

He staggered toward her with open arms, with the white goo already emanating from his palms and drooling down the sides of his mouth. Cheryl barely had time to register her disgust when she realized that she was in the middle of a fight and was, in fact, fighting. The white goo shot out from his hands as though the time in the cocoon had fully weaponized it, and morphed him into a genuine predator. She felt adrenalin surge and slapped the two streams back instinctively; the goo splattered and sprayed like fireworks as her palms splashed the gushes away, the goo turning instantly to dust as soon as the dispersing particles made contact with the floor or walls. She could feel the wetsuit reconstitute suddenly over her skin, then a second layer, an unconsciously summoned outer armor, maybe an inch or two around her clothes and hair. Knowing that this was an attack-response, her temper flared and in a blast of uncontrolled fury, she went for him; one hand out, the other raised in a fist. He advanced also but was more experienced and punched her hard, directly on the bridge of her nose before she knew what was happening. He advanced as she recoiled hopelessly backwards, but she felt only a little pain on what surely should have been an excruciatingly broken nose; the outer shield had buffered that, but the force of it still sent her two steps back and onto her bum, again feeling that she should have felt a lot more pain, and more than a little shocked at the whole thing happening in the first place. Then, as he bore down with his hands extended, white and glistening with goo, she was possessed with a sudden and highly disconcerting realization; she did not know how to fight. She had never been in one, had never had to. Her whole life… she'd barely even scrapped with the other kids in the schoolyard! Everyone had either liked her, occasionally teased her, or stayed clear. In a way, that had been the advantage of being… just Cheryl. An ordinary oddball. Nobody was passionate about her either way, so she'd never been too badly hurt. Not there; not at school, anyway.

She scrambled back a bit, toward the basins, unable to think of a spell to summon. She wanted the water to come and save her but she couldn't think how; where had it come from before? Why had it appeared? She had summoned it just by wanting it and; *what was she now, anyway?* She asked this of herself again; *what had she become?*

She bumped the back of her head against a basin and realized she had nowhere left to retreat.

He came at her, and she heard the other women screaming and calling out; just a mish-mash in her mind. His suit really was completely intact, she saw as he grasped at his long dong, hanging from the unzipped pants, and paused as though about to urinate over her. After everything, she was still totally shocked at this, at the profanity and degradation he intended upon her, and that flared her temper again. It was as though something had worn off; the audacity of his disrespect trumped the mild stunning caused by his punch and she suddenly saw his dick as just a thing, just another appendage. She had been intending to grasp him by the neck when she had attacked, and shove her fist down his throat, with… water, or something, a summoning, or a flow; just, *her new powers*. But she just reached up and took it, grabbed it as she would take his hand, yanked it as hard as she could and punched up underneath it, into his balls. He cried out, and there was an expulsion of the white goo, gushing down and out of him as though Cheryl had somehow scuppered him, and she withdrew the fist before she could get too much of it on her. The goo vanished to dust almost instantly anyway, but now she saw, and thought she understood, that he wasn't human, that he was some kind of tulpa, or drone, just an animated sac filled with the goo. He dropped to his knees before her with a wide-open mouth, and she punched again, returning the favour and landing him right on his nose, right in the middle of his shocked expression, then again, and again. He didn't react as a person would; didn't bleed or even recoil too much. It was indeed as though his body were not a real body, not solid, not muscle and bone and sinews like a human body. The outer layer of his faux-handsome skin, that was not skin, started to bend like dough. She was going to call the water but she suddenly didn't know where to call the water down from; didn't really know where the wetsuit came from; the atmosphere? Just particulate water in the air? But she balled her fist tight then, and punched him in his still-gaping mouth, shoving her first right in and…

The water didn't come.

Cruise bit down; there were no teeth, but a strong sensation of her wrist being gummed, like a thick rubber band had been suddenly tightened, and her hand felt completely consumed by the whole lower half of his head.

'What the f – ' Cheryl used her other hand to force herself upright. '…you have a fucking sphincter for a head?'

She pulled on it; it didn't give so she used the purchase to hang on his open-mouthed grip and punch him in the face again; two, three, four more times until his upper head and eyes were like dough, his eyeballs right beside themselves, almost touching as they stared inward at each other, and then the white goo poured out of where his brain should have been.

'You *giant*…!'

Yet the sphincter around her wrist tightened more; it was painful now, closing in even on her wetsuit, and wetshield, so she reached in and grasped it, using the hideous malleability of his destroyed features to penetrate his very cranium and find the offending sphincter ring with her fingertips.

' – *giant* – !'

But it was too tight, way too tight and closing in; and she understood that it would do damage soon, that the water molecules, twice around her, could be reduced, and become gossamer thin with this terrible pressure, that it would cut off circulation, and eventually break her wrist, even pulverize it. But the panic, the fear, the confusion of the potential of suddenly, and quickly, losing her hand to this thing, would again not allow her to summon the water from the air as she had; the fear was over-riding her anger.

*Think it through Cheryl, always think it through.*
*Because that, in itself, makes you angry.*
*Working out why things are the way they are –*
It came from her lower gut, but she felt it through her blood –
Almost always –
And it came from her heart to her blood, and the energy that created came through her skin, out of her pores, and bonded with the air. And there was always water, always some water somewhere. But she would have to be careful, because if she was careless commanding, if there was not enough in the air, it would take the water from her blood, and the rest of body –

'*– giant –*!'
*Almost always made her angry.*
She remembered to close her eyes as the thing's head exploded.
'*– arsehole!*'
Water appeared around his head and smashed in, as though his face were a pressurized deep-sea pod that had lost integrity, and then the water was all there was, drenching what was left of his head, and her fist. When she opened her eyes, there was a kind of rubbery loop, attached to a rudimentary nervous system, hanging from her wrist and attached to the thing's fake human, besuited body. She could see things twitching, the glands all over its body attempting to reactivate, to create more goo, to in turn create another shell, to create another head, another body.

That would take a while. But something about it, its basic nature, suggested it would succeed if left be. Yet the goo that had covered her, covered the floor and walls, was already becoming dust again, and only the water that she had summoned from around her, that had blended with the goo, prevented it all from just vanishing without a trace.

'…insubstantial…' Cheryl uttered to herself. She slipped her hand free of the loose sphincter and kicked the headless body onto its back, where it lay twitching, legs spread and knees up. The she looked across at Candle.

'That's what Shilling wanted?' Cheryl shook her head. 'Jesus, he is ten steps ahead, as bloody usual…' She stood again and looked Candle in her eyes. 'Waiting for my boon, testing me when it arrived. Well, fuck him and his fucking five-dimensional cosmic chess…!'

Candle stared back.

Cheryl still felt tired, but she was coming back into herself. Perhaps the fight had sharpened her, or perhaps this was all just quickly becoming normal, her new normal, the way constant strangeness did when it occurred. She saw now that Candle had dark brown eyes that were like polished wood, with streaks of ochre and honey.

'Don't, Candle. Don't look away. Look at me, Candle. Shilling won't let you be this. He will contain, and drain you. I've seen him do it. He infiltrated us, back then; Heather's Circle, and that's what he did. I thought he was okay, just a bloke, a kind-of cool guy. He's not. He's the closest thing to The Devil we have in human form. So don't join him; *join me*. You and me; we'll create the five.'

'How?'

'We'll find the missing three; if they're gone for good, we'll find replacements; we'll work spells and bring them to us – if all this is *so meant to be*, in the City of Light, you and me, then *they should find us*, it should all come together; and that's what *he doesn't want*. That's what he is *trying to prevent*. Why would you not try and stop what evil incarnate is *trying to achieve?* Join with me, Candle! We have a ready-made coven and my two best friends are the most powerful sorcerers in the country! Say yes, and this game you're all so keen to play, this game that is fucking trapping us all in this city right now with no choice but to play, will never know what's hit it! Plus! If you hook up will me, and my crew, and them...' She pointed up. '.. who are also my crew now, she, Madame Shirley, will give you...' Cheryl spread her arm. '...a bad-ass fucking sorcerer costume!'

Candle was shaking now; her lips were trembling. 'You... you don't even look like you're wearing a costume; you just look cool!'

'You're in then?'

Candle was visibly trembling now, all over. 'There's something they do, in the mansion. When you live there; I wanted to know. I needed to know. You want to go in, you want to be a part of it...' She shook her head, like she was trying to shake off the notion. '...Feather kept saying. You want to go in, you want to be a part of it... the sex. The sex; you can feel it; you want it; it feels like it will be... bliss, when you get in there...'

Cheryl started to untie her.

'What are you doing!?' Shirley protested.

'I've seen it before... she's in his thrall, coming out of it. Can you guys get down?'

Candle was loose.

'I'm sorry,' Cheryl offered. 'Will you trust me? Can you?'

'I don't even know... who I am any more... how can I trust you?'

'Well, you have your brain back, at least...'

Cheryl looked over her shoulder, down the corridor to the front of the salon.

'Come with me.'

'No.'

'What?'

'I mean; not without Karri.'

Cheryl looked up again. 'What about Shirley?'

'I don't care; I mean, I do; but – she hasn't told you?'

Karri shrugged down. 'People tell me the truth. It's my thing. But...'

There was an awkward pause.

Shirley sighed. '...every question she asks; she falls asleep for an hour, not long after.'

Cheryl frowned. 'That's your thing?'

'Every truth I force out of someone, costs me an hour.' Karri shrugged. 'I go to the astral. It's not so bad.'

They found the ladder.

Then they found Feather.

She was behind the reception desk with Pitt.

Candle gasped when she saw them. 'Feather!'

They were making out in the receptionist's chair, Pitt reclined back, Feather straddling him. Their mouths were wide open, and Feather was sucking Pitt's tongue like a lollipop. It might have seemed like a perfectly normal, passionate, drunken office tryst if it hadn't been for the white slime that covered Feather's face, and that was dribbling down her cheeks, chin and neck. The white goo was clearly emanating from somewhere deep in his gut; regularly burping and repeating out of his mouth as his hands pasted her hair back with it, as he combed and groped his fingers all around her head and face.

'Sorry…' Feather gasped when she saw them. She could barely find the breath to speak, and couldn't stop kissing him. 'We just couldn't hold back any longer…'

Feather was delirious; clearly she thought she really *was* having a drunken fling at an office party; both were oblivious to the shrieking of the wind outside, which became much more apparent as the women approached the front of the store.

'Feather…' Candle sighed, shakily. 'What… what are you doing? You said you could control these things?'

The front door bumped from what sounded like tremendous pressure outside as a fierce whistle shrieked through a gap somewhere his in the front cornice.

'What things? Those things in the well?'

She smooched some more.

'Jesus, I am no prude…' Shirley gasped. '…but that is as sexy as a gall stone.'

Karri stepped forward and raised her hand.

'It helps, doesn't it?' Cheryl noted, quietly to herself. 'The hand thing?'

Karri smiled but Candle scoffed. 'Der. It's the main thing we have them for.'

Shirley raised an eyebrow. 'Not her, apparently…' She shook her head. 'For Christ's sake, somebody ask a question before they stray any further and she takes out his big white pecker!'

Candle snapped. 'What was our real mission here?'

Karri echoed, but amended. 'Tell me everything Shilling wanted you to do here.'

'Shilling? He said if I wanted to be the jewel in the crown of the new feminine energy, then I had to lock as many of the coven as I could find, as many who were here, any anyone else, in the shaft, no matter who, and then make Cheryl Equinox fight the two White Men. If they killed her, he said to put them in the shaft with the witches, if she killed them, he said seduce her and

432

bring her to the hotel. Either way, leave the witches to go mad in the sewer.'

'The hotel?' Cheryl asked. 'Which one?'

'The Hilton. He lives there. In the middle square, the energy centre.'

Candle snapped again. 'You were going to throw me in there? With them?'

'I need a better lover for my consort; he thought you would be more use to him driven mad by the ghouls in the well. That was the plan, after bringing you here.'

Karri lowered her hand. 'Seems I've lost an hour for nothing; she's not afraid of talking.'

Cheryl sighed. 'Shilling… he does this… plans and uses, and then has a backup plan, and a backup use; five times over.'

Candle paced back and forth in the short space. 'I should never vie for power; I always do the wrong thing; I always sleep with the wrong people!'

Karri gasped. 'You did sleep with Feather!'

'Of course I did; look at her, she's a gorgeous bloody goth princess! Everyone's slept with her; she sleeps with everyone!'

Karri frowned.

Cheryl stepped in. 'Shilling doesn't bother with people he thinks are too filled with light; he thinks they're corrupted; he just kills them.'

'Oh…' Karri shrugged. 'That's okay then…'

'Where are the others?' Feather suddenly asked, still half-smooching.

Pitt grunted something and belched out a vomitus flow of white goo that covered Feather's entire head.

'Ohhhh…' Feather groaned in ecstasy. '…*God*!'

Karri screamed and Shirley backed away into a corner, bending over to retch.

'What is that?' Cheryl demanded. 'What's he doing?'

'He's loving me; I will love him forever now.' She pulled up her three layers of tank tops as the goo started running down her chest, encouraging it to cover her breasts as she smeared it into her lily-white skin with her other hand. 'It seeps into my pores; so I can give him children.' Pitt started mouthing the breasts, one then the other, repeatedly. Then he vomited directly over them. She dropped the tops and let him go. 'They're very strong, and aesthetically pleasing. Easy to breed and hard to kill. Shilling wants them all through the city. I see now he wants me to be the brood mother. It's such an honour…'

'You poor bitch.' Karri raised her hand again. 'What did you mean 'the others'?'

'The ghouls…' Feather was starting to gyrate her hips. '…from the shaft…?'

'They already escaped…' Cheryl told her. She looked back to Shirley, who was wiping the corner of her mouth. 'Didn't you see them?'

'Oh no, that was just the plug…'

'No…' Cheryl corrected. 'There were hundreds…'

Karri lowered her hand again. 'The plug?'

'That's right…' Feather agreed. 'Just a few hundred. But there are thousands; all the people who've died in poverty or pain, or blame…' She suddenly groaned in pleasure, and Cheryl saw that Pitt's hands had started to wander evermore southerly. '…they should be here soon…'

There was a horrendous smashing, and a loud creaking from the back of the salon, accompanied by a wailing from above. Cheryl looked up. They were there, all of them, the hundreds that had raced past her, and Candle, all of them up on the ceiling, looking down, watching.

'Oh Jesus.'

'Quickly!' Shirley shouted. 'Out!'

'It's locked! Candle screeched.

The creaking and groaning of old wood continued from the back of the salon, amplified as though it were happening just around the corner instead of three rooms away. Then came the sudden splintering of wood and they heard the door, then another, then another smash down. Candle fumbled with a key from her pocket and went for the door. A gush of wind blasted past them all, and boomed into the glass frontage of the salon. Then another, that knocked them all to the ground, even Feather and Pitt, and then one, solid, continuous blast that blew out all of the glass and pushed everything and everyone out onto the street.

At first Cheryl resisted; she fell hard on her side, but her wetshield was there and there wasn't a lot of pain. But there were things, flashing past. Bottles and blow driers and brushes and disorientation as the ghouls from the well rushed over her and into the night. As the gushing blast slid her along the checkered floor, toward the front of the store, she tried to stand but then realized that even if she could get to her feet, the blast would only topple her, and send her spiraling into the shattered glass that was by now all over the street. As she tried to stabilize herself on her hands and knees, the still-continuous blast, or perhaps something in it, carried her up and out of the front of the store, then dumped her past the glass, over the footpath and onto the street. The blast didn't stop though, and she rolled across the empty street and into the concrete rise that was the edge of the tram stop, crashing hard against the edge with her exposed ribs as she raised both arms to cover her face and hands, shouting in pain with the wetshield mysteriously vanished.

She dared open her eyes and saw that the others had been dumped unceremoniously on the street as well, all except for Feather and the White Man, whom she couldn't see. The enormous gush release billowed out, a wind tunnel of sand and dirt so thick that you could practically see the path of the rushing air, see the spirits, the ghouls, escaping and ripping up and sideways and over, into the night, into the city. She thought it was about to end, and she tried to stand, but then there was another, massive blast and she heard more windows break, all up and down the street; the hotel next door, the office buildings on the other side, the hotel over the road, and then the World Casino as well. She tried to hold onto the edge of the concrete rise but it was too rough on her hands, on her fingers, too painful, and the wind was too strong. She felt herself carried up, over the other side of the street, perhaps a meter or two in the air, and when she felt sure she would hit the sandstone wall of either the Casino or the Station and break every last bone in her body, just before, she remembered the water.

Water came rushing to her at her summons, through the debris, from every direction, but it was all over the place, swirling with her. To her shock, she went straight through the wall, straight through the Casino; only she didn't, of course she didn't.

Cheryl was in the air, a floor high, and she could see the familiar walk bridge across the main Adelaide Railway Station concourse but knew she would not be carried there, that she would not catch the rail, catch that break, that she would fall short, and instead as the wind that was carrying her finally died, she grabbed for one of the long, hanging lights, for the second time in a hour – huh! – but it could not take her weight and she fell, with the wire zipping out, and the other lights rising and jerking abruptly along the line, along the ceiling, then something snapped and she fell, and hit the marble or concrete floor, or whatever the hell kind of *hard* it was, the impact of which she was sure would kill her instantly, but then much shorter than she had thought, in her disorientation, into what felt like a child's paddle pool that evaporated instantly upon impact.

She took a breath.

Barker was looking down at her, with an expression that was a candidate, for sure, for the most shocked she had ever seen him.

# PART FIVE
## MOVES AND SHAKES

# CHAPTER THIRTY-SEVEN: DASH

A few seconds passed before Emerald could speak.

When she did, she sounded amazed.

'You followed me here?'

'Yes.'

She felt hurt. She was surprised how much.

'You – led him here? Led Manny to me?'

The portal was still open, still purple, and still had Manny standing in front of it.

'Led him?'

Micro responded sharply, in a hushed tone from the back seat.

'No! Of course I didn't! And don't speak!'

The engine of the Ford Taurus was still running. Emerald kept her hands on the wheel, gripping more tightly with each passing second. She swallowed, hard. Her tongue clicked on the roof of her mouth. She'd gone dry. Manny didn't look any different. Still in the same ordinary clothes; grey, pale, cream, Bill Gates, tech-billionaire, Mark Zuckerberg, just-normal clothes. He didn't even look angry. It was like no time had passed for him.

All that running, for nothing.

She closed her eyes.

She had no thoughts.

She opened them again.

The gun was still there, still extended between the two front seats from the back seat of the car. But a second hand passed her water bottle through.

Micro spoke again. 'How could I lead him here? I didn't know where you were going. Drink.'

Emerald removed a hand from the wheel and reached down. She looked sideways, tried to see her.

'Don't!'

But Emerald had already realized.

'That gun's not… not pointed at me, is it?'

'What? No! Of course not!'

'Then…'

'Don't move your mouth so much! He'll see you're talking! Drink the water!'

'How did you…?'

'After I left you at the lobby on Fifth… I couldn't stop thinking about you.'

Emerald took a swig of water and listened.

'I had such a bad feeling. And; such a good feeling. I never wanted anyone so bad in all my life.'

Emerald gulped the water. 'Oh?'

'Look, it's okay. It's not like that. I know you're not… *that girl*, but, still…'

Her accent was dense to Emerald's ears, and she liked it.

Kind'a; *Noo Yawk*.

'…I just… never felt so bad, about leaving someone in their own goddamn protection…'

Emerald was a little offended.

'I got this far…!'

'Sure! And here he is; waiting for you, right at the end. How far did you run to get away from him, only to run right back into his ever-loving arms?'

Emerald heard herself sigh, then growled.

'Look at him there. Smug bastard. He thinks I won't run him over…'

'Don't talk, just mumble.'

'Okay. I get it.'

'Good. I had an idea he would try and track you. He has surveillance on everyone. But he's such a goddamn male asshole, he didn't expect to be followed himself…'

'Yeah. He was always a bit like that.'

'Okay. So, you have backup. All right?'

'All right.'

'Okay. So, to get through that thing, you'll need to run him down, run him down and through it. He knows you won't do that.'

'I…suppose.'

'That's where you're going, isn't it? Through that thing?'

'He *thinks* I won't do that.'

'You're not mumbling. Here.' She slid a phone through to her. 'Pretend you're talking on it.'

Emerald lifted it to her ear, and spoke a little more clearly. 'The only reason I haven't run him over yet is; he might survive. I don't want to take him with me, half-dead on the hood.'

'You don't mean any of that.'

'Don't I? Plus, I don't know where it goes. It might be the middle of London. With lots of CTV.'

'You don't know where it goes?'

'It's like… I traded.'

'Traded what? Your life? What is this – witness protection for woo-woos?'

'I need to get away from him. From everything. I accepted a mission at the other end of this portal. At least, I think that's what I did. I was pretty exhausted and very keen to be moving along, off this continent. But I have my own plan.'

'So did I. Pie shop in Nebraska, remember?'

'Look, I traded being someone's agent on the other side, in return for being able to start again. But I don't know where. It's just… the way it had to be. Okay?'

'I watched you talk to that old guy in the bar. The one who gave you the take-out. He has no real identification anywhere. That's very rare for someone who has dealt with so much municipal planning.'

'You were in the pub?'

'The old guy clocked me. He knew I was there. He watched me watch you, he watched me leave and follow you.'

'You were waiting for me? How? And how did Manny even find me here? How did he get up here? You really didn't tell him?'

'No!' She hissed. She was insulted.

'Sorry; I'm sorry. I know that, I'm grateful you're here. It's just – a shock! This is not how this was supposed to go. Nobody even knows this level of the building is here…'

'Well, then I could just shoot him. Or I could throw him off the edge. People would assume he came up to the floor below, and jumped off that one. You drive on, go on through the purple ring thing, nobody's any the wiser.'

Emerald kept staring out at him, holding the phone to her ear.

He seemed oddly calm. Creepily calm.

'He shouldn't have been able to find it.'

'When you left. You called me Micro. Why?'

Emerald took a second to remember. 'I saw the way you were looking at me whenever I went through the lobby; you were reading my micro-expressions. It was my way of remembering you.'

'Huh.' She shifted a little. 'I like that you wanted to remember me. I don't have a real name anymore.'

'That's sad.'

'But – I don't like that one.'

'Sorry.'

There was a pause. A strange pause.

'It's the beanie, isn't it?'

'Process of elimination, huh? When you left, I put a nano-tracker under the rim. Hooks into the weave, looks like a baby spider.'

'You just happened to have one?'

'I have ten different kinds of ten different devices on me at all times. You think that's just a phone you're holding? Most people have no idea what their *ordinary* phones can do.'

'Wow.'

'Like I said, I was worried for ya, Mo-Cap.'

'You tracked Manny too?'

'I always track my clients these days. Always like to know where they are, what they're up to; sometimes they decide – no witnesses. So, since that happened, I always track 'em. From the first meeting, I track them. I have good tech, y'know?'

'Obviously…'

'Really good tech.'

'Again…'

'Hermann Devane is just a games guy. He thinks he knows tech, knows hacking. But he isn't CIA, or Black Ops, or Dark Government. He overpays surveillance people who put on a good show, who tell him they're better than they are. I'm way better than that; I mean, not just morally, as a person. I am way better *professionally* than the people who do that. Way better. Simple as that, and I know that, because these days I look for easy work. I saw the others he hired in the first round. Look-alikes?' She laughed. 'Jesus Christ! Circus clowns! I thought; you gotta be fucken kidding me!'

'But, you're not freelance… you made that call.'

'Loose alliance. Flexible agent. But look; what I told you in the lobby, that was true. You saw that, right? When I saw who turned up on his *last round* of hiring. That wasn't right. But I wasn't prepared to get killed over it.'

Emerald sighed. Micro… whatever her name was, whoever she was; little bit masculine, little bit striking, little bit… well, *little*, she supposed, which was why she hated the name Micro… and a big bit *tough*, and *smart*, had come all this way for her.

'Thanks…' Emerald whispered. '…for coming.'

Micro cleared her throat.

'Is it one of those psychic things? That big purple ring? Real magic? Or is it like; a laser show?'

'It's real. That doesn't creep you out? In New York, I got the impression…'

Manny suddenly lost patience and called out. 'I don't care who you're talking to on that phone! I don't care who or what you bring here! Neither of us are leaving here until we talk!'

Fuck, Emerald thought, now *that*…

'*That* creeps me out…' Micro confessed. 'Right freaking there. Oh, I know what's what, Mo-Cap. I know this shit's real. I've been probed by psychics before. I'm obstinate; I don't give anyone up, and it hurts. But I don't care that it's the psychics, the sorcerers, the psychos, the cops, the bad partners, the bad parents, the bad fucken film producers, the bad fucken shop keepers; even if they *are* things that other people say don't exist; I don't care what kinds of power people abuse. It's that they abuse it, that's what counts. That's what creeps me out.'

'Cover me.'

Emerald reached for the door handle.

Micro sounded anxious. 'I need a safe word. One that tells me to come out shooting.'

'Well, that doesn't sound exactly safe to begin with.'

Micro didn't respond.

'Okay.' Emerald nodded. 'Dash.'

She lowered the phone.

'I'll say Dash.'

# CHAPTER THIRTY-EIGHT: THE WATCHERS

Emerald watched Barker as he talked to the thing on the Railway Station concourse.

It seemed that it was true, what she'd been told.

What the Trader had implied, what virtually everybody else she had spoken to or contacted since arriving here had implied.

These things were everywhere.

Shaping every city, shadowing every sorcerer.

But here, definitely here, they were active in a way that…

Quaker manipulated the remote, held with the same weapon-like authority as every man she had ever met had held one. Barker's picture came up as a hologram now. He was a flat image with the illusion of depth that hovered without any apparent framing screen, right there in the space between her and the traditional security monitors. This technology had seemed amazing in science fiction movies ten years ago, was available to the very wealthy now, and would be an everyday possession in another ten, probably five. If she lived, and based upon the more and more likely chance that she was to have grandchildren, to whom she could tell her story, this part would seem quaint; where she was mildly impressed by holographic screens in her rich soon-to be's security room.

'There *is* something else going on, isn't there?'

Emerald could see the shimmering mote-body of the demon that Barker was talking to.

But she didn't think Quaker could.

'What are you thinking?' Emerald asked blankly, trying not to see it as a form of a lie.

'From his stance, from the body language, it looks like there's somebody else there, down on the concourse, that the cams aren't picking up. Either the third person has scouted and secured a sweet spot that Station security hasn't…'

Emerald looked at him. He was no fool, he was simply not properly educated in the reality of mysticism. At the moment, that was his problem, but he didn't know it. That was *the* problem. But Emerald had learned. This was why, even if he did propose, she would not tell him. She would not Samantha him. She would have sex with him, maybe even properly fuck him, make sure they both enjoyed it, just like his ex-wife had told her that day, and if she were really lucky, she would end up actually making love to him. She would marry him and have a child with him, for him she would put her body through the ordeal of giving birth, an apparent natural joy for which she had no apparent natural magnetism toward; and in return, he would hand her the finances to create the system of education, and the infrastructure throughout society, designed so that nobody; man, woman, child, whatever, would have to go through what she had been through… as the saying went; ever again. Only then would she reveal what the whole thing had been about.

'…or, the third party has enabled themselves with some sort of… digital cloaking? Something military? That would be my educated guess. But why someone with that level of tech is negotiating with Barker Moon…? Let alone negotiating in there, in a Railway Station, like it's still the Cold War, at this time of night…?'

Suddenly, the demon was gone.

It had just turned, dematerialized its mote-body, and was gone.

'Why is the sound so poor? I'd like someone to scrub this later; I want to know what they're saying.'

Barker was doing it. His powers were coming back. What she'd heard about him was true; and his powers were truly coming back. Down on the corner, she had seen it. Seen that he was radiating with power, barely able to control it but holding on; a mystical power overload, stressing his mind and body and spirit… whatever the occult jargon term for it was.

The Bull?

He had seemed so attractive to her then and there, so powerful yet so vulnerable. She had almost opened up to him, told him.

*I'm not who you think I am!*

*I'm not doing it for the reasons you think I'm doing it!*

Down on the concourse, Barker had been obscuring the conversation unconsciously. Perhaps it was the demon, but all of this, the security footage from tonight, could be wiped if he wanted. Either of them could do it, with one focussed spell. All either of them would have to do would be to create that spell.

How many levels was Barker aware of? Was he playing? Without even knowing?

He hadn't seemed frightened of the demon at all; she'd been nervous, but it was half a block away. She'd heard that they could turn their vibrations down, the ones that turned adults into terrified children. She supposed that might be true. How else could people speak with them at crossroads, to make deals?

She wanted to know.

She turned to Quaker.

'I think –'

Quaker had been looking at her, and was still looking at her very curiously. It wasn't jealousy, as such. It was more that he realized he would have to destroy Barker, at least in her eyes, if he were ever to fully possess her. And Emerald could see him weighing it up; was it necessary to fully possess her? To possess her physically, have a child, then have it on record that he had possessed her physically; to empower her with what she wanted, and have that be something he had permitted, allowed, endorsed… with all that, orbiting a woman as beautiful as Emerald Tarragon, did it really matter that she was lusting, at the very least, after a younger man? Was it enough that she would sacrifice that lust, and that he was the one thing that could stand in its way, and make her do it?

She knew; he knew; neither would know until it played out.

Quaker spoke.

'The man on the bridge is a Chief Inspector. He was with the drug squad, but I suspect he's moved on. Nobody seems to know what department he's with any more.'

'I know him,' Emerald confessed. 'I sounded him out when I first arrived. Psychics often develop drug habits. Nice man, very world weary, but in the end, he wasn't much use.'

'I don't think this bodes well, Emerald.'

' – I think something is going to happen very shortly. I think you should close the casino for the next few hours; until daybreak at least. There are only a couple of dozen people here. I can have them cleared in under two. Is there anyone up in executive?'

Executive was something she tried not to think about.

'No, Mister Wade has been quiet tonight.'

'Mister Wade?'

The casinos were her way in; into the part of the world she needed access to.

She would scorch the earth on her way out.

She had not known about the Executive Rooms when she'd come in; it was something that had, for some reason, never appeared on her radar. And Quaker never spoke about them.

But that was her deal with herself, how she remained here.

Scorched earth; end it all.

'Mister Wade came with the casino. He handles the Executive Room. The state government refused to budge on that; I tried to phase it out, just maintain the High-Roller's Room. But, in the end, I agreed to keep Mister Wade, and the Executive Room. To keep the peace.'

Quaker moved in, toward the hologram, and stared at Barker; he was still talking to Parry.

'I know when someone says my name. When I got my first job I learned to lip read. Micro-expressions weren't a thing then. All the smart people learned to lip…'

He stared at Barker keenly then, who was still talking up to the Detective Inspector.

'Just about all I retained was the ability to know just a handful of words when I see them. *Quaker doesn't know…?* What do you think Barker Moon, and the people he is speaking with down there, think I don't know?'

Emerald didn't know. She didn't want him distracted from the information she suddenly found for some reason bizarrely absent from her entire world here; a place that otherwise she had made sure that she knew like the back of her hand.

'Mister Quaker, you've never spoken to me about Wade before tonight. At least, you've never mentioned that name.'

'We agreed that your business would begin on the first two floors. There will be time for –'

'I need to see him. I need to see his face.'

'His face?'

'It's really, *so important*, that you listen to me right now.'

Quaker looked at her squarely.

He really was so handsome.

And, he really was so dissatisfied with the way things were going.

'Very well.' Quaker crossed to his desk. He had one of those illuminated keyboards that was built into the surface. He also had a traditional one, she knew, that was plugged in beneath, in a slide-out desk; always with the backup plan. She'd learned that from him. She was, in the end very grateful for him.

He sat down and started typing; she was surprised how at-home he looked; one might expect a man of his perceived stature to feel that working a keyboard was beneath him. But the way he attacked the keyboard suggested quite otherwise; this was just another aspect of his world that he commanded.

The image came up before Emerald.

At first she was relieved.

She had thought that she would see a face, and behind that face she would see eyes that she recognized, eyes that would make her frightened, despite herself. For a split second, that was not what she saw. Then, a split-second after that, it was precisely what she recognized; only, these were not the eyes she thought she would see, and fear. These were the same, but different. And the face was the man Barker had been talking to down on the concourse.

All this time, a demon had been running the Executive Room; a whole section of the third floor, right beneath her. And she hadn't seen it, hadn't sensed it, hadn't even suspected it.

Percival Wade.

She didn't bother reading the bio, the work history.

'I'm more than happy to try and get rid of him again. If you have anything on him, I'm completely open to a conversation about how we can make that happen.'

Emerald heard herself.

*'Holy shit…'*

There was a bright flash of purple on the monitor, and they saw the Chief Inspector jump from the bridge.

'Jesus…' Quaker exclaimed, genuinely horrified. 'Did that cop just kill himself?'

This was immediately followed by a tremendous explosion from somewhere; outside the casino, Emerald sensed. The whole building shook. On the monitor the purple light had calmed, but it was still there, Emerald could see it.

A dimensional portal.

Just like the one in Montreal.

*Barker Moon had just opened a dimensional portal on the concourse of the Adelaide Railway Station.*

They could see a tremendous breeze blow Barker – and the Chief Inspector; he was standing just beside Barker as though he had just whizzed down a slippery-dip. Then a bigger, more massive gush of wind staggered the pair backwards as a woman,

all in blue, seemed to fall from the ceiling, and land heavily at
Barker's feet.

'Well, that can't be good…'

Emerald turned around.

Percival Wade was at the door of Quaker's office.

Emerald held her breath.

Then she uttered, clearly, albeit with a little fear in her voice.

*'Dash…'*

# CHAPTER THIRTY-NINE: TALLER

Barker looked down at Cheryl. 'What kept you?'

Cheryl looked up. 'You're late.'

Barker kept looking down. 'You're blue.'

Cheryl kept looking up. 'You're much taller in person.'

Barker extended his hand. 'Didn't see you down there.'

She accepted. 'Saw your light on, thought I'd drop in.'

Barker pulled her up. 'Next time try knocking.'

Cheryl brushed herself down. 'I was thinking about renovating the old place…'

Barker looked around. 'Well, you've certainly opened the place up a bit…'

Cheryl looked at the portal. 'Back to your old tricks again, I see?'

'Apparently.' He gave her hair a little, fluttering wave. 'This is new, though.'

'Makeover. Took a bit longer than I thought.'

'Are you taller?'

'Heels.'

'But…? What's all the…?'

'Blue?'

'All the cobalt and sapphire and azure? Do boons do that now?'

'I'm thinner, thank you, Steve Rogers Thesaurus. But it's kind of… athletic. I always thought; lithe. I wanted to be a little more *lithe*, you know?'

'Well, instead of lithe, you got athletic and blue. But you still look a little bit show-tunes; you like that, right?'

Cheryl shrugged. 'Meh. We play the hand we're dealt.'

She stared at the glowing, open, bright purple portal. It was perfectly round and about four meters, top to bottom.

'So, we're really doing this again, are we?'

Barker had opened the portal beneath the foot bridge, basically between the two access tunnels; the platform cavern and the tunnel-ramp, and they were standing between it and the big stairs leading up to North Terrace.

'Doing what? The portal thing? Thought I'd give it another go; seemed like it had a lot of life left in it, a pity to let all that practice go to waste. Didn't go... *exactly* to plan...'

'What else is new?'

'...and...' Barker's face lost all of its humour. '...Carlton's at the other end. He's stuck in Argent.'

'Argent?' Her deep blue eyes darkened. 'Okay – ' Cheryl slammed her fist into her open palm. 'Let's do this thing!'

Parry grinned. 'I'm too old for this shit!'

Barker and Cheryl both turned to him, as though they had forgotten he was there.

'You're not Danny Glover, whoever you are...' Cheryl informed him. Then she turned to Barker. '*Argent?* How'd he get there?'

Parry spread his hands. 'But, I'm *actually* an old cop.'

'Long story...' Barker sighed, looking at the portal. 'There's a girl involved...'

'Of course there is...' She turned back to Parry. 'No way; I'm Danny Glover. You're Joe Pesci.'

'I am not – !'

Cheryl seemed affronted. 'I am Murtaugh! He is Riggs! You are – whoever Pesci was supposed to be!'

Barker frowned to himself as he held his hand out toward the portal.

'*Why won't it....?*' He turned to Cheryl. 'Can't you be Rene Russo?'

'Riggs' girlfriend?' Cheryl eyed him suspiciously. 'You want to sleep with me now I'm blue and empowered? More empowered than you maybe?'

Barker looked over to Parry. 'You can be Murtaugh.'

Cheryl seemed to change her mind.

'Rene Russo, huh?'

She leaned over and gave Barker a kiss, a nice but solid peck.

Then she stepped back, a little surprised.

'Oh…' Her fingers touched her lips. 'My-my. What was that? I actually *felt* something…' She gasped. 'You bloody liar! *You do want to sleep with me!*'

'Cheryl, I swear, I don't – I have The Ox…!'

Cheryl's whole body sagged for a second in sheer relief. 'Oh thank God!' Then she turned to the portal. 'Is that why there's something off with the portal? It looks… different…?'

Parry tried to save him.

'We haven't been formerly introduced. Chief Inspector Parry. Ah, basically, I just jumped from the bridge up there onto this… circular, expanding ball of purple energy here; basically I was pretty keen to avoid the clutches, I suppose it would be fair to say, of a demonoid bat-winged security guard.' He shrugged, keeping the hand out. '…there was a not inconsiderable degree of trust involved at that point, you understand, but I think it's fair to say I can trust the two of you…?'

Barker nodded at him, as if to say, *it was nothing*.

With his unaccepted hand still outstretched for Cheryl to shake, he looked up and around the arched ceiling.

'Ah… not sure where it's gone. Maybe it flew out of those doors you… literally blew in on.' His hand was still extended. 'Does that costume come with a hat? Very fetching, I'm not denying, but it looks like, a hat, over the bandana? And if I am not mistaken, while there is a suggestion of some kind of hair; upon closer examination, the expected ponytail, seems to be… you might even say – invisible?'

Cheryl stared at the mustachioed man for a not inconsiderably long few seconds, nodded three times, with tight lips, and then turned back to Barker

'We work with cops now? Since when do cops understand the supernatural? Cops put people like us into psych wards.'

Parry was still willing to give it another shot. He adjusted his stance, but kept the hand of friendship firmly extended. 'I will make no claim to understand it, but I will make some not inconsiderable claim to having witnessed and accepted it; returning your attention to said, massive ball of purple energy currently billowing away there…'

'I can see that!'

'Well, I wasn't really sure what you might be able to see; your eyes are really very strikingly unusual.' He looked at Barker. 'Is she always like this? This is Cheryl *Equinox* I assume?'

Cheryl scowled. 'Is he your new assistant now?

'Be polite Cheryl, the man's shoulder must be very sore by now, keeping his arm up for you to shake his hand all this time, and he's been very patient and polite, not to mention extremely helpful tonight. And I would never, ever, call you an assistant, particularly as you're all super badass-blue now. And the only reason I said he could be Murtaugh is that he *really is* a Chief Inspector, and he's older and wiser and grumpier; kind of. Probably close to retirement, too.'

'Nowhere near it…' Parry was nonplussed. 'And I think I've taken all of this… *paranormal activity* with an incredible *absence* of aging surliness, I'll have you know.'

Barker nodded. 'It's true. He seems really very well-adjusted in the face of what is, to be honest, quite an enormously confronting level of supernatural activity. I wonder why that is…?'

'Ah; well. Full disclosure; I might be said to have had a pre-existing relationship with the… the aforementioned newly-blossomed paramour of one Mister Craven.'

'The girl?' Barker stared at him. 'Fiona Pitcher?'

Cheryl gasped. 'He's back with Fiona Pitcher?'

Both Barker and Parry turned to her and demanded simultaneously.

'*Back?*'

'Yeah… they had a fling. Like, a year ago. He didn't tell you? He was pretty happy about it… he said the sex was like rocket science!'

'Please…' Parry groaned. 'That's my *niece*.'

'Your *niece*?'

Suddenly Parry seemed to be taking things *extremely well*.

'She was concerned that she had been drugged by her husband; perhaps hypnotized somehow… she called me one night, about six weeks ago. Said she had developed athletic ability that she had no memory of training for, knew things about people she couldn't have known… realized she could do… other things, as well.'

'What did you do?'

'I thought it sounded crazy. But she's always been very straight-ahead, level-headed. I thought he probably had drugged her. Either that, or she was breaking down.'

Cheryl frowned. 'And…?'

'I hadn't heard from her for years. Not outside of family things. Not just out of the blue like that. Then she invited me over. When I got there… I really did think she'd become mentally ill or something.'

'Why?'

'She'd made a target range out in her back yard, just bottles and cans and stuff. She wanted me to see. She started throwing. She hit one, then another. Then ten in a row. She told me to go and look. You could see where the rocks had hit the cans. You could see; she had one hundred percent accuracy. And not just that; uncannily on target. I mean, she could hit the dot on the 'i' on a can of Sprite from across the back yard of a quarter acre block. I stood there while she did it, again and again, for a good twenty minutes. I didn't even get bored. It was bloody amazing. She said she could do it, make it that accurate, for as far as she could throw; and that she could throw a lot further now than she ever could…' Parry shrugged. 'She threw the rock that hit my car windscreen. God knows where from; it was her way of telling me to stay back, that she was on to something.'

'On to something?' Barker frowned. 'Like what?'

'I don't know; this Argent place maybe? But; long story short, she led me to Carlton Craven, which in turn, led me to you two. The rest has been, as they say, the strangest night of my life.'

Barker had been staring at the portal as Parry spoke.

'You implied before that you were looking into this, for the department.'

Parry smiled, a little wry, a little grim.

'Let's just say…the strangest night that actually makes sense, anyway.'

'She's beautiful, Fiona Pitcher…' Cheryl uttered. '…she was never bitchy. We used to walk home together sometimes; and then she ended up with that idiot…'

'Zinc…' Parry uttered, with clear distaste. 'Currently wanted for questioning on a number of different matters. Most of them minor. But, adding up to more than the sum of their parts, it seemed. More and more.'

Cheryl turned and regarded Parry again.

'I guess he seems okay.'

She extended her hand.

Parry raised his hand again and they shook.

'Any friend of Barker's…' Cheryl smiled.

'Does not belong in a psych ward, understood.'

Cheryl turned back to Baker. 'Well at least you *could* open it! And this seems to indicate that we're in a…' Cheryl went fishing. '…slightly better…?' She shrugged, hoping that was right. '…place right now than we were only a few hours ago? When you dropped me off in the city and we were essentially powerless shadows of our former selves?'

Barker spread his palms. 'You tell me.' He made a face. 'Apparently Fenner Shilling is alive?'

'Yes, I heard.'

'That's got to sway things fairly convincingly toward a negative imbalance, you might think?'

'Yeah…' Cheryl's shoulders sagged. 'Yeah; I thought that.'

'Do something about it, shall we?'

'Mindless positivity…' Her blue-lipped smile beamed. 'I really missed that about you, Barker Moon!'

He shrugged. 'Still got the demon thing to deal with. More than one now.'

'The demon thing? Of course. I am still totally on board for that. I mean…' She put her hand over her heart. 'I just released two centuries worth of empirical oppression in angry spirit form into the city grid.'

'You did?'

'Oh, absolutely; I mean, and I have like three new admirers, and a coven to take over, and on top of that I might also like girls now.'

'Really?'

'Really might!'

'New energy?'

'May – be.'

Parry cleared his throat. 'Could that possibly be why we can't see all those hanging lights up there anymore?'

'Because I like girls now?'

They all looked up.

'Oh, right. Because I just released two centuries worth of empirical oppression in angry spirit form into the city grid. You did well spotting that, Chief Inspector.'

'Yeah…' Barker uttered as he stared upwards. 'He's an inspector, he's observant…'

'So do you two magical people see… a kind of phantom, angry, agitated, swirling? I see a definite kind of *mass*, of… *paranormal activity* up there?'

'Yep…' Cheryl nodded. 'Sure is.'

'Cheryl…?' Barker scratched his head, still looking up. 'Did you say *girls*?'

'Sorry?'

'You like *girls* now?'

'I *might* like girls now, too.'

'Because they look like ghouls to me, not girls.'

'No, totally unrelated. I might like girls, but I definitely freed the ghouls.'

They heard movement behind them; several security guards had arrived at the top of the Railway Station staircase.

'You think they're here to help?' Cheryl asked doubtfully.

'Might be. I count five…' Parry assessed.

'Not sprouting wings yet…'

Barker turned to look at them.

'Give it time.' He looked back to Cheryl. 'You know that this place is about to transcend dimensions and become very, very strange, right?'

'And… we're just talking about this because we want to avoid the obvious.'

'Which is…?'

'Which is…' Parry sighed. '…that if this portal thing was working properly, you would have gone through to save your friend by now….' He looked at Barker. 'Something's wrong.'

'The Persuader played me perfectly….' Barker nodded. 'He *wanted me* to open it.'

And with that, a savage blast of red-ochre dust, blown by a fierce wind, billowed straight through the middle of the portal and coated them all.

# CHAPTER FORTY: MASTERS

Nothing happened.

'I said kill the blonde and bring those sticks to me!'

Still, nothing happened.

The children didn't move.

Carlton smiled. 'They must have reached that terrible, rebellious age...'

Fiif almost smiled as well. 'A bit far advanced to be the terrible twos...'

'You will obey me!' Echidna screamed again. When nothing happened, Echidna looked around, revealing the edge of being somewhat startled. 'Why won't you obey me!?'

'We don't like you anymore. We like the frightened one with the booby-bags.'

The children were moving out of the darkness. Fiif could see the two little girls, who seemed to lead the gang, almost clearly now.

'You promised you would bring more; bring more Mummies and Daddies.'

Both the girls had shoulder-length blonde hair. The second one was a little shorter, perhaps the younger of the two sisters. They had to be sisters, not twins; somehow Fiif could see it in their frames.

'We see you bring them in, the last seven years we watched them come in, from all over, and even more now; but none for us! Always for the house!'

'The house?' Carlton scowled.

Echidna moved toward the girls, like a mother at the end of her limit. 'I told you; when you come and live in the house, you can have whatever –'

A little boy stepped forward, like the two girls, almost into the light.

'When! When will we come to live in the house!?'

'Our master lives there now!' The first girl chimed in again. 'Our master lives there now, and he never comes to see us anymore!'

'I am Echidna; the consort of the great one, your master's master! And you will do as you are told! Kill the stupid woman!'

Carlton had edged forward a few steps toward her. Fiif had a feeling that he would be okay, so long as he didn't step off the grass, and onto the road. But Echidna could see that he was trying to get a better look, and spun about, pointing her long index finger at him.

'*I see you!*'

Carlton spread his arms and shrugged. 'Look, I was never any good at school…' The children all turned to look. '…and if we did classics, I either slept through it, or stared at Mary Herbert's side-boob, or Clara Thompson's legs…'

'God, how the hell did she get away with those short skirts!?'

Carlton winked back at Fiif. 'I know, right; I never heard a thing in maths class, still don't even know what an integer even is! But my God – those thighs!' Carlton rolled his eyes goofily, then turned back to Echidna. '…so; just, would you mind? Just, remind me? Echidna? That isn't just the Spiny Norman type of not-hedgehogs we have running around out here in the bush – is it? Echidna was the wife of – someone? Important?'

'You ignorant *shit*!'

Echidna suddenly stalked forward, having whipped two daggers from behind her that had been tucked into the back of her skirt. Fiif saw him make some kind of connection with daggers; he was appalled.

'*Where did you get those, Echidna?*'

He turned to her; no, not just appalled, he was massively angry as well.

'We have to get to Barker.'

She could see he meant it. Even if it killed him.

Then he turned and pointed the kali sticks at Echidna.

'Confess your love, Echidna!'

'What? I…?'

The children laughed and came forward. They sat in a ring around Echidna, as she grasped at her throat, as though attempting to prevent the words from forming in her larynx. Fiif saw them now, the children. They were really quite beautiful, but it was as she had suspected.

'I love him – yes! Fenner Shilling, I have loved him since the very day we first met! Before!'

Carlton's arms drooped, and he sighed.

'He has made me Echidna! I shall be Echidna to his Great God! The Great God  he has summoned, the Great Old God he shall become and make A New God! And we shall be As The Gods! We shall rule and – !'

'You shall do what?' The first little girl asked.

'You heard her…' Carlton grinned. 'I wondered what this was all about…'

The first little girl was still staring up at Echidna, cross-legged at the front of the story-group.

'I think our master might have something to say about *that*!'

Echidna leaned down, her tall frame lowering like a weird, black flamingo, and stared at little girl, right into her upturned face.

'Fenner Shilling is your master now!'

The girl was outraged.

Her hand snapped up and grasped Echidna by her long throat.

'I – don't – think – so!'

Echidna immediately and violently reciprocated. She grasped the child around her neck and raised her, holding her up before her, even as the little girl dug her claws deeper into Echidna's neck. They were still face-to-face; Echidna could not extend her arm, or the child's grasp would tear out her throat. But they held there, neither killing the other, snarling like wild animals.

The other dominant little girl, the younger sister, got up and turned around to Carlton and Fiif.

'They do this. She ripped my brother to pieces once and he needed a new child. So we had to let one of the others live, so he could live again.' The little girl smiled at Fiif. 'You've guessed it all. You're smarter than he thinks you are. And he thinks you're smart.'

Fiif looked over. 'Carlton?'

The little girl laughed. 'No! He doesn't know what to think of you. Other than he wants to put it in you, a lot. No; I mean the man at the house who's living with our master... Funny Shitting!'

'You'll pay for that; he has no sense of humour...'

'We have children's senses of humour because we still have their brains; the funny little children. But we know what we know; we are old, so old!'

'So old we don't have a name for you...'

'You did; the humans before you. The ones who disappeared knew us as well...'

Fiif looked into her face.

'The legend says there was a town here...' Carlton probed. '... built for the gold mine. But they found something else, didn't they, once the gold was gone.'

'The gold's still there. We like our gold.'

'The mine's still there?'

'Lots of mines are still here. Down, under. All over. From all over.'

The little girl was a kind of cross, so far as Fiif could tell, between Pinocchio and a vampire. Her skin looked hard, the woody texture yellowish-brown with a swirling grain through it like polished timber. Her eyes looked bloodshot, with dark amber irises, like glistening tree sap. Her hair, and the rest of her little body seemed real though, all the weird kind of wood-flesh of her face; although her teeth were sharp, enamel, like a classic bloodsucker.

'You said…' Carlton ventured. '…in my mind, I had part of the story right… it's that part, isn't it? Early twentieth century. The town was isolated out here. The people were terrified. And the demon they found in the old gold mine, it was bored and it wanted to come out and play. It used the Spanish Flu pandemic to scare them. It told them, nothing could get them up here; but their children…'

'One of us had a cold.'

Fiif cringed. 'One of *you*?'

'…and it used the cold to make all the parents believe their children were going to die. Unless it let the demon take care of them.'

'That's… so sad. So horrible.'

Carlton proceeded. 'You're the demon's servants, its brethren from a previous age, aren't you?'

Echidna looked away from the child she was still holding. Fiif saw that Carlton had gotten the reaction he was looking for.

'They're *what*?'

'They're you, Echidna. Whoever you *actually* are. You, in thousands of years.'

The child in Echidna's choke hold laughed.

'You'll never be as old as us!' She laughed some more. 'He'll never love you as much as he loves us!'

Echidna's other hand came up to strike the child, but she kicked up with both feet and they lost their respective holds. It was curious, Fiif saw; they were each too scared to murder the other, even though they were at any given time only seconds away from the act. There were scratches in the child's wood-like neck now, and blood dribbling from Echidna's flesh, but neither seemed seriously hurt.

'You all… need each other for some reason…?' Fiif uttered, accidentally aloud.

Carlton threw his right-hand stick in a twirl then caught it with a slap.

'There's a balance…'

Fiif took a guess. '…and so the thing, from the mine, persuaded the townsfolk that he would keep their children safe. Forever. And somehow… locked off this town. But occasionally… attracted people here?'

'Because just like their master… they need blood. Did your master go willingly?' Carlton addressed the little girls, as they returned to each other and held hands. 'Or did Shilling drag him out?'

'Shilling is his superior!' Echidna shouted. 'He is the superior of every one and every-thing, every being and every-nothing! He will take the thing –'

'The what?'

'The thing!'

'Our master?' The girl demanded.

'The thing master what?' Carlton taunted.

'Ceea'gha!' Echidna shouted. 'He will take the demon Ceea'gha and –'

Echidna stopped suddenly, realizing that all the children in the circle had just stood simultaneously, and were staring at her. Unanimously angry.

'You said the master's name.'

The boy who had seemed to be the second to the two girls tensed, then spun about at Carlton.

'He knows too much!'

Then he leaped; down the last stretch of street and across the lawn at Carlton with such speed that Carlton barely had time to raise the kali stick. The boy exploded in blood, all over Carlton. What remained was a stick creature, a strange kind of bark-thing that was like some withered ventriloquist dummy. The ghastly Vaudevillian thing, still wearing little boy's clothes which were way too big for it now, was all woody, and covered in a kind of stringybark so as to look almost fur-like, like a wolf-boy. And it still had fangs. The fangs seemed less enamel, less human now, and more like little wooden stakes as Carlton held it back, as it clung with its tiny hands to his shoulders, to his leather jacket.

Carlton cried out in alarm and fell backwards, then Fiif stomped over and kicked the stupid little fucking thing in its head. It flew to the side, tumbling over the grass and onto the start of the street that led up to the dead church.

Then it stood up again, turned and adopted a kind of fight stance; shoulders high, fists balled, feet braced, and growled.

Carlton pointed the stick at it.

It growled some more, but didn't make a move. The rest of the wooden children were frozen now, staring back at Fiif and Carlton; she counted maybe twenty in the street, with three, then four more appearing from the darkness, coming down from out of the foliage, from inside the houses behind the trees and shrubs. Five, six… a dozen more.

There could not have been this many children in the town, not in 1918, when the Influenza epidemic hit. Most of the young men would have been off fighting in, or have been killed in, the First World War…

The demon, or these wicked, murderous little vampire tree-people, had forced those who remained to breed, and had used the resulting children for blood, or allowed them to grow, for spare bodies.

They were going to do that… to her.

Make her breed with Carlton.

Keep them here.

The girls stepped up again.

'Again…!' The elder one smiled, with all her teeth and neck as though to show off the scratches that Echidna had left there, in her wooden skin. 'Fiona Pitcher knows! She is so smart! She is going to have baby after baby after baby; just like the ones who thought they were our parents did, just like the ones we let live, who were their children, the ones we didn't drink until there was nothing left, after all the babies! And their children, and then their children! You have at least ten children in you Fiona Pitcher! If we keep you sleepy and dreamy, and far away in your mind, maybe more!'

The little wooden boy was about to attack again, when the hinges on the church doors behind him, up at the top of the hill, creaked open as though a woodsman had smashed a massive axe down on a brittle log; first one door, then the other.

Everyone looked up.

'He is here!' Echidna shrieked. 'He has come!'

The sky turned darker as the stars and the moon suddenly seemed less bright. Then everything turned orange, then red.

A man Fiif assumed to be Fenner Shilling, accompanied by five women, was coming out of the church. The women wore bright, lipstick-red robes, long and billowing but body-hugging, almost supernaturally so, it looked to Fiif, by the way the dusty-red wind was helping to reveal each woman's figure. All five of them seemed totally high, and blissfully unaware of the danger they were in; whose influence they were allowing themselves to be guided by. They were dancing, slowly waving their arms like stoned hippies, their dresses in the dust storm making it seem choreographed, terrifyingly so, as they following Shilling from the church like their messiah.

The children all gathered at the bottom of the decline, and a few ran toward him.

'I shall make them all in my image; you shall have them all for yourselves, my children! Consume my offspring! Inhabit them! Become them!'

Only the oldest of the children remained, and she was staring at Carlton. But her demeanor had changed, completely.

'I see in your mind, Carlton Craven… this man… who he is…'

Fiif stared up at the sky.

'Did he cause this dust storm? Did he dress those women that way because of it? How can he do that? How can he know that!?'

Shilling cried out.

'Fiona Pitcher – how I have waited for you, all these years! Your coming, heralded by the dust storm that heralds the rains!'

Carlton was staring at him, backing into Fiif, clearly horrified.

'I'm sorry Fiif...'

'You told me... they see ahead. He dressed them for this moment because he saw that he would come here, for you, at the time of the dust storm...'

The two of them backed away, as the children, now numbering more than thirty, ran up the hill to their new mothers; their breeding animals.

'He wants you to know, to see he can do it.'

The children's little-girl-leader still couldn't take her eyes off Carlton, nor remove her mind from his, as he and Fiif backed further away from Shilling, more toward her. Fiif looked into her eyes as they blazed at Carlton; keen amber eyes, ablaze with intense concentration. Then she spoke.

'This man Shilling is three, four, five steps ahead... psychopathic, they call him; the human demonic, but oh, so clever and fast and...'

The red night air was becoming thicker with the dust as it swirled down Argent's main street. Then the red was suddenly mixed with bright purple from the end of the street; and for a second, before he turned around, Carlton was reminded of Shilling's horrific orgy, and realized; Shilling was breeding – dividing batteries from fuel, yes, but the energy from this town, the supernatural machinery of this town, was all in there too, all compacted into Bridger Mansion; creating those tree things, and impregnating the women to come here for... Christ it was awful, all of it! Carlton turned toward the purple light and was shocked to see that it wasn't more of the girls from the house.

*There was a bloody portal at the end of the street!*

Fiif looked back at the child; she looked strange.

'I see this man; I know his plan, I know who is coming – run Carlton Crowe – run through the portal, run to your friend – this man Shilling; he must be sto –'

Echidna stepped out of the red, dusty darkness and decapitated her wooden head with a savage double swing of both knives. Now Echidna was standing between them, and their run to the portal.

Fiif looked back at Shilling. He and his entourage had met the girls halfway down the road that descended from the church, and had paused there. The children had begun to dance with joy, adoring their new breeders, and dancing around them as though this were some quaint English village at Mayday. But now, suddenly, the children had started to notice what Echidna had done. Shilling had seen too, and had come to a full stop as he stared down the hill, onto the street below. The five girls around him stopped, too dazed and confused to be shocked, but they seemed amazed and even aroused at the sight of the huge purple ring at the end of the street, just before the street light, and the darkness beyond.

'The portal is open!' Shilling laughed. 'I knew he could not resist! Return his compassion with what it deserves! Kill whoever comes through that portal! My creatures – wait at the portal! Kill Barker Moon! Kill everyone when they come! Kill! – kill! – kill!'

Carlton grabbed Fiif's hand and tugged, and they went back a few steps, toward Echidna as the children streamed down the base of the hill toward them, then past them, almost taking flight, leaping over one another to get to the portal.

Across the chaos one of the breeding girls that Shilling had brought, who was caught up in the rush of excitement, looked right at Fiif, and she heard herself say in a tone of complete shock;

'Amanda?'

# CHAPTER FORTY-ONE:
# EXECUTIVE


'*Dash…*' Emerald repeated, staring at Percival Wade. '*Dash it… darn it…and…*'

'Of course, it's always better if the people working for us have no idea.'

'*…damn it! Damn it to hell!*'

'Whatever you're telling your security people, Miss Tarragon, they are all gone by now. Dealing with your friends on the concourse.'

Emerald stood very still; her whole body had tensed and locked.

'The Executive Room.' Quaker stated. 'I don't know why I allowed it…' He scoffed. 'What is all this, anyway? What are you talking about, Percival? Emerald has total control over the security personnel of this casino –'

'Only a few…' Percival smiled. '…are mine. Just enough. The rest…'

*Please don't tell me you killed them…*

He smiled at Emerald, skimming the irrepressible fears of her mind. 'I sent home.' Then he smiled at Quaker. 'And, you did not allow anything I have done here, Mister Quaker. Before or after you arrived. You had no choice. None at all, Mister Quaker.'

Emerald turned to Quaker.

'Ernst, I am hoping that this is going to be the first in a series of apologies tonight…'

'You're hoping to apologize? For what? This brazen egomaniac?'

'No. Not him. But; I do hope to apologize. Because, if I am not apologizing, it means…' She turned back to Percival Wade. '…it means you are under the influence of –'

'Miss Tarragon; Mister Quaker is no more under the influence of my kind than the rest of the world. Which is to say; almost completely. However, not to the direct, personal extent you are thinking.'

She felt herself relax, just a bit. She hoped that was true.

'Executive Rooms, or, whatever they are called, in whichever casino they exist, exist in almost every city in the world. They exist for one reason and one reason only; to exploit people, people with psychological vulnerabilities; vulnerabilities of a specific nature. They exist to milk these people of all they have. Casinos themselves, as a general idea, are set up for this too. But the Bleeding Rooms are another level entirely. You see; people are so in love with the notion of escape, with the opportunity of winning big, that they will allow almost anything to ensure the casino's continued presence. Its taxes feed the governments, its kickbacks entertain the governing elite, and for the gen-pop in their social cages, it represents that enormous 'lotto win'; their potential 'deus ex machina' – God's mercy, the win out of nowhere, the magical save at the last minute; *the boon*.'

Percival chuckled, charmingly.

'People are so in love with that idea, the symbol of it in the heart of their existence, that they are willing to allow an appalling corruption at the heart of it – a room designed specifically for those identified to have psychological imbalances, who cannot stop gambling; to exploit them to the furthest limits of their existence, to the furthest extent that the law, and the government, and the society, permits. I mean; can you believe it? There are laws that restrict the exploitation of the vulnerable – *so that it's not seen to go too far!*'

Emerald felt Quaker tense up as well. He was unaccustomed to being spoken to, or at, in such a way.

'Mister Quaker is no different; he understands that this is part of the deal. The bitter pill that must be ingested and digested, that must alter the DNA of a city and change its very root structure, in order for 'good times' to be available to all. In order for the potential 'money fountain' to be given free rain. Or is that 'reign', like royalty? Or, rein, like, letting a horse go, so it goes and goes, without 'reining' it in? I can never remember. We take the reins off so it rains, and then it reigns; no matter, we can have it all, can't we? Or at least, the potential – provided there is a casino in the middle, and poker machines on every corner, and living power cells to drain, so that the promise of the big win always remains, at someone else's expense.'

Emerald nodded. 'I've seen enough of them…'

'Yes…' Percival smiled. 'You made your way here leeching from them, didn't you?'

'I'm not talking to you…' Emerald kept looking at the thing, but was addressing Quaker. '…I've seen enough of these things to know, Mister Quaker, that if they speak openly in regard to themselves and their plans, then it is from a Bond-villain level of supreme self-confidence. I'm sorry, Ernst. I set a trap for a demon; but I was unaware that I built it around another demon. And now that demon is locked inside the trap. Inside here. With us.'

# CHAPTER FORTY-TWO:
# TOO-OLD AND NOX

Coughing through the red dust, Parry stared up at the ceiling of the concourse.

'What the hell was that!?'

Cheryl Equinox was blowing it away from her face.

Moon seemed to just ignore it.

The whole concourse was a dusty ochre; the deep, rusty orange of the Australian desert, now totally filtering the dull neon glow of the surrounding city and the shimmering purple of Moon's magic circle thing.

Parry remembered from the radio in his car, as he was falling asleep.

'There are fluke storms coming tonight; once in a century thing – big dust storm, then a massive thunderstorm…' He scratched his head. 'Okay. Right. Not a fluke at all, is it? It's the mad bastard on the other end of the purple donut.'

'So…' Cheryl moved closer to the portal. '…the dust storm just hit Argent?'

'Argent's just up in The Hills…' Moon uttered. 'Can't be more than eleven, twelve k's away.' He turned back to Parry. 'How fast do those things move?'

'Dust storms?' Parry shook his head and took an educated guess. 'If that thing leads to your haunted town in the Hills; a few minutes I suppose. Ten at a pinch.'

Moon looked to Equinox again.

'Shilling's summoning something; something bigger than the thing he summoned last time. What the hell do you think it could be?'

Equinox groaned a little, as though the very idea of contemplating that question made her incredibly uneasy. She looked up and around at the dust, as though that could help, as though it and their surroundings would make it easier for her to guess.

'What the hell could it be? Hell's probably not far off...'

Parry looked up with her, looked over at the security guards, still gathered at the top of the stairs, but staring now, as though gathering their collective courage. But something else snatched his attention.

'Those things up there...' Parry could still see them in the red dust, as though it had made them more visible; like long feathers, with huge, fanged faces, forever circling an enormous drain. '...they're getting restless...!'

'They're ghouls!' Equinox snapped. 'Some of them have died horribly and been angry about it for more than a century; all they know is anger – of course they're restless!'

Well, Parry wasn't talking to her again for a while. A bit snarky that one. But he could have sworn...

'Moon; I think they're getting lower...?'

Moon ignored him again. Whether that was true or not, whether it was just a hallucination, the swirling shapes, the giant feather-shaped people, all around the top of the concourse was definitely becoming wilder. He looked to Equinox and sighed inwardly.

Well he had to talk to *someone*.

'Nox! Can you see faces...?!'

'Yes! Lots of face – *what did you just call me?!*'

Moon stepped back again, gritting his teeth, his arm and hand still extended toward the portal. Then he snapped, exasperated.

'I can feel it...!

Whatever the hell that meant.

' – it's just like it was – but it's not...!'

Parry had no idea.

But he hated just standing there.

'Well – *what's it supposed to do…?*'

Moon shook his head. 'We should be able to see Argent…'

Okay, Parry thought; well…

'Well what does Argent look like, then?'

'Nobody knows!' Nox snapped at him.

Jesus; what was it with these people? It seemed like a perfectly reasonable question.

The security guards started snarling again.

'Get behind me!' Nox ordered him.

He ignored her; he could see them, shuffling around in the broken glass doors, starting to confer. There was no proof that they were those demonoid things; for all they knew, or could really tell, the guards were just five ordinary blokes, just poor minimum wage bastards trying to figure out what the bloody hell was going on. And after all, there had only been one of them before, and he had just flown away when Moon had –

'It's just one way…' Parry heard Moon utter.

'Nox; maybe they're just real blokes…?'

'Too-Old! I said get behind me…!'

The guards seemed to reach a consensus, all of them nodding and grunting. Parry hoped they weren't going to charge down the stairs with their truncheons or anything. Then all five of them hunched and pushed their shoulders back and sprouted their demon wings, ripping them through their shirts and World Casino jackets almost simultaneously. Okay, now he really hoped they weren't going to charge down the stairs. The one in the middle took a few extra steps. Yep; that was him. The one who'd been behind him on the bridge. Fuck. His wings were hovering on either side of him like leather sheets, rising from a clothes line on a windy day.

'You were saying?' Nox snapped.

Three of the ghouls above them growled as the lead-demonoid thing descended a few more stairs.

Parry looked up at them. 'Maybe they're with us!?'

Then one of them suddenly changed direction and swooped savagely down at Moon, slashing his outstretched hand.

Nox turned to him. 'Too-Old! Shut the fuck up already! You're jinxing us!'

He looked back at Moon. There was a gash across his hand, but he was still holding it out at the giant purple-circle portal, with a kind of semi-clawed tension that made it seem like he was trying to crack the knob on a giant invisible safe.

But – what the hell was this now?

Through the purple and lavender and violet and white, through all that shimmering and rippling that seemed to recede into the distance that *wasn't the real distance*; behind it, there was something in the *actual distance*.

There was a woman, or something; something in the shape of a woman at the other end of the concourse, out by the road under the street lights. She looked like another one of these people who weren't quite totally normal.

'Nox – Moon!' Parry pointed through the portal. 'Down there; who's that!?'

Nox saw it, then Parry saw her eyes glaze over, and he knew that suddenly, now, she couldn't see anything else.

'Nox – what's wrong? Who is it…?!'

Parry saw Nox's expression. Transfixed, appalled; but nevertheless, somehow radically empowered, with her blue skin glowing, and shimmering.

'She's trying to tell me something…'

'Who?'

'The portal's blocking her… nothing can get through from that side…'

'What – who is she?'

Nox ignored him again, but he could see that she, like Moon, was concentrating as hard as she could, focusing her mind, with all her might, at the thing she was trying to understand.

Snarky, sure. And snappish. But she was pretty feisty, this one.

You kind of wanted her on your side.

'Barker!' Nox yelled suddenly. 'Even here on this plane – nothing can get through; nothing can get through from that end of the concourse – the portal's creating a flat-out total block!'

Barker started walking closer to it again.

Parry turned around.

The demonoids were taking it one step at a time, but they were sneaking closer down the main stairs. They were probably wise to be afraid of the two sorcerers, or witches, or whatever they were, but he knew this kind of movement. The not-very-bright preparing to rush. Sure enough, the bravest, perhaps their leader, was about ten steps down, halfway down the first section of the forty-odd steps, with the others creeping up behind. But the swooping shapes from the ceiling… Nox called them *ghouls*, right? The ghouls were swooping around, scaring them off, or at least making them keep their distance.

'Of course!' Moon cried out.

Then he dropped and sat, cross-legged and still.

Parry couldn't believe it.

'Moon!' Parry looked at Nox. 'What's he doing!?'

All five demonoids were halfway down the stairs now; and the ghouls were clearly seeming less and less intimidating to them. But Nox was just transfixed by the woman at the other end.

'Oh no…' Nox uttered. 'They *can't have…*'

'What?' Parry demanded.

'No…!'

'*What!?*'

'It's the river! They trapped the river spirit!' Nox turned to him, tears in her blazing cobalt-blue eyes. 'Somebody trapped the spirit of the river in the lake!'

# CHAPTER FORTY-THREE: PERCIVAL WADE

'Trapped?' Percival Wade smiled.

Emerald was starting to shake.

But she raised her hands anyway.

As though surrendering.

'Don't try anything, Emerald.'

The demon's warning was serious. Emerald gasped. Her heart was already pounding in her chest. She could feel it; she thought that the demon must have been able to see it, her heart, through her black tee and bra, thought the pounding must have been pulsing the line of her lapels.

She checked herself.

Shoes… made for walking around, standing all night.

Made for purpose, made very deliberately, for walking the floor.

Every night for ten hours, five in the afternoon until three in the morning, six days a week for the past two years.

Okay. That was okay.

Not heels. The shoes fit, so to speak.

Fit for purpose.

Hold it together.

'What the hell is going on?' Quaker demanded. He was feeling it; the fear the demon emanated naturally. It wasn't quite as bad, Emerald thought she knew, hoped she knew, was telling herself, when they were in mote form, in semi-human form. That was part of the risk she was taking; when it was no longer in human form, that would be… well, they would see. Or, it would kill her, and Quaker, right now.

'Wade...' Quaker growled. '...we had a deal, it is part of the arrangement that you keep your... vile chamber business to yourself! What are you doing up here!?'

Even Quaker wasn't immune.

'Not fully immune...' Emerald heard Percival Wade tell her. Again, reading her broadest, largest thoughts, her frontal-fear thoughts, the ones she couldn't help; par for the demon course. 'This one, this Quaker is one of those genetically descended from the kings of the old worlds, with his big ideas, big personalities...' Jesus. He was talking to Emerald about her thoughts about Quaker, as though he wasn't there; as though he were irrelevant. '...he cannot be influenced by the likes of me – not without a lot of time and effort. A lot of focus; and he must be inherently malevolent to begin with. Unbalanced or damaged. Hurt and vengeful. But you are correct – what fear he feels now, from my natural *perfume*, manifests as anger – and results in what I believe the British enjoy calling – *front*.'

'Mister Quaker...' Emerald spoke, clearing a frog in her throat as she did. 'I really need to apologize.'

'Or – *bottle*.'

Quaker whispered angrily. 'There is no need, Emerald...'

'I'll pay for the damages...'

'For the concourse? You're hardly responsible...'

'No – for these.'

There was a wet thud as the tip of a long blade jutted out of Percival Wade's chest.

'Again, sorry.'

Part of the classic casino-owner's personal security room, and office, that had been retained by Quaker was a glorious old full-size pool table that had been with the building since its inception; since it had been an actual Railway Station, with a lounge and waiting section that had been, to all accounts, as sumptuous and comfortable as it was elegant and well-appointed. Powerful business men had knocked back intoxicating liquor from crystal brandy balloons, and smoked the finest hand-rolled Havana cigars around the pool table, or billiard table as it had once been called, for more than a century, and by keeping it just in the next room, Quaker had maintained that tradition, and a connection to that chain of powerful men.

Emerald enjoyed those kinds of thing about Quaker.

Quaker had enjoyed the fact that Emerald would request permission to enter and use the table once or twice a week, and had always done that for the two years they had been in business together. He had taken it as a sign of their interest in not just each other, but also in their like-mindedness, their love of focus and precision.

Emerald vanished before him as she turned and sprinted into the next room. Percival turned and his hand flashed out. Emerald leaped sideways onto the table, dodging some kind of fireball that had soared from Percival's hand, and was upon the table and in one swift movement, snatching her personal cue from the top of the table-length light shade. But she knew that she had screwed it; not fast enough, and the second fireball would – she gasped as she realized she was dead, dead now – smash her, right in her back, and kill her. It flew past, way off the mark, and exploded on the wall in front of her, destroying the top of the pool room wet bar; then she was rolling over and out of sight.

She wondered what the hell Quaker must have thought at that moment, as she whipped the two ends of her staff out of the leather cover, dropped it and was on her feet again, looking over the table, no time to even cast the spell for the cue to automatically connect, each end extended at Percival Wade.

There was no need; Dash was thrusting him forward; she had undoubtedly saved Emerald from a second fireball in the back by shoving the body of the thing further into Quaker's office. But Dash had taught her that, as she had taught Emerald better fighting skills over the past two years. Trust your backup; to stop you getting killed, to be at the rendezvous on time, to execute whatever it was, their part of the plan, and get on with yours – or the whole thing falls apart.

Dash ripped the dagger out of Percival's back then, accompanied by a nauseating squelch that was foul-smelling and inhuman, and as Percival turned to try and identify his attacker, she smashed him in the face. Dash was a lot shorter but Emerald had forgotten how she could pack a punch, how she used her body and the angles, shifted her weight correctly, and of course wore the brass knuckle-dusters. Percival's jaw was plainly broken as she punched him again, and again, then broke his nose square-on, but it didn't seem to matter. He did not go down, and in the confusion of being attacked physically for the first time in a body he did little else but walk about in, the demon was momentarily lost.

Emerald threw, and the wand-half of her staff seared across the room. It sliced past Quaker's face and impaled in the side of Percival's neck, then as she made the smooth, snatch-back gesture for it to return, she simultaneously launched the club with her other hand. It soared again, as Quaker stepped back, smashed Percival in the side of his head, cracking his eye socket, then soared back at Emerald. She caught both, one after the other, then was over the table and coming at Percival with the club held for attack. Percival's hands went out at each of them, but Dash had each of her hands on each of his wrists. The fireballs intended for each of them went up; the one that would have melted Dash's face went into the ceiling, and the one intended to smash square in Emerald's chest went down and blasted the carpet, searing and burning a massive patch and giving Emerald pause, skidding her to a halt, before she came forward with ruthless determination and struck hard at the demon's fake, mote-head. It cracked, and the stench was like an abattoir that had lost its air-conditioning in high-summer.

Dash simultaneously gutted him with the blade, stabbing hard and up into his belly, then again, and then a third time with added grunt, each producing the same sickening squelch, and the awful stench increasing the pungency with an added sulphurous punch. Then she raised the blade in both fists, raised her leg and kneed him with all her might, so he fell backwards onto Quaker's desk. With the demon's head lolling continuously side-to-side, its mouth open and gaping, Dash brought the knife down hard into its chest, and pinned it there, prone on its back as the legs came up and tried to catch her. She grabbed the left one and shoved it hard toward the table, cracking whatever held it there, under the fake skin and flesh, breaking it almost off, one would have thought, with Dash shifting her body down in the maneuver just as a spray of bright gold-yellow jetted out from the thing's crotch, burning through the suit pants, arcing a spray over Dash's shoulder. The bright yellow hit the carpet behind her and exploded like napalm, searing her up the back of her right leg and burning away the back of her own pants. She didn't make a sound but turned with Emerald and ran, as the stench of sulphur, of rotten and decaying flesh, spread throughout the casino.

'Quaker!' Emerald commanded.

He ran after them, leaving Percival Wade failing on the desk, his flesh contorting all over as though he had been subjected to some kind of flight-speed test.

The elevator was there, open and waiting and they clambered in, Dash hitting the button. At the other end of the corridor was a window Quaker had installed; just a plain floor to ceiling window of a dozen rectangular frames.

Emerald pointed the wand at it.

*through*

The spell blasted the glass and frame out in shattered fragments, into the cold of the night and onto the roof; a person-sized exit hole, almost comical, almost from the old cartoons.

'I don't have a choice; I have to take it out.'

Dash didn't argue, but was not pleased.

She snarled. 'But it's not *him*, is it?'

Emerald stepped out.

'I know. But we have to deal with them as we find them.'

She looked at Quaker.

He would have read nothing in her expression.

'I'm sorry.'

She turned to Dash.

'Get him to safety.'

The doors closed on Quaker; he was assessing her with the same cold, unreadable expression that she was offering him, reflected back at her.

# CHAPTER FORTY-FOUR: FETCH

'Manny…'

Emerald closed then driver's door then stood beside the Taurus.

'Emerald…'

'How did you find me?'

'An algorithm. I know how you love your music, Emerald. Your weird, eclectic taste. Most people stick with the music from the decade in which they were teens. Most even stay within a few years *within those years*. They defend those years, that music, *as the only good music*, for the rest of their lives. Defend it like they defend their sports teams. But not you. Not you, Emerald. I knew you could not last without your precious playlists.'

He stood there, basking in the smugness of his triumph for a few seconds.

When Emerald maintained her silence, he proceeded.

'From there, it was simple. Once I realized you would not use a credit card, that you would need to download your music illegally, I simply sought a pattern, sought out your most obscure favorite songs and waited. After three weeks, I had it down to three different people; if you had not downloaded Manfred Mann's *Watch*, some way across the Canadian border, I would never have found you.'

Emerald nodded. '*Drowning on Dry Land.*'

'Exactly.'

She shrugged to herself. Oh well. Totally worth it.

'What do you want, Manny?'

'Manfred *Mann*?' He guffawed. '*Watch?* Well, of course – I took it as a sign! Perhaps an unconscious sign, but a definite *sign*. I know how you love your *signs*, Emerald.'

'It wasn't a sign. Unless I wanted to be done with you once and for all, before I vanished forever. I doubt it though.' She didn't. She didn't at all; she knew that it was a sign. But it was a sign for her, not for him. One that told her, indeed; *you must deal with him before you vanish forever.* But there was no way she was telling him that.

'One more time; what do you want, Manny?'

He was getting cross now.

'I would have thought that was totally fucking obvious, *Emerald.*'

She tried to breathe, calmly.

'Coveth, is that you?'

She could not feel Coveth.

It, Coveth, would be instilling fear by now; or well on the way. But she was not afraid.

If it was there, however, and she named it, it had to say.

For the first time, she noticed a small wicker picnic basket at the side of the nearest concrete pillar. She tried not to let him see that she had seen it.

'I was able to retrace your movements that evening; one of my security personal let you go, I know that. She misrepresented herself; I have my best men on the case, and my people will find her eventually.'

'I'm sure they will.'

'Then, retracing your path of murder and destruction along Fifth Avenue. Your flight toward Madison; and, of course, you were also helped by a woman in a warehouse showroom. An Instagram personality. I forget her name. But that was where we lost you; the move with the SIM cards. Off to Seattle. How Not To Be Tracked, One-Oh-One!' Manny smiled and nodded. 'So, we shan't forget her, either.'

Manny turned and went to the basket.

Emerald's heart skipped a beat.

Oh, Christ.

Was he *that bat-shit?*

He lifted the lid.

Had he *Se7en*'d her?

He reached inside.

Was… was Galena's head in there?

'But her best friend's name…'

Oh, God. It wasn't Galena! He had Gavin, her dog!

*He had her little dog's body in there!*

He took something out.

No. Not quite that bad.

The item Manny lifted out was a dog's collar.

For some reason, Emerald had assumed that Gavin was one of those tiny Chihuahua-type lap dogs. But from the size of the collar, he would have eaten a meal twice the size of any of those little yappy breeds every day for breakfast. Nevertheless, this what it was; a bright yellow dog collar that Manny could have worn as a headband, with the name Gavin emblazoned upon it.

Manny smiled as he held it up. '…now, what was her best friend's name again?'

Emerald shrugged.

'What is this, Manny? You expect me to give a shit? The dog collar of a woman I met for five minutes and exploited to evade you? Please tell me that's not all you've got?'

She hoped it was, she really did.

Her instincts were fried, but… she couldn't help feeling there was something else. After all, this was so bizarre. They were standing on a magically secluded floor of a major inner-city parkade, in front of a functioning, open, multi-dimensional portal, and he was all-but pretending it wasn't… it wasn't there.

'You need to understand, Emerald. You can't leave me. I need you. You're mine, now. Forever mine. He said you were mine, and that I had to protect you. Everything I did, I did it for you.'

'Don't Bryan Adams me, Manny, you know I can't stand movie ballads.'

Manny snapped. 'He took everything! Everything, Emerald! But when I asked him, he couldn't even remember who you were. It was like you never existed. He used you, to leap through all those others, to me, and then finally, from you – to where he is now. And now, I have nothing…'

'The game?' Emerald was curious. 'He took the game?'

'No; he…' Manny slumped a bit, becoming more emotionally depressed. 'He made it mean nothing. It means nothing to me anymore. All I could think of was finding you. Finding you, and seeing you again, and trying to figure out… what was it?'

Emerald frowned. 'What was it?'

'What have I done? Just for you?' Manny held up the dog collar. 'I kidnapped her dog, and made her…'

'Made her what, Manny?'

Manny stared at her.

'You're just a woman. You're… not even that beautiful, when it comes down to it. It's just; the strange arrangement of your features…' He squinted. It was like he was seeing her for the first time. '…the illusion; the aesthetics…' Then he held up the collar again, in front of his face, and stared at that.

*Alas, poor Manny.*

'That's…all it is, isn't it? The arrangement of flesh, or genetics, of the features that a clash of DNA jumbles together; the reality of their appearance as they emerge from the womb and form and grow, as the lottery of puberty changes them… and some people get lucky. The hardwiring in the rest of us makes us want…' He turned back to her, allowing his arm to drop to his side. '…you. Want to please you, yes, but really… it's nothing. A biological desire to contain and impregnate, and, why?'

'I don't know why Manny. You tell me.'

'Because beauty has an advantage? And always will?'

'But you just said I wasn't really beautiful…'

'But – what is, Emerald? Pick something apart; deploy the critical eye, the formal appraisal – one can always find a flaw, just one small flaw… your weird eyes or your gross lips…'

Emerald rolled her eyes and tightened her lips.

'…and from there we pick, we pick at the flaw, until it is a crack, and into it we slide the thin end of the wedge, and apply

pressure, on and on, until, ultimately; we destroy, and tear it down.'
He nodded to himself. 'Our… *thing on a pedestal.* I thought I had
you…'

She'd heard enough. But she was waiting.

He still had an ace, she was sure.

'You did, Manny. You're right. You did have me. You had me
completely, until a demon found that flaw in you, and picked you
apart – until I couldn't reach you anymore. Until I was forced to
run from you…'

'Can we try again?'

'Try again?

'Please?'

'No, Manny. The thing will always find me. If I go through the
portal, I can't be traced. Nobody will know where I am. Not even
demons can trace the path of a portal, not unless –'

'I'll tell him! I'll tell him you were here! He will find you from
here!'

'No; he won't. You're not listening. You're not hearing. I go
through there; nobody can find me.'

'You won't stay?'

'No.'

'You won't take me with you?'

'No, Manny. It's too late for that.'

Manny's shoulders slumped.

'You're right. I don't really care about you either. Not any more.
He took it. He took it all.'

'Manny, its not a he. It just takes that shape. They're all its.
Its. And they do that; they all do that. You have to wait, Manny.
I know it feels like shit right now, but you just have to wait. The
feeling comes back. Just – hang on. I'm too close to recovering
from it myself, I wouldn't be any good for you. But you have
millions of people who know how amazing you are, with what
you do. They'll get you through. Go online, like you used to. Do
an AMA. Get your ego boosted. Fight some trolls, get angry.

Your passion will come back. It's like poison, or like a bad trip… you just have to wait for the demon's influence to wear off.'

Manny huffed.

'You're not who I thought you were.'

He hadn't heard a word.

'Manny, I am. But neither of us are who we were; not right now and perhaps, not ever ag –'

'I was going to pay them off.'

Emerald tensed right up again.

'Pay them off?'

'But now I don't care.'

'Pay who off?'

'I thought, if you came back with me, I would pay them off. If you didn't; serves the bitch right – and I'll give them to you. But now, I just don't care.'

Manny dropped the dog collar.

It seemed to be a sign.

The Trolls had each been hiding behind a different pillar. It was *spoiledbitch*, the woman she'd clocked unconscious between cabs before she'd even spotted her, and *wontfuckingforget*, the fourth agent who had been mysteriously absent during the entire chase; the one who had rape fantasies about her (about almost every woman he ever met, she realized now she was clearer) but particularly about her, and especially in the past few weeks. They both had guns trained on her, and *wontfuckingforget* had a second one aimed at the back of Galena's head. Her mouth was taped, and she appeared to be wearing thick, banana-patterned flannel pajamas. Pajamas that she had been sleeping in, Emerald had to assume, when they'd found and kidnapped her.

Christ; how many more people would be dragged into this?

Dragged down by the demon's wake?

'I'm not this person, Manny.'

Galena looked right at her. She'd been there the whole time, heard what Emerald had said about exploiting her. She had hurt in her eyes; six different kinds, over how all this had all gone wrong. Emerald could see it. She hadn't meant what she'd said. She had liked Galena, straight away, and she had wanted…

Manny sighed. 'Not what person, Emerald?'

Emerald was more tense than she had ever been. Her neck felt half its usual length, the muscles had contracted so much. She could feel the muscles on her shoulders acutely on the fabric of her tee, they were so tight. All the way down her back, into her gut, across her chest, tight. Her thighs, her calves; even her toes ached with the stress, and the outrage at what was occurring.

'I am not this person, the person you're trying to make me into, right here and now.'

'You did this to yourself, Emerald.'

'I'm not this person, Manny. This isn't my story. I don't try to get away, get everyone killed, and then go on the rampage. I save everyone, then get revenge. It's very important, Manny, that you know that. That you hear me clearly in this moment and understand what I am saying.'

'And what's my story, Emerald!? I get caught in your wake – because you're in the wake of a fucking demon!? What is that anyway!? They don't exist! This doesn't exist – this place, *right here!* It's not on any listings or entries! Not anywhere! This floor! This thing behind me!'

'Manny – when I'm gone, go to the bar. Okay? You know where I came from? The Old Port? Whatever they call that area – go there, find them. They'll make it okay for you, I promise.'

'Shut-up!' *wontfuckingforget* demanded.

Emerald turned to him. Galena was still staring at her, wide-eyed, terrified.

*Forget* was very tall, slightly taller than even the stunning giraffe that was Galena, but he was all muscle, and mean with it. Emerald could tell from the way he was holding her, like he'd done it a million times before, over a thousand lifetimes.

'Where did it go!?' *forget* demanded.

Emerald was surprised. 'Where did what go?'

She saw that they each had a knife, sheathed at their side. The same kind *gagonit* had possessed, that had been in his hand when she'd crushed his chest with the cab door, that she'd kept, that had been in the bottom of the croc bag, that had been sent on. She hadn't had the time, or mind, to examine the glyphs… but what the hell was this now?

She suddenly realized.

'The demon?'

'Where did it go?!' *spoiledbitch* demanded.

Quite the demanding bunch.

'You're… hunting it?'

'Tell us you fucking spoiled bitch and I'll kill you before he takes you and has your body – he doesn't care either way…'

Galena was crying now, whimpering through the gauze tape across her mouth.

'You came after me with those daggers because… you thought I was one of its brethren…? That's why you were so determined?'

'Tell us where it went! Our Master will brook no pretenders in the city!'

'Your Master… is a demon from New York City?'

*Spoiled* sneered. 'Don't pretend you don't know…!'

Manny had simply wandered off, past the edge of the portal toward the next empty lane. Coveth had depressed him to the point of emptiness. Emerald watched him, the shadow of the man she had loved, probably for the best part of eighteen months…

She would never, ever Samantha anyone ever again.

The two assassins had come up to the edge of the portal now, taking her brief lack of focus upon them as some kind of attempt at sorcery.

'Your magic won't work on us; we've been made immune!'

*Spoiled* informed her of this as she came closer, holding the gun out, stiff, not giving her an inch. She held out her other hand.

'The pool cue. Hand it over.'

She wondered if she was immune to objects *propelled by* sorcery.

Her friend on Fifth Avenue certainly had not seemed to be.
'Give it to me. Slowly.'

Emerald scoffed. 'It's in the car. Take it after you shoot me. I don't know where the demon is. It's called Coveth. Horst was going to hand me over to it, so he could keep me like a sex zombie, so I tried to take him out. I didn't finish the job and Coveth tried to possess his body. So I called in some higher forces and destroyed his body. Coveth won't find me when I'm gone; at least, he won't find me unprepared now I know who you are, and what you do.'

'You're not going through there, you spoiled fucking bitch. Not with your fucking head on your shoulders, anyway.'

'Dash.'

A shot rang out and *wontfuckingforget* fell, dead.

The shot echoed, followed immediately by a dog barking.

*miss*

Emerald felt the bullet fly past her ear, to the extent that it blew and singed her hair, then she was wrestling *spoiled* for the gun.

Gavin raced past. At least, Emerald assumed it was Gavin; a massive Great Dane without a collar. The dog ignored Galena. She was just standing where she had been, *forget's* body at her feet, trembling. Perhaps Gavin hadn't seen her. Instead he targeted Manny, barking as he ran toward him. Manny, distracted, was shocked. Anyone could see the dog was just playing, but Manny ran from the loping beast as though it were a saber-toothed tiger.

'Hell hound! Hell hound!' Manny screamed. 'Keep the Hell Hounds away from me!'

He ran straight to the edge of the carpark without looking where he was going, looking behind him all the way, terrified, unable to take his eyes away from the perceived threat, hit the edge of the concrete rail at a decent speed and flipped right over.

Then he was gone, without even so much as a yelp, as the giant dog ran up to the concrete rail as well, then sniffed, and turned back. Spotting Galena, he ran toward her in just the same dopy, friendly lollop.

Emerald and *spoiled* had been grappling with each other, but had managed to see what had happened. Emerald was about to point out that *spoiled's* chances of getting paid had just radically decreased, but suddenly *spoiled* was wrenched from her. Emerald heard a series of thuds and crunches, then *spoiled* dropped her gun and clutched the back of her head, crouching in pain and staggering around, until finally she fell to her knees.

Micro was behind her, clearly furious.

'Fucking devil worshippers.' Micro leaned in and did something, put some pressure on *spoiled's* shoulder, and she screamed. 'He was okay that bloke – dumb, and a man-child – but he was okay until you fuckers played with his head!'

Micro smashed *spoiled* in the back of the head again, but stopped her fully falling forward as she somehow managed to hog-tie her while she was still kneeling. Micro had clearly had just as much practice at this kind of melee as the others, but… Emerald had to tell herself, at least she seemed to be a psycho for the good guys.

She let out a breath and found she had tears running down her face.

She wondered if she would ever smile, or laugh again after this was done.

When Micro had finished, Emerald leaned into *spoiled's* line of sight; but not so close that the demon's assassin could take a bite at her nose, or lip, or anything.

'Any other demon emerges in his territory, and your demon sends in the fucking clowns, is that right?'

*Spoiled* screwed up her face until it was beetroot red, then shrieked at her face, in a tone that sounded like a three-year-old in a tantrum.

'*He's going to have wild horses take turns fucking you while you're spit-roasted alive!*'

Micro looted *spoiled's* pockets. She was dressed in basic, casual, black paramilitary gear and had all sorts of knives and bullets and packets of who-the-hell-knew-what secreted all around her person.

*'He'll find you! He knew about this place! He knew you'd be here! He'll make that dumb fucking dog crawl up inside you cunt-first and eat out your brain from the inside, then wear your hollow, spoiled bitch fucking corpse around like a dog jacket!'*

Emerald really didn't know what to say as she went on.

*'You're not going parallel! You're not ascending or descending or leaving the planet, you dumb spoiled bitch! You'll still be on the planet! Feg'hak will find you! He'll find all the people you love and… spank them! Until they hate you! They hate you, hate you, hate you! He has destroyed all pretenders to Madison Avenue for five decades now! He will find you! He will find you, wherever you are – and you will pay for this!'*

Micro looked up at her. 'You just needed the name, right?'

Emerald nodded. 'And the blades.'

'Good.'

Micro did something terrible to her again, made her face contort in pain, somehow with just a hand on her neck and a hand in her back, then cut the hog-ties with the long blade that she had already commandeered, and forced her to her feet. Before Emerald could even enquire as to her intent, Micro had forced *spoiled* across the parkade, following in the path of Manny and Gavin, right up to the concrete rail, flipped her over and let go.

Emerald was shocked.

'There might be people down there!'

Micro looked over, then swung back to Emerald.

'No – they've cleared the area. It was over a few feet from poor old Manny. I assume they won't find this place? They can scrub the eighteenth floor all they like, and make up their own weird suicide narrative from whatever they find. Not sure what to do about rape boy over here, with the exit wound through his nose.'

'Rape boy? How did you know about that…?'

'About what?'

'It was in his head – the whole time. Everyone he looked at, right at the front.'

Micro walked back to her, pointing over her shoulder.

'Free the gazelle.'

Emerald looked behind her. Galena was sitting cross-legged now, her hands still tied behind her back, crying with the tape on her mouth. Gavin was whimpering, licking the clear-running mucus from her nostrils and the tears from her cheeks, just as fast as she could cry it all out. Emerald gently pushed his enormous canine head aside and pulled the tape off.

'Good boy.'

'Ahw…!' Galena gasped.

'Sorry…'

'Emerald! I was so scared!'

'It's okay now…'

'I though he was going to kill you!'

Emerald almost cried herself then.

'Me? I thought…'

'We all got through it, it's all good, huh?'

'You knew these people?' Galena asked softly as Micro knelt behind her and untied the knots. 'This one who had me; he assaulted you?'

'Yeah. He got me.'

Galena's hands were free and the strange foursome stood around the assassin's body.

'Three years ago. Came in my sleep.' Micro stated it so matter-of-factly. 'I woke up, and… he was already there. I fought him off, after. Tried to kill him, but he got away.'

They watched the blood run from the bastard's gaping head wound, then tried to stop Gavin as he tried to lap it up.

'Gavin!' Galena cried out. 'Not that blood! That's horrible blood from a horrible man!'

Gavin didn't seem to care.

Micro stared down at the giant, lapping tongue. 'I could never find him again. When I saw him in New York; I was terrified. But I don't think he even recognized me. Or if he did, he didn't care. Demons don't scare me. This guy… '

'Gavin, no!'

'It's okay, Galena.'

Emerald put and arm around her shoulder and guided her toward the car. Micro watched Gavin for a few seconds more, then lifted his giant head and slipped the yellow collar back around his giant head.

'Come on, mad boy.'

Galena looked up at Emerald.

'Was it worth it? Are you safe now?'

'You did what I asked, didn't you?'

'Sure.'

'I'm sorry, Galena. I'm so sorry.'

Emerald opened the door and grabbed a water bottle from the back seat.

'Here.'

'Thanks.'

'You like cold burgers?'

As Micro led Gavin over to the car, the rapist's body suddenly squelched.

Gavin spun about, but Micro kept hold of his lead.

Emerald stared as Galena spat water in shock.

The rapist's body had deflated, as though all the bones had suddenly liquefied. All that remained was the head, and the gaping hole in it. Then it proceeded to slither. Wriggling like a snake, the head lolling but slightly raised, it made a break for the portal.

Even Micro was astounded.

'Holy – *fuck*!'

She was up, and running at it, blade in hand. The slithering body was almost there, but as she reached it, the head reared up and she swung the blade down and across, decapitated the head in one savage slice. Still, it slithered on, with the decapitated head gurgling a final, disgusting threat.

'I will find you! I will faaagghhh…'

Then the mouth was filled with blood.

Galena grasped the second blade from the ground before Emerald. The thing was right near the portal now, and moving quickly. Micro slashed down again, then Galena began to hack savagely away at the whole body with a raging bloodlust that seemed, quite perversely, to urge Micro on as well. Together they sliced the thing at first into log-like chunks; three, four, then five slams each, each penetrating right through and reaching the concrete beneath with a high-pitched, clinking strike. But gradually, as they quickly diced what remained into random-shaped chunks, as the remaining fluid seemed to dissolve the clothes, the whole of the thing seemed to melt, and liquefy completely. Within a minute or so, they found themselves chopping nothing but darkly stained concrete, still a good meter or two from the portal, as the remnant of what had once been the flesh and bone of a full-bodied male human finally evaporated, like the last skerrick of brandy set alight on a demolished Christmas Pudding.

Emerald looked at them. One of the tallest, and one of the shortest women she had ever seen, working together to… well, working together.

But then Micro saw behind her; the head, decapitated, shoved aside, and even with the massive bullet hole and exit wound, was still rolling at the portal.

She skipped forward and kicked it hard, like a soccer ball, and it flew right across and over the portal, landing with a thud somewhere way beyond.

Chasing after it, Gavin ran straight through the portal.

'Gavin!'

Galena cried out.

'No!'

And then she was through the portal, after the dog.

'Oh…' Emerald groaned. '…shit.'

# CHAPTER FORTY-FIVE:
# PLOT

Emerald glanced sideways at Percival's flailing body, attempting to free itself from the desk, as she ran to the end of the corridor, toward the shattered window. It was almost there, pulling itself apart to get upright again. The thing, the demon, whichever one it was, would come back hard now; it had been surprised on its own territory, humiliated, but now it would marshal.

The shattered window exited onto the outer roof of the fourth floor. The penthouse exterior was only a few meters of rooftop rim that Quaker had not expanded the penthouse out to, just to tick the box and make it legal.

She stormed into the freezing cold night air, with the broken glass smashing under her shoes, and jumped over the edge of the roof, ramming the club-end of the cue onto the edge of the right-angle corner and slamming her shoes onto the wood as her staff met the side of the building. She slid right down, sparking green, her hair shooting up, almost vertical, black jacket billowing, pulling the cue tip up in a slight panic as she realized that her emotional urgency was influencing her speed, braking then hitting the cement canopy over the Railway Avenue-North Terrace corner, right above the entrance to the ramp, hard enough that she staggered forward in a kind of collected run across the top of it for fear of slamming forward, head-first into the concrete. She didn't know how old the thing was; at least back to the twenties, or if it would take the weight of a person, let alone someone jumping and stomping wildly across it at speed. Still, she ran straight to the corner, discovering aluminium over the solid concrete, her footfalls gonging like a temple bell, jumped and rode the cue again, this time down the pillar closest to the casino entrance. Hitting the footpath, she glanced back, down the ramp tunnel, whipping the cue under her right arm as she bolted down Railway Avenue for the three pillars and the casino entrance.

Down the tunnel, she had seen red dust billow from beneath the gate, and the purple light of a dimensional portal flash around the edges. If the freak, predicted dust storm, ahead of the rains behind it, had reached the hills and come through the portal, it could only be… what? Minutes? Before it hit the city?

*Barker can handle it, Barker can handle it, Barker…*

There were stragglers outside the casino, addled addicts, wondering if they could go back in.

Emerald tore past them.

'Closed forever!'

How she wished.

She pushed through the glass doors, through the old marble lobby, out of the vestibule and pushing again, into the main casino. She had built this trap to kill a demon; Feg'hak, or Coveth, or even the horrendous thing, demon or whatever it was, that the mad bastard up in the hills was worshipping at Bridger Mansion; whoever came after her first. But the last thing she had expected was that there had been a demon here, the whole time, right under her nose; and that she would have to kill it – or as close as was possible – in its own house.

How could she have missed that? How – the – *fuck*?

She ran into the main room.

How…?

Because it knew, and had known all along; because it had wanted her here.

That was the only reason.

She panted.

Empty.

She didn't think she had ever seen it empty. Not even during the renovations…

The gambling screens were all there, shining. The sounds of those infernal matrix banks were coming from upstairs, from everywhere now; every single inch of spare space they could fit another one of the evil things into.

And the roulette wheel.

Right there in the middle of the huge room.

But the whole place was quiet, eerily quiet.

Too quiet.

As they say.

'I'm sorry...'

She said it to the building.

'I don't know if you were good or bad as a proper Railway Building...'

She looked around. Hardly any sign of what it had once been.

The beautiful stone.

The old world.

'But no building deserves to be forced into this.'

There was a groan from somewhere within the stone.

Maybe this wasn't such a good idea.

Luring and trapping, then banishing was one thing.

Banishing something on its own territory...

But then, there it was, coming down the escalators, and Emerald knew that it was too late to turn back. If she ran now, if she showed fear, if she confessed within herself that the thing could, that it *was going to* defeat her, then it would.

*It would.*

It was still trying to put the body back together, but it was on its feet; it must have seen first to repairing the leg that Dash had broken. Broken off, almost, Emerald had thought. From here, the head still looked battered and broken.

Jesus, these things...

Then it collapsed, halfway down the escalator, and lay still.

Just as the demon that Barker had spoken to appeared before her.

Emerald started to shake.

*It would; this was it, she had pushed it too far, and she had made a terrible mistake.*

She was surprised to find that, over her bubbling terror, she could still speak.

'I – I thought it was you…'

'You quite took me by surprise up there. That blade… where is it from?'

'New York.' She tried to be brave. 'Ever been there? Your kind of town.'

She knew that her sassy smile was crooked and false. It was too late. This was over. She couldn't win.

The thing shrugged, regarding her through its mote body. He was allowing it to ripple, reminding her of its power; just collected dust, reflected light, congealed with water… he was allowing the motes to weave and spark, to unsettle her.

'I have not been there in the world as it is now. I would not find my purpose there. I can make it anywhere; why would I be drawn into trying to make it there? Los Angeles lures desire, New York lures ego. Masterful construction, that continent; no more of my kind are required in either city.'

Emerald nodded. 'We're all ageless, you know. All of us, in the end. It's not such a boast.'

'I doubt you will find me a braggart, Emerald. I am The Persuader. I am here to make you an offer.'

'No.'

'No?'

His – *its* - mote body congealed suddenly. It was excellent; it would pass for real, and from her studies over the past two years, Emerald understood that this was rare. They were too often too keen to influence, and their mote-bodies lost discipline, and integrity. People found them out; took them apart like she and Dash had tonight, and they had to start again. Or they got too accustomed to jumping flesh-bodies, and taking possession, and didn't manifest their mote bodies often enough, and again; people saw through them. This one though… he had been using this a long time, and often. But it was also very similar to the flesh body. He must have been using that a long time too; holding it together with motes as well, but building on it a long while.

She wondered who it had been, originally.

'He was willing.' The Persuader smiled, reading her broader thoughts. 'You are well-versed. My dust body, and the original body I keep, stuck together from decaying, they appear the same. You know our kind, at least superficially well; to tell them apart.'

'Why… have you been…?'

'Hiding from you? Oh no; now, these two you cannot tell apart – the difference between hiding, and waiting.'

He smiled as Emerald's heart sank.

Now she knew, for sure; that he had known all along.

He, it, had deliberately concealed himself from her, Quaker, everyone.

Because he could; that was how powerful he was.

Like every demon, hiding in plain sight at the center of every city.

'I have been intending to speak with you for some time, Emerald. But two years, it is nothing to me. Not that I wanted you here, of course. Not at the start.'

'Why didn't you just kill me?'

The last two words caught in her throat.

Running. Still running in to the arms of evil.

Not home after all.

Never home.

'To finish the thought; certain people, like Quaker, cannot be possessed. People like yourself, Emerald. Men like that handsome, shaggy-dog sorcerer downstairs, and the blue witch. You come from somewhere else, and you always resist us. Look at you all; let's not forget the drunkard and the bimbo, who've gotten themselves trapped. All huddling together.'

He was hiding something.

Right there.

But she was too scared to see it.

'Men like Quaker can be relied upon to act a certain way. I wanted to see how you and he played out; if perhaps you could be made to help us. I gave it a while to play out, to cook. It seems the buzzer had gone off. Time to stick a knife in it.'

He held up his hand. The blade that his dormant flesh body had dropped when he had abandoned it bounced down the escalators, making a terrible racket, clanging and pinging, and with each metallic impact jolting Emerald's whole body.

'See if it's done!'

The blade hit the lowest escalator stair and flung upward in a huge arc.

It was heading right between her eyes, she could see it. But then the tip thudded into the floor, exactly between her feet, sticking up between her legs. He was toying with her, but as he looked down at the blade, he suddenly shifted his gaze across the floor. West, toward the railway concourse.

'What is happening down there?'

He looked up.

'The dust storm will hit… minutes.'

Then down again.

'That man in the Hills… time he was dealt with.' He looked back to Emerald. 'Which returns my attention to you, Miss – Emerald – Tarragon.'

Emerald could barely think, she was so filled with terror.

Rational, irrational, it didn't matter.

It was what these things did.

'Now. Without people of your kind, without our...' He glanced up again. '…natural enemies, to guide you…' And he glanced back to her. '…my kind would run everything. And there would be no game, no sport, no conflict, no friction. No power. Do you see?'

'Yes.'

She did, but she would have agreed with him, regardless.

'These people we can never fully inhabit, never fully persuade. We must reach deals. Agreements. Contracts.'

'Frighten us. Hurt our friends.'

'If you disagree, quite so, I am afraid. Or is it you, who are afraid? We do – *mean business* – you see.'

'Yes. I see.' She was shocked that she not only had the power to speak, but to speak against it. 'Mean business. Cruel business. The evil that men do.'

It smiled.

'I will make you an offer. But I fear we will have to war with you, and kill you all tonight. But I am willing to open negotiations. I am open to an agreement, or even continued employment. What do you say?'

'No.'

He was quite astonished at this.

'No? Emerald, I can quite easily take you out of the game right here and now. You knew that as you came in; you have entered my temple and demanded satisfaction. That is suicidal. You *know this*.'

She betrayed herself then, allowing a hopeful glance below.

'Barker Moon? Barker Moon will be dead before the night ends. He has been dead a long time, Emerald, but doesn't quite know it. You know it though. You have known it since the moment you met, just over there, at the bar that is no longer there.'

He came forward and smiled.

'You, on the other hand; you are willing to fight for your continued existence on this plane. That is why I wish to employ you, rather than kill you. You can marry Quaker, control him for me with your sex, with your child, with his desire. That is a time-worn and true arrangement that will see you survive very well. Here, in this place. I can train you. You will always work here. In twenty years, you can be working the Bleeding Room, and I will move on. You can have children that will work here. I will train them also; Quaker's children, or the children you have with another, after his decade, and your marriage has dissolved.'

Emerald gulped.

She'd been offered something so similar, not so long ago.

She had been a fool for not accepting, she knew this now. By now she would have been married to a handsome French-Canadian. She would have been pregnant, and happy; reading the good people who came to her for help, sending them off better than they were.

'You stole those weapons from others, did you not?'

The Persuader smiled; thoughtfully, with a slice of cunning.

'People, occult mercenaries who fought on behalf of the demon they served, no?'

'No...'

She gasped, the word choking in her throat. The more she thought of the life she might have had, back in Montreal, the more it hurt. The more she seemed to be losing, here and now; the more that frightened her. Then she focused again, and forced her throat to relax, again, as he stared at right at her.

'I mean – yes.'

The Persuader nodded.

'Here is my offer. Marry Quaker as you intended. But rather than receive the safety he provides, I would have you influence him as I say, on my behalf, and it will be *my protection* you receive. I would have you as my right hand; those you have recruited here; the big dumb one, the little feisty one; those others you like, that you have collected around you, who have seen the horror we represent but think you can protect them; they are your pilot fish, and I will allow you to keep them if you so choose. I will create weapons for you, and them, that will kill my rivals, and their brethren, even more efficiently than the one you used upon my body this night. If you submit to me in this way, I can make you more powerful than any of those others you have seen who serve the others of my kind.'

Emerald suddenly felt her fear diminish. It was as though her mother had come to her childhood bed, and whispered into her ear that everything would be alright. Suddenly she could speak, collect her thoughts and utter them.

'Speak now.'

She cleared her throat.

The fucking thing.

The *fucking thing* had dialed down its fear projection.

Just like that.

*Just like fucking that.*

But it was something.

She had thought all this through, over and over.

She collected her thoughts, quickly, and dug deep.

This was it.

It.

'I have been chased by a demon my whole life. A young one, who had just appeared here after fighting his way up; he built his power, his existence on Earth by taking the energy of the men who loved me, then taking my energy, as my spirit drained, with each failed love affair…''She could feel tears in her eyes as she confessed this aloud. '…I have waited here for two years to kill it. I defeated and escaped it in New York, the last time it came for me.'

'Kill it?'

'It's the same; sending you back to your source. That's what happens to us, to humans, mortals, when we die, we go back to… some kind of source. If we call that death, you must as well.'

'Hmmm.'

'I said no. Maybe I was too hasty.' Emerald shrugged, pathetically. 'Maybe I should reconsider.'

*She didn't even know any more.*

*Was she pumping the demon for information?*

*Or, was she really considering this?*

*How many more demons could she send back, could she kill, if she had the protection of one? Maybe she had been too smart, after all?*

'Persuader; if I have your protection, I could kill them both, when they come here. I could lure them here, openly; you could help. This city is a grid for channeling and focusing power. The sigils and daggers on the blade… you said could make better weapons. Could you teach me how to improve them?'

The Persuader shrugged, examining the blade, still upright between her legs.

'Perhaps I spoke too soon as well. They would not require *too much* improving. They are exquisite. Yes; I can help you. We can turn this place into a trap...'

He grinned then.

'...or, an arena! A demonic arena!'

He walked away from her for a second.

'Yes! I can inherit the power of those we lure here. It's true, competition between spiritual forces is one of the things the grid was created for... but who is to say which of us that conflict should be between...?'

Emerald wondered, did this creature fully understand the city?

He had been here long enough.

Who was to say that what he described had not been the original intent?

'Indeed!' The Persuader plucked that thought directly. 'Indeed; you are a smart one! Most in your position would have abandoned their own ideas long ago, especially in my presence! Very good; yes! Yes, I will keep you!'

He nodded beside her, to the roulette wheel.

'This is all piecemeal; I pay little attention to what occurs down here, in Quaker's domain. I prefer the Bleeding Chamber upstairs. That is art. But I have seen how you enjoy it here; watching these fools come through, to part with their money. You enjoy seeing them part with it, yes? I will give you this place, you may retain these floors; you may have Quaker, and between us, we will see to it he denies you nothing; *nothing*!'

Emerald looked to the roulette wheel, still too scared to move.

'This wheel; I like to come down here and be the spinner, or the croupier sometimes. I took the time, to learn how to spin it, to deal cards, to throw dice. I like to spin the chocolate wheel, as well.'

The shimmering dust and water body before her vanished again, as the flesh body at the end of the escalators rose. The demon had returned its essence to the reconstructed physical form she had almost ruined. It spoke as it walked back over to her, past the machines, past the tables.

'Of course, I would have done something with you eventually. But it is interesting that I underestimated you. I did not anticipate your arrival. You were sent; that is interesting…'

She began to feel the dense fear again.

She remained rooted to the spot. Her body was still terrified, still prisoner to her primal brain, that thought being still and not drawing attention was a viable survival skill.

'…you built your lure, your trap; the casino with your prints all over it, without knowing I was here, then when you realized, tested the blades on me…' The Persuader nodded. 'Idiotically brave, but classically foolish. Textbook human sorcerer.'

The flesh body might as well have been human again, she saw as he drew closer. Then she saw deeper, as he came right up to her, and realized that it had combined the two. Its mote body and flesh body were somehow fused; and it made it look more than human, somehow. Stunningly… handsome and desirable.

She gulped, swallowing hard, dry.

It was right up close again now, as it leaned down and withdrew the blade from the floor, pulling it sharply, then slowly rising it, hovering the flat under her crotch.

'We have a deal?' He stepped back and regarded her, holding the blade in his palm. 'Come aboard as my first, then! Open your wrist for me here, now.' He extended the blade again, then pointed the tip down. 'Bleed into the floor of this building. Bond my essence with your iron life-fluid, and nobody will ever challenge us for this building again!'

Emerald heard as the building groaned a second time.

This was not reality; her consciousness had shifted and they were part way into the astral now. Where these deals counted for something. Where words echoed and formed potentials that became solid, and anchored back into reality. She was on the very edge here, where the universe was listening, dealing with her spirit before a demon; not completely fearless, far from it, but rational enough, able to form thought without submitting to total, primal terror, because he wanted her to have that reason.

To be aware of the consequences.

To act with free will.

She had to pull back, think.

*Had she genuinely considered the unthinkable?*

*A deal with a demon?*

Keep thinking; *back here, where he can't hear.*

*Keep asking.*

*He wants a blood deal, but he would not hand over the blade…*

*He doesn't believe you…*

*But keep asking… they like it when you ask…*

'Why now? I could have made this deal with you two years ago, when I first got here. You could have taught me so much in all that time; you can read me – you know what my intent has been, since I first got here. The blades, the sigils and glyphs, my research says they sever the dimensional channels from the lower levels; the sigils represent connection to extremely powerful earth energies. The glyphs are from the Inner Earth, from another age almost. They're left over from the civil war in Hell that ended the Third Earthling Humanity.'

'Oh… is that… so?'

'They sever the power of the demon from the denser, darker dimensions. That is the power you exploit, that you require, to maintain your hold here, in our reality, correct? You lose your connection to those demonic realms, those Circles of Hell, whatever they are, and you lose your influence over the structures you've claimed here; you become trapped in this physical density. You lose the true, deeper, denser power that you exploit to establish yourself here in this dimensional reality. Isn't that right?'

He regarded her curiously.

'Where have you learned this, human?'

'Once that is so, you're gone, right? You fall back to Hell.'

The Persuader sneered.

'There is nobody here, listening. I would know. Nobody behind me with a blade, waiting to strike as there was at the Quaker's door. Nobody coming to save you. You are jabbering.'

'You're misunderstanding my intent; I will help you, but what I mean is; some demon in New York is actually handing these out, just to kill human demon brethren. Can you believe that? I mean, just the blade part will do that, will kill a normal person, demon-affiliated or not; wielded efficiently. But; the arrogance!'

The Persuader looked curiously at her.

'Or – the plot.'

Emerald stopped.

She stopped talking, stopped thinking, stopped trying.

She started feeling the fear again, despite herself.

It, the thing, the demon…

It was on to her.

It grinned.

'But; no. I thought you were like all the others. Mistaking this town for a small pond, running down stream; to be the big sorceress… in a little city. Find a man who cannot be whispered to, as your five previous lovers were whispered to… but I have… underestimated you.'

Emerald's fingernails suddenly stung, as though she had just struck a stray splinter, but with each of them, simultaneously. The awaiting magical power that she held there, that would emanate from them, was turning on her and hurting her; she had never felt this, her power turning against her, not even in this small regard. She could feel, up and down her arms, the muscles contracting, tensing, across the back of her neck, and down her throat so that she couldn't speak. Under her clothes her nipples were erect, but so sensitive that the inside of her bra made it feel as though they had searing-hot clamps attached. Her gut was twisting, like the first signs of food poisoning.

The Persuader no longer seemed charming.

'Why did you come back in here? You should have run.'

He smiled. The soles of her feet felt as though she were standing on a hotplate. In her mind, the entire floor was like this, all around for an expanse of eternity, and she would walk forever with this level of pain; forever at least until they turned up the heat. Needles, needles between each toe now. Under each toenail. Her toes, skinned, the upper layers slowly peeled back one by one.

And there would be more.

It didn't make sense; how could her feet be this hot forever, until they became hotter?

Christ; *eternity.*

Eternity, she realized; The Persuader was promising her the bizarre, unreal torment of forever-pain, of an eternity in pain, in Hell.

'Yes…' The Persuader smiled. 'This has been but a second, and you understand, because conceptually, you are well-disposed toward it…'

Her kidney on one side, her liver on the other, one pulled slowly out of her anus, the other from her vagina, but which? He hadn't yet decided.

But somehow she remembered what Barker had said, when she had been listening to him down on the concourse; *they have to tell you.* Somewhere in all their rambling…

But she couldn't maintain focus. She was; she was well-disposed, pre-disposed, because; she had awoken to this. To the mystical, the supernatural… she could see and understand and knew what to expect and –

*She had to know, she had to believe; this was all in her mind.*

Back, and back; the idea of eternity like that, forever receding, it was just fear, it was just an instilled fear; there could be no such thing because she knew that she had been wrong, *wrong about it all,* that there *were* other dimensions and there *had been* other lives, and while a human could conceivably torture you to death and make it seem like an eternity, it was not possible to take a soul and do the same; a mind, yes, but not the soul because…

She heard her voice wavering as she spoke.

'Yo.. can.. hav… me…'

Her mind was reeling with the fear of the promises he – *it – the thing* – was making; he could keep her here for ten minutes and make it seem in her mind, make her remember it, as though it had been years, the way a dream is a day in the dream, but is just a minutes or less in real-here-time; he would make it *decades*, an ageless torment that she would never forget and never recover from, that she would always remember when she woke from it. She would be traumatized from it for the rest of her life, and take the pain into the next life, and the next, so she would seek it out, seek him out in her next life to beg him to stop it; and the knowledge of that would eventually see her fall, and become hospitalized, and live out her life…

'I can have you?'

'Y-you…'

'I did want you. I was thinking about it. Making you my trophy human, like Quaker will. I considered setting you against Shilling; oh yes, I know Shilling! That is what he wants, after all, to use the city as a playing field, to bring in a power that will destroy me, destroy the thing he is bargaining with, up in The Hills there; to claim it all as his own… that is what I thought you were doing; claiming your territory, Emerald. But human – so wonderful – never content; Shilling himself wants to become one of us. And not simply one of us; *The One of us.*'

'…cahhn…tuh!'

'Did you…' The Persuader actually seemed a bit shocked. 'Did you just call me a *cunt?*'

'– *can't* – !'

Emerald kept telling herself.

It can't be possible; this is a trick, a *trick*.

'*Can't – have – me!*'

'Oh, Emerald; it is possible and I *can* and will do it. I can kill you here and now and keep your spirit in the building for as long as I see fit. For as long as I live; which is a long, long, long time.

Until I forget about you and you become worse than all those ghouls out there; your stained spiritual memory stuck here in the gross third density; and your true spirit in the astral, roaming life after life, caught and imprisoned; century after century watching in pain. This pain I cause you now, ever-escalating, because even though the human body is only capable of feeling a certain dimension of pain, even though the human spirit can only feel so much sorrow, and the human soul so much torment; for as long as I have your psychic imprint burned into the stone walls of this all-enduring building, I can keep you here, and I can make your psyche forget that you have experienced the summit of agony, I can make your spirit and your soul confused and spin them in time, so that you forget, again and again…'

'..spuh…'

She was losing.

Losing her own bet.

He hadn't done this to Barker; she did not think he would do this to her.

How; how had it all gone so…?

'So wrong? You have come into my lair and challenged me directly; Barker, I was just interested in manipulating. He had begun playing on the board again, making moves. Making him open that portal was something I required. Something this grid requires. Shilling wants to pit me against Ceea'gha, while he brings forth his champion; he wants the portal open so I have a direct link to Ceea'gha, and he to me! He thinks we are like territorial wolves, and we will immediately attempt to devour each other! He thinks we will wear each other out, spread our power all over the city as we fight, through the suburbs and hills and beaches and people, the cats and dogs, and roos and emus, the crows and galahs and wombats and foxes, fighting for supremacy, extending too far; and then the thing he brings forth will devour us, at our most extended, and diluted. He is wrong! *I want him to do it!* But he could not do it unless Barker opened the portal; and now he has. Now, as it was designed, the power on this board, the power to play for, the prize; it is greater than anything humanity has seen since the Norse demons made their final play and turned Europe into a slaughterhouse of epic proportions! And it will rise, that game, that game again – from here! From here where nobody will see it coming!'

He lifted his hands, and Emerald rose into the air.

Clutching her staff, still, for dear life.

'And you, Emerald, have played your part! *You* – have challenged more of them to come! The grid will fill! We shall destroy those angels who reside here! Those higher beings; those witches and sorcerers – and all the others!'

She was hovering about a meter above the floor now.

'Yes…' The Persuader examined her. 'A fine specimen!'

He walked up to her, closer. He lifted the blade again, beneath her crotch.

'No…' Emerald whispered.

'No?' It smiled. 'I can make you feel pleasure as well, Emerald.'

Then suddenly she did. Her whole body began to relax. The hovering, the weightlessness, being tethered to him like a balloon, started to feel pleasant, if not a touch erotic. A touch, yes. He would touch her now. Touch her in the places only she knew, in the combinations she told only her most trusted…

She held her breath and tried to calm down.

'This is the oldest trick in the book, Emerald. Pain, pain, pain; and then just a little pleasure. A touch of salve on the rawness feels like… Heaven! Yes! Sensitivity! How brutal it can be! How electric, how – *lovely*. After all that pain, it feels so wild, so arousing! But; the real trick; the pleasure makes you forget the pain. And we start again, all over; all over again, all over your body, pleasure and pain. Wonderful brains, wonderful, stupid, blind fool evolution! Leaving you little apes so vulnerable.'

She swallowed. Easily. Now her dry mouth was filled with saliva. Now her tongue felt wet and slippery, ready to be deployed.

'A kiss, Emerald? A kiss before you go?'

'Play me…'

He laughed, unbelieving. 'What?'

She kept her breathing.

'Play me… gamble me… make me your prize!'

She was delirious, clearly. He stared at her.

'Black; take me on my back. Red; I give you head!'

He kept laughing. 'Wh-wh-wh-*what?*'

'Red for my pussy; black for my ass!'

Christ she was so turned on; *this had to work.*

Some demons had sensual desires, some did not. There was only one reason for him to have maintained his flesh body. It was handsome and desirable; it was a genetic freak body he had claimed. Just like everybody said about her body.

He liked it. He liked himself in it, and he used it.

'Please…' Emerald moaned.

*Please be right.*

She leaned forward in her floating euphoria, and swung her cue down between her legs, riding it softly, like a parody, like a sexy witch. Finally, she was Samantha; more, she was the erotic dream of Samantha. She enunciated clearly with her big, wet, freaky lips.

'Ride me like a demon; fuck me 'til I'm *red raw*; spank me 'til my *ass is black*! Spin me 'round; fuck me in my ass, spin me round, fuck me in my mouth; spin me, spin me, spin me!' She was spinning herself now on her broomstick, spinning and spinning, around and around, upside down and up again, her hair whipping about, riding the bronco, writhing on the stick. 'Spin me, spin me, spin me!'

The Persuader was laughing and laughing, raucous and desirous, clapping his hands.

'Oh, yes! Yes, yes! The Ice Queen of the World Casino *finally melts*! She does not respond to pain, but to pleasure! Oh yes, yes, Emerald! We have a deal! Black, I have you; red, I have you!'

He reached forward and spun the roulette wheel with a massive swing of his arm, and a final flourish of his wrist, just like the game show host he was.

And it all stopped.

Emerald fell straight to the floor with a thud.

She felt nothing; no pleasure, no pain.

No fear.

She lay on her side, clutching the cue, still embracing it between her thighs, and in her arms like a lover.

*'Oh thank God.'*

She kissed the cue tip with her big, wet, beautiful lips.

The wheel spun, the ball clattered.

The Persuader staggered back slightly, then looked down at Emerald. He raised the blade, ready to bring it down on her head, but cried out as it stung him. He dropped it and it hit the floor, the tip once again impaling in the wood, right beside Emerald's cheek. She came to her senses and snatched it right away, rising and stepping backwards, away from The Persuader, away from the roulette table she had been trying so desperately to get near, but been too scared to move towards, to show her hand, all that time.

But she had won; she had played her hand, played it, the thing, The Pretender, and beaten it on its own ground.

At least, she hoped.

Emerald nodded to herself. 'Or – the plot.'

Emerald reached over and held her hand over the roulette wheel.

Just as it was seeming to slow.

'Why!?' The Pretender gasped, staring at her, his hands up before him as though he were trying to frame the scene of the spinning wheel, as though it would make more sense, focus him more. '…are you…?'

Emerald held the dagger tight, and spun her staff in the other hand, just casually.

*'…doing that…?'*

She took a deep breath.

'Like I said; I have walked down here for two years. Walked and walked. I have spun this wheel. I have dealt those cards. I have thrown the dice and counted the chips. But; truth be told, the roulette wheel, mainly.'

She looked back behind her.

The chocolate wheel was still there, propped up against the wall.

Waiting for the weekend, when it was used.

'That too.'

The Persuader smiled, trying suddenly to flatter her.

'I see. You basically own this room.'

Now he was the one at odds; now he seemed a little anxious.

Then his expression changed, and Emerald felt her chest tighten as he stared at her. He still had it, still had the terror.

'Of course you do. Little sorcerer woman… but the universe heard you. You agreed; I could have you – black or red! You wanted me to spin that thing; but in order to convince me, you had to sell yourself! Sell yourself and there is no way out for you! Black or red, red or black! I will fuck you into eternity and back again, until you can't tell the difference between pleasure and pain or desire and despair!'

The clattering seemed to slow, as the spinning of the wheel declined.

Once the momentum ran out, Emerald knew, it stopped fairly quickly.

'All that talk…' Emerald smiled. 'I was defining you. That is what I do; I play with a toy, until the toy and I are one. I spin the wheel, until I know the wheel, how it feels, how it spins, the pressure and the speed. How long it takes to complete, at what pressure. I know these carpets, these walls; I know this place. My ability is special. Few have it. I walked and walked around down here, using it all; all the *real things* that are remaining. All that while; you said to me, don't look up here. Pay no attention to the man in the Executive Room. So I didn't, and Quaker didn't, and nobody did. The whole city; nobody pays attention until it is too late, and you have destroyed another life. But still; the spell you cast is so powerful; even after all the lives you destroy; *nobody pays attention.* It's like you're not even really there, *and the people have done it to themselves.*'

'You… you can't have planned this!'

'No; I didn't know you were here!'

'Then –'

'You demons – you love to talk – I listened to you talking to Barker, and he told me; you have to tell us. So I let you talk, talk and talk – I thought you had me, I really did! I thought I was doomed, and dead, and in an eternity of despair…'

'You did? You were! I had you! *You – were!*'

'Yes! But I thought my way out of it, as you talked and talked and talked, until I realized; that is the way out! Now, I know who you are as well as anyone, or anything in this building. I know your style, your plans and desires, and you have bragged and threatened and – I know who you are and what you want and why you are here!'

The ball clattered for one final series of spring and rolls, all over the red and black numbers, and then it clattered once more, just once more, and it stopped.

'But you have made me an offer! You have gambled your way out of your own plan! Red or black – one or the other – and you are mine! Now bow before me, Emerald Tarragon! You – are – mine!'

His whole mote body flashed, and he was standing before her, naked with bright red, muscular flesh, huge ram-horns and a black beard, furry calves and a long, forked tail that was black on the end.

'What!?'

At first, Emerald thought it had been deliberate, he was doing this in order to tell her to suck his great, big, red, demonic cock. And it was right there; and it was. But The Persuader seemed just as stunned as she was.

'What – is – *this*!?'

'From my studies, buddy; your true form. Your true, physical form, in third density, severed from your power by all the symbols and glyphs and runes and whatever the hell else was on those knives, that I have taken two years to carve into the reverse side of that wheel; ever since the renovations. This is what you are, in the human dimension. Without access to the magical dimensions below us, down in the darkened density of the cruel earth!'

'Red or black! I still have you – red or black! How can this be!?'

His voice sounded deeper, and he already sounded less sophisticated.

His cloven feet stomped over to the roulette wheel.

'Red or black – oh!'

He saw it.

Emerald smiled, letting out a deep breath.

' – or emerald.'

'No!'

'Or whatever colour the green zero is. Emerald sounds good though, doesn't it?'

'Nnnnnnno!'

'This is my room. Always bet on Emerald.'

He spun about to her.

She suddenly realized; he was real. He furious bull-man, about ten-foot-tall, all muscle, and real.

Real in this dimension.

Coming right for her with fists the size of bowling balls, clenched for vengeance.

'Oh… shit.'

# CHAPTER FORTY-SIX:
# TEN

'Oh…' Emerald groaned again. '…*shit.*'

Micro took a few steps forward, toward the portal.

'I… I didn't mean to…' She turned to Emerald. 'Where do you think it leads!?'

Emerald stared at her, mouth agape.

*'I don't know! That's the whole point!'*

Then she pulled herself together.

'Get everything you can in the back of the car. If it closes, or if the direction is programmed, I hope it doesn't close, or reset, until a car goes through; he told me – *drive through.* Or… I don't care, just get everything into the car!'

Emerald took a few steps toward the portal as Micro obeyed.

'Jesus I hope she's okay and not…'

Emerald concentrated hard, focused with all her might. She probed out, the way she had been taught; but nothing got through. When she turned back, all signs that there had ever been any kind of incident, other than the weird black blood stains on the concrete, were gone. But they would dry, she knew, and turn to dust.

Micro walked out from behind a pillar.

'Done. There are actually all sorts of things, all along here behind those pillars. Personal items, messages carved in; reminders that they do not want to be followed.'

'Thanks again, Micro.'

She squinted.

'I'm sorry.'

Emerald stepped forth and embraced her, tight, the side of her face between her breasts. She held it as long as she dared.

'I have to go.'

Emerald released her and went to the driver's side, without looking.

'I don't know how I can ever repay you, but if I can, I will.'

Micro didn't say anything.

Emerald got in. When she was in position, and ready to start the engine, she couldn't see Micro.

She'd stepped away.

She wasn't one for goodbyes; Emerald knew that.

'Okay… here we go.'

She started the car again and drove forward, slowly rolling closer to the portal.

She was about four car lengths from it now. Three, rolling on; two.

It was bright.

So bright.

She stopped.

She'd count to ten, she thought.

That was standard.

Ten, nine…

Would she do it?

Eight, seven, six…

It was up to her.

Five, four…

The passenger door opened.

Micro got in and sat, looking forward.

'This is why you stopped, right?'

Emerald sighed. It had seemed like the right thing to do.

She hadn't expected to be so relieved.

'…three; two; one.'

Micro smiled. But, Emerald realized; Micro really wasn't right for her.

Micro, the name, was all wrong.

Always had been.

'Seeing as you don't have a real name, I'm going to call you Dash now.'

'I like that. A lot better.'

'Well, Dash, we made it in New York.'

'Made it *out of* New York.'

'Quibbling with terms. Let's see where we need to make it now.'

'Anywhere, apparently.'

'Amen.'

Emerald drove through.

# CHAPTER FORTY-SEVEN:
# PACK

The alert Emerald had given out when she had first realized that Percival Wade was the same demonic creature that Barker had spoken to on the concourse, placing the first cracks in the spell that the demon had cast in order to go unnoticed, had summoned Dash, who was never far anyway.

*Dash it* summoned her, while *darn it* was code to tell the rest of her crew to hold back until further notice, and…*damn it – damn it to hell…* told them all that there was, finally, a demon in the casino, and that they should all remain on standby until she and Dash had assessed the situation.

Now, as that very same demon manifested in the dense physical form of the human world, came stomping toward her across the main casino floor, she raised her phone again, hit speed-dial, and once again alerted her loyal right hand.

'Unleash the hounds!'

Then she pocketed the phone as she made two long strides, stretched her right arm and grasped for the central turret of the roulette wheel, gripping it hard, like the hilt of a sword.

The roulette wheel had been in the original casino bar of the Railway Lounge since the nineteen-twenties, and retained as part of a National Trust heritage deal when the building had been recreated as a full casino. It was beautiful, hand-crafted sometime in the nineteen-twenties from rare West Indian mahogany, so when she had taken it apart and crafted a weapon from it during the renovations, under the guise of having it restored, she had been very careful. She had worked with a retired roulette wheel repairman in Monte Carlo, with herself masked and anonymous over Skype, to ensure she did nothing to damage it; at least, any more than she had to.

But what she had to do, had to be done, and so, that was that.

Given Emerald's own brand of magic, her own tactile ability with magical energy, the idea to use the roulette wheel as a kind of distributor for the power of the daggers she had collected in New York had come to her almost immediately upon entering the World Casino. She had walked in and seen the beautiful old wheel for the first time it and realized, with militaristic malice aforethought; I can weaponize *that*, for a start.

Emerald was very familiar now with the way magical energy worked, at least in her hands; like the modern alchemists who physically handled solids or gases or liquids or plasmas; say, masons or anaesthetists, bartenders or electricians. Emerald had become aware that magic had its own natural properties, and even seemed to have its own will, or consciousness at times, just like firemen said about flames, or botanists claimed about plants. The different forms and stages of magic, in themselves; as the energy moved through one's body; as the spell formed in one's mind; as the two combined and fused and departed the body; the wielding of the tools or symbols; as the energy transformed and was propelled, moved into, through and eventually altered reality; these were all different stages and states in which it took different skills and approaches to understand and negotiate, and a sorcerer had to balance all of these at once.

Magic, majik, mystical energy, spiritual energy, occult energy, whatever; solid, gas, liquid, plasma, *source*, Emerald seemed to want to call it now; now, Emerald had finally understood that *source itself* was a force to be reckoned with.

Similar to the way water followed the path of least resistance, although not always the path of least resistance you had located and assumed to be the one it would take; or the way that life consumed matter that allowed its continued existence, but did not always bargain on the hidden side-effects of that matter; or an earthquake could leave a tin shed standing when disaster-proofed skyscrapers had toppled; the practice of sorcery existed within the sometimes fickle, always malleable, but *absolutely comprehensible bounds* of source, that had been hidden from humanity for centuries.

But Emerald had seen the way that the roulette wheel could seem to concentrate, then spray magical energy; spray luck after focusing it, and how it was almost always at the center, being the main attraction, of not just this one but any classically designed casino.

After that realization, she had then spent months online; for the first few weeks intensely studying the creatures she had been running from. Rather than simply hoping that they would not come again, find her again, and destroy her again, she would find a way to deal with them when they did, inevitably, come. Rather than hoping that the information was not all bogus, and fantasy, she sought out the people who had written the information, again over the internet, to assess their veracity, their sanity, and real-world experience, to ensure that *they* were not all bogus. She had learned, where she could, what the glyphs and runes and sigils on the daggers meant; what their size and placement and subtle, eccentric differences signified, and she had come to realize that it was all rather fluid, that it all pretty much depended upon the will, and subsequent personality, and individual styles, of the practitioners in question.

She had discovered that they were real, these creatures. They came from somewhere, had a genuine presence in the world that could be observed and measured and recorded. Studied. Therefore, they could be dealt with.

They could be stopped, or sent back to source, if not outright killed.

She had been particularly mindful of this, after long periods of focused intent, when she had attached three of the demon-killing daggers she had retrieved from the vile assassins to the underside of the roulette wheel, each divided equally and pointed to the secure base of the central turret. Then she had been mindful again, and focused again, as she had carved not just many of the same symbols, but others of her own discovery, and a few of her invention, and even some inspired by her contemporaries, into the mahogany around the daggers.

So when the giant red thing came at her, and she was able to respond, The Persuader was shocked. Emerald clutched the central turret and lifted the top of the wheel. The wheel was essentially a large bowl, rimmed with an inward-curved lip that prevented the little balls from flying out as it spun. She had inlaid several other spells within the base as well, made to correspond with her commands.

*a >apart< part*

And there it was. Lifted, apart from the base of the wheel, a part of her; a shield she could hold grasping the turret, her elbow settled into the lip, bringing it down across her chest, under her chin, with the knives and her carvings facing out; facing the thing as it came.

It reeled backwards as though struck, falling onto its back.

She advanced as the hounds arrived.

They came tearing in, almost falling over each other for their first chance at prey, the mother and father at the rear, allowing their offspring the initial advance. They savaged The Persuader, ripping into its red devil-flesh, tearing and, at first chomping, but then simply engaging in savage pack-frenzy. The Pretender threw one of the dogs aside and Emerald heard it hit the casino wall and yelp; its mother then went for The Persuader's face, and took a slash from its horn.

'No!'

Then The Persuader was on its feet again, bits of its own flesh hanging off almost every part of it, shredded and ripped over all parts of its body, dripping with demon blood and chunks of bright white and dark black meat.

Emerald heard their owner cry out again.

'Regroup!'

And although one remained for one more rip at the demon's flank before bolting away from a mistimed, retaliatory swipe, they all returned obediently.

Emerald drew the roulette wheel back, as far as she could, then swung as hard as she could, releasing it with all her might.

*sever*

The flesh-torn demon leaped back with extraordinary speed, but the wheel still caught it under its throat, jutting up with a crunching wallop, accompanied by another slap of ruined, severed flesh; but the blow did not complete its task. The Persuader's head was not severed, nor was its connection, at least not fully, to this density, nor the lower realms of darkness.

*The damned thing still lived.*

It gurgled a cry and the fleshy body began to disseminate, rising upwards.

The wheel wobbled and came unstuck, flying backwards onto Emerald's arm, knocking her a few steps backwards and jarring her shoulder quite sharply. Damn. She'd have to work on that. But that had been the other vital spell, she had realized quickly upon designing the roulette shield, near the start; finding a reliable additional spell that countered mass, and stopped the thing weighing fifty kilograms. She drew back again but it was too late; she knew what it was doing. It was returning itself, the fastest way possible, to the third floor. Back to the Executive Room, where it lived, had lived for almost two hundred years probably, where it would be essentially impenetrable, and unkillable for the foreseeable future.

Then it was gone, and the dogs were back, lapping up the demon's blood they so craved.

'Did we do it?'

Emerald turned around, and there was her friend.

'Almost, Galena. Almost.'

'Almost?'

'Is Michael okay? Was it Michael that got thrown?'

'He'll need stitches. Uriel too. But the thing…?'

'We'll have to fight it again, but we did well. It's retreated, further back into its lair. We won't be seeing it again for a long time.' She looked back over her shoulder. 'Bring the pack. Call the others. We need to help Barker.'

# CHAPTER FORTY-EIGHT:
# A LOT GOING ON

To be honest, to Parry, the river spirit looked like an Aboriginal woman, wrapped in a blanket, and caked in wet mud. But then, he supposed; that's what a river spirit, trapped in a lake for a hundred years, would probably, or at least, might very well look like. He supposed.

'Are you sure that's what it is?'

The imperial government had treated the indigenous people of this continent appallingly, and to this day they still did not fare that well. He'd seen a lot of homeless over his long career in this city, a lot of them alcoholics and druggies; this did not look like one of them, but on the other hand, it didn't look completely unlike one of them either.

Either way, it was a tragic image.

Another figure appeared; somewhat less tragic but no less weird. Emerald Tarragon, the woman who ran security at the World Casino and was the rumoured paramour of no less than Ernst Quaker himself (and considered by many to be the main reason he had set up shop here) sprinted onto the footbridge, her long hair flowing behind her, looking down keenly at them as she slid to a quick halt somewhere near the middle, over the top of the glowing purple portal. She appeared to be carrying a pool cue, and what looked like an upturned roulette wheel, brandishing them as though they were a… well, it had to be said, as a shield and spear.

'Barker!'

Moon remained cross-legged on the floor, in front of the portal.

He ignored her, which could not have been easy.

Parry hadn't realized, but a lot of noise had built up, being generated from the ghouls, who were absolutely increasing in number, and at the same time growing a lot more swirly, if not outright restless, all along the ceiling now, pretty much completely filling the massive arched chamber.

'Cheryl! Cheryl Equinox!'

Cheryl took her eyes from the captive river spirit and looked up at her. Then Tarragon seemed to piece it together that Cheryl had been focusing past the portal, and she turned and saw the figure standing at the other end of the concourse. Then, for a few long seconds, Tarragon seemed to become suddenly embroiled within her strange mesmerism as well.

'What!?' Tarragon finally yelled at it.

Then she turned back to Nox, who was clearly stunned that Tarragon appeared to be able to have achieved successful communion.

'Use the creek! She says; use the creek! The creek runs through Arthur!'

'Arthur?' Parry asked himself.

Tarragon shouted down again. 'Who's Arthur!?'

There came shouting from the stairs.

Several women were descending behind the demonoids. The most arresting of the group was a sixties beehive at the front, who was wielding a short-sword in each hand, and a tall, voluptuous redhead at the back, who was carrying a smaller, busty blonde woman in her arms, who might have been wounded, but looked for all the world, for some reason, as though she were fast asleep. Around and between them were several others, all brandishing weapons of some description; a long sword, a spear, and some long daggers. They all looked pretty authentic. It was all becoming a little bit concerning to him.

They went for the demonoids, but the demonoids backed off, dodging their spears and swords, flying up and back over them, swooping away from the aggressive ghouls, then out of the building and fleeing into the night. Then the women came charging down the stairs, about eight of them in all, and ran toward him, and the others, and ultimately Moon and the portal.

As though this were not enough, a pack of wild dogs, enormous ones, headed by a Great Dane, and one of those enormous black, shaggy Russian things, the others probably being their litter by the looks of things, burst out of the casino and along the footbridge as well, followed by what looked like a supermodel. From the hotel side, several of Tarragon's security people emerged, also brandishing relatively strange weapons, it had to be said, for this day and age.

Tarragon turned to the supermodel, then to the woman at the head of her security detail, a short and stocky but very striking dark-haired woman. They seemed to know what to do and came up to Tarragon, each standing at her side, and then the trio vaulted the rail and jumped off the footbridge, all three at the same time.

Tarragon shouted something that sounded very odd, something that his mind couldn't translate or process properly, but it made him feel like he had just had a belt of really excellent whiskey, laying back on a lover's feather bed, late on a Sunday afternoon in midwinter. The three of them jumping, and simply surviving without injury, would have startled Parry at lot more if he hadn't done the same thing himself, just fifteen minutes or so earlier. They landed as though dropping in slow motion; still having to catch themselves as their feet impacted, but okay. Then the three of them were right in front of him then, and Tarragon was right up in front of Cheryl.

'Can you do it? Can you do what she's saying?'

The woman with the beehive hairstyle was approaching from the stairs.

'What is she saying? What is she asking of you?'

Cheryl turned.

'She says that the creek that runs through Argent can be made to force open the portal. She says it will run through to here, through the portal, and back into the lake.'

Shirley looked over Cheryl's shoulder.

'We've tried to free her before this; we even tried talking to the Town Council.'

Cheryl shrugged. 'She says the water that runs through Argent is magically empowered. It's dark magic, because of Argent; she feels it, even when it's flowed all the way down through The Hills and suburbs to get to her, here. But the further away from Argent it gets, the weaker it is. If I channel it through here; it will be strong enough to break Shilling's spell, and she says she can do the rest.'

'Shilling's spell?'

'Well; the spell he's maintaining there.'

'He must have modified it…' Shirley frowned. 'I don't like this. This is fiddling about with the balance of this city before we know…' She looked down at Barker. '…he's up to his old tricks again, then?' She went over to him, glanced him over as though checking his meditation posture, then crouched beside him and stared into the purple light, addressing his left ear. 'You can get into Argent, but you can never get out. That's why the portal won't open. We can all go through, if we want. But we'll still never be able to get out, and we've no idea what's on the other side. But the water will come through?'

Barker opened his eyes and shook his head.

'I don't know. I think it will. Is Cheryl ready for this?'

'No.'

'Maybe I'm not.' Cheryl went to them. 'But we don't have a choice – we know that evil bastard is going to torture them, if he's not killed them already!'

Barker folded his arms and sat up straight, his legs remaining crossed, still without taking his eyes off the portal. 'Just… give me a minute.'

Tarragon came forward. 'I suppose we have to hope that whoever is on the other side figures this out, once the water starts running through it. Although; I mean, it's winter. With this big storm coming, that everyone's talking about? How much water is coming through exactly? I mean, there's been flooding upstream, hasn't there?'

The tall redhead came forward.

'Cheryl; I'm sorry for everything. I will make amends, I promise. But; remember what happened at the shaft?' She pointed up. 'With the ghouls, remember? If this is that old magic, if this is that water, from the deep earth… and it's been through Argent, as well?'

'That's right,' Shirley snapped. 'Is the water dark, or old? Is the energy dark, or old? And just because our friend the water spirit over there is feminine, and has always been here, there is no reason to assume she won't kill the damn lot of us, once we connect her old energy with whatever Shilling's doing in Argent, just for being the descendants of the people who…' Shirley waved her two short-swords in the air, for lack of being able to do it with just her hands. '…Great Mother, I don't know! Even if we *can* get the damn thing open!'

They heard a motorbike in the distance.

Barker stood. 'I've got that covered…'

Parry looked over as Moon's bike appeared at the top of the stairs.

It seemed to be riderless.

Although; Moon's not-pet koala was sitting on it, clutching onto that long branch of wood that Moon had seemed so keen on keeping.

Now that, Parry thought to himself, even though there really did seem to be a lot going on around him, really was something you didn't see every day.

# CHAPTER FORTY-NINE: LAST DITCH

'Amanda!?'

Fiif felt Carlton pull her back, toward the portal. She looked back through the dust storm for a second, past Echidna, as they stepped over the headless wooden girl and moved past her sister; still, staring, blank. The dust storm was really coming in thick now, the way they did once in a while over seemingly random parts of Australia.

'There hasn't been a decent one like this to hit Adelaide for years…' Fiif heard Carlton utter. It was getting harder to hear. 'Seems like a real doozey; clearly some kind of mystically-summoned superstorm kind of doozey…'

The wind howled and the air swirled about them; she could feel it on her skin, on her cheeks and forehead, on the backs of her hands, like sunburn.

Echidna strode forward, up the street, blocking their path to the portal, and attacked. She was furious, with her hands up, as though prepared to channel, cast and throw down the world's hottest and deadliest spell at them. Carlton saw the words form on her lips and, as close together as they had stood so far, recognized her face from somewhere distant, but real. But there wasn't enough time to see through the glamour; there wasn't enough time for anything. Echidna was no novice; she knew that Carlton had the sticks. She was simply trying to out-draw him. Carlton threw the instant-karma-kali-stick at her as Echidna flung her hands forward in a classic, theatrical, bad-ass, bad-witch spell-cast, and whatever she had intended for Carlton exploded back in her face, half-formed, half-delivered, immediately setting her hair on fire. She screamed and clutched her head, then staggered backwards like a birthday cake sparkler on legs and ran, at first backwards, then turning and leaping like a gazelle, into the darkness, toward the creek.

Fiif let go of Carlton's hand. She stopped and turned, swinging his backpack off her right shoulder as her left hand dived into it, then she swung her arm back out in a wild arc and screamed some kind of outraged incoherence. Three big rocks flew out, apart but roughly in the same direction, spreading as they flew, hitting three of the wooden children between their eyes and knocking each of them back off their feet. They screamed like outraged piglets. Carlton saw where things were headed and moved swiftly in front of her now, as three more wooden children leaped again, practically flying through the air. He took two of them down with the kali sticks, just as the relatively ordinary weapons he had trained with, one with each stick, cracking them across their heads with a dual snapping sound, like a clapperboard, and Fiif countered the third with a swipe of the backpack itself.

All six were back on their feet in seconds.

None of them appeared hurt, but they gathered and regrouped, snarling and snapping, as more came down the street after them, ahead of Shilling, all of them closing in now as Carlton and Fiif again started to back away.

'Amanda!'

The four other girls looked to be around the same age, but they were all radically different in appearance. He'd selected a very broad spectrum of ethnicities and body types. They were gathered around Shilling like puppies around their mother, like they were afraid to stray too far from him in case they missed a chance to suckle.

'Ignore the humans!' Shilling bellowed, his arms high. 'Surround the portal while I deal with them!'

The children ran past, snarling and snapping but not touching them, until suddenly another two went for Carlton. There was a crack-crack of wood meeting wood again, and again they spiralled away, slamming into the ground; two of the same ones who'd attacked first. They were up again, but Carlton was kicking them up the road, like dolls, into the bushes. A third flew right at Fiif, arms extended, but she ducked and slammed it into the bushes with the backpack.

'They're not fully…'

'What?' Carlton had only half-heard Fiif.

'…his control – like wild animals!'

'Wild animals who don't know how to fight! They're probably just used to swarming, overwhelming people.'

Carlton took a pause as he tried to figure the next play; eerily, the children were ring-a-roseying around the portal now, some having joined hands, dancing and running around it.

What the hell were these things?

Ancient wood demons or possessed children?

The second little girl, who had once seemed so evil, and taunting, had been staring down the whole time at her decapitated sister.

'We don't know either.'

Fiif spun about to her, as though that had meant something, then looked back to Shilling. He was staring at her; right at her, into her eyes. He and the five girls were at the base of the hill how, at the end of the street near the grass, and the street light, and he was going to devour her, in some way, she was sure. But he was taking his time, making her feel it; making her understand that there was no escape, no hope, that she was his, and his completely, to do with as he desired.

Then, Shilling tensed suddenly.

He seemed to sense that there was something in the air.

'Amanda!' Fiif cried out again, hearing the desperation in her own voice; yet clearly sensing an opportunity for the girls, a break in Shilling's focus, for all the girls to get through. She tried again. 'Amanda! For fuck's sake!'

Shilling was staring up to the sky now, his arms spread. Fiif turned back to see if the wooden children had been affected as well. They had not; they were still dancing around the portal, for the most part, while the dozen or so who hadn't joined in were simply watching the others. She looked back; Shilling was turning on the spot, still with his arms raised. Fiif moved toward him a few more steps, and for the first time she got a good look at him; she saw how handsome, but how clearly devilish he was. He was Lucifer as a middle-aged man; you could see it, it was obvious. Something about his stance, the confidence that radiated from his every physical move, alerted Fiif straight away.

She could see them now, after Zinco.

'Yes!' Shilling exclaimed.

She could spot these fucking psychopaths a mile away.

Her revolting husband and sickening marriage had left her with that, at least.

'Yes!' Shilling echoed himself as he turned fully away from her, and the portal.

She stepped forward again, toward him.

She needed to hear what he was saying.

The five girls were stepping away from him as he spun, his adoring acolytes, and creating a pentagonal formation around him that she had to assume was somehow either directly controlled by him, or had been installed within them. Stances complete, they simply stood with their hands at their sides, their eyes upturned to his glory.

Carlton hadn't seen her move closer. He was still staring at the portal, and the children, still trying to explain.

'They know it's a funnel...'

She was only half listening.

She could feel the moment approaching; when she could act.

Someone had to.

*Someone had to try.*

'...wider on one end; things can only go through, and things can only come out this side, the side it had opened toward...'

'...is it Barker...?'

'...it has to be Barker... but we should be able to see him!'

'Well, why can't we!?'

Carlton turned back to her.

She didn't wait for an answer; she went toward Amanda again.

'Fiif!' Carlton snapped at her.

She looked back; he was telling her – don't.

She didn't have to read his thoughts; it was right there on his face.

*Don't do it. Don't fuck with Shilling.*

Telling her this, with one foot braced toward the portal, the other toward Shilling himself; almost ready to take Shilling on, but not willing. Unwilling, even though there was a small stream of water, dribbling down the middle of the road, that was being separated around the toe of his shoe, the shoe that was placed, tense toward Shilling, the water that was heralding the storm that Shilling had summoned; the dust, then the rain and whatever horror that would bring with it.

So here it came, here came the storm.

Carlton wanted to do it, she could see; he so wanted to do it. They both did – kill the fucking sick bastard. She could see it, his desire; and now she saw Shilling, she understood. He was a super-smart psycho with the power of sorcery. She got it, she could see how he'd manipulated her wanker boyfriend Zinco into proposing to her, using her, marrying her, preparing to dispose of her. She could tell how Shilling had manipulated Zinco's fuckhead mates as well; she could see Bourkey, the so-called smart one, listening to Shilling's bullshit, taking it all on board, Zinco realizing that Bourkey understood, but using his own charisma to ensure that he still maintained control of the gang… she could see it all, understood the whole thing, and she could see the same fury in Carlton's eyes as a result.

*This man killed all my friends.*

'Yes!' Shilling had his back to her. 'I see! He comes! I see!'

But she and Carlton were regarded as such a non-threat to him now, as merely pathetic, disposable things that he could have killed just then, but now could kill a bit later, after this much more important thing, that he was at this moment completely ignoring them.

The red dust was swirling about him, thicker than it had been. Swirling around the five girls, but focusing about him, in the middle. Centralizing like he was the eye of an ochre hurricane. And the girls; none of them were conscious. None of them seemed to even truly realize where they were, or what they were being asked to do.

'Typhon! Typhon I embrace you!'

Carlton scowled. 'What!?'

Fiif thought she'd heard it. 'Typhon?'

'He said that, didn't he?'

*'Taiiii – foaaaaahhhnnnnn!'*

'Sure did.'

She accepted her instinct to take a few steps backwards.

Something about what was happening; Shilling's confidence, his intensity, and after that last call, complete insanity, snapped her out of her vengeful fury and changed her mind.

Carlton gulped. 'Typhon… the storm…'

'Isn't he… like, the Ancient Greek Satan, or something?'

'Or something…?' Carlton did not seem thrilled. 'The portal, okay? While he's distracted?'

She looked back, as though to ensure that he still was distracted.

The ochre dust was beginning not merely to center around him, but to attach to him. It was hard to see through it now, but as the wind came up savagely and the dust blew up, into the core that was starting to form above his head and upstretched arms, they had a sudden, terrible, clear line of sight.

His suit was starting to fray as the dust whipped; the girls' skin was reddening with it too. But the dust was actually beginning to stick to Shilling's skin, like clay. He started ripping his clothes off. The grey jacket first, then ripping the waistcoat and then his shirt from his chest, the buttons flying, like a man possessed with desire for his lover. As though via some psychic command, the five girls started stripping him even more quickly, dropping to their knees and taking his shoes and socks, pushing down his pants and underwear, making quick work of the ripped upper garments, then returning to their preprogrammed pentagonal positions.

The dust had thickened his skin now, turned it dark orange. At first it was like a ridiculously dark fake-tan, but then she began to understand; it was blending with him. He was becoming something else with it; his muscles were expanding, he was becoming taller, and his features bigger, more pronounced. More alien somehow, more like…

Fiif heard her own gasp.

'…more like a *beast*.'

The girls came forward again and began to caress him. The continuous top layer of the new skin, the new flesh, the new body, was malleable and they ran their hands all over him as though he were some grossly exaggerated he-man muscle-champ, and the new, soggy dust was body oil.

'Yesssss….!'

Fiif looked down; the trickle of the water down the street, the rain coming, had increased but remained minimal; the liquid to make the ochre dust clay must have been coming from Shilling's own body, from his blood, his flesh, his piss and semen and bile, all his inner fluids. The fluid must have been drawn out of him somehow, mixed and congealing. It was horrifying, disgusting; but here it was, happening right before her. The dust swirled up again.

She could tell that Carlton was even more frightened of him now; not only did massive sports egos fall to him and do his bidding, but the psychological stain of him having murdered – she didn't know how many people, how many of Carlton's friends, to make this happen – was in the end too powerful a mental block for him to overcome.

Poor bastard. Poor Carlton; she understood.

How could any of them overcome any of this?

Any of what had been done to them?

But; what was happening to Shilling?

What was being done to him?

Was he…? He was.

He was becoming something else – let alone how.

*What* was he becoming?

Something horrifically more powerful than he already was? The *already was* that Carlton, and Barker, were scared of? Becoming Satan on Earth? Well, Greek Satan, anyway. But surely that was bad enough? Even if actual Satan, Ancient Greek or otherwise, was bestowing some kind of terrible – was *boon* the word? – upon him, before her very eyes – that was surely enough?

And she, she and Carlton were here, just watching it happen.

Could she live with herself? Could she stand before anyone else after this and say that she had been here, watched it happen, Satan becoming embodied on Earth, and – her hand was already groping in the backpack for the biggest rock she could find – *done nothing?*

But – she thought, *she really thought* – she could do something, make something happen, and that there was a chance.

She could see it; she thought, *really thought*, that she could see, *see what could be done.*

And if there was a chance, that she could make this stop…

Make it all stop.

Then…

Fiif flung.

# CHAPTER FIFTY:
# SKYLIGHT

'Mainwaring! Bach!'

Both the bike and the koala had gotten the gist of Barker's telepathic effort, and responded from the parklands at the other end of the city. If they all survived this, Barker knew now, he'd be able to get through to them both telepathically now, give Mainwaring and Bach basic remote commands, while at the same time allowing Mainwairing his freedom in the local gum trees. This had been a tall order for the big little guy; or, more like a tricky request actually. He had asked Mainwaring to pick up the piece of wood, get on the back of Bach with it, lay down on top of it and clutch the sides of the seat to keep it in place. Simultaneously, he had telepathically asked Bach to come down the probably trafficless four-AM North Terrace to deliver it, as soon as she could, without freaking Bach out or causing an accident. It had taken all that time to get through to them, and he doubted it would have worked, that his telepathic reach was capable of stretching that far again just yet, given that it had never been great in the first place, if he hadn't thought of using the Botanic Astral Gate as a kind of psychic signal booster.

There were a lot more people in the Railway Station now. Half a dozen of Emerald's people, most of Shirley's coven, along with Cheryl and Parry.

They'd all seen it; the black and lime-striped bike shudder down the railway steps, with the big male koala on top of it, hugging the bike seat with a five-and-a-half-foot-long branch of ghost gum underneath him. The koala rolling, and dropping casually off the phantom bike right after it had stopped, the branch dropping, the koala grasping the end and lackadaisically, but quite deliberately, dragging it a few meters across the concourse floor and letting go of it right at Barker's feet. Barker leaning down, scratching the koala behind his ear as he grasped the wood, firmly in the middle, and the koala turning around and sitting casually on the floor beside him as Barker stood up.

Barker did a couple of basic twirls with the new staff, keeping his eyes on it.

The bike revved.

Barker looked up.

'Everyone!' Barker shouted.

Everyone was already looking.

He had hoped that.

'The war you've heard about, it's going to start! As soon as we open this, we're challenging Fenner Shilling to come kill us all, plus whatever exists, up there in Argent. Anyone too freaked out, we'll all understand, but you'd better get out now!'

His voice echoed throughout the hall, through the red dust, and made the ghouls staring down on them flutter and spin again.

One of the security team turned and ran out. Emerald sighed.

'He has a family...' Galena reminded her.

Then one of Shirley's coven dropped her spear.

'I'm sorry! I didn't sign up for this!'

She ran up the stairs, but turned halfway before vanishing into the night.

'I thought I was going to use spells to make men fall in love with me!'

Shirley and Candle exchanged glances, as beside them, laying on the ground, Karri woke, blinking in the red dust.

'Uhgh...' Karri groaned. 'Classic Narelle.'

Candle helped her to her feet, and she saw Cheryl standing in front of the portal with her eyes closed and her hands raised. She was shimmering all over, a translucent sliver-blue.

'Holy shoot...' Karri rubbed her eyes. 'What did I miss?'

'What did *I* miss?' Barker's eyes widened as he gasped. He looked back at Shirley. 'Seven years' worth in one night?'

Shirley nodded. Barker looked back.

'I'm not sure this is such a great idea after – '

'It's starting.'

Emerald pointed with her cue-tip to the floor at the front of the portal.

Water was trickling through, pooling a little, then spreading. It had the same shimmering look that Cheryl's wetshield was emitting, but it was crystal clear. Any one of the group gathered before the portal with any magical ability could sense the power in it.

'Cheryl?' Barker stepped toward her. 'You okay?'

Cheryl spoke with a clipped delivery he'd never heard from her before.

'There's a crack forming; use your staff.'

Barker stood with his left side to the portal, facing Cheryl, and spun the wood before him clockwise, then counter-clockwise a couple of times between them, creating a magical circle that generated from his gut, from where his adrenalin, his anticipation, anxiety and excitement was building. On the third counter-rotation the staff came down with a slap into his extended left hand as he drew his right hand back. Purple energy crackled along it, threading down his fingers from under his skin, electrifying the air around the left-handed grasp, then the right.

Barker could see the crack right there.

The water; high, sacred water from the rains that were behind the storm…

Holy fuck.

'Cheryl; there's something behind the dust!'

'Open it!'

The crack was low, coming through the bottom of the portal, where the circle touched the ground. It was as though a mouse had chewed a hole through the other side of a wall, and now the rain was dribbling in. He kept this image in his mind; down the wall of the house, the rain would come. He had lived in many old houses. It dripped into the house, onto the other side of the ceiling, onto the floor of the attic, from the roof; from a broken or displaced tile; something like that. He made himself see the portal as a house, an old house. In that instant he saw how old, how very old, Argent was. The human houses there were nothing. The thing that had been there, that was now at Bridger Mansion – *the thing he had called to Bridger Mansion, been forced to summon to Bridger Mansion* – had been here, with its horrible little evil wood sprites, for thousands and thousands…

'The house, Barker!' Somebody placed a hand on his right shoulder. 'The tile; crack the tile!'

'The thing that was there, it is so old…' Barker saw, could not help seeing. 'But the thing that is coming after the dust, with the rain; that is older…'

'*Crack* – the *tile*.'

He was in Bridger again, in his mind's eye. He saw them all; his friends, saw them draw the daggers, and the blood.

But he had to ignore it.

He knew he did. He could, But, this would help.

He looked up.

The balcony.

People looking down.

Things, creatures, looking down.

Higher, higher; to the tiles – but the weird skylight… *that would do.*

'Oh, shit…'

He heard Emerald say it and knew it was her hand on his shoulder, that it was she who could share his vision, and she who had focused him when he had needed it. She understood that he had no choice, but what would happen when he cracked a skylight instead of a roof tile?

'Barker – now!'

Cheryl said it.

But Heather said it as well.

Everyone was watching.

The staff swung up from his left-hand grip, was upright, tight in his right, and he planted it on the concourse floor; the energy went up like a mortar shell, through the skylight. The skylight shattered and everything – light, water, people, creatures; everything poured through.

# CHAPTER FIFTY-ONE: FRENZY

The fling hit Shilling's left temple, and at first he didn't seem to notice.

Carlton realized now that he was going to die here.

There was nothing he could do.

Not against Shilling ordinarily, not against him in this demonically-enhanced form, and certainly not as pissed-off as he was now, in this form.

And certainly, not against Fiif's righteous anger.

The rock hit had splashed some of the clay-flesh from the top layer of his newly-formed skin.

But really, Shilling had barely noticed. The five women had paid more attention.

*Okay, he hadn't noticed.*

*Nice try, but maybe they didn't have to die, maybe –*

Fiif flung again, and hit again.

This time, Shilling turned fully to them.

He was still recognizable, but oddly like some giant Muppet version of himself.

Fiif flung again.

*'Hurt!'*

The rock smashed into the middle of Shilling's chest where, if he had one, his heart would be.

She threw again.

*'Hurt!'*

It hit there again, and Shilling roared, in… what surely, *had to be* pain.

She threw again.

*'Hurt!'*

And this time, again hitting his chest, there seemed to be blood.

The heads of all the wooden children, still ringing the portal, turned at once.

The five women started running down the street toward them, shrieking insanities, completely deranged and outraged.

Fiif pulled from the backpack and threw again; this time she just shrieked, hatefully, and the rock struck Shilling once more, this time in the middle of his forehead, right between his eyes, sending him reeling backwards with his face to the sky, roaring in guttural fury and pain, as a fountain of blood showered high into the air, like a woman in a hair commercial.

Carlton cried out.

'Oh – fucking ay!'

Three of the children raced past from behind him, one of them almost knocking him over. Fiif ran after them, going straight for the five women, clearly intending to take them on all at once, single handedly, and get through to deliver the fatal blow to Shilling while he was down. Carlton knew better; they'd had the benefit of surprise, of catching him vulnerable, delirious with his own success, distracted and underestimating. The children zig-zagged past the women, and one of the women turned to chase them, seeming to get wind of their treacherous, primal intent. Fiif rewarded the first of the young women to reach her with a savage backhander. She fell, her body twisting with the impact to the side of her face, but the next woman pounded into Fiif with both hands extended, clamping them around her neck with insane force. Carlton would have helped her, but the other two were upon him, and thrust him backwards onto the road. He had the presence of mind to keep his head locked up as he fell, but the impact on his upper back was for a second stunningly painful. He kept clutching the sticks and they made a good effort to at first wrench them from him, then one of them bit deeply into his right hand as the other started smashing his left wrist against the ground with her fists. Somehow he registered that the road was wet beneath him, before he smacked them both across their heads with the respective sticks, unable to clear his mind to come up with a decent magical command.

They each reeled away, screaming in pain.

Carlton was up; the women were trying to kill him, trying to kill Fiif, he couldn't deploy the instant-karma, or it would kill them; these were innocents, under possession. He went forward, as more of the children from the portal ran toward Shilling –

He cracked the kali sticks over the upper arms of the woman who was trying to strangle Fiif, and she retracted, squealing like a child, although Fiif still had hold of her wrists and would not let go. Then the one who had bitten him, who still had his blood around her mouth, ran after the children as well.

'No!'

He tried to assess the situation; he looked back quickly at the portal. Half of the remaining children were running toward him, but passed him, while the others started brawling amongst themselves, splashing about in the water that had formed around the base of the portal, and was pooling like a blocked drain. He looked up the road. The children who had run to Shilling were descending upon him savagely. He started roaring, in what sounded like more pain and frustration. The ochre clay, the flesh and blood and mud, were spraying everywhere.

Of course – his blood!

They feed on blood!

'It's bloodlust!'

'Amanda!'

Carlton got it.

The portal behind him flared and he turned; it was opening.

Really opening.

But then, Carlton saw past them all. Past Shilling, past the end of the street that went down, into the darkness, that followed the creek down into… somewhere, somewhere *bad*.

He'd known it, somehow, when he'd seen it, when they'd first arrived. Or had Maz known it? When he or Maz or they had seen these two roads, they had known that that church had been open, but now it was closed. But neither of them could have known; neither of them could ever have been to Argent before.

Unless… was the church even, really – in Argent?

Where were the boundaries here?

But his thoughts were jumbled, he wasn't thinking right.

Was he really seeing what he thought he was seeing?

The creek; the whole creek, was rising, rising over the bank, down the lower street, as though it had a life of its own. It did; in mystical terms, but really like it had an – animal, conscious – life of its own. The water rose up like a giant squid, lumbered out of the bank and slapped back down on the ground. The flow didn't proceed; it seemed to swell, and dam, rising and rising around the fork in the road where he had sat with Fiif and astral travelled to Bridger, but moving, slowly moving, past that, down the street, past where Shilling lay, where he was roaring and being overwhelmed by the children who had gathered to devour him, passing them just as he started to throw the children off, finally, with chunks of his new, failing flesh in their tiny mouths, coated in his blood.

The living creek water formed a shape, like the head of a serpent, with a mouth opening, and Carlton saw that he, and Fiif, and Amanda and two of the other girls stood between it and the portal, and the pressure, the magical force, that the river was pushing onto the portal, to force it open.

He spun back, as Fiona wrestled with Amanda, as the remaining two women looked up and screamed, their terror at the massive head of the creek serpent over-riding their adoring need to fight for their hideous master, and then he looked again at the portal.

It cracked.

Something deep in the earth beneath them trembled.

There were people, he couldn't see who, at the other end.

Three of them standing there, forcing the portal open.

He made two brisk strides up to Fiif and Amanda, who

alternately were struggling to strangle, and not to be strangled, shoved his right-hand kali stick into his back pocket and grabbed Amanda by her hair, from the back of her head, and wrenched her backwards. She screamed like a child. Fiif let go, staggering backwards as Carlton grabbed Amanda's left arm and wrenched it down behind her back. She screamed again, then he turned her about and pushed her hard toward the portal, where more of the wooden children had emerged from the shadows, and the bushes, and the houses, keeping hold and walking behind her, their feet splashing in the pooling creek water, three inches deep now at the end of the street, and shoved her through.

She vanished.

He turned, saw Fiif aghast, saw Shilling on one knee, pulling more of the children off him, throwing them into the bushes, into the water, down the street toward Fiif, and saw the tree creatures from Bridger Mansion start marching, one by one, out of the doors of the old church and stomp-running down the hill, coming to the aid of their master.

He extended his hand to Fiif and she took it as Echidna came running out from the empty creek bed, as more ochre-red dust blasted down the creek bed behind her, and then even more down the street with the tree creatures, into Shilling, past Shilling toward them. The screaming women were paralyzed. Carlton grabbed one by the hand, then Fiif grabbed the other. They dragged them; as Echidna descended; as Shilling finally stood again and locked eyes on them; as the remaining children turned their attention to them once more, their brief rebellion nothing more to Shilling than a pack of mad puppies who needed to be trained better or drowned; as the tree creatures ran past Shilling with their terrifying faces leering right at them, shaking and screaming and in complete hysteria, toward the portal. They were almost there as the serpent began to lose integrity, as the creek began to restore itself into a creek again, ignoring the millennia-old path of least resistance it had carved through the many centuries, following now its new, magically attracted path into the portal. Carlton felt the creek water begin to rain down, knowing there was a small ocean behind it that would blast through after them, but then suddenly he and Fiif were through the portal and out of Argent, staggering into a giant red room, the first people in almost a century to escape the long-lost town's once-certain promise of a prolonged and ghastly death.

# CHAPTER FIFTY-TWO: RECKONING

She had sensed that Barker needed help; she had, to an extent, shared his vision, but had shared it without the emotion of it, just the practicality of what he had needed. Just like the Trader's map. It was possible to give a boon; it was possible to deliver a kind of energy into the body of a sorcerer, or a witch, or any mystically prepared person, but as to its use, its deployment, that was another matter. The boonee had to figure that one out for themselves. In reading the map to the carpark in Montreal, she had been shown a style, a form of magic that was purely technical, in a way; rational magical energy, she supposed, as opposed to the normal, more passion-infused magic she had become so accustomed to, that had always come with emotional baggage, had always come with some kind of fear, in some shape or form.

She removed her hand from Barker's shoulder, but remained standing with him, albeit from the other side, crossing to check on Equinox, to look into her face. You could see she was struggling. Her eyes were no longer closed. They were intensely cobalt blue, with quicksilver pupils.

'Christ – Cheryl!'

'Nearly there, nearly through – he's coming; have to hold it, have to dump it on that fucker!'

Emerald had no idea what she was talking about.

Emerald did it again; she placed a hand on Cheryl's shoulder.

She saw; she was saving her best friend. The river spirit from the lake was feeding her power, and she was handling it, but she had not rebooted, she had not slept after receiving the boon.

This would kill her.

'Oh, Cheryl…'

She looked over at Barker.

Barker's eyes reflected the same sorrow. 'I know!'

'I won't have this!' Emerald was surprised to hear herself shout that.

But; these were her people.

This was her tribe.

Shirley came up to them.

'We need to get her to the Botanic Astral Gate – as soon as the portal closes! We can save her! But we must be fast!'

Emerald's hand was still on Cheryl's shoulder.

'She's trying to kill that sorcerer!'

A woman in a flimsy, bright red robe came stumbling through the portal, falling flat on her face as though someone had shoved her through with a kick to the backside.

Emerald saw – the massive creek serpent.

She saw all the water Cheryl was holding back, she felt all the energy from the river spirit in the lake, that the spirit was allowing to pass through Cheryl's body in order to hold the water, and form the water serpent there; the immense pressure the serpent contained, magically summoned and endowed, that Cheryl was holding back.

She saw two, no four people running, about to come through, saw that Cheryl was hoping to dump all that pressure on the man, Shilling, who was now half of one of those creatures that The Persuader had turned himself into, a demon in third density form, the classic red and black horned-muscle-man-thing, and she was disgusted, but –

'Cheryl! Don't kill yourself just to piss him off! It won't kill him! Believe me!'

Cheryl grumbled through gritted teeth.

'Fuck it… I know. I know!'

'We can save you! I won't let you die, Equinox! I swear; not after this – *I – won't – let – you – die!*'

Emerald took her hand off Cheryl's shoulder

Carlton Craven staggered through the portal, followed by –
*Fiona Pitcher?*

They each had dragged another woman through with them, but they released them immediately and they all fell to the ground.

Barker dropped his staff and the two men embraced in a giant, mutual bear hug, slapping each other on the back, the way men do.

Emerald caught that emotion, heard herself gasp, and allowed herself a tear.

The two friends separated, and Carlton addressed Barker very quickly.

'Fenner Shilling's a ten-foot demon now, and he's got a child army of fifty or more vampire Pinocchios at his disposal, plus a small army of tree people who mean fucking business – good to see you mate, let's get the fuck on with it!'

Then he fell to his knees.

Fiona was immediately with him.

'I'm okay...'

Barker was going to help, but was distracted when Emerald spun about and raised her pool cue staff, and her roulette shield, and addressed the seven women of the coven.

'Everyone! Get to the top of the stairs! Evil is coming through – riding a savage river!'

The coven turned.

There were now at least a dozen of the demonoid creatures at the top of the stairs – that they could see. The whole coven turned back to her. She looked up to the footbridge. Galena's dogs and her people were trapped; there were those demonoid things at each side, closing in. The dogs began to snap and savagely bark, snaking between her people; Jürgen and the others, who had agreed to stay, and fight, to protect them.

'Ladies...' Emerald growled, loudly. 'It's quite possible the war has already started, and we have the fight of our lives on our hands, right this minute.'

'You heard the nice sorceress, ladies!' Shirley cried out. She raised her short-swords high, locking eyes with Emerald, then spinning about to her coven. 'Are we ready to *take these fuckers on!?*'

Her coven collectively shrieked with the ferocity of an army of banshees.

Barker felt Mainwaring push closer against his leg. He squatted down, picked up his staff and with his free arm lifted his koala into his arms. He came willingly, and clung to him.

'Listen to me!' Barker shouted as he stood. 'I can't close that portal! Cheryl can't hold the water much longer! We have to get out of here!'

Several of Emerald's people on the footbridge got the gist. Jürgen jumped down, sliding as Parry had off the edge of the portal, and ran toward the glass doors, and the river spirit, at the other end of the concourse.

'I can't hold it!' Cheryl gasped.

Jürgen hit something; some kind of force barrier around the river spirit.

'I can't get through!'

'It's…' Cheryl gasped. 'She can't drop it, until the water comes!'

'Jürgen!' Emerald yelled. 'Take Shirley – see if the platform gates respond to magic!'

Jürgen obeyed; Shirley and half the coven followed.

Barker turned to those remaining, the koala still under his arm, clinging to his chest.

'The ramp!' They were already moving. He turned to Emerald. 'That's higher ground – and the creatures can't get through the barrier!'

Emerald saw that the cop, Parry, was suddenly embracing Fiona Pitcher like they had known each other all their lives, as Craven slowly got to his feet, looking pale and weak. Then Pitcher released the cop and turned around to see if Craven was still okay.

Then, Pitcher saw her. Their eyes met.

'I know…' Emerald exclaimed. 'I know! I know you said you'd kill me next time we met; but, can we – ?'

Barker went over to Parry, completely blocking Fiona out, cancelling their reunion and its charge of negative energy toward Emerald. He stood close to the Chief Inspector and addressed the koala.

'Go with Parry.'

The koala transferred his long limbs to the detective and clung to him, as Barker spoke quietly, but deeply.

'Parry, you have no magic to protect you; Bach can get you out past those things. Save Mainwaring.'

Parry said nothing, but nodded gravely and walked immediately for Barker's bike.

It started itself, and revved.

'Bach – ram those things! Get our friends out of here!'

Parry sat on the bike and grabbed the handles. The koala, Mainwaring, and she completely got that, turned and clung to him around his torso and chest. Fiona was watching, her lower lip trembling, as Craven took her hand. But he was watching Cheryl.

'God speed!' Barker shouted.

Bach took off.

Cheryl groaned and started to collapse.

Craven moved to her, but Emerald and Barker were still on either side of her and got there first. Then Craven, pale as a ghost, passed out, completely this time, and Fiona caught him. She nearly dropped him, but Dash had remained at Emerald's side, and moved in to help.

Emerald and Barker had caught Cheryl simultaneously, and were now embracing her tightly from each side. It had been accidental, but they had embraced that as well. Cheryl's arm remained extended, still controlling the portal, and holding back the water, but she was barely conscious. Her mind had locked into the spell, the loop between her, the river spirit and the creek in Argent, and it would not break until she completely lost consciousness.

Emerald shouted at Dash, as she and Barker tightened their embrace around Cheryl.

'Dash! Can you get Craven up the ramp?'

Fiona and Dash moved away, with Craven half-stumbling between them.

'Everyone get as far back as you can! Get ready! Here it comes!'

'Aren't you coming!?'

Dash's call was filled with incredulous concern.

They could all hear the dammed, redirected creek now, rushing from the other side of the portal.

'She can't move! Barker shouted. 'Until the spell's done! We're going to shield her against the water! We'll be okay!'

Emerald's fists were pressed tightly onto Barker, the one squeezing her cue on his shoulder, with her roulette-shield facing the portal, against his hip; she could feel his tense muscles beneath his coat, like rock.

Cheryl's hand remained extended between them, but she was only just conscious now, the spell still keeping her anchored to the spot.

She could feel Barker's clenched fist acutely on her lower hip, his staff right down her side, and his free, open hand under her neck. It was almost as though Cheryl wasn't there. She could feel his touch, his urge to protect not just Cheryl, but her as well. She could feel him, even more so, fighting the urge to look into her eyes, over Cheryl's shoulder and see, finally, into her.

Barker tried not to. He tried to be professional.

'Ever shielded against this much water before?'

She hadn't.

Of course she hadn't.

Probably nobody had in this day and age.

She sighed.

'The Trader promised me a reckoning… I suppose; here it comes…'

They both felt Cheryl pass out.
Her arm dropped.
Emerald saw that Barker was going to look into her eyes.
She braced herself for that, more than for the water.
And then, finally, came the reckoning.

# EPILOGUE: SAFE

The Taurus went straight through the portal without obstruction.

There was a bright flash, then the car was moving down the end of a dark driveway, surrounded by high, overgrown trees and dense, tangled bushes.

Emerald pulled up, almost right away, as they reached the end.

'Just like that?' Dash demanded. 'No special effects?' She looked around through the windscreen. 'It's getting dark. Sunset…'

The driveway was white gravel, and they were outside a very big house.

'Is this a sorcerer's house? Will someone meet us?'

Someone came around the corner. The trees were so thick and overgrown that it was difficult to see very far. But it was Galena, and she walked up to them with Gavin at her heel. She shrugged, sheepishly.

'He's usually so obedient!'

Emerald cracked the door open and got out.

Dash got out as well.

'Are you okay?' Emerald asked. 'Is Gavin okay?'

'Yes, he's fine. He's been chasing another dog around.'

It was hot. Emerald was suddenly way overdressed.

'Where are we?'

There was barking in the distance.

Dash looked around again.

'Well, it *was* mid-winter, now it's mid-*summer*. Makes it Southern Hemisphere. Probably Australia, with all the gum trees. Might be New Zealand or South Africa, I suppose, but, probably Australia.'

Galena handed Emerald a sheet of paper.

'Australia. Adelaide Hills. This place was up for sale. One of the last complete colonial mansions and grounds in the Adelaide Hills, it says. Adelaide is *South* Australia. I have fans here. I should be able to find us a place to stay.'

Dash raised an eyebrow. 'Fancy.'

A huge, black, shaggy Russian Terrier came rushing up to Gavin and the two started sniffing each other.

'Uh oh…' Dash growled. 'I've seen that look bef – uhp!'

Gavin had mounted the Terrier and before they knew it, there was some very intense, rapid repetition of movement, then the deed was done.

'Hope it was good for her, too.'

Emerald laughed, but she was still staring at the house.

'Gavin…' Galena frowned, a little disappointed.

Gavin looked very pleased with himself, and the two dogs proceeded to run around the car some more, staying near the three women.

Emerald frowned. 'Doesn't look like anyone bought it. Or if they did, nobody's living here.'

Dash shrugged. 'Do we wait here for a contact?'

'We've got food in the car, if no-one shows up, we can hole up here for the night until we figure out what we're supposed to do. Some of those portals shift people in time; it might not even be the same year.'

Galena moved closer to Emerald.

'Looks creepy. But I guess I'm supposed to be here?'

She was looking to Emerald for reassurance.

Emerald reached out and touched her arm.

'We'll figure it out. It's an adventure, Galena. You like adventures, right? Gavin seems pretty much at home already.'

Galena smiled, but they could both feel a prickly vibe from Dash, which diminished the second Emerald stopped affectionately rubbing Galena's arm.

Emerald shot her a look.

'What?' Dash shrugged.

Emerald shook her head. 'We can sleep in the car. Or, I think I have a tent in the trunk. Hardly the first time I've slept rough. Main thing is, we're out of danger.'

'Are you sure about this?' Dash was persistent. She had a phone in her hand. 'No reception. Where the fuck do you have to be these days to get no reception? Maybe we should just drive the fuck out of here, huh?'

Emerald was so tired of running.

Maybe this place was her new home.

Maybe The Trader had seen the need for that within her, and sent her to one.

She couldn't tell.

She was done, for now.

Tonight, at least.

'I need to be somewhere quiet a while, Dash. My brain's completely scrambled, and totally overloaded. They wouldn't direct the portal to anywhere that wasn't safe, would they? If there's nobody here who can help us, we'll leave first thing in the morning…' She looked at the sales brochure again. 'Look, this place even has a name. Bridger Mansion. Sounds fine to me. One night. What could possibly go wrong?'


## TO BE CONTINUED…

Emerald Tarragon will return...

And in fact does.

In...

*Saga of The Urban Sorcerers –*
*Book Three: The Shaping of Cheryl Equinox*

# www.GalexyTales.com

(OR SEARCH "GALEXY TALES"
AT AMAZON...)

## Acknowledgements

Enormous thanks and all my love as always to Melissa Sheldrick.

Huge thanks to Michal Dutkiewicz for the wonderful cover. Thanks and gratitude to Adam Dutkiewicz for the formatting.

Gretel Newman-Sugrue was way ahead of me in regard to her suggestions, as usual – but this time the title was her suggestion. 'Reckoning' was not on the list of ten or so other words I was considering. It was 'Judgment' for a long time, 'Gamble' was in it for a while, then I really had settled on 'Calculation' (sorry, Chris!) – but when Gretel got back with 'Reckoning' it fitted with everything the book was about, and like all great titles, when you hit upon it, it changes the book in subtle ways that are so cool to discover along the way. So, Gretel: thanks again!

Thanks again to everyone who helped.

Raechel Carroll – brilliant and amazing!

Anne Ruwoldt – amazing and brilliant!

Special 'you know what you did' thanks to – Stan James, Gennie James, Chris Collings, Angeline Collings, Darren Koziol, Gillian Koziol, Adam Vale, Tom Kafa, Kay Leanne, Travis Pollard, Melissa Stokes, Alexandra Champion, Regan and Nicole, Mario Kukec, Karen Carlisle, G.R. Thomas, Stacey Logan, Kimberley Clark, Andrew Irvine, Kylie Chan, Mark Custance, Walter Rhein, Jacinta Maree, T.R. Kester, Alan Pinder, Michael Lickorish, Nat Karmichael, Sam Elsegood,

Nick Talbot, Claudia Ienco, Zoe Clare, Dave de Vries, Petra Elliot, Lucia Stanzel, Greg Gates, Matthew Pilkington, Anthony Fagan, Cherie Davy, Veronica Gaunt, Peter McNamara, Pat McNamara, Greg C. Grace, David Bradley, Dan Foley, Big Pete Wagner, Jon James, Chris James, Tash James, Dawn Sheldrick, Mearns Sheldrick, Belinda Sheldrick, Mike Cooper, Haley Snook, and Dave Baker.

Joanne Bouzianis-Sellick – for heaps, going way back!

And Rushelle Lister at Ingram-Spark – many thanks.

And really, really many, many thanks to all the cosplayers who pose with me, all the people who've bought my books at cons and expos, and to all the people who come back! I love the people who come back!

## About the Author

Alex James is a writer who lives in and is inspired by Adelaide, South Australia.

Alex studied European History, Classical Mythology, Film Studies and Screenwriting under the Communications and Liberal Studies banners at the University of South Australia.

Between 1992 and 2005 he wrote many, many, many outlines, treatments, concept documents, bibles, pilots and screenplays, for just about every active Australian production company there was.

From 2008-2014 he was an in-house writer for Angel-Phoenix Media, who published his first two e-book novels, *The Pandora Sequence* and *Venus AI*, both of which were launched at the 2013 San Diego Comic-Con.

Alex's most recent works are epic novel sagas which include *The Saga of The Urban Sorcerers*, *Amazon Seven*, *Dark Streets*, *The Chronicles of The Terraguard*, and *The Ascension Sequence*.

He publishes via his own independent imprint, Galexy Tales.

**Novels by Alex James:**


**THE ASCENSION SEQUENCE:**
VOLUME ONE
The Pandora Sequence
VOLUME TWO
Book One: The Pandora Inheritance
Book Two: The Pandora Arcana (Pre-order)
Book Three: The Daughters of Pandora (Pre-order)


**THE CHRONICLES OF THE TERRAGUARD:**
Book One: Maker of Rules


**AMAZON SEVEN SAGA - VOLUME ONE:**
Book One: Mission Queen
Book Two: Queen Renegade
Book Three: Intergalactic Ingenue (Pre-order)
Book Four: Princess Executor (Pre-order)


**SAGA OF THE URBAN SORCERERS:**
Book One: The Summoning of Barker Moon
Book Two: The Reckoning of Emerald Tarragon
Book Three: The Shaping of Cheryl Equiniox (Pre-order)


**DARK STREETS SAGA:**
Book One: Agents of Fear
Book Two: Avatars of Wrath (Pre-Order)


Venus IA

**www.GalexyTales.com**

(or search "GALEXY TALES" at Amazon...)

www.ingramcontent.com/pod-product-compliance
Lightning Source LLC
Chambersburg PA
CBHW070729120726
47910CB00001B/33